RAVAGE & REQUIEM

S H A T T E R

S. WHITTINGTON

Ravage & Requiem: Shatter

First Edition printed October 2022

Cover Illustration © 2022 by Shawn Christopher Whittington

ISBN: 979-8-9865545-2-5 (hardcover)
ISBN: 979-8-9865545-1-8 (paperback)
ISBN: 979-8-9865545-3-2 (eBook)

LCCN: 2022919211

Printed in Poplarville, Mississippi (USA)

Published by Inward Crossing Publishing
www.swhittington.com

For my father,

my brother,

and in loving memory of my mother

1956 – 2018

Table of Contents

I: The Great Wraith

Spathi's bloodshot eyes wearily scanned the darkened, volcanic wastelands of the Tauldren province, with Vrashri, the holy Selebane sword, sheathed on his aching back. For days, he trudged through Raktogin's doomed deathscape.

Or was it weeks? Months?

He didn't care anymore. He just wanted to die. Finding and killing Constanvol would simply be a minor bonus to his inevitable demise. The heat was unbearable! Nausea and dizziness plagued him, despite the sun's rays being unable to penetrate the thick ash clouds above. His lips were badly chapped, with his face, fingers, and neck having suffered burns, the dead skin peeling from his blistered flesh. Everything stung, throbbing. It was a wonder he hadn't puked yet, even though he had tried to retch here and there. Yet nothing would come out. His stomach was empty…like the rest of him.

Empty guts. Empty head.

Empty soul.

His efforts yielded nothing.

Like they ever did anyway.

Here he was, led by some songbird he only *thought* he saw in the rain the other day, thinking it were a sign, thinking that General Jenaya Devral's Bonsai tree was also some sort of good omen.

Fuck it!

There was no hope!

This was it! Everyone was dead! All dead!

Feshta was eradicated. Van De Yoth was annihilated. The Enpherom were extinguished. The Vauphec were exterminated. The Enoshah were extinct. His family was gone, his grandfather, his mother. Staea.

His wife.

All were dead.

Why couldn't the world just explode already? Why was it taking so damned long? The war was lost. Drixilo had won. The devil had taken everything away, consuming and assimilating all to his whim. And the fall of the last holy city appeared to be a scathing indictment of heaven's true intent. The triune god of the Unleztruv seemed nonexistent. Unzelkoyte was long gone. And perhaps Astrekiah and Arczellius were dead as well?

Deven was certainly dead.

All the other angels had probably died with him.

What did it matter? Soon, Spathi would be dead with them, yet he still managed to shamble through the geothermal mires, sloshing through the shallows of salt lakes, witnessing the petrified remains of birds, antelope, and humans. All he could do was drag his feet around like a ghoul.

One sore foot…in front of the other.

He didn't even mind losing his spare Selebane sword and scabbard to a river of lava far below trying to climb along the sides of a volcanic canyon, the strap having been scraped away from his belt by a jutting piece of obsidian. All sentimentality had eroded away, especially of when he was a knight centuries ago. A knight. What a joke! Who gave a damn? Memory was useless now. Perhaps it always was…and he was only realizing it now, here at the very end of days.

Pathetic.

Onward, he meandered through the wastes, cutting down Ravaged Drixiles here and there, stoked by moments of wrath, yet even his fatigue was slowly robbing him of that. The attacks had already tattered his long coat, yet the demons were no match for his new Sevelurnum implements. Their maggoty blood would spatter on Vrashri's luminous edge and his plate mail, the fluid and larvae scorching to nothing on contact.

But he didn't dare sample a drop!

He was done with the Ravage. He was clean—and he intended to keep it that way. Nevertheless, he was starving…and gravely dehydrated. He had even collapsed a few times and had fallen unconscious, only to be awakened by the distant rumbling of quaking earth or the cries of more Drixiles far off.

It didn't make sense. It defied all logic. He should have died by now. What was holding him together? And why wouldn't it just let him die? Why was it tormenting him? What was this cruel living nightmare called existence?

He was alone. All alone.

Just like Malroc, the High Lich, had once sneered at him.

As much as Spathi craved death, he was far too stubborn to take his own life. Why kill himself when the Drixiles would eventually do it for him? Self-affliction would only bring more pain. And even if he did commit suicide, who was to say that Malroc wouldn't transform him into one of those accursed Torpids? He was loath to simply join their ranks, especially out of weakness! Yet there were moments where he pondered what it would be like. Though he had been infected with the Ravage before, he had never been fully converted into a rabid servant of Drixilo.

Would he even be aware of it? Could it possibly be better than this?

To join the enemy?

The same enemy that tortured him with his unholy influence, the same enemy that demolished his homeland, the same enemy that massacred those he loved, his allies, his friends, his family.

His wife.

Staea.

The choice was obvious.

To keep from being tempted to sup on blood, he had torn a portion from the bottom of his ragged long coat and wrapped it around his mouth and nose as a makeshift scarf. He refused to taste another drop of blood. The sounds of the screaming woman in Vider still haunted him, the one he mutilated after Empress Noshva's lobotomy attempt. Along with the bald Enoshah soldier on the dreadnought five years earlier and all the blood that had been donated from the military for his sake, it was all too much to bear. He hated it. He hated himself! He hated being beholden! He hated who he was, what he was.

A blood-eater.

Aspiring in vain to be a knight in shining armor once again.

He was no hero. He never was. He never would be. How he wished he had some sort of purpose! How he longed for some sort of sensible reason to justify all this mayhem, this agony. And at the same time…a part of him was glad. Everything had reverted back to a morbidly comfortable meaninglessness, untethered by the bounds of loyalty to anyone living. All ways were now open to him at last. The panoramic uncertainty was as mortifying as it was exhilarating. He was free to indulge himself, free to roam, free to fight.

Free to crave.

And free to fight the cravings.

He cringed, grunting—convulsing! His ears rang!

He felt as if being torn apart, riven in two!

Violently, he growled and shook his head, struggling to regain his composure, trying his best not to pass out and flop onto the smoldering silt and peat beneath him. His pained heart thrummed in his chest like tired pistons in a failing engine. The ringing slowly abated. The adrenaline was up now, coursing through his veins. Fuel. His stinging eyes surveyed the dark lands again, much more alert now, paying more attention to Tauldren's unforgiving environment.

He just wanted to hunt now, to slay demons.

And find Constanvol.

The baron had mentioned strange things to him the other day, after Gyeno had been captured and absorbed back into Drixilo. Virgin cosmos. A copious mother. A stern father. And the Mulya-Sheloth? Succubi within the moon? Was *that* what the whispering women he had heard actually were all this time?

His eyes widened.

Had Staea been one of them? This whole time?

She, too, had drawn power from the moon, even without the circle tattoo that was once etched across her chest. But that would have made her a blood-eater by nature, unlike him who was bitten by Constanvol. Yet Spathi never discerned where *he* came from. Perhaps he never would.

Perhaps…he didn't want to know.

But it was preposterous! Staea, a cosmic moon whore? And Constanvol, half Drixile, half…whatever the hell else. Who gave a flying shit anymore? His mind was too broken to calculate anything. And he didn't want to. He was sick of thinking. Thoughts had gotten him nowhere.

He was done, finished.

Shattered.

All he wanted to do was hunt demons…until he died.

That was all a lunatic like him could ask for now.

Kill…or be killed.

He observed the obsidian landscape of igneous rock and mummified sagebrush. Stubs of obliterated jungle plants jutted from the ground near charred stumps and gurgling calcium pools. His impromptu scarf failed to filter out the strong odors of sulfur, ash, and rot. The sun was setting in the North, hueing the clouds in the horizon with deep orange and red outlined in pink. In the distance, gargantuan stratovolcanoes disgorged their pyroclastic rage down from their summits while strangling the heavens with colossal, bulbous pillars of smoke. The fire mountains' cooked slopes were all marbled with cracks oozing with bright crimson wrath, as if Tauldren itself was ready to buckle and collapse from Empress Maethel's livid influence. Some of the molten rock streams gushing from the stockier craters had ignited with sulfurous blue flames, giving the lava a spectral aura.

Hellfire. Brimstone.

He treaded further, passing the scant ruins of ancient pagan temples, the foundations of modern buildings, and the rusted frames of cars halfway sunken in old lava flows. The magma had not touched everything but had carved out various wavy gouges through the barren mire. Tar pits burbled nearby with smoke and mist rising from the bituminous sludge, the repulsive stench like burnt feces. Through the toxic haze, Spathi noticed a fiery glow before him.

A new river of lava.

The gorge cut by the running molten rock was several yards deep, making it difficult for him to notice from afar earlier. Small ventifact islets of charred stone stood over the churning magma like thin sea stacks, most of their flat tops level with the ground where Spathi stood; each one was crowned with a dead tree blackened with soot. Under his feet, the ground seemed to move like a serpent's rippling scales, gradually forming fractures in the earth. Scalding steam rolled out from the fresh cracks. He looked behind him, then back at the infernal ravine before him. If only he had seen it earlier, he would never have come this way.

He chuckled, with a madman's grin widening beneath his scarf.

What a lunatic he was. And all he could do was laugh.

Just laugh. And laugh. And laugh.

Giggling. Snickering uncontrollably.

It didn't matter if he died. The lava would offer a nice, abrupt ending if he was unable to evade it, in exchange for a few last moments of indescribable pain. As far as he was concerned, it was a win-win situation. He couldn't lose anymore at this point even if he tried. If failure did, in fact, have a proverbial "rock-bottom," he had certainly discovered it by now. And he made for quite a spectacular failure. Actually, he couldn't help but be quite proud of it, however morbid it was. Not only could the man not live right, he couldn't even die right either! He was simply terrible at everything.

And what did it matter? After all, there was also the chance that this was just another one of Empress Noshva's petty "simulations" anyway. Sensation, emotion, and thought were all just meaningless parts of a flamboyant illusion called life. Just another computerized dream.

Right?

Yet, the eerie digital dusk-blue tinge was oddly absent.

But why would that be a tell-tale sign?

What could he possibly know about anything anymore?

He was beyond broken.

The ground shifted more under him. Nearby, he spotted a brick staircase leading up to one of the taller islets over the lava river. He sighed. Though he wanted to die, there was no sense in just waiting around for death. Might as well put some sport into it.

He was going to die anyway. Why not have fun with it?

The earth shook. As the rock came apart beneath him, Spathi sprinted up the steps and lunged onto a nearby ventifact. The bottom of the rock column snapped, tilting away from the crumbling staircase. Like a frenzied flea, he leapt from stack to stack, each pillar falling apart under his weight. More adrenaline coursed through his veins. Life. So alive, on the fringes of death, whether it mattered or not. The very feeling, real or not, was so invigorating. He couldn't get enough of it. To live. To breathe.

To thrive.

And hunt.

Spathi finally landed on the lava river's other side as the remaining ventifacts fell into the magma behind him. The quake lessened to a smooth, steady rumble under his feet. He peered back up…and furrowed his brows.

The skyline was even darker than before.

All the volcanoes in the North seemed to have vanished, as well as their ash clouds, replaced by a malefic blackness that put the night to shame. Then, something flickered a few miles off: a dark-blue glint that appeared to carve right through the wall of shadows, followed by rolls of sharp booms.

Constanvol?

Crouching low, Spathi crept toward the suspicious glimmer. The hunt was on. Yet the barrier of darkness pulsated, rasping a long, ghostly sigh, producing a brisk, chilling wind that almost knocked Spathi off his feet. As he braced himself, the sound of crows cawing far off and cicadas chorusing fluttered through the haunting gale. Even the lava's glow dimmed from the shadow barricade.

Then his eyes darted around, looking.

Searching for the dark-blue light.

"Damn it!" Spathi cursed.

He glared at the darkness, then froze. His eyes widened, noticing fractal lines of twisting bones and ribs surfacing, like the skeletons of snakes and spirals of nautilus shells. They shone like a hazy harvest moon, gilded and ominous. Clusters of conjoined jaws and eye sockets crawled through the macabre monstrosity, gaping out like dead barnacles on a ghost ship's decaying hull. Crooked limbs and claws unfolded downward, kneading the air. Another malign wind blew, generating a sickly fog across the geothermal land. More unseen crows and cicadas chimed as Spathi ducked behind a boulder, gawking at the titan before him.

A giant reaver.

Spathi squinted at the wraith colossus before him...then he remembered. He had heard tales of this entity from sailors at the tavern near the ports of Van De Yoth ages ago, about a sudden black smoke that would rise from the sea, infested with evil spirits of otherworldly bones that would consume vessels without leaving a trace, never to be seen again. They had even given it a name.

Moldrus. The Vauphec word for "rot mist."

As a knight back in Ancient Raktogin, he had never believed such stories. And Lena had been right: Drixiles had rarely showed their true forms...until now. Only now could he see that the sailors weren't always full of shit, that it wasn't just another nautical myth.

The legends were true.

Immediately, the wraith wall invoked the gripping fear of Malroc, the High Lich. That merciless grim reaper. There were fates far worse than mere death. But wasn't this a simulation? Did he not believe that this was nothing more than a dream? Yet, why wasn't his self-substantiation in this "simulation" waking him up, just as it did in the boreal kingdom of Vider? Why wasn't his self-awareness not making him omnipotent, enabling him to override the boundaries of a place that was purported to be false?

Unless...this *was* all real.

And that all his family and friends...*were* all dead.

Even Staea, his wife.

He sobbed! If nihilism wouldn't take him, the crushing weight of sheer grief and despair would. He *was* awake! This *was* all real! A living nightmare! Part of him wanted it to matter. Part of him wished this were nothing but fiction. Regardless, it was all true, all reality.

And he was being torn apart! Right in two!

Creeping low, he followed where the dark-blue glow had been, slinking around dead shrubs and rocks. In the foreboding sheen of Moldrus's aura, Spathi could make out the outlines of segmented pinnacles leaning, pointing toward the South.

Sevoliths.

Appendages of the World Choker.

The precipices were badly corroded by acid rains, rust, and wear and tear, littered with circular cavitation. Some of their pointed tops had broken off, resembling headless snakes frozen in place; others had been reduced to serrated nubs. As Spathi skulked amongst the vicinity of the Sevoliths, he noticed the face of Moldrus shift, swirling.

Forming a maelstrom.

Out from the torrent's center, a gigantic reaver's yawning face emerged, opening its melancholy maw wider and wider, its throat emitting a tainted pale luminosity. The unified choir of the spiraling reaver faces uttered an ongoing moan, a single, horrifying note that drowned out all other noise. The horrific pallid light in Moldrus's giant mouth contorted around, morphing into a sphere.

Then into a funnel.

Feeding directly into the reaver's jaws.

The land quaked as gravity's pull inverted towards Moldrus's undertow, syphoning rocks, lava, and decaying trees all into its ravenous throat. Spathi grunted and grabbed hold of a nearby Sevolith with both hands, doing everything he could to stay grounded. Yet it was to no avail. The obsidian and silt beneath him cracked and fragmented, floating upward into Moldrus's funnel. Spathi yelled a soundless scream, with his feet instantly flung into the air, his hands still gripping the corrugated siding of the eroded Sevolith.

But the tighter his fingers gripped the leaning monolith, the more he could hear the low whisper, a menacing rasping in his mind.

Sevthiel…Sevthiel….

Spathi cringed and bit down on his jaw. Of all the deaths he could hope for, being slaughtered by reavers proved to be one revolting fate, agonizing beyond words. Being slain by the minions of Malroc was only the beginning of *true* torment rather than the end. In fact…life suddenly became so valuable. So precious. So priceless. The very infernal essence of wraiths was a traumatic dread so thick and suffocating, producing the helplessness and isolation one felt while being paralyzed in a psychotic nightmare. It was fear that made Spathi cling to the Sevolith.

And from terror…came the yearning to live.

What wretched irony.

Sevthiel…Sevthiel….

"Sev…ahh!" Spathi spat soundlessly, feeling cold, unseen hands attempting to manipulate his jaw to speak the vile name.

He glared and saw the skull-like scales carved on the Sevoliths all turning and gazing right at him. These things weren't dormant. They were alive! He had awoken them, yielding to the World Choker with his embrace, clinging to this immeasurable monster for aid against death.

Anchoring himself to a false god.

Sevthiel…Sevthiel….

Spathi looked at Moldrus's maw, drawing closer. He released one hand and unsheathed Vrashri, then he shut his eyes, trying to muster just a sliver of hope, trying to breathe one last time, trying to picture Deven, his friends, his family.

His wife, Staea.

The edge of Vrashri burned with its faint nebulous blue aura. Underneath him, the earth shuddered even more violently. Yelling mutely, he let go, flying up to Moldrus's massive face. The reaver wall's extremities readied themselves as Spathi raised Vrashri high over him, preparing to cleave the wraith…or perish trying.

One final drive. One last fight.

Boom!

Moldrus's funnel vanished. Gravity reverted to normal as Spathi tumbled to the ground, crashing through rotten tree limbs. The volcanic ground sundered, with enormous golden-brown hydra heads erupting from Raktogin's crust. Moldrus screamed and combated the appendages of the World Choker as Spathi scurried to his feet and ran for cover. The mandibles of the serpents' skull scales opened and inhaled, absorbing the wraith barrier and its fractal array with ease. As they devoured the phantasmal black reaver smoke, each bony face emitted a spectral gasp. Sound steadily returned to Tauldren, with Spathi sprinting away from the cosmic hydra. The monstrosity's bulk swayed, crushing his derelict Sevoliths, then the heads belched a series of horrifying screams, a twisted din like that of banshees, dragons, and dying whales all melded together. Spathi ducked behind a boulder, eyeing the World Choker's heads. Yet, the hydra atrocity seemed to ignore him, focusing instead on a few golden structures about a mile off in the North. Spathi turned…and saw it, gleaming in the dim magmatic glow of the volcanoes' fire.

Maethel's palace.

He struggled to catch his breath. Sweet breath. Sweet life. It was his instinct to crave life, whether he liked it or not. And it *was* real. All of it. Real pain. Real anguish. Real regret. He scowled and gritted his teeth, gripping Vrashri in both hands, sickened by the sight of the World Choker, nauseated by what he had done.

He had coaxed him here. It was all his fault.

If only he hadn't touched the Sevolith.

If only he hadn't thought of the damned name!

Of the World Choker.

Sevthiel.

As he caught his breath, the man's sinister voice stabbed his mind again in a malicious whisper, burning his conscience with unbearable shame, chuckling, mocking Spathi by uttering two simple words.

Thank…you….

II: Trenches

The hydra raged out another series of baleful cries as Spathi fled to a nearby gulch for cover. His eyes shifted around frantically, putting his back against the jagged crevice's outcroppings. With teeth clenched, he shut his eyes and let out a long, low growl. Why did he have to be so foolish? And why was it so easy now to summon the World Choker? Had the thin veneer between planes of existence finally been obliterated, merging together in these heinous final days?

A loud din roared from the North.

Cautiously, he peeked over the gulch's top, watching Maethel's towers teem with movement. Legs. Thousands of legs and arms skittered across the surfaces of the gold pagodas, with the stingers, Sunoc's brood, taking flight with their wasp-like wings, all swarming around dark-blue flashes around the ramparts.

Constanvol.

Laying siege to Tauldren's capital.

Spathi eyed the closed drawbridge standing over the crumbling moat of lava. The magma churned upward like river rapids, lapping against the intricate walls, quaking and growing increasingly unstable from the World Choker's writhing movements. It was only a matter of time before Maethel was aroused from her dwelling to retaliate.

The World Choker only sat there. Watching.

Waiting.

Then its gilded scales fluttered and emitted the dissonant chorus of millions of cicadas. Spathi grunted and held his ears, trying to keep the unholy insect stridulations from digging into his mind. As the World Choker's unbearable chittering rose, the hydra's ridged extremities slowly coiled around like giant rattlesnakes, as if anticipating Maethel's imminent arrival.

Spathi glared. Everything was about to become one chaotic mess! The whole damned place was about to go up in smoke. Yet he was unable to locate another way inside the palace walls. He took a deep breath, then belted the air right back out. It was going to be one hell of a long shot.

But it was the only way.

He refused to turn back. He refused to let Constanvol go.

Not after what that loathsome bastard had done.

He gazed down the gulch again and darted down the winding path, turning right down another empty fissure. The dice had been rolled. The ante had been made: his life. A life he previously didn't care about, an existence he had deemed meaningless just a few minutes ago. What was this peculiar thing called instinct, driving him, overriding his will to surrender?

But this *was* his will, wasn't it? To survive? Against all odds? It was just mere instinct. Yet he wasn't an animal. He still had a choice. He was still in control. Right? He scoffed, puffing for breath. All he knew in that moment was that his feet were moving, one in front of the other, scurrying down one obscure chasm after another, a zigzagging maze of igneous crevasses and gleaming obsidian. As he crept, he stopped and listened. Above, something else was rumbling, a distinct noise…like the sonic boom.

Of an engine.

He peered back up at the fissure's top, scanning back and forth. The World Choker's heads belched another sinister, mournful roar. Spathi sighed; the volcanic fumes must have been getting to him. It was becoming more difficult to breathe through the scarf. Impetuously, he pulled the cloth away from his face, gasping for breath, inhaling the toxic air from the nearby fumaroles within Maethel's imperial caldera. More toxins billowed from the crevices beyond, halfway flooded by the waters of an adjacent salt lake recently ruptured. Spathi made out figures, standing shin-deep in the reddened pools.

Humans. The old corpses of resistance soldiers from who knew how long ago. Some had been mummified from the scalding minerals, lying in pieces half-submerged, along with a skeletal menagerie of animals, including birds, deer, and even a few feral cats, all fossilized by the unforgiving land. Yet some human cadavers still stood, some with their heads and arms broken, with some leaning against the walls, the saltwater trickling on their melancholy façades, forever petrified.

In pewter.

These had been victimized by Maethel's irate gaze.

The clashing of steel rang out above. Spathi looked up. The palace walls were closer now, the rampart's many braziers flaming brilliantly in the volcanic night. Another dark-blue flicker blasted, knocking a few of the great torches away, spraying hot coals and embers on squealing stinger Drixiles. Like ants, the Tauldrenians skittered towards the intruder. Spathi gritted his teeth. It had to be Constanvol.

A great shriek rang out!

Then a massive, winged shadow tore through the choked skies, flapping her sleek, gilt wings. Her six nether dragon heads were fixed on the World Choker. All four of her arms were outstretched, each equipped with a gold-plated blade.

Maethel.

Like a meteorite, she soared directly at her cosmic adversary, her throbbing blood vessels glowing with molten light beneath her thick scales and armor. An entire fleet of Ravaged stingers sailed with her, swarming around their furious queen. With all her might, her eye sockets spewed out a thick jet of her solidifying yellow blaze, conflagrating on contact against the World Choker's heads and spreading into a voracious inferno below their necks. The hydra wailed, yet their serpentine flesh seemed unfazed, refusing to be converted to lifeless stone.

Boom!

The ground quaked violently. Spathi looked around. Lava oozed and slopped through the walls on both sides of the fissure, the charred stone wrinkling towards him into curved orange rivulets of incandescent death. Frenetically, he pawed his way up back to level ground, the obsidian shards scorching and cutting his exposed fingers. He bit down so hard on his jaw fighting back the unrelenting agony that he felt as if on the verge of cracking his teeth to pieces. As he finally hoisted himself over the top, his eyes gawked at the unsettling sight before him.

A fresh fumarole had formed about half a mile away, bursting through the earth and flinging magma everywhere. Yet another fiery ulcer on Raktogin's crust had been born, exsanguinating its flaming blood in bulging rivers of boiling rock, forking everywhere in scathing deltas. One smoldering stream was headed straight for him. Spathi surveyed the area for a ledge, seeking any way to avoid the incoming lava flow.

He groaned. Maethel had certainly carved Tauldren in her fierce image.

The usurped land was her callused canvas, her ungodly ire her vicious paintbrush.

Heavy chains clacked to his left.

Spathi turned and glared. The drawbridge was opening. Yet whatever platform that was previously meant to catch its end on the moat's other side had evidently eroded away, leaving the bridge protruding only halfway over the unstable fire trench. He couldn't make that leap. No mortal could. It was insane! As he frantically sought out an alternate route, another swarm of stingers burst forth from the yawning gate, along with a flock of huge bats.

Necromantids. Ravaged. Almost the size of dragons.

As they soared out, some of the stingers split up.

Diving right towards him.

"Took 'em long enough," Spathi grumbled, raising Vrashri.

Impetuously, he lunged over a bulbous stream of lava, then another, narrowly missing the molten rock. The radiating heat was beyond excruciating, threatening to cook the meat right off his bones! As he made his way to the drawbridge, the stingers swooped down, lashing their scorpion tails down at him. He ducked, then flashed his spirit shield from his left arm. The demons squealed and flocked upward from the holy light. Wearily, Spathi lowered his arm. The shield was much weaker than before…and it was draining him of his stamina; he wouldn't be able to hold them off much longer.

To his right, one of the World Choker's head bashed Maethel away in midflight. The empress screamed and went sailing, crashing into one of the drawbridge's chains with a loud crack. As she propelled her bulk back up into the air, one of her blades inadvertently fractured one of the rusty links.

Then busted with a loud clang.

The drawbridge creaked—then clanked and bonged, tilting downward!

Spathi panicked, seeing more lava from the moat gush and lap onto the other corroded chain, steadily wearing the metal down. He looked back up at the stingers and necromantids, making another round for him.

Maybe he could hitch a ride on one.

The necromantids had grown to the stature of the Enpherom's teratorn vultures, large enough to mount. Yet he would risk being bitten, being infected with the Ravage once again. He may not get another chance to be purified. One could only tempt fate so much.

But it was either gamble or burn.

He eyed the rupturing moat again, growing wider by the minute with the magma splattering against the palace walls in violent waves, melting the detailed golden murals and etchings. Surely a demon as vain and avaricious as Maethel would not be *this* reckless as to destroy her ancient wealth and lavish regal dwelling. But maybe she wasn't doing this.

The power of her volcanic lands had been hijacked.

By the World Choker?

Why now? Why were they fighting each other? And why wouldn't the cosmic Uden-then hydra make any attempt to attack Spathi? Hadn't he summoned him by accident in the first place by merely thinking of his accursed name? Was Spathi not the Drixiles' public enemy, the only adversary Drixilo had left?

Was he not the last dying ember of defiance?

The storm of Drixiles sailed at him again. He leaped up and tackled a necromantis, slashing away the airborne stingers. The female demons shrieked, repelled by Vrashri's light. Then the necromantis grabbed hold of Spathi's legs in its claws and carried him upside-down high into the air, over one of the gushing fumaroles. He didn't dare cut the huge bat, yet he struggled to gain control of the creature, flexing upward. The necromantis's claws were loosening, on the verge of dropping him into the molten pit below. Around them, the hot winds blew from the Northwest, stymieing the bat's flight. Spathi grunted, flailing his arms and sword around, trying to grab one of its wings.

Shing!

The necromantis screeched.

Spathi looked. One of Vrashri's scythe-like barbs had dug into the creature's back. The necromantis plummeted, headed for the volatile moat, magma splashing everywhere in thick geysers. He strained onto the bat's dorsal side and sheathed Vrashri and extended the necromantis's membranous wings, manipulating it like a crude ornithopter. He steered the failing wingspan to the palace entrance. The other drawbridge's chain banged loose as the metal platform toppled, its tip sinking into the flaming slop below. Spathi squinted, trying to glide down, trying to land inside the palace.

It was going to be close.

Clang!

The necromantis splattered on the drawbridge! With all his might, Spathi hiked up the steep, submerging bridge, the gold smelting and snapping beneath.

The bridge broke off!

Spathi lunged…and grabbed the ledge.

He heaved and pulled himself upward as another earthquake rampaged through Tauldren. A massive whale-like roar bellowed. Spathi turned. One of the World Choker's heads burst forth from the magma—and bashed itself against the wall and struck at incoming stingers. The palace gateway crushed, its golden pieces collapsing. Spathi ran into the stronghold, dodging beams of metal, wood, and gilded shards of the ceiling. All grew dark as the palace entrance caved in while the seismic tremors rived parts of the tiled floor to pieces under him. He flew down into the darkness, tripping over stone furniture and smashing through unseen pottery and statues as the mayhem of screeching metal and crushing rocks chased him down a long corridor.

Then the rumbling lessened…and ceased.

The hail of debris finally halted.

And all grew quiet. All Spathi could hear was his hoarse wheezing and coughing. Sweat and grime dripped from his face and fingers as he swallowed and caught his breath. He looked around.

Where the hell was Constanvol?

Everything was silent. All too silent.

Then, something grumbled at him from the blackness, inside his mind, morphing into another conniving chuckle, the same laughter he heard outside earlier.

An insidious male voice.

Good, the telepathic voice taunted. *Very good….*

III: Lurkers

Spathi clenched his teeth at the ominous snicker in his mind. Then the menacing voice vanished, yet its presence still somehow persisted, a shadow prowling around in his conscience. All that was heard was the cavernous draft of the palace interior and the dull booming outside. As his eyes adjusted to the dim lighting, chills skittered down his spine.

He knew he was being watched.

Where had Constanvol gone?

Boom.

He turned to the right. Something large bonged against the palace walls, then screeched against the golden parapets above, as if trying to squeeze through a crevice or a hole. Maethel, most likely. Or the World Choker. He squinted. Why was only Drixilo in league with the Udenthen and none of his servants? Why had the World Choker consumed Moldrus just now? Had Constanvol spoken true? Was the baron a true renegade, opposing both heaven and hell? Spathi sighed. He had to find him, but only because his morbid curiosity pestered him all too much.

He no longer wanted to live. But he didn't want to die, either.

How torn he was!

He shook his head and scanned the vast palace halls. Maethel's stained-glass windows immediately drew his gaze; each pane was a mass of enormous claw-shaped rubies, the shards ornately cut and jutting upward, constructed like lotus petals stacked on top of each other. In the faint firelight, the walls glittered of black quartz with jagged veins of pure gold running all through them like lightning forever petrified in stone. The empress's extravagance was nauseating.

All this treasure. All this might. All this privilege.

And *still* she was bitter and petulant!

For Maethel, there was no such thing as "satisfaction."

He peered down. Debris consisting of wood splinters, fragments of statues, and glass lay strewn across the polished tiled floor. And dead bodies! Hundreds of corpses of female Drixilac cultists in armor lay mangled on the floor, many sliced in half while others were mutilated beyond recognition. Some were rendered mummified, drained of every last drop of blood, undoubtedly Constanvol's handiwork.

A fresh genocide, meticulously wrought.

He was hunting quite a monster.

Old news.

Amongst the bloodied women's guts, a few dishes of dented gold and shattered cornucopias lay strewn, along with squished pieces of fresh fruit. A print from a boot marked the flattened skin of a crushed plum. Spathi crouched low, examining it, then stroked the moist texture with his bare fingers. He recognized the imprint.

The boots…of the Enoshah military?

Ludicrous!

He shook his head again and sighed. It was impossible for any of them to be left. The Enoshah were extinct, as were the Enpherom and Vauphec. It was most likely from a pair of boots that one of Maethel's Drixilacs had stolen as some sort of joke. He studied the shoeprint more closely. Maybe it wasn't military. He also failed to rule out it being from Constanvol's boot.

The baron had to be close.

Spathi scoffed and stood back up, glancing around.

More elegant braziers and sconces lined the corridors, with the holes and slits in their plated sides fuming with strands of lazy smoke, wafting with sweet spices of cinnamon, roses, and incense. Opulent bowl-like chandeliers adorned with pearls and diamonds hung from gilt chains overhead, swinging in the gentle draft. Curtains and tapestries of crimson silk swayed around in the dark, with Tauldren's bat-like insignia embroidered in shimmering gold on each; some of them lay recently tattered and even smoldering in a few places. Green palm plants, tropical flowers, and other lush vegetation sat in tall vases of carven obsidian and brass; some had been toppled during the debacle earlier. Countless white candles were placed all around gold idols depicting smiling serpentine goddesses sitting within archway niches in the walls; the thick draperies of their pale wax caked around the pagan effigies' scaled waists, oozing all the way down to the floor. Massive pillars engraved with elephants, bats, and caryatids of cobra women supported the lofty ceiling.

Gold. Jewels. Wealth. Abundance.

Decadence beyond measure.

If Spathi hadn't known any better, he would have thought he were back in Ixod.

Above, intricate clerestory windows of orange, white, and red gemstones displayed the grim light of the volcanoes outside, just enough to make the crystal shards visible; somehow, not one speck of soot was evident on the panes, no doubt Maethel's ignorant and naïve "initiates" were meant to risk their lives to clean and preserve the dragon queen's vanity.

Just like Silda once did.

Before him, the floor ended into a small set of steps of solid pearl that led into a steaming rectangular pool of glassy water. Lotus flowers of various colors and sizes drifted calmly amongst lily pads, each one carrying a small tealight; their ignited wicks flittered like burning fingers coaxing him to the water. He looked. The pool ended at another petite staircase, up to a decorative mirror that reached up to the vaulted ceiling.

A faint orange light seeped out from a horizontal crack at the bottom.

A door?

Spathi peered at the shallow water. Crystal clear, yet it was gradually being reddened by the cultists' spilt blood. But there were no stingers. No tentacles to drag him down. Nothing. He took a deep breath and drew Vrashri, then eased into the pool, quietly sloshing to the other end. The lilies, lotuses, and flickering tealights twirled on the surface to his cautious wake. He eyed the walls next to the bath, at more of the candlelit idols in their gawdy niches, decorated with mosaic patterns and other ceramic statuary. Smoldering scars were carved on some of them. He squinted, looking back and forth for Constanvol.

Something wasn't right. The corridors had become all too quiet. Even Maethel's battle with the World Choker outside seemed to have subsided, along with the volcanoes' raging. The eerie draft in the halls sounded more and more like the ongoing unified groaning of countless ghostly women, all humming in long, cacophonous, soughing notes from afar that occasionally rose in pitch, only to sink back into its disturbing undulating moans. The farther he crept through the water, the more the corridor reminded him of Id-Zix's haunted aqueduct five years ago, all the while having to suffer each jaundiced wraith that was chained to the rusty sconces.

But this was almost worse. The opulent serenity only mocked him.

Something was waiting for him, prowling about in the shadows.

He could feel it.

As he drew closer to the mirrored end, he noticed the remaining archways open up to other hallways of niches...with men bound to the idols by chains. Live men.

Dismembered men. Castrated. Armless and legless.

With their eyes and tongues cut out. Each one had an apparatus like a gas mask, with a translucent feeding tube stretching up and disappearing into the darkness of the ceiling, spewing a substance down their mouths that resembled snot, vomit...and heaven knew what else.

Spathi's eyes bulged as he watched the men's writhing torsos twitch to creatures scurrying across their flesh: tarantulas. Huge tarantulas! They had spun webs around their hosts while laying egg sacs in their skin; some had burst open, revealing their thousands of progeny crawl around the tormented captives. He looked down the other prison halls, each one stretching down what seemed like at least a mile away down into the blackness of the palace. His eyes shifted back and forth; there were ten hallways on each side of the pool. Like the "coffer silos" of women in Ixod, Maethel also had accumulated a cache of victims throughout the centuries to feed on, doing so in her own way, basking in the agony of men, "empowered" by their pain and despair. He debated whether or not to put the men out of their misery. This was a fate worse than death! But there were so many of them, and he still had to find Constanvol before he fled Tauldren. He scowled so hard that his face hurt.

Maethel was no better than Id-Zix.

A worthless gender war that had gotten nowhere.

Anguishing mortals, men and women both.

An infernal travesty.

Ping! Ping-ping-ping.

Spathi swung around back to the demolished entrance, his legs splashing, then he glanced at one of the larger hallways, gripping Vrashri tight. His eyes darted left—then right—then left again. He held his breath, listening, watching. All he could here was the peaceful rippling of water around his shins and the grotesque slurping of the men's feeding tubes. He stared at the busted gold dishes on the floor, then he quietly exhaled a quavering sigh. Maybe it was just another piece of debris falling from the ceiling. Reluctantly, he turned back to the mirror door and slowly stepped out of the pool.

And finally noticed his reflection.

A normal reflection!

No skinless visage, no exposed muscle tissue, tendons, or bone. Just a regular image. With his wide brown eyes, he approached the polished silvery surface and examined his armored body. He hadn't seen his own flesh in so long! The wastelands had abraded and grimed his tan skin, with sweat matting some of the strands of black hair on his forehead, cheeks, and neck, but at least he could see it for the first time in forever. Strangely, the Sevelurnum armor had maintained its brilliant sheen…for the most part. Alas, even the holy metal was not invincible, having already suffered claw marks from Drixiles. He grimaced at the mirror, examining his remaining fangs. Four were still there, two on top, two on bottom. Constanvol's blood-eater curse still lingered, a contagion to his existence. Hopefully, killing the baron would end it.

But then what? Wouldn't he just be mortal?

Powerless? Unable to fight?

What if being a blood-eater helped him withstand Malroc? The last thing he wanted to be was a damned reaver, or to be dragged down to the Nevarifta, or to suffer that hellish void again! He didn't want to live. And he didn't want to die. He was truly trapped. Was there such a thing as solace? Freedom? Would being a blood-eater actually aid him in this losing battle? Part of him wanted to simply succumb. And yet, part of him wanted to endure as long as he possibly could.

Oh, how torn he was!

And…feverish. Lightheaded….

His body pulsed, his head throbbing. He grunted, cringing, feeling as if his skull was splitting right down the middle. Then he gazed at his reflection again.

The figure was no longer corresponding to his movements.

Then it roared!

Its mouth yawned like a reaver's drooping face as its eyes flared red. The skin turned the color of ash as insect proboscises jutted out from both its arms. Spathi swung and bashed against the mirror's surface, fracturing it more and more with each thrust.

Then it smashed. Shattering.

Spathi wheezed and coughed, leaning on the demolished mirror's jagged edge. Small cuts striped his cheeks where the flying shards had nicked his face. He sputtered and retched, recovering from the strange episode.

"Took you long enough," a familiar smug voice echoed from the room beyond.

Spathi caught his breath, then glared into the chamber, then up at a huge idol resembling a creature that was half woman, half spider. On the statue's lap, the dimly-lit shape of his target sat.

Constanvol. With a golden goblet in his hand and a gilded bowl of grapes next to him. The left side of his face was spattered with the blood of the Tauldrenian cultists he had slaughtered.

"Help yourself, won't you?" the baron mocked, gesturing to a long altar of food before the idol. "You look quite famished."

Spathi stepped into the vast chamber: a temple illumined by thousands of white candles. The sanctuary seemed even more opulent than the corridors before, the walls gleaming with more gold, rubies, and garnet. Yet parts of the wall were packed with vertical tubes of dried mud all around, seeming like crude organ pipes.

Reeking of fresh insect pheromones.

Like the hallways before, the marble floor was littered with the dismembered bodies of female Drixilacs. Overhead, the clerestory windows shown clear with elaborate polygonal etchings decorating their panes. A large rotunda loomed over the spider goddess idol, adorned with coffered mosaic tiles and stained glass. On the sprawling altar before him, many exotic flowers and dishes of fruit had been offered to the idol: apples, grapes, pitayas, guava, cherries, mangoes, pineapple, berries of many sorts, and broad cylixes and goblets of wine and red blood. Yet a few platters had some sort of charred creatures on them. Spathi grew closer and examined them.

Then he wanted to vomit.

They were not animals. They were children.

Cooked newborns, given as grisly sacrifices.

Spathi retched again. Was this the fate that Flora, Silda's baby, would have suffered had he not said anything to her pregnant mother that fateful night at Drixilo's reincarnation ritual in the desert? Was this the 'offering' to Maethel that Silda had referred to?

But she was dead anyway, along with her infant daughter.

His words had been to no avail, simply delaying the inevitable. Nothing he did mattered. He didn't want to live…and he didn't want to die. He was just another flesh slave subjected to this complicated sham called existence, born simply to die.

Just like the rest of them.

Constanvol popped a few juicy grapes into his mouth and chewed soberly. "Beginning to think you wouldn't come."

"Why wouldn't I?" Spathi said. "You are my prey."

"And you mine," Constanvol said, ingesting another grape, then he took a sip from the goblet and eyed him quizzically. "You know…just because you're a blood-eater doesn't mean that you're restricted only to blood."

With one furious sweep of his arm, Spathi flung the offerings off the altar, sending the dishes and cups binging and clanging to the floor. "I'd rather starve to death."

"Well…that is a pity," Constanvol quipped, on the verge of eating another grape.

Spathi chuckled. "You truly are your uncle's nephew, aren't you?"

The baron scowled, then cast the bowl and goblet down and rose to his feet, standing on the idol's folded arachnoid knees.

"Did I strike a nerve?" Spathi sneered.

"If only you had," Constanvol snapped. "What a relentless little shit you've turned out to be. You just keep coming back for more…and more."

"Damned straight," Spathi growled.

"Well," Constanvol said, "I'm not going to fight you. Not yet."

"What?" Spathi blasted.

"We both have the same enemy, you idiot."

Spathi gritted his teeth. "If you honestly think you can swindle me to side with you, especially at this poi—"

"I know nothing of 'sides,' Spathi Ansdari!" the baron blared. "As long as Drixilo lives…it's just going to interfere with our feud. The last thing I'd want to do…is to side with the likes of you. And you feel likewise about me."

Spathi throttled Vrashri's hilt.

"But we cannot deny that we both want to kill Drixilo," Constanvol hissed. "I cannot express just how badly I wish to cut you down—*but*…as long as Drixilo lives…I refuse to combat you. Once Drixilo is dead…then—and *only* then, should we finish our vendetta." He scowled harder at Spathi. "And I refuse to allow anyone other than myself kill you, especially Drixilo."

"I'm right here, Constanvol—take your shot now!"

"Damn it—you're the only one who can stop him!"

Spathi's eyes widened, almost dropping his sword.

"Though you are among my bitterest of enemies," Constanvol admitted, "even *I* must concede I have witnessed your uncanny power time and time again. You are my adversary, Spathi Ansdari, but you have proven to be a worthy adversary."

"How touching…and desperate," Spathi spat. "And why should I take your word for anything? How am I to know that this isn't some cheap ploy to catch me off-guard?"

Constanvol looked up at the idol's face. "Do you know who this is?"

"Just another worthless shit-fucker like you."

Constanvol leapt down onto the altar, with Qualkytdle's sleek scythe blade folded under his arm. "It is Anayoc, empress of the former kingdom of Dyvadros and was once the Dranixile of the stingers. 'Twas a lush empire, prosperous and powerful." He gazed upon the spilt sacrifices. "Then the wretched, codependent romance of Id-Zix and Maethel played itself out. They were once lowly Drixilian servants, nothing more. He promised her that together, they would usurp Enerbiez in Ebenex, modern-day Ixod, and take her as his queen. But he betrayed her, used her…yet, she toyed with him as well. When Tylphon-Teno got word of their unsanctioned debauchery and the murder of Enerbiez, both Id-Zix and Maethel were placed on trial in House Oxil. Tylphon-Teno pardoned Id-Zix, claiming that Enerbiez was too weak to defend his province, thus appointing him the new Drixilian tetrarch of the Penterium's southern province. Maethel still had to answer for her crimes. Livid with the Scion's decree, she fled to these very lands, hiding amongst mortals, where she demanded that Anayoc help her overthrow Id-Zix. But the spider queen refused." He paced back and forth. "In her wrath, Maethel killed Anayoc, taking her throne…and appointed Sunoc as the stingers' new archdemon. Dyvadros became Tauldren with the first mountain she ruptured with her anger. As a result of her treason, Id-Zix and his army of conquerors came to lay siege to her by order of Tylphon-Teno himself, but with her newfound ire, she held him off with such ferocity, so much so…that

Tylphon-Teno remarked that she fought like the Udenthen themselves; thus, he reinstated her in the Penterium and blessed her…with the form of a dragon…and six draconic serpents to safeguard her…nether regions from Id-Zix—or anyone else—from ever violating her again. Her ire is the reason these lands suffer the volcanic rage you've witnessed."

"What does that have to do with anything?" Spathi griped.

"Everything," Constanvol claimed. "The Penterium, or what's left of it, is one morbid, dysfunctional family. But I refuse to be like any of them, cannibalizing one another, only for Drixilo to take control and consume everything in the end." He squinted at Spathi. "If we try to strike each other down now, the victor is most likely going to die soon after, but if we leave each other alone until Drixilo is slain…then there is hope."

"I refuse to lay down my arm for the likes of you!" Spathi roared. "I will not have you lecture *me* about 'hope,' you hear me? And besides, no one can kill Drixilo," Spathi argued. "I tried to in the desert ritual. He can't be stopped."

"He can be stopped only with the copious mother and the stern father."

"Wh-what the hell is that supposed to be?"

"Melendraenin."

"What?"

The baron sighed. "Unzelkoyte's two-edged helix sword, the two halves: Chau Lepha and Vren Dotha." He peered up at the clerestory windows. "The sword of creation…and the sword of destruction. Each one is a sentient essence, far unlike the crude weapons of you mortals. When joined together, the two blades form balance, matrimony, two halves of the same divine will: abundance and retribution. Mercy and vengeance. Grace and judgment. After the First Quarrel, Unzelkoyte disappeared, sealing Drixilo away, leaving only two parts of his triumvirate self: Astrekiah and Arczellius. Yet, Melendraenin separated, divorced, its two halves vanishing into the virgin cosmos, a place only Unzelkoyte himself has set foot in, none other."

"How do you know all this?" Spathi questioned.

"Because Gyeno tried to find the two blades and reunite them for himself," Constanvol went on. "He thought his schemes were so well hidden, yet I confiscated his notes in his private study, a chamber that lay near a mercury well in the basement of his research facilities. He found an entrance to one part of the virgin cosmos, but he failed to enter it." He turned to Spathi. "That's why he experimented on you for five years. He postulated that your 'third eye' reacted to the portal, but he caught me spying on him, so he decided to have me executed, to silence me and distract the others in the Penterium. That, and with Drixilo about to assume a corporeal form in Raktogin, it forced his hand. That's why he staged your escape that day. He could delay his plan no longer."

"What makes you think that this so-called 'third eye,' or whatever the hell this is in my forehead, will do anything?" Spathi snapped.

"That was *his* theory, not mine," Constanvol told him. "I doubt if it even did affect the portal. But at this point, I'm willing to put it to the test, regardless."

"I bet you are," Spathi said, squinting at him. "And you also escaped that day, so how am I supposed to know that you're not—?"

"Believe what you like, but I wasn't part of his plan," Constanvol retorted, jumping down from the altar. "I was just a symptom of his desperate maneuvers. I was just in his way." He glared. "And he experimented on me for *far* longer than what he ever did with you. I am a descendent of one of the Mulya-Sheloth, a moonchild, the ones you mortal savages call 'blood-eaters.'"

"There's more?" Spathi said, raising an eyebrow.

"He thought that my connection to the moon would be the key to unlocking the virgin cosmos," Constanvol said, "but he failed, much to his chagrin. I will never forgive him for what he did to me."

Spathi glared at the baron, growing more suspicious.

"As I said, only Melendraenin can kill Drixilo," Constanvol told him. "Nothing can withstand its divine wrath." He looked around. "But Drixilo seeks the two halves as well. It is the key to unlocking the gates of the Mionia and claiming the Thruus Dyla, the throne of heaven."

"And after Drixilo is dead, what then?" Spathi snarled. "You'll kill me and attempt to ascend to godhood? Do you still think me a fool?"

"Once Drixilo is dead," Constanvol said, "if I claim the Thruus Dyla, then it is destiny. If I fail…then I am not worthy, and I will have no choice but to accept that."

Spathi uttered an acerbic laugh. "You self-righteous little shit! Think yourself 'worthy' to be a deity simply because you've survived this long, or because you think you know how to wield a sword?" His face tensed in fury. "Or is it because you're some bloodthirsty bastard son of some alleged 'moonchild?' The devil's blood still runs in your veins, have you forgotten?"

"Perhaps you'd like to take the Thruus Dyla yourself, Spathi Ansdari," Constanvol breathed coldly. "Maybe you'd like to succeed where Unzelkoyte failed."

Spathi chuckled mordantly. "I'm not the one pretending to be a god."

"So you claim," the baron jeered.

Spathi only tightened his glare at the demon.

"I sense much more turmoil in you than before," Constanvol taunted. "Like a smoldering wick, about to die."

"And I sense cowardice and weakness in you, like a scared rat about to be dragon fodder," Spathi taunted. "Is that what brought you to Tauldren? Are these sword halves here?"

"The *key* to them is," Constanvol said, looking at the ceiling, "unbeknownst to that thickskulled dragon heifer—and I'd like to keep it that way. Ol' Queenie locked him up in here, using him as a mere power conduit."

"Him?"

The baron squinted at him again. "The Nalx."

"You mean…?"

Constanvol nodded.

Spathi belted a long, grating sigh. "I had a feeling he wasn't dead…but I'll believe it when I see it."

"Suit yourself," Constanvol quipped. "Just try not to die. Not yet." He looked to the door to the left and walked towards it. "I'm going on ahead. Try not to fall behind this time."

"Hey, where the hell do think you're going?" Spathi spat, raising Vrashri and running towards him. "Don't you turn your back on me, you—!"

Shing! Bang!

With one deft motion, the baron bashed Qualkytdle's blade against Vrashri, sending Spathi sailing against the wall and into a mass of mud tubes, crashing through them like dirt clods.

Constanvol scoffed and folded Qualkytdle's blade, then he resumed his casual pace to the doorway. "You may have grown stronger, but you desperately need to hone your intelligence. And work on your swordplay. You've grown sloppy since our last duel. It's revolting."

As Spathi dug himself out of the tubing of dried earth, a loud, mournful roar rang out from above. Constanvol stopped and whipped around, gazing upward. He extended Qualkytdle's blade at the stained-glass rotunda. Spathi rose and readied Vrashri, wincing and glaring at the ceiling.

Boom!

One of the World Choker's heads crashed through the dome and burrowed into the Anayoc idol. Spathi struggled to shield himself with his weakened flaming spirit aegis while Constanvol deflected pieces of gold and boulders. Then the hydra head moaned and rose up from the deep hole it had bored...and eyed Constanvol with its fierce cyclopean eye. Spathi looked down at the hole, stained with steaming black bitumen and saw a circular vault lined with various royal tomb-like niches.

A sepulcher.

For something monstrous.

Spathi gazed back up at the hydra appendage's immense serpentine bulk and its Udenthen head: two horned melons, one on top, one on bottom. The bottom was eyeless yet riddled with symmetrical cavities all the way down its armored mandible, the holes emanating a deep, foreboding yellow glow resembling ghostly candlelight deep within a cave. A noise like a colossal rattlesnake's tail emitted from its gaping fanged jaws, steadily changing to the horrible chittering of countless cicadas. As Spathi cringed from the insect stridulation, he noticed smoldering scars on its neck. And some of its flesh had been petrified as pewter, chipped away.

Like bleeding scabs, freshly picked.

A winged form screeched from above—then pounced on the head. The Udenthen roared again and thrust its head up into the roof, bucking and swaying as Maethel crawled towards the hydra head's eye. With a great flare, her eye sockets spewed forth her wrath and crystallized the entire Udenthen extremity—then severed it from the World Choker! Spathi turned and looked.

Constanvol was gone.

"Damn you!" Spathi blared.

He darted down the hallway to the right as the hydra collapsed onto the floor and down into the catacomb opening. As he sprinted, he looked for the baron, running down another corridor, scanning for any sign of his adversary.

"You coward!" Spathi growled.

Ping!

Spathi looked down the hall, at a four-way intersection, then he raised Vrashri, grasping the sword in both hands. Slowly, he inched towards the corner, preparing to cleave the baron in two. He refused to be manipulated into another demon's schemes, especially this one. Yet he couldn't help but be baffled by Constanvol's confession.

He at least knew that Spathi wasn't a man to be fucked with.

But perhaps that made it all the more amusing to the wretched baron.

He stood at the corner, about to turn, heart drumming in his chest. Someone else was right there; he could hear their nervous breathing. He could feel the blood course through their veins.

He turned—and slashed!

Bing!

Both weapons ricocheted off each other, then Spathi beheld his opponent.

His eyes widened. And she widened hers.

"Spathi?" she rasped in disbelief.

Spathi dropped Vrashri to the floor and staggered. "Staea?"

IV: One with Five

Spathi and Staea beheld each other in the dimly-lit hallway, mouths agape and eyes wide. Neither one could believe that the other was alive…causing them to squint at each other in suspicion. As Spathi shook his head, Lena emerged from the right corridor, her Selebane sword drawn, then she shared in their shock. What was this cruel illusion Maethel had prepared for him?

And where the hell had Constanvol gone?

Had he been right about the Nalx?

Was Sile here?

"The hell y'all lookin' at?" a familiar twangy drawl sounded.

Spathi looked. Alehi stepped into view—and jerked back! Then Tyri, Haandin, and even Silda appeared around the corner, holding Selebane blades and having stringless Sevelurnum bows strapped to their backs. All of them had a few leather satchels and wore a special ancient Sevelurnum armor beneath their tattered military fatigues. Spathi's breathing quickened, then he snatched up Vrashri from the red carpeted floor and aimed the cleaver at them.

"No," he said. "No, you're…you're dead. You're all dead!"

"Nice to see you, too," Tyri snarked.

"Spathi, we survived," Staea claimed. "We managed to take refuge down in the caves of Mount Zevania."

"Mount Zevania erupted!" Spathi snarled. "I saw it from the desert!"

"What?" Haandin snapped. "Wait—that's impossible! You can't see Mount Zevania from the—!"

"Get back," Lena said, pointing her weapon at Spathi. "It may be a trick."

"*You're* the trick!" Spathi growled. "My friends are dead! The whole mountain range went up in smoke—volcanoes, blowing ashes, everything!"

"Wait," Lena said. "Where exactly were you when you saw this?"

Spathi sighed. "I don't…I don't know. Tauldren's ashes had blackened half of the sky. I could see Van De Yoth's mountains in the East, and they exploded. It had to have been Mount Zevania!"

Lena shook her head. "No. What you just described sounds more like the Lut Ve Brista range…or one of the nearby sierras—*those* are volcanic, but they hadn't erupted in ages…until now, apparently."

"How'd you get so far out?" Silda asked.

"I don't know," Spathi said. "I can't really explain it. Some supernatural energies with that gravity sword in Eregatho's back came together and tore some vortex in the air—I don't really know."

"Yeah, I saw that!" Alehi said. "What was up with that?"

Spathi shrugged.

"Told ya it took 'im all the way out here." Alehi grinned.

"Damn," Tyri said.

They all lowered their weapons.

Spathi looked at Lena. "Mount Zevania is…intact?"

"It was when we left," Lena said. "I don't know about now. We took one of the few surviving cruisers and flew it here, but we got into a meteor shower, and it knocked us down, crashing into one of the palace courtyards earlier. Been trying to find a way out of this damned place."

Staea sheathed Chauvien, her holy Selebane spear, and ran to Spathi, embracing him, tears streaming down her face, kissing his neck. Spathi wrapped his arms around her, kissing her scalp. Both of them held each other for what seemed like minutes, with her ear pressed against his chest.

"It *is* you," she said. "I know that heartbeat from anywhere."

"Look, I hate to be a mood killer, but we need to get out of here," Tyri said.

Spathi let go of Staea and stepped forward. "Not yet."

"What?" Staea questioned.

Spathi looked at them. "Constanvol."

"That little shit's here?" Haandin said.

"Yeah," Spathi replied. "He's trying to swindle me into a scheme, but I'm not falling for it. Says he knows a way to kill Drixilo."

"Pfff! Sure he does," Silda mocked.

"What did he say?" Lena asked.

Spathi turned to her. "Chau Lepha. Vren Dotha. That mean anything to you?"

Lena gasped. "The copious mother and the stern father."

"He said the same thing." Spathi looked around. "He claimed that Gyeno knows where they are, in some…virgin cosmos or something."

"There's a bunch of virgins in outer space?" Alehi said.

Lena sighed. "He means 'virgin' as in unexplored, uncharted."

"Ah." Alehi nodded.

"Where did you get those armors?" Spathi asked.

"The Silver Armory," Haandin said. "The ancient storehouse of St. Grae beneath Mount Zevania. The seal finally opened up." He groaned. "You know what *that* means."

"It means Raktogin is officially a ticking time bomb," Spathi grunted. "Global volcanism. Earthquakes. Seas boiling. Meteor showers. It's finally happening. Well, that explains why Maethel's volcanoes are going extra crazy."

"I'm afraid so," Lena said.

"Well," Silda said, "in that case, we'd better get mov—*khoouff*—khoouff-khoouff!"

She bent over, heaving and hacking in a hoarse voice, then the coughing fit subsided.

"Medicine must be wearing off," Lena said, grabbing a leather flask with its strap slung around her shoulder. "Sure you don't need another—?"

"I-I'm good—I gotta…I gotta ration it." Silda gulped. "That's the…that's the last of it, right?"

"Unfortunately."

"Where's Flora?" Spathi said.

"She's with the others in the caverns," Staea said. "They've been migrating, south of Vider, I think. Snow's been melting…along with the glaciers."

Spathi looked back at Silda. "Surprised you left your baby to come all the way out here to find me."

"Get over yourself, honey," Silda jested, then she raised her Selebane battle-ax. "Don't get me wrong, though. I'm glad you turned up. But Mommy has a score she has to settle."

"Maethel," Spathi said.

Silda nodded.

Spathi sighed, eyeing the elegant, unconventional Selebane bows on their backs. "I hope all you tenderfoots know how Sevelurnum *really* works."

"*I'm* trying to get the hang of it," Alehi defended.

"Good, because you're gonna need it," Spathi said.

"So are the others," Lena told him.

Spathi glanced at her, knowing full well the harsh gravity of the situation she was referring to. He knew what was coming. And it was going to be uglier than the siege at Van De Yoth.

Far uglier.

Tyri scoffed. "Can't be *that* hard to use a bunch of swords, axes, bows and—"

Boom. Boom-boom. Boom.

The earth shook. All the etched gold paneling, chandeliers, and ruby lotus petal windows clattered to the gradual quaking. Spathi and the others tensed, their eyes darting around the four hallways. Then, slowly, the seismic rage lessened, then ceased…followed by a deep, distant, mournful roar.

"World Choker," Spathi said.

"*That's* what that thing is outside?" Staea replied, her breath quavering.

"Yeah," Spathi breathed.

He stepped and continued straight down the hall, with Staea and the others following, their eyes vigilant to anything that moved. The hollow, jar-like chandeliers faintly swayed above them, each one riddled with decorative holes, seeping out more sluggish plumes of smoke emitting a strong, sweet incense. More braziers and sconces of gold lined the corridors, flicking out tiny tongues of dancing flame. As they ventured further, something shrieked from somewhere far behind them.

They all turned and froze, listening.

Another screech resounded from the direction of the temple, then another, each one growing more and more distant…followed by the faint chorus of skittering legs, seeming to scurry in a helter-skelter stampede in the rooms above.

"I can't wait to get the fuck outta here," Alehi rasped, eyes shifting around.

Spathi turned and noticed the hallway several yards up ahead become a narrow staircase leading upward into one of the loftier pagodas, the way lined with arched windows that were fitted with clear panes. He waved the others forward, all of them stepping carefully to the carpeted steps. As they trudged to the next sector, Spathi noticed Vrashri's blade.

The sword's bluish glow was virtually nonexistent.

And his spirit shield was nowhere near as potent as it was during the attack on Van De Yoth, however long ago that was. What was wrong? Constanvol could have diced him to nothing in Anayoc's temple earlier. Though his desire to kill him was still quite evident within him, it no longer burned like it once did. The effort he made to slay him just now was nothing short of absolutely pitiful.

He had fought far more fervently on Zevania that day. Back when it mattered.

Back when everything was at stake. And it still was.

Wasn't it?

He knew Constanvol meant to use him, albeit indirectly, yet astoundingly, the baron made no mystery of it. He wished for Spathi to know upfront precisely what his intentions were. Unlike Gyeno. Perhaps that was the point. Maybe the demon was *that* eager to display his alleged dissension from his infernal peers, especially the Drixilian Scions. But it did not absolve him, and Constanvol did not intend for it to. He only wished to corral Spathi and his friends to help him kill Drixilo, as a mere means to an end.

Not if Spathi corralled Constanvol into fighting his devil kin.

Could the baron actually be of some use, even as a temporary diversion for Drixilo. Yet if the devil claimed and assimilated Constanvol, it would only make him stronger. How he hungered for Constanvol's demise! And at the same time, the urge for restraint was growing just as strong. Part of him wanted him dead now. And yet…part of him wanted to spare him, temporarily, as his most unsavory ally.

What was this foul division?

How had he become so riven with such ungodly conflict within?

And the Ravage was gone, as was Malroc's influence! He had only himself to blame now. He no longer felt like himself. At all. But, then again…who was he to begin with? Where had he come from? And where was he going? Where was there *to* go? To hunt Constanvol down?

Or to follow him?

He looked at his comrades, at least…he hoped that's what they were and not demons wearing their forms. Even if they were genuinely his family and friends who had survived, he felt no comfort. He only felt shame for his wayward thoughts…and suspicion for this purported reunion.

Paranoia.

Their arrival here was far too convenient…and unlikely.

What was this morbid trap Maethel had set for him?

And why wouldn't his Sevelurnum radiate light anymore? Had St. Grae abandoned him? Deven was dead. The angels had washed their hands of him. Unzelkoyte was nowhere, and Astrekiah and Arczellius had evidently forsaken him as well. Was he to be consumed by fire like the godless thralls of Drixilo, while Raktogin exsanguinated its fiery blood and blasted out its ashen breath from its rocky lungs to suffocate the skies? Had the grace of the Unleztruv been depleted for him? Had he squandered the last of heaven's mercy?

He didn't want to die. But what else was left to live for?

He eyed Staea again. Could it be her? Or were these stingers just itching for the right moment to stab and poison him? Were they waiting to drag him down into Maethel's "man coffers" to dismember his genitals and tear away his limbs, only to fasten him down into one of those nightmarish niches, as another idol.

Another one of Maethel's playthings?

He growled deep down in his throat; he was so sick of all this. Without warning, Spathi stepped ahead of them, quickening his pace, then stared out the windows.

And stopped.

The others joined him and gazed in awe at the sight outside.

No longer was the moat present; it had overflown to a giant lake of unstable lava, splashing and lapping at the palace sides and towers. And the flooding magma was only growing higher. The ornate pagodas stood like titanic fusiform domes, each segmented story adorned with elaborate serpentine dragons with flaming crests and colossal spikes of ivory and white marble, made to resemble the gold-tipped tusks of elephants. Yet, the towers were tilting, sinking.

And neither Maethel nor the World Choker were anywhere to be seen.

Then something shrieked from above!

They looked…and a white fireball screamed through the ash clouds and smashed into the top of one pagoda, obliterating the shrine and several levels at the top. Spathi and the others shielded themselves as smoldering metal and pieces of splintered lumber bashed near the windows. Glass shattered, knocking everyone back into the wall opposite of the panes. Spathi and the others groaned, rising back up to their feet to see the pagoda's remnants topple into the lava like a dead tree. More stars fell, a brilliant shower plowing into Tauldren's volcanoes and the barren marshes beyond.

"More meteors?" Tyri asked.

Lena shook her head. "Those aren't meteors." She peered up at the celestial volley colliding with Raktogin. "I remember something in the Aurixla describing something about angels in the last days descending and hurling fire and lightning from the heavens onto the earth." She huffed. "Guess it meant that in the *literal* sense."

"Can't they wait?" Silda barked.

"Evidently not," Spathi snapped, stomping up the steps. "Come on."

They followed him up the steps, leading into the adjacent tower and down a darker corridor. Most of the sconces had been snuffed out, only adding to their anxiety. The floor shook—then shifted. All of them staggered, then regained their footing.

The entire palace was sinking.

"Is this the way outta here?" Alehi questioned.

"Where are we going?" Haandin griped.

"To find Constanvol," Spathi said.

"Let him rot," Staea said. "We need to get out of here."

"Then you go," Spathi said. "I'll catch up."

Staea glared, then slammed him against the wall. "You look here. We have traveled many a mile for days to come find you. I'm not going to have you brush us off like we're just some pesky flies or—"

"Yeah?" Spathi spat. "How do I know you're the *real* Staea? Or them?"

"Oh, shit," Silda moaned, rubbing her face.

"C'mon, man—don't pull this crap on us!" Alehi snarled.

"Well, how do we know this is really Spathi?" Tyri protested. "He keeps wantin' to lead us to 'Constanvol,' so how do we know he isn't leading us into—?"

"Well, clearly we've all reached a damned consensus that we don't trust each other!" Spathi yelled. "So, I'll go my way, and you can all go yours. How's that sound?"

"Stop shouting!" Lena said. "I don't know what else is after us in—"

"Oh, spare me—they know we're here!" Spathi growled. "I'll yell and shout all I want to." He turned and continued down the corridor. "I don't need anyone's damned permission or their approval."

All but Staea followed him at a brisk pace. Haandin shook his head at the stubborn blood-eater couple and sighed. Lena rubbed the bridge of her nose. Tyri rolled her eyes as Spathi and Staea vanished down the dark hallways beyond.

"Well," Alehi said, looking at Lena. "What are your orders, Cap'n?"

Staea huffed, closely pursuing her husband.

"What are you doing?" Spathi griped at her.

"Shut up," she hissed, passing him. "Careful, I might turn into a demon."

"Likewise," Spathi scoffed. "Try not to trip."

"Follow your own damned advice! Horse's ass."

"Beginning to think you *are* Staea." Spathi gripped Vrashri tighter in his hands. "You sure do piss me off like she does."

"Yeah?" she sang, flicking her dark, wavy bangs out of her face. "Thinking the same about you, pet."

"How sweet."

Both of them stormed through the hall, then the corridor widened substantially with vaulted ceilings and disheveled decorum. More pewter statues of humans littered the hallways, mostly busted to pieces. Many of them were missing their heads and arms; others lay crumbled on the long crimson rug beneath.

The carpet was stained with fresh footprints of bitumen, still sizzling.

Up ahead, Spathi saw a great orange light pulsing from a massive room, the glow gleaming on the gold walls. He and Staea eyed the gilded etchings and murals, marred with draconic claw marks and blood.

"Wow, she is one sloppy bitch," Staea cursed flatly.

"Yeah," Spathi agreed.

Cautiously, the two entered the colossal chamber: the hollow, boxlike interior of one of the pagodas. Spathi squinted; this was the most lavish portion of Maethel's palace yet. Around the walls, hundreds of steps on the walls led high upward to the pagoda's roof, presumably to a shrine on the pinnacle outside. To their right, a tall flight of stately golden stairs led from the room's center stone platform all the way up to an enormous regal door carved from a huge garnet.

Large enough for the dragon queen to fit through.

The royal door was engraved with snake women and dragon goddesses, shining from the bowl-like braziers ablaze with thick wisps of fervent fire. Along the stairs, more of Tauldren's silk banners and jewel-studded tapestries flew on the walls from the draft the sweltering volcanic heat produced. Around the chamber, a moat of lava lined the walls, already overloaded with the magma seeping from outside and sputtering beneath a bridge that led to the tower's central platform.

With a scrawny man shackled to an abstract polygonal idol.

Spathi's eyes widened.

Constanvol had spoken true.

"Sile," he whispered.

The Nalx was on both his knees with his wrists chained by manacles enchanted with pulsating demonic runes; the geometric grooves on the idol shone with the same energy as from the glyphs, bristling with blue and red energy.

The five closed eye slits across his torso burned with the same luminosity, depicting a cosmic sand dollar branded on unholy flesh.

With his mouth slit open where Spathi slashed him at Feshta the other morning, Sile resembled a gangly mummy, no longer swelling with bulging muscles; even the long, grimy feathers from his deformed wings had been plucked. His scraggly gray hair partially veiled one of his eyes as he turned and beheld the blood-eater couple.

"Blights," Sile said, speaking through his bony mouth. "All of you."

"Shut up," Staea said. "You're not Enpherom."

Sile chuckled a wheezing laughter. "You are still blights, nevertheless."

"Oh, how heartbreaking," Spathi mocked.

"I agree, love," Staea said.

"I told you he was here," a man's voice called from above.

Spathi and Staea looked up at the pagoda stairs. Constanvol stood perched on the steps over the entrance to the opposite hall, the gateway barred by a gold-plated portcullis that appeared to be jammed with a small gap beneath its golden spikes. Like a conniving cat, the baron studied the two, then he glanced at Sile.

"Your parents are dead," Constanvol spoke.

Sile turned to him. "And you have come…to kill me as well?"

"I come to give you freedom," the baron claimed.

Sile wheezed another chuckle. "You Drixiles are all alike. We are both a means to an end, you and I. We always were." He turned to Spathi and Staea. "I suppose you two are as well."

"The hell's he talking about?" Staea whispered to Spathi.

"The world…it is full of the users and the used," Sile croaked. "But even the users are tools themselves. All are manipulated. All become stagnant and depleted. Soon, I will be diminished…as will be the rest of you." He turned back up to the baron. "I know what you *truly* seek, Son of Veliath."

"Not if I kill you first!" Spathi snarled at Sile.

"That would be most unwise, Ansdari," Constanvol admonished.

"I hate to say it," Sile said, "but he is right."

"What?" Spathi spat.

"What the hell are all of you talking about?" Staea growled.

"I can take you…to the virgin cosmos," Sile claimed. "I can open…the door, where only Unzelkoyte himself once walked. But strike me down now…and the world will only stagnate under Drixilo's rule, with or without Melendraenin. The Aordrixis is fracturing under the weight of the final days…and the Udenthen are slowly escaping through its cracks. Once free, they will unleash the remaining Uxuclique…and the Unleztruv will be lost, along with the angels…and their precious, spoiled souls in heaven."

"Sounds like a big crock of shit!" Haandin said behind them.

They turned. Lena, Haandin, Tyri, Silda, and Alehi arrived in the pagoda as the moat below sloshed more, steadily threatening to erode the pagoda away.

"He must be sacrificed at the gate," Constanvol explained. "Only the purging of great evil through an oblation of justice grants access to the virgin cosmos." He squinted. "And seeing you as the bastard child of two lecherous fallen angels, that makes you quite the candidate."

Sile laughed again. "Speak for yourself, moonchild."

Staea glared, then raised Chauvien with one arm, aiming the holy spear at Constanvol. "Why not offer *you*?"

The baron almost smiled. "You sure that'll work…Amaiphynie?"

Staea gasped and dropped Chauvien. The Selebane spear clattered to the platform as she stood stock-still, then she quivered and squeezed her eyes shut.

"Staea?" Spathi said, grabbing her shoulders. "Staea!"

"Staea, snap out of it!" Lena shouted.

"The hell did you do to her?" Spathi roared.

"Her name is not 'Staea,' you imbeciles," Constanvol sneered. "You haven't the slightest inkling as to what you're married to, do you, Spathi? Not even *she* does, apparently. How rich. See how her *real* name causes her such terror?"

Staea emitted an ethereal shriek, generating a small transparent shockwave throughout the pagoda, shattering the ornate stained-glass windows above. Spathi and the others stumbled back a few steps as Staea recovered, her mouth agape, with the jeweled shards hailing down and smashing onto the platform. For a brief moment, Spathi could see the irises of her eyes flare like bright magenta coals staring at the ceiling, then the light faded. Slowly, she relaxed, panting, sweating, and scowling up at Constanvol.

That damned wretch.

He looked back at his wife.

"Staea," Spathi breathed.

"What's goin' on with you?" Tyri asked.

As the echo of Staea's scream faded, a myriad of ghostly female whispers slithered back down from the pagoda's peak, as if…responding. All but Constanvol looked around wide-eyed, with the baron rolling a muffled, smug laugh in his throat.

"Do you hear them, Amaiphynie?" Constanvol taunted. "They miss you."

Lena just shook her head in bewilderment. "No. That's…that's impossible."

"What's impossible?" Spathi barked.

Immediately, Staea snatched Chauvien from the floor and aimed it back up at Constanvol, gripping the spear with both hands.

"*Two* moonchildren," Sile's voice grated.

"Shut up!" Staea railed.

"Moonchildren?" Silda questioned.

"Look, either you come down here in the next three seconds, or the Nalx's head comes off!" Spathi blared up at Constanvol. "One."

The baron flung Qualkytdle's scythe blade forward with a loud, steely clack.

"Two!" Spathi growled.

"Wait!" Staea queried. "What if we *do* need him?"

"What?" Spathi sniped.

"It's just a…feeling is all," she claimed.

More of the female whispers resonated throughout the pagoda.

Spathi's glare tightened up at Constanvol. "I need him like I need a hole in my head."

"Careful what you wish for, Ansdari," Constanvol hissed.

Crack! Boom!

The entire pagoda shook to an earthquake, splitting the platform and walls in various places. Lava gushed from the rising moat as rubble fell down the hallway they had come from. A falling stone crashed through the abstract idol, freeing Sile's chains. The Nalx stood and swung the links around like whips, popping and flashing with energy with each strike. Constanvol staggered as the steps around the tower toppled and fell to the molten slop below. The platform grew more unstable, severing away from the small bridges. Silda slipped and fell, yet Lena grabbed her arm just in time. Spathi and Staea rushed over to help the knight-captain hoist her back up on the wobbling platform, trying to dodge falling debris.

Sile saw his chance and ran towards the royal staircase—then lunged onto the steps, ambling upwards on all fours. Haandin snatched a Selebane bow from Tyri's back and aimed the weapon. Ten ethereal shafts of blue and white light formed in a neat arc formation around the stringless bow as the Vauphec knight launched them one by one like javelins at the Nalx. Each arrow smashed near Sile, most of them missing their mark.

Then one jabbed his leg!

Sile wailed, favoring the wound, bleeding luminous blue and red. As Haandin waited for more arrows to appear, Constanvol vaulted towards the Nalx, grabbing one of the loose chains and raising Qualkytdle's blade up to him.

The rebel baron gritted his teeth. "You're coming with me, y—!"

Clank!

Sile swung the other chain, the links rattling and coiling around Qualkytdle. Then the Nalx yanked and hurled Constanvol back and forth against the riving walls with what little uncanny speed and strength he had left, then bashed him through the busted panels, sending him sailing outside. Spathi gawked at Sile. For an emaciated shadow of his former self, the Nalx still proved to be all too formidable.

Yet the runes on the chains were gradually fading, drained of their potency.

High up above, the garnet throne room door opened one quarter of the way, then the door stopped as if jammed. Sile continued to clammer upward for his life, enfeebled by the Selebane arrow as he bled all over the carpet, setting it ablaze with spectral blue fire.

"Come on!" Spathi yelled, running and leaping over the moat.

Staea and the others followed, barely making it over onto the steps. All of them sprinted up the stairs, up the lofty ascent to the palace's tallest pagoda, avoiding Sile's flaming vitality cascading all over the place. Overhead, the Nalx crouched and slipped underneath the door, vanishing into the darkness beyond. Spathi and the others panted, finally reaching the entrance. Breathing heavily, he looked down at the massive hole where Constanvol had been cast outside. He couldn't be dead. Not *that* easily.

Demons had a pernicious habit of surviving deadly falls.

Far below, the glow of the voracious magma radiated closer, on the verge of consuming the entire palace. The heat was driving him insane! It was a wonder the meat hadn't been cooked off his bones. Sweat dripped from every pore of their bodies. And the higher they were, the more Tauldren's wrath seared their skin. From a nearby torn gash in the wall, he watched more of the strange white comets streak downward from the heavens to Raktogin, parting the clogging ash clouds above and pummeling the sprawling deathscapes of the world. Soon, there would be nothing left.

Soon, it would all be over.

Reluctantly, he bent over…and entered, with Staea, Lena, and the others following his lead. He groaned as he stepped into the dark chamber, dreading why the Nalx sought shelter in here. A gut-wrenching reason.

And it wasn't because the palace was sinking.

V: Ire Queen

Spathi and the others stepped into the dim chamber, aglow from Sile's luminous blood speckling the gold tiles of the floor. Shards of orange and red stained glass were strewn all over the place. They all locked eyes on the Nalx's quavering form on all fours near the base of a thick, stocky, round pillar upholding a shadowy draconic idol with six arms and two membranous wings, with fine silks and pillows draping the statue's darkened lap.

A gawdy shrine.

For the false goddess.

Two saucier-like braziers sat before the gilded dragon effigy, one on each side, freshly snuffed out, with sluggish smoke and embers still crackling within their obsidian bowls and reeking of sweet incense and potpourri. Twin female snake idols sat fenced off by lattices inside arched niches in the walls, one on each side; each lay beneath a broken rose window, illuminated by a myriad of white candles casting an eerie glow in the shrine chamber. Curtains and tapestries were frayed and billowed in the volcanic winds outside, the torn silk banners flicking around on the floor like dead serpents. Over the main idol, an elaborate symmetrical stained-glass window loomed over them; the pane was already busted somewhat in the center, revealing the lofty ash clouds of the sky and the orange Udenthen sky cage above, burning like molten ribs beneath the charred surface of the heavens. The window's jagged panes jutted upward, similar to that of the jeweled lotus bloom frames from earlier. Spathi scoffed. The glass's lavish display reminded him of a massive crimson agave plant of solid ruby nestled among crystalline palms, gleaming like ravenous fanged jaws in the sparse candlelight.

Ready to devour all.

Spathi took a few steps forward to Sile, aiming Vrashri down at him, with Staea gazing at her husband with concerned eyes. Only Silda gazed upward at the large dragon idol, wringing her gauntleted hands around her Selebane ax, glaring in silent terror at movement in the shadows.

Something…slithering.

"Spathi, wait," Staea pleaded.

Spathi looked over his shoulder and squinted at her. "Why are you suddenly so eager to spare him? Especially after what he's done."

"Aye," Haandin said, holding the Selebane bow with fresh floating arrows aimed at Sile. "Let's waste 'im."

"Shoot 'im!" Alehi said, then raised an eyebrow at the ethereal projectiles. "And you gotta show me how to do that with the arrows."

"Later," Haandin agreed. "Spathi? What ails you, lad?"

"I don't know," Spathi quipped. "Shall I? Can we all reach a unanimous decision?"

Tyri glanced at Silda, then stared at where she was looking…and her eyes widened, taking a step back.

"I can take you…to the virgin cosmos," Sile croaked.

"Right," Spathi huffed. "And I can sprout wings out of my ass and fly to the moon. Seriously, what the hell is the virg…?"

He trailed off, then he stared into space. The virgin cosmos.

Constanvol wasn't the first one who told him. Something else had. Five years ago.

In the belly of the Udenthen, right before he crashed into Ixod.

"Seize the virgin cosmos…" Spathi whispered. "Release yourself…."

"Uh, guys…" Tyri said through clenched teeth.

"I shouldn't have come back here," Silda rasped timidly, peering up at the huge, writhing shadow.

A low, monstrous thrumming rolled from the idol's lap as Spathi finally caught the undulating movement of rippling scales along serpentine bodies…and her large tail coiling around. The silhouette of her huge dragon wings unfurled upward, then her magmatic veins pulsated like iron in a forge, radiating from underneath her scales…and exposing several scars and gashes still bleeding.

From the World Choker.

"Ssssilda," Maethel hissed. "Welcome home."

"Fuck you!" Silda shouted.

Maethel roared, her eye sockets and throat aglow with infernal heat! Spathi and the others dropped their weapons and covered their ears from her deafening din, the noise blasting them back. The force of her railing caused the throne room door to slide down shut, fracturing the windows even more. Her six dragon heads snapped and squealed down at their prey as Maethel's snarl slowly quelled, her imperial eye pulsing to the beating of her vile heart.

Pulsing.

Like a dying sun about to detonate.

Spathi bent down to pick up Vrashri.

"Touch it…and you're stone!" Maethel growled, her eyes bristling with her petrifying fire, scowling right down at him.

Spathi froze, then he reluctantly rose away from the sword, then he squinted up at her. "Why was the World Choker after you?"

"You and that bratty dissenter brought him here to kill me," Maethel sneered. "The Nalx stays with me. Drixilo requires it."

"What for?" Spathi demanded.

"Like you'll live long enough to see," Maethel mocked. "Men. How insecure. Always wagging your tiny, little dicks around, but when a woman obtains a stately position, you can't bear it. Spineless. Weak. Useless."

"You? A woman? Hah!" Lena jeered angrily. "I don't need the likes of a slimy, man-eating whore to speak for me."

"You would actually defend those wretched pigs?" Maethel barked.

"The blokes have their flaws, I must admit," Lena said, then glowered and cocked her head to one side. "But a pig would be a strict upgrade for you."

46

Maethel groaned, then she erupted with wild laughter, then breathed in a disturbing, wraithlike gasp. "You amuse me, Vauphec. So bold. So strong."

The tail snatched Lena up and plopped her in Maethel's lap.

"Shit!" Alehi griped.

"Lena!" Staea cried.

"Mother!" Spathi yelled.

Maethel's tail constricted tighter around Lena. The Vauphec grunted, imprisoned in her coils while the empress rolled a more sinister laughter, eyeing Spathi.

"Didn't realize you brought your dear ol' Mommy with you," Maethel mocked. "How quaint. I see she still has to hold your hand through it all. Man-child! Just like Id-Zix was. Honestly, I thought you to be stronger than that, Ansdari. But I see that the more your little dick shrinks, the lower the levels you stoop to." She leaned closer to Lena's struggling form. "Hope you weren't planning on tucking him in tonight…Mommy."

Tyri reached for the Selebane bow.

Maethel roared at her again! Tyri backed away, watching her slowly crush Lena.

"That's right," Maethel chided. "Just a scared little girl with shiny tinker toys. Not so big and tough without your belt of grenades. You think I've forgotten what you did at Glasora?" She looked back down at Lena. "All of you will make for excellent statuary…but why rush things?"

Lena shut her eyes.

"There, that's it. Pray. Pray to your dead god!" Maethel taunted, peering up at the ceiling. "See if there is there's *any* god who can hear you. Nothing more than the fanciful shit of a failed patriarchy." She leaned even closer to Lena. "*I* can answer *all* your prayers, any time you wish. You lay right in the caress of a lovely *goddess*. I'm faith that you can touch and feel. I'm real. I can give you whatever you desire, all without guilt or remorse." Her forked tongue licked her fangs, hissing like a snake. "All you must do is submit t—"

"Here!" Spathi roared.

Maethel looked up…and glared down at Spathi.

With Sile in a headlock and Vrashri aimed at his throat.

"If he dies, so does she!" Maethel barked.

"If you kill her, he dies!" Spathi railed. "Now answer me: why was the World Choker after you?"

"You summoned him!" Maethel screamed.

"He has no allegiance with us. And I have no allegiance with Constanvol," Spathi protested. "The entire time I was out there, the World Choker paid me no mind. He could have crushed me easily, but he went right after *you*. Why?"

Maethel uttered a more hostile thrumming in her throat as Staea and the others retrieved their weapons from the floor.

"Ahh," Spathi said. "Looks like somebody's been a naughty androphobe," he glared down at Sile, "keeping Drixilo's prize all to herself. Just drinking him up with her new-fangled powers as one of the Ravaged." He peered back up at the demon queen. "Is that right?"

"What would a weak man like you know of *true* empowerment…or Drixilo, for that matter?" Maethel bickered. "The Thruus Dyla needs a *queen*, not some pompous trinity who abandoned his creation—who can't finish what he started!"

"So," Staea said. "Ol' Queenie's a rebel, too."

Maethel said nothing, then squeezed even tighter on Lena. She squawked, her face turning pale-blue.

"Lady Maethel, wait!" Silda said, casting her battle-ax to the ground and bowing on both her knees. "Forgive me. I was blinded by these Unzelites."

"What?" Spathi spat.

"A bit late for that," Maethel jeered. "You always were a kiss-up. You think I don't know what you're doing, you petty sycophant? Pathetic."

"Are you really going to crush this beautiful, strong woman and let these…pigs get the better of you?" Silda beseeched. "The Maethel I know would never do such a thing! You taught us that solidarity is the way to overcome the patriarchy. Will you let them divide us, sweet Maethel? Will you let them win?"

"Silda…no," Lena wheezed. "What're you…doing?"

Maethel squinted down at Silda and emitted another thrumming noise in her throat. "I *did* teach you solidarity."

As Spathi watched them, he noticed a figure climbing through one of the smashed stained-glass windows out of the periphery of his vision, creeping through the shadows. He eyed Silda, then glanced up at Maethel; the dragon queen was calling her bluff.

Or was she actually backsliding?

So much for "settling a score."

"I will honor your petition, Silda," Maethel said, "on the condition you renounce Unzelkoyte."

"Silda, no!" Haandin rasped.

Silda said nothing and stooped towards the dragon empress as if in a trance, visibly traumatized. As she drew closer, Maethel gradually relinquished Lena from the coils of her tail—then she snatched up Silda! Lena plopped down and coughed and gagged. Spathi dropped Sile on the carpet as he and Staea rushed to his gasping mother. Sile wheezed and tried to amble for the door, but Alehi pressed him to the floor with his foot.

"Slow down, Sticks," Alehi grunted, pointing his Selebane sword at the Nalx's neck.

Maethel stroked Silda's face, the redhead's expression softening to an almost catatonic state. A succubus dragon queen, only interested in depraved affairs for the sake of corrupting souls.

Just like Id-Zix once was.

Tyri squinted up at Silda. The redhead slipped her hand down her trousers around her crotch, fingering something on the inside of her thigh.

"You missed me, Mistress?" Silda cooed.

"Of course, my love," Maethel sang.

Spathi eyed the figure in the shadows above, readying a curved scythe blade emanating with a dark-blue aura. He knew it. He knew that bastard couldn't be killed that easily.

"You know what I miss the most about you?" Maethel asked.

Silda grabbed the object inside her pants. "What?"

Maethel scowled fiercely down at her. "That pretty golden chain I had around your scrawny neck!"

Constanvol lunged from the shadows and dove down at Maethel, yet the dragon queen deflected, sending the baron tumbling to the floor. As the empress and her six dragon heads snarled down at them, Silda unsheathed the hidden object: a Sevelurnum dagger.

Glowing with a faint blue light.

And jammed it through Maethel's imperial eye!

Maethel wailed as Silda stabbed her repeatedly, rabid with vengeance. Haandin raised the silver bow and fired more arrows at the queen's two eyes, smelting them shut. Maethel shrieked and tossed Silda to the floor, then she collapsed from her idol throne and fumbled on the floor like a dying snake, spewing orange blood that ignited the carpet. Silda sheathed the dagger and grabbed her ax back from the floor as the dragon heads tried to bite them. Tyri and Silda lunged, hacking two of their heads off, with Spathi, Staea, and Lena joining in the fray as Alehi held Sile prisoner. Even Constanvol assisted the others as they decapitated each dragon head, one by one.

Maethel squealed again, then Spathi stepped up onto the blinded queen's bleeding torso, aiming Vrashri down at her throat.

"I must say that I agree with my wife," Spathi sneered. "You *are* a sloppy bitch. Think you're so invincible. Can't you breathe fire, you spineless gecko?"

"Let's don't tempt fate, Spathi," Staea groaned.

Constanvol leapt up onto her with Spathi. "If only Id-Zix could see you now. Broken. Beaten. I'm sure he'd find it quite arousing. Oh, how he'd bathe you in his excrement."

"You're mistakes! You're all rotten, little mistakes with legs and mouths!" Maethel gurgled. "You won't live long enough to seek the virgin cosmos."

Constanvol pointed Qualkytdle at Maethel's forehead. "I beg to differ."

Spathi glared at him. The baron only turned to him with a satisfied glint in his eyes.

"Do you see now, Spathi?" Constanvol said.

"If it is true," Spathi said, raising Vrashri up at Constanvol. "The Nalx goes with my comrades and I. As for you…."

A loud, mournful roar reverberated from outside.

All of their eyes widened as they looked around frantically.

Boom! Crack!

The pagoda swayed, creaked, then leaded down as the World Choker's heads burst into the throne room, shattering the room to pieces and opening their jaws. The hydras' mouths radiated with kaleidoscopic light, syphoning them all down their serpentine throats, including Maethel's defeated form. Spathi screamed as the yells of everyone else resounded away. He tumbled, then his fall grew more and more inert.

Drifting. In solitude.

In a vibrant void.

VI: Unstable Tread

Spathi peered ahead, breathing short, nervous breaths, watching the World Choker's innards manifest into an endless abstract matrix of fractal rows and segmented columns of iridescent crimson. Each pillar was fixed with four porcelain masks, carved to resemble the emotionless head of a bald man; each façade faced a different direction, as if corresponding with the cardinal directions of a compass. Glyphs of strange symbols flickered in the air within the spacious aisles before him. In the distance, he saw the silhouette of Maethel's mutilated body neatly frozen in stasis.

Then she evaporated like a ghost.

What was this garish, cosmic nightmare?

Was he finally dead? Or was it yet another false alarm? Could he escape?

And what became of the others?

Spathi raised an eyebrow as the psychedelic realm fluctuated around him. Somewhere, he could hear several screams dissolve away in stammering echoes around him. Staea, Lena, Haandin, Tyri, Alehi, and Constanvol, even Sile, all of them had vanished in the vivid chaos of the World Choker's bowels. As he tried to decipher what was happening, an insidious voice rolled a low chuckle like rasping thunder.

The menacing male voice.

Of Sevthiel.

Spathi squinted his eyes. "What are you?"

"You've been sleeping," Sevthiel said. "*Now*…you are awake."

"Oh, shut the hell up!" Spathi snarled. "Is gaslighting the only trick you demons have? I don't know if you know…but it's getting really old."

The thin air crackled, then roiled like the surface of water. Spathi turned around and tensed. A geometric tear formed in the space before him, spraying embers everywhere. From the otherworldly gash before him, a stoic ceramic mask breached through, the same face that was depicted on the rows of pillars.

Closed eyes and lips. No ears.

The head was encased in a transparent star tetrahedron of gilded fluorescence, with a glowing red and orange halo of elaborate polygonal webbing that seemed to sprawl for eternity, with just as many strands zigzagging and fusing to every single column in the surreal realm. Around the mask's edge, something seemed to writhe around, concealing the atrocity beneath.

Spathi swung at the mask. With…air?

He looked at his hands.

Vrashri was gone!

He checked and felt around him. It didn't feel sheathed on his back! He stopped and looked down. His Sevelurnum armor had disappeared as well. He was nude! Yet his flesh was somehow unscathed. He glared harder at the giant floating face, panicking, trying to breathe the scarce air, then he screamed at the porcelain head. Sevthiel only rolled another deep, sinister laugh.

"What did you…do to me?" Spathi croaked.

"You?" Sevthiel said. "There is no 'you.' You have no name."

Spathi's head steadily throbbed, aching, growing heavier and more excruciating with each passing second. Instantly, it became virtually impossible to concentrate or even think. He barely knew how he got here…or why.

He couldn't even remember his own name.

"What'sss…" Spathi slurred weakly. "Wh…where'ssss…"

"*This* is reality," Sevthiel claimed. "You are a finished dream, perfected and luminous, inoculated of lies from the finite…woken from the nightmare of limitation. This is enlightenment. You do not seek. All will seek you. *Now* you are awake."

Spathi wheezed and gasped, then he breathed less…and less. There was no air. No gravity. And no point…in anything. Did he…really need to breathe?

What was it to breathe?

Spathi's face contorted. "What are you…doing to me?"

The huge head approached closer. "I have awakened you. Time for you to know. Time for reality. Time for you…to transcend."

Spathi blinked. Suddenly, all the paths twisted and came to him, rather than he to them. He levitated over the glyphs, then lines of red fire appeared, zipping and stuttering rather than roaring and crackling. Each individual flame contorted into a cube, then they all spread out in a sphere around him and constructed themselves into even more corridors stretching in all directions, above and below, the paths infinite.

Spathi looked. The corridor shifted sideways.

The plane around him unfolded into a tesseract of overwhelming detail, made of pillars of heads burning bright red and white. The newly-formed columns were made of two faces, one on top, one on the bottom. Each top head was upside-down, conjoined with the forehead of the bottom face; each one shared the same third eye, swirling around as a maelstrom of multicolored incandescence, shaping into ribbed spirals. Each mouth spoke in a language he failed to understand, the syllables like distorted lightning. The symmetrical veins in their faces and necks were ridged like thin copper cords, pulsing with ultraviolet light. He sampled the color spectrum across his tongue. Sounds fluttered visibly around him as geometric wings. In front of him, a twirling ring of green and orange eyes appeared in the distance, along with stars. How he longed to reach it…and he failed to understand why.

Hovering in place over the vibrant mayhem, the vast tesseract of faces, stars, and barbed spirals traveled to him. He didn't have to move.

He didn't have to breathe. He didn't have to think.

Things came to him. He was the center of it all.

Was this wisdom? Enlightenment?

The tesseract became even more complex and intricate. Everywhere Spathi turned, a geometric shape appeared showing a glyph he did not understand.

"What is this?" he gasped, trembling. "Where…am I?"

Somewhere, a scream rang out again: a woman's terrified voice.

"*This* is enlightenment," the porcelain face repeated, bobbing beside him. "*This* is what transcendence is. You have reached it. The dream is gone. You are released."

Spathi halfway closed his eyelids. "Released…re…release…"

Release…. Release….

Release…something…. Something release….

Release…self?

Spathi squinted his eyes, struggling to recall what told him that.

"Enlightenment!" the face almost snapped, "This. Is. Reality. Not what was *before*. Do you understand? You were *dreaming* before. The past is *behind* you now."

Spathi gazed lazily at the face, now blurry. "No."

"Yes," the face laughed. "You will feel it."

"You…make me…sssssick."

"Sickness is beneath you."

"You…."

The face turned as the tesseract shifted around him.

"Everything you need is here," the man's voice said. "I will show you knowledge. Knowledge you did not have before."

Something screamed again, far away. Spathi felt something unseen brush across his skin, inside his face. A scarce nudge, against his face. Somewhere. In his forehead. Nudging left? Or right? Up? Or down? Sideways?

Something… Something on…something….

What was it?

Deep inside him, he heard someone speak. A murmur.

Get up…. Get up…. Do not lose yourself here….

The tesseract darkened to purple. Then to gray. Spathi failed to move on his own. The realm controlled him. A puppet to life. A tool to circumstance. His skin was so uncomfortable. How he wished to flay it all off, a claustrophobic soul trapped within flesh, one step closer to death with each relentless second.

Things…moaned around him, an odious droning, a sound like ghouls.

Then he heard them: cicadas. Louder than ever.

Everything grew darker. And darker. And darker.

Spathi wheezed and retched.

Sweating.

Dying.

The giant face before him disappeared. Then the tesseract's pillars of heads now showed empty sockets and drooping mouths glowing with fiery light, diabolic fumaroles groaning out at him.

Get up…. The murmuring continued. *Get up….*

"The voice isn't real, Ansdari," Sevthiel claimed.

Get up…. Get up….

Spathi clenched his teeth and shut his eyes. Something shrieked around him: a man's angry roar, followed by a woman's maddened scream. Both resounded, drawing closer.

Closer.

Spathi held his head. "What is all this shit?"

Darkness cannot take you…. Go to the place of impalement….

Spathi opened his eyes. Sevthiel's voice grumbled in unclear, haunting syllables. Slowly, the realization crept over him, icing his blood. He knew where he was.

Go to the city…. Get up…and go to the place of impalement…. I will show it to you…. Go to the city…. The time has come…. Go….

Spathi looked up. "Wake me!"

The celestial murmuring faded.

Something thrashed around him.

Spathi turned.

Thousands of Udenthen hydra heads came at him! Fish eyes swayed in lines and grooves like fleshy waves of putrid stars along the countless skull-shaped scales. As they lashed towards him, Spathi grasped something at the air. He felt it materialize in his hands again: a sword hilt. Vrashri melded back into existence, spewing embers all around him.

He looked. From the corridors, Staea and Constanvol barreled to him like comets, she from his right and he from his left. In the baron's hand, he gripped the two mystic chains, pulling Sile's limp form behind him, the alleged "key" to the virgin cosmos.

One hydra head came. Spathi swung. Blue light gashed into the scaly membrane. Golden blood sprayed forth. The horrible whale cry rang out all around them, a noise that threatened to split Spathi's skull to pieces. Constanvol slashed another head.

Spathi cleaved at more of the heads as his armor reappeared on his body. Then some of the hydra extremities finally constricted around him. The yawning ghoul heads of the tesseract detached from the pillars and flocked towards him, closing in fast.

Constanvol dodged the heads and fled to a corner in the psychedelic corridors. Staea slashed at the faces with Chauvien, defending her trapped husband.

"We will rise!" Sevthiel roared.

"If one is to rise," Constanvol snarled, "it shall be me!"

"Fuck off!" Spathi yelled.

Constanvol jabbed Qualkytdle through the tesseract membrane and carved.

The whale moan sundered all around them as white light poured through the gash. Spathi and Staea decapitated the coiling Udenthen heads and felt themselves syphoned towards the gouge. The sound of rocks and tidal waves crushed all around them. The realm ruptured as the twisting bowels of Sevthiel quaked. Gravity shifted, flinging Spathi and Staea through the torn hole and into the obscure spaces beyond. Through stars. Through darkness.

Then through water.

Deep saltwater.

They looked. Lena, Haandin, Tyri, Silda, and Alehi also appeared as the dark silhouettes of Sevthiel's worming, bleeding appendages retreated into the murky ocean depths away from the shore, his abominable roars fading away. With their hearts pounding in their chests, they all looked up and swam helter-skelter, making for the surface of the raging polluted waves above, unable to hold their breaths much longer.

Unable to breathe.

Anticipating the worst.

VII: Devil's Aggressor

Spathi and his allies swam for their lives, paddling upward to the ocean's surface, with the night sky strangled by something blood-red…and foreboding. Unclear crimson forms congregated in the storm above, their ominous shapes rippling and distorted by the sea's raging aqueous surface. Spathi and the others stroked upward, higher. Higher.

Breaching. Gasping.

Air! Oxygen at last!

A large wave emerged from behind—and slammed them onto the sand, their bodies tumbling and gagging amongst dried reefs covered in old barnacles, dead coral, and decaying red seaweed. Groaning and aching, they sheathed their weapons and rolled onto the shore, wheezing and coughing. Finally, their breathing regulated, their throats parched and burning.

Though drenched in saltwater, they somehow felt…dry. And grimy.

Spathi closed his eyes and inhaled, the quavering brine whistling through his irritated nostrils while his hands rested on his abdomen. He breathed. Sniffing. Sniffing the rancid sea air.

He opened his eyes again and glanced around.

No sulfur. Nothing volcanic.

And no Constanvol.

He furrowed his brow. "This…is not Tauldren."

"What?" Haandin looked at the cliffs behind them, then blew a sigh and placed his head back on the sand. "Shit."

"Red seaweed," Staea said, eyes wide at the reefs.

"Ixod?" Lena said.

"You gotta be kiddin' me," Alehi rasped.

"No way," Tyri said.

"No, nah-ah—no-no-no-no-no-no," Silda said, then pointed at the bay with a shaking finger. "You mean that…that thing puked us up…all the way—?"

"On the other side of the planet," Spathi groaned, sitting up, glaring at the sickly gilded light shining like a toxic sun pillar into the distant thunderheads. "Guess they don't call him the 'World Choker' for nothing, do they?"

The horrible whale cry tore through the heavens!

Spathi and the others scurried to their feet and saw it, far off in the contaminated bay. Sevthiel. The World Choker. The Udenthen hydra. The monstrous brother among the five Uxuclique.

Demonic parasites.

The dark golden-brown light shown up into the storm clouds as the black outlines of the coiling heads emerged from the ocean, vomiting black smog from their jaws up into the sky.

Into red…feeder bands?

The smoke and phantom bones of Moldrus, the conscripted Royal Arm of Tauldren, ascended into the ribbed cyclone overhead. The tempest's extremities absorbed the colossal wraith, assimilating it, grafting its entire being into the hurricane.

Becoming one.

Spathi groaned again, feeling the filthy brown mists of furious, oily precipitation blow around the beach. He knew what this was. There was only one storm that could produce this putrid slobber. Slowly, they all turned and looked above at the coastal cliffs.

The sea level was far lower than it should have been. The watermark of the cove showed on the wall of demolished stone docks, with a slope of debris leading up to the original shoreline. Spathi eyed two forms climbing the rubble towards a staircase leading to the crag's top.

Constanvol.

Pulling Sile behind him. The baron had wrapped the chains around the emaciated Nalx's wrists, yanking the chains in one hand, with Qualkytdle's scythe blade drawn in the other.

"Is he…taking that Nalx guy to…you know who?" Tyri asked.

"Let 'im," Alehi scoffed. "We need to get outta here if *that* asshole's up there."

"No," Spathi said. "We need to get him."

"Why?" Haandin questioned.

"Son, you can't trust demons," Lena rebuked.

"Yeah, forget those fuckers," Silda agreed.

"I'm not disputing that," Spathi told Lena. "But we need to get Sile away from Constanvol *because* I don't trust him." He looked back up. "I hate Sile too, especially for what he's done to our loved ones, but there's no telling what sort of evil Constanvol has planned for him, exploiting him for power. Even worse," he turned to them, "if Drixilo gets a hold of him…then everything we've fought for *will* be lost for sure."

"Spathi's right," Staea complied. "Nalxes are no joke. They're not like the other Drixiles, even ones weakened like Sile." She squinted up at their two adversaries. "We've got to stop them."

"And then what?" Tyri snarked. "Try to be friends with him?"

"Yeah, right," Spathi quipped back, looking at her. "We bring him to Shojem. Get him to cough up some answers. That little imp knows far more than what he lets on."

"I don't trust that mummy shaman at all," Haandin said, crossing his arms.

"Neither do I," Lena concurred.

"He's definitely not Enpherom—I don't know what he is." Tyri said.

"He's a little shit," Alehi snapped. "A damned smartass, that's what he is."

"Wait, you mean that…stubby little papier-mâché guy with the two tattooed ghouls?" Silda raised an eyebrow. "That guy gives me the creep-khoou…*aukhooou*-khoou." She coughed, then cleared her throat.

"Well, if we don't hurry," Spathi said, starting up the slope of debris, "we're not gonna live long enough to figure out jack shit. Come on!"

They all grunted and followed him, pawing up to the cliffs, watching Constanvol rise up to the weathered staircase that once led to Ixod's palace. As they scaled the ruins, Spathi peered up at the eye of the hurricane, the clouds billowing, breathing like lungs, flickering with fiery light. The skeletons of Moldrus entered the pulsating eyewall, completing its grisly merging with the beastly storm; their jaundiced, glowing appendages were gradually transmogrified with crawling sinews and scarlet blood vessels splaying over the giant ethereal bones and skulls. Streaks of red lightning flared behind the cliffs' tops, chased by the vicious roll of otherworldly thunder that ended in a ghostly rasp. As they reached where the disheveled steps began, Constanvol and Sile disappeared around the bend at the top. Spathi quickened his pace, with the others struggling to keep up. Yet, the further he went up, the more he could hear the abysmal din of an infernal throng, one he had never heard before.

And he would never be unable to unhear it.

Time was running low.

And he dreaded the things that lay on the crags' other side.

The spidery legs of fear ran up and down his spine, as if something unseen was strumming his vertebrae, antagonizing him...and savoring every ounce of Spathi's terror. As they turned the corner, reaching the final steps, he heard it.

The ring of sharp steel. And the shrill cawing.

Of Dather.

He stopped and looked. Constanvol pierced and impaled the shadow bird against the rock with Qualkytdle, gritting his fangs at the fluttering creature.

"Tell your 'master' that this Nalx belongs to me," Constanvol sneered. "And if he wants it, he can come pry it from my dead fingers!"

"Have it your way, you whelp!" Dather gurgled.

With a rageful swipe, he flung Dather against a nearby stone. The bird exploded in black flames, then morphed into a flock of angry crows squawking up to where the palace once was. Spathi gawped at Dather's form, at a blue scar on each crow's torso.

The baron actually managed to wound him?

Dather existed after all?

Spathi reached Constanvol, drawing Vrashri. The rebel turned to him and squinted, yanking Sile off his feet.

"Don't even bother," Constanvol sneered.

"All that talk about wanting to kill Drixilo, and here you are about to hand-deliver the very thing he wants!" Spathi snarled as his allies arrived next to him. "Of course, I already knew you were full of shit to begin with, but that's neither here nor there."

"He knows we're here, you fool," Constanvol rasped.

"Then why march right towards him, idiot?" Staea barked, catching up to them.

"I came up here to seek a vantage point," the baron claimed.

"Like hell you are!" Staea hissed.

"If you recall in those little minds of yours, this place is an archipelago," Constanvol snapped. "Or what's left of it, rather. Traversing the beaches would only lead us in circles.

Our only chance to navigate these islands is to elude Drixilo through either the aqueducts…or possibly find a land bridge, but I doubt the latter is likely…at least right through this area."

"You're full of shit," Spathi repeated, shaking his head.

The baron sighed and pointed at the bay. "Look there. The waters have receded. The earthquakes are causing the seafloor to split open, creating trenches that are causing the sea level to sink rather than rise." He shrugged. "But by all means, try your luck at escaping elsewhere if you wish. I won't impede you. *I'm* going this way."

"No. Not with the Nalx, you're not," Spathi growled.

Sile uttered a feeble chuckle on his knees. "You are all fool enough to try and outrun the demon host?" He laughed harder. "This is going to be spectacular. What an extraordinary travesty this shall be." He grinned up at Spathi. "And I shall get a front-row seat."

"Shut up!" Staea kicked him down.

"'Our' only chance?" Spathi scoffed.

"What's with this 'we' and 'us' crap?" Alehi grumbled.

"Don't get angry with me because we wound up here!" Constanvol barked, aiming Qualkytdle at Spathi. "There weren't enough Drixilacs dead in Tauldren to coax the World Choker from the Anli realms quite like that. I had no plans to invoke that wretch!"

"Neither did I!" Spathi blared.

Staea and the others looked at him.

Constanvol squinted at him. "You touched one of the Sevoliths…didn't you?"

Spathi shook with rage.

"And you spoke his damned name."

"I didn't speak that name!" Spathi roared.

"Well, *I* sure didn't bring him here!" Constanvol spat. "You almost got us all killed," he looked to his companions, "including your friends…that is…if you care about that sort of thing."

Spathi glanced away as Lena gawked at her son in shock.

"Spathi," she breathed. "You didn't…did you?"

Constanvol lowered Qualkytdle's blade. "How much proof do you need that not all demons are on the same side? Had we not banded together minutes ago…the World Choker may not have prematurely regurgitated us onto the shore just now."

"For the last time, we have no alliance with you," Spathi's voice grated.

"No," Constanvol agreed, "but we share the same enemies. The question is…how much longer do you want to live?"

"How much longer do *you*?" Staea griped.

"Just remember what I told you, Spathi Ansdari," Constanvol said. "I know you're a good fighter. Who knows? As long as you don't fuck up any more…I just very well might have a change of heart…and appoint you and your comrades as royalty in heaven…when I claim the Thruus Dyla."

"Unzelkoyte rebuke you, devil!" Lena growled.

The baron flinched back, hissing at her as if she had flung acid on his face.

60

"Gee, that sure is a tempting offer," Spathi mocked Constanvol coolly, getting into the rebel demon's contorted face. "If only it didn't reek of absolute horseshit—*ahh*!"

A flash of blue and red from Sile's bound palms knocked them all back. Constanvol staggered and released the chains as the Nalx scooped up the slack and sprinted over the crag and down the slope below.

"Get back here!" Constanvol snapped, chasing after him.

Spathi and the others pursued the baron, hiking up the remaining steps. As Spathi descended down on the other side, he skidded to a halt, as did Staea. One by one, they all stopped in their tracks, with Constanvol crouched behind a rock beside them, watching Sile flee to the abominable gathering below.

"Hey!" Silda rasped, running with Haandin. "Wait, why are we stop…oh, my sweet, holy Astrekiah."

They all scurried behind a few rocks as their wide eyes beheld the horrendous sight below. Ixod's sprawling crimson rainforests no longer existed; not even stumps or puddles remained. In the distant plains, two more Ot Kharden tetrahedrons had been erected. North. South. East. West. The four sets of the twin monoliths were established for whatever mysterious grim purpose, no doubt they were all aligned with the remnants of the Penterium Hinge in the North. Every stone structure, Enpherom and Ixodian, was rendered to dust, with the islands reduced to flat, barren plateaus jutting up from scalding, bloody tar where water once washed against the jagged cliffs. Spathi squinted down.

The sea was bleeding, as were what was left of the drying rivers trickling from the exposed aqueducts, somehow still intact. He shuddered, witnessing yet another sign of the apocalypse's final phase.

On the eroded isle, a huge congregation of transformed humanoid warriors stood, both Drixiles and Ravaged mortals. Tenoc, the Ruin Chief, played a ghastly melody with his syrinx, with no drums present, as his mutated mockers, the goat men, reveled around the huge, broken body of Maethel; the queen writhed helplessly on the dusty rocks as she lay on a hecatomb circle carved in the stone, along with a few Rinyox fanatics bound to glyphs in the ring.

Sunoc, the Swarm Mother, stood with a monstrous royal female Drixile that resembled a gigantic tarantula that was heavily plated with a ridged black and rusty-red exoskeleton; a grisly yet somehow elegant woman's torso was fused to her bulging, quilled, arachnoid abdomen. Twin gnarled scorpion tails swayed behind her, arcing high over her lithe humanoid parts. A crown of iron, brass, and garnet was upon her head.

Anayoc?

Had the World Choker resurrected her? A replacement for Maethel?

Near the eyewall's edge, a vast host of tattered white wraiths glided round and round in a circle like a school of piranha, moving in unison. They were scrawny and legless and garbed in bloodied robes, with their arms caked in gore and blood veins; the drooping maws of their leathery skulls were perpetually agape. Behind their heads, each one had a lengthy mane of scraggly silver hair that suffered a mutilated receding hairline, the strands wisping like smoke. In the storm's eye above, the silhouettes of Zilan and

Tylphon-Teno drifted, along with Gyeno's new form, reconstructed with pieces of Ere-gatho; their daunting visages were mostly obscured by the swirling mists. Yet the one thing Spathi did not see was just as disturbing.

Drixilo's large red diamond eye was missing. As was his cocoon.

Where was the demon host?

And where was Noshva, the ice empress of Vider?

From the tempest, Malroc's unsettling hooded form draped downward just below the Drixilian Scions with his forked arms outstretched, grinning up at the hurricane. The High Lich's bony hands moved with slow, sickening motions similar to that of worms as if…conducting a choir.

Spathi's jaw dropped. He had never seen reavers like this before.

Each one had a palpitating spike jutting from its sternum fastened with tendons, flexing like a praying mantis's claw.

"Insatiables," Constanvol rasped.

"What?" Staea snapped at him.

The baron turned. "The final stage of the Ravage. They've hatched out of their Torpid cocoons." He shook his head. "Once they've reached this stage, they're irredeemable, no going back."

"I think the sun's rising," Haandin said, turning to the bay in the South.

Constanvol scoffed and looked at the Vauphec. "You realize that's the World Choker's aura back th—?"

"No," Spathi said, turning around. "He's right. Look."

They all peered toward the bay and at the horizon beyond the World Choker. The faint bluish-gray glow of dawn shone on the clouds, gradually growing brighter.

"That might work to our advantage." Constanvol faced the demonic crowd again. "One of the many drawbacks of having the Ravage is that they can't—"

"Be out in sunlight," Spathi finished.

"What about Drixilo?" Tyri asked.

"I don't know," Spathi said.

"He'll be weakened, but only slightly," Constanvol claimed, looking to Spathi. "Not weak enough to fight, though. If he finds the Nalx, he'll make for the boreal regions in the East, where Unisylis once stood."

"How do you know?" Staea griped.

The baron squinted at her. "I'll show you."

"I don't believe one word of it!" Lena retorted.

"Suit yourself," the baron chided. "But I refuse to let Drixilo depart with the Nalx. Once that sun rises…I imagine that's when he'll move out, with his Insatiables taking refuge in his hurricane." He squinted at them. "Flee if you wish, but I'm going down there to retrieve that Nalx."

"Oh, no you don't—I'm going with you!" Spathi spat. "I'm not letting you out of my sight for anything."

"I go, too," Staea affirmed.

"We *all* go," Lena snapped.

"Do what?" Silda squeaked.

"Uh—wait a minute, now," Alehi protested.

"Do as you wish," Constanvol sighed. "Just don't slow me down."

"I thought you said Drixilo knew we were here," Haandin said. "This is a trap."

"Then be ready for anything," Constanvol quipped. "Unless you prefer to go make friends with the World Choker?"

Haandin grumbled and rolled his eyes.

"Shit," Silda hissed through her grimacing teeth. "Oh, shit—oh, shit, shit, shit."

Spathi looked back down at the revel below. He had never felt so sick in his life. What the hell was happening? Could this really be it? Could they truly be that close to it? The end? The end of time and history itself was nigh, after five long centuries, heralded by the Second Surfacing.

The end was coming at last.

Even after all the hell on earth he had endured, after all the death he had wished upon himself and others, after all the yearning for the bullshit of the world to be washed away with fire…he just wasn't ready yet.

And if Unzelkoyte wasn't here to fulfill what he had promised…then that was it. This wasn't how it was supposed to be. Unzelkoyte was the one to be victorious, not Drixilo. Not the devil. And deep down, only now did he sense the egregious temptation he struggled to swallow: to actually align himself with Constanvol, a demon.

His nemesis.

A forbidden alliance.

He shook his head. Too many demons had competed for godhood, and some still were. Drixilo. Sevthiel. Gyeno. Id-Zix. Maethel. Constanvol. And no telling who else. The Drixiles spoke of the Thruus Dyla as if it were an empty throne, not one occupied by a responsible, loving triumvirate god of the Unleztruv, not by Astrekiah, not by Arczellius. And definitely not by Unzelkoyte. With the nightmarish things going on in the world fraying to pieces before him, he was only tempted to believe heaven's "power vacuum" more and more.

The trinity was incomplete. Severed.

If that were truly so…then all was doomed.

Little wonder then that so many sought gods elsewhere, much to their folly. Even more foolish were mortals and spirits who attempted to elevate themselves as deities. Nevertheless, Spathi found it increasingly difficult to blame them, considering the insufferable circumstances.

But what was that voice he heard within the World Choker just now? What in the damned hell was that soft murmuring, commanding him to go this way and that? Why couldn't he discern it? And why couldn't he hear it all the time? Would he want to? Was it even holy? Was it anything good, if anything at all?

Or was it something…evil, masquerading as an angel of light?

All this time?

Constanvol scanned a path down the slope, then he crept down to infiltrate the hellish carnival below, with Spathi, Staea, and the others reluctantly pursuing. More red lightning crackled above, yet it was originating from a nearby precipice rather than the sky, the voltage being fed up into the storm. Something pulsed from the cliff, darkness emanating like black sunlight rather than shadows, ebbing all space around it.

Like a black hole.

Pulsing….

Pulsing….

Pulsing….

Spathi stopped and turned, then peered up at the dark sphere…and the one within it.

And he wished he hadn't.

Standing at least ten times the height of a mortal man, the towering entity loomed, arrayed in a hooded, cocoon-like cloak of segmented moaning shadows, their faces squirming in the malefic material. Though the black aura devoured virtually all light around it, the figure spared just enough of a glow, channeling it beneath him to shine up at him with dim crimson luminosity. Two barbed arms hung at his sides, wriggling with serpentine arteries throbbing with molten hatred. Behind the robed silhouette, six wings of black and red metal feathers arced around him, three folded on each side like a demonic seraph, with some of the steely, swordlike plumage shaped like goat skulls carven to depict yawning reaver faces. The crows of Dather fluttered and unified into his shadow avian form, then perched on the robed creature's shoulder. Staea and the others also froze, gazing up at the entity; even Constanvol halted and stared up wide-eyed in terror.

The robed figure turned slowly to them, revealing his face.

A mask. A scream in nature.

Perverting creation itself.

A wrinkled, petrified face of dead, ashen leather showed, forever weeping red blood and black ichor, with an elongated maw and empty eye sockets and nasal cavities permanently stretched to resemble crooked teardrops. Around his head, he was coronated with the most regal and insidious of demonic crowns, adorned with seven spikes all around his skull. A gaping hole showed exposing his sickening chest's innards. No lungs. No heart.

Only a ghostly red diamond eye, burning like a dying star.

Drixilo himself.

The demon host.

Enemy. Intruder. Defiler.

The ultimate traitor of heaven.

The source of all anguish.

And his eye sockets locked onto Spathi's face.

"Ansdarion!" Drixilo raged, raising his arm.

Boom! Boom-boom-boom!

Thick lightning rioted from the devil king's grotesque palm, blasting Spathi, Constanvol, and the others from the cliffs and down into the makeshift arena below. All of them rolled into the blowing sand as the mockers and Rinyox raised their weapons at them. Tenoc ceased playing his tune. Spathi looked at them in disgust. The skin of the goat demons' faces was gone, as were their sunken eyes, showing their decaying, yellowed enamel underneath; each now had four horns, curling down like a jester's crude motley smeared with ashes and oil. Each one gripped a smoldering scythe rather than a trident, ready to reap and harvest what remained of the mortal resistance. The possessed Enpherom demoniacs no longer looked human. Their heads were disfigured to appear like reaver skulls, engraved with nihilistic smiles for eternity with their teeth fused together, forming grills along their exaggerated angular jaws. Each arm was either a sinewy blade, a claw of bones, or a deformed rifle grafted to their arms and metamorphosed by the most infernal of magic. The huge bat wings of necromantids were folded behind their backs. Constanvol looked at the leader and recognized him.

"Jaeanos," the baron scoffed, shaking his head. "After all that talk about renouncing Drixilo. But I figured as much."

The Insatiable Ravaged above roared in hysteria as they paused their circuit overhead, hovering in the hostile sky.

"Ansdarion!" they all screeched, pointing down at Spathi. "Ansdarion!"

"Ansdarion?" Spathi barked. "What the hell is going on?"

A low, wraithlike chuckle erupted from Drixilo. They all turned and peered up at the ruler of hell. The demon host unfurled his six abominable wings and outstretched his arms. With a sound of warped time and space, Drixilo tore right towards them, leaving a fleeting vector of a thousand black shadows frozen in place, caught screaming in agony before fading behind him. He landed, seeming to stand even taller than before, gliding to the impending hecatomb where Maethel lay.

"Lord Drixilo, have pity!" the dragon queen begged.

Drixilo only grated another low laugh. "Yes…plea for me. Your agony is a hymn of justice, sweet and pleasing to my ears."

"Lord Drixilo, my liege!" Maethel squalled. "My lord, I beseech you—have mercy on your servant!"

"And mercy you shall have," the demon host sneered with sadistic glee, his spectral voice echoing, each diabolic syllable lacerating the air like razor-sharp steel.

Spathi cringed as Drixilo raised his hand. The circle and glyphs flared with sulfurous blue hellfire, shrieking with the cacophony of damnation. Maethel cried out, yet the demon host only chuckled again. The devil's servants went wild with crazed euphoria.

"Rejoice, my sweet Maethel," Drixilo said. "Your debt is paid in full."

Spathi and the others shielded themselves as more voltage and blood-red fire railed from his palm, striking down Maethel, each unforgiving bolt steadily rending her and the bound Rinyox to oblivion. The dragon empress's wails fragmented away in the wind as Drixilo's wrath dismembered wings, scales, flesh, bone, and all, sending the screaming spirits of the Rinyox up in a geyser of blazing brimstone.

Then the geyser inverted, imploding and burrowing deep into the ground.

Tearing a hole.

All the way to the Nevarifta itself.

Spathi strained to use his spirit shield to protect his allies, yet the devil's ire was too great, singeing their minds, bodies, and souls. The gate crackled and roared, quaking with the racket of stampeding hooves, drawing closer to the surface.

"Arise, my child," Drixilo commanded, gesturing his hand upward. "Arise and awaken from your confinement. Your sentence has been served. Arise and taste angel flesh!"

Boom!

The army burst forth! Demonic cavalry surfaced, astride skinless horses with skeletal snakes for tails. Each rider was an emaciated humanoid torso, no saddle, yet they were unlike centaurs; their legs were merged with the forelimbs of their mounts, with a goat's skull wrapped in rotten sinews for heads. Flames plumed from the horses' nostrils as they galloped around, kicking up dust with their cloven hooves. Like the mockers, each cavalier gripped a scythe, yet theirs had straight shafts and longer blades. They were all led by a general, more decorated than the others, armored with spines and horns and a long mane of silver hair. Only his head resembled that of a human skull, retaining some of the flesh…and the gray-blue eyes of a corpse.

Across his chest, a swollen imperial eye showed, scabbed over with a scar all the way across, as if…demoted. Scorned.

"What the fuck, man?" Silda cursed, covering her head.

The general corralled his troops into a circular formation around Spathi and the others, then raised his scythe.

"Halt!" the general blared.

The riders obeyed and stomped to attention, the devil steeds braying in horrifying, warped noises, blowing more fire from their noses and throats. The fire from the gate cleared, allowing Spathi and the others to stand. They all drew their weapons, all facing the dark legions.

"Veliath!" Constanvol yelled, stepping to the general.

"Stop where you are!" the general snarled.

"Father!" the baron glared.

"Father?" Tyri snorted.

Spathi glanced back and forth at Veliath and Constanvol. The Scion general regarded the baron quizzically, trotting towards him. Drixilo rolled another vile laugh.

"Qualkytdle," Veliath groaned in disbelief.

"I am your son, Constanvol," the baron said, kneeling before him. "Son of Minaya."

"Minaya?" Staea almost shrieked, traumatized, twitching in psychotic rage.

"What?" Spathi snapped. "Staea!"

Staea shook and shouted with eyes closed, a montage of strange visions zipping through her mind. She struggled to snap out of the conniption while strangling Chauvien in her hands.

"What is this?" she sobbed. "What is…I…?"

"Staea!" Spathi said, shaking her.

Her eyes opened and beheld her husband.

The general gazed at Staea. "Mulya-Sheloth."

"You wish!" Spathi roared, stepping in front of his wife.

"Father, come with me!" Constanvol said, rising to his feet. "Together, we can finish our work, our revolution! Drixilo has wronged you, depriving you of your birthright! Let justice be done upon this tyrant!"

Drixilo only laughed louder as Veliath scowled down at his spawn.

"Father…" Constanvol pled.

"I have no son," the general's voice grated.

"What?" Constanvol blared.

"You reek of the Mionia…and its fickle whores!" Veliath turned and aimed his scythe up at the moon. "Mark my words: Minaya, the moon succubus, falls by my hand and *my* hand only, by the will of Drixilo himself!"

"You wretched pig!" Constanvol fulminated.

The Drixiles cheered maniacally. Drixilo rumbled with another low, dissonant chuckle with arms outstretched. Spathi's eyes darted around, looking for an escape, an opportunity—anything! But there was nothing. Nothing but their imminent demise.

He still didn't want to live. But he didn't want to die, either.

And he couldn't let his family die.

Not like this.

"She is in your hands, my child," Drixilo granted. "You have my blessing."

"Thank you, my liege." Veliath knelt to his master, and his cavalry with him.

"Praise be to the demon host, the *true* god of Raktogin and the Unleztruv!" Tenoc declared. "Everything in the earth and everything above it and beneath it belongs to him!"

"Praise Drixilo, master of all!" The Insatiables blasphemed in unison.

"Sing for him!" Malroc crowed above.

"Praise Drixilo, sovereign and heir to the Thruus Dyla of heaven!"

"Sing for him!" Malroc called again.

"Praise Drixilo, ruler of supreme might and majesty!"

"Sing for him, my faithful!"

"Praise Lord Drixilo! May he consume all and make all things new and beautiful in his glorious swath, for his time has come at last! May heaven bow to him and despair!"

"You!" Constanvol roared, lunging at Veliath with Qualkytdle.

The general's scythe bristled with red electricity and embers and bashed the baron away, sending him plopping to the dust. Spathi squinted at Constanvol, then back at the horseman.

"Qualkytdle is a relic, you maggot!" Veliath scourged.

"Step aside," Drixilo seethed. "Let Ansdarion come forth."

Veliath complied and backed away. Spathi stared up at the devil, his tall stature slithering towards him, pulling a pair of chains from his darkness. All of them gawked as they saw Sile dangling from the links.

"This…is what you wanted," Drixilo said, "isn't it?"

Spathi only clenched his teeth, glancing around for a weak spot on the devil.

Drixilo cast Sile over them, landing before Tenoc.

"Anayoc," Drixilo called.

"My liege," Anayoc chittered.

"See that the Nalx does not escape," Drixilo rasped. "He is in your hands. Do not fail me like Maethel did."

"I will not fail you, most exalted liege," Anayoc replied, grabbing Sile's chains.

Drixilo turned and gestured to Sunoc. "Behold, your servant, Anayoc."

"My liege," Sunoc knelt to Drixilo, then rose and turned, then bowed to Anayoc. "Under Drixilo's watchful eye, as I served you in the ancient days of the Dyvadros Empire, I serve you now, my queen."

"I welcome your service once again, Lady Sunoc," Anayoc stridulated. "Rise."

"I think I'm gonna puke!" Haandin sneered at the horde.

"You rotten, stinkin' shitbags!" Alehi yelled at the Drixiles. "Ya think you're all so fancy and cordial and all—"

All the demons roared at him in an earsplitting din! Alehi and the others jumped a mile, then the Drixiles all cackled at them, delighting in their victims' trepidation. Only Spathi managed to stymie his tremors, turned and glaring back up at the devil.

"How long I have waited for Ansdarion to appear before me," Drixilo said.

Spathi simply tightened his scowl. Ansdarion?

Was he mishearing the demon host?

"What ails you, Spathi?" Drixilo said. "Come at me."

"Fuck you to pieces!" Spathi growled. "All the way to hell where you belong!"

Drixilo laughed. "That's not very chivalrous of you…is it?"

Spathi only roared at him.

"You are no saint, Spathi Ansdarion," Drixilo mocked. "I sense the turmoil within you. All the people you killed…just like you killed Treth."

"No," Spathi grumbled.

"Murderer."

"May Unzelkoyte damn you!"

Drixilo squealed and backed away a few feet, then he erupted with the most diabolical laughter yet, as all his faithful joined in his maniacal merriment. Spathi's legs wobbled, his morale evaporating to the winds.

"'Unzelkoyte damn me,' he says!" Drixilo sneered, then he snatched Spathi up by his throat. "There is no Unzelkoyte! I killed him! And Astrekiah! And Arczellius! Heaven is empty, and its usurpers are slain! Why do you think you suffer so? Do the angels hear your pleas? Behold the world before you!" The devil's voice grew disturbingly zealous. "How I long to save you from your misery and your wanton religion! I yearn to clothe you in my mighty glory, everlasting pleasure, glorifying me in your endless hunger and self-indulgence!" He dropped Spathi the ground. "Why do you hesitate to receive my blessings, brittle fleshling?"

"Spathi!" Staea screamed, running to him.

"Staea!" Lena shouted. "Come—*aughk*!"

Drixilo grappled her torso in one hand and rose her to his gory, yawning mask and uttered another chuckle, then looked down at Spathi.

"If there is an Unzelkoyte," Drixilo taunted, "then pray. Pray for your mother. Pray to your imaginary dead god! Save her! Pray for her salvation, Spathi! Pray for her before she dies! Can your trinity save her from me?" He tightened his grasp around Lena as she grunted. "Or am I the only god there is? I'm the only one who stands before you. Call unto me, and I will answer your every prayer."

Spathi and Staea rose and charged at him, jabbing and hacking into him with their weapons, while Haandin launched more arrows at the devil. Yet they had no effect, passing through him like smoke; even the projectiles did nothing, the ethereal shafts dim and feeble. Spathi's eyes bulged in horror at Vrashri. What was wrong?

Why wasn't it working?

Where was the light, the blue glint?

Drixilo merely raised his other hand and launched a volley of chain lightning, snaking and crackling through Constanvol and the knights. All of them fell down and cringed, crying in agony, their pain amplified by the cackling of the Drixiles and the Insatiables. All the demons pointed and guffawed, threatening to deafen them and rive their brains apart. Then the lightning finally subsided, their squirming bodies smoking. Slowly, the laughter died down to a low droning racket…followed by an irritable groan from Drixilo.

"Accursed Sevelurnum," the demon host snarled.

Spathi and the others moaned, all rising on their hands and knees. He looked at their armor. The holy silver had taken quite a beating, corroding around some of the edges; the lightning was too much for it. Constanvol stood up on one knee, gasping for breath, his cloak tattered. He looked at Spathi.

"You'll…do," the baron coughed, nodding at Spathi. "You'll do…."

"What?" Spathi wheezed, grabbing Vrashri from the ground.

"Your forbidden union is futile, Constanvol," Drixilo scorned, "but amusing, nevertheless. It taints you all. Why can't you all see the error of your ways?"

Lena muttered something, steadily wedging her Selebane from between Drixilo's fingers, trying to raise it up. Spathi saw it, trying to muster his strength. They had to endure. The devil was only toying with them, withholding his full power, reserving it to besiege the Unleztruv.

But they had to endure.

"You'd best be careful about killing me, Drixilo," Spathi sneered. "You wouldn't want my 'third eye' to—"

"To hell with your third eye!" Drixilo sneered. "I no longer fear it. All that remains is to traverse the virgin cosmos and—*aahh*!"

With her Selebane luminous, Lena stabbed Drixilo's arm—then impaled his ribs, barely missing the diamond eye. Drixilo squealed again, dropping the Vauphec woman as she landed on her feet. The devil staggered back…then something screamed from the sky. They all peered up.

Another white comet tore through the heavens, striking right through the hurricane.

And landing, blasting dust everywhere.

Unfolding five angel wings.

From the crater, an unknown Aurixell emerged with brilliant armor and a mask shining like a platinum sun; in his hands, he brandished a massive, flaming two-edged sword. Drixilo gasped as the other demons went into a furious uproar, parting where the archangel had landed.

"Your line has been broken," he Aurixell's silvery voice keened at the demon host in a loud whisper. "They are retreating."

Drixilo roared at the angel!

"Wait, what line?" Spathi demanded.

The archangel turned to them. "Go. Take the Nalx to Unisylis. Two messengers will guide you. Go! Run!"

Spathi waved his comrades to a gap in the crowd of demons, leading down a hill into a cave. All of them ran, including Constanvol, carving their way through demons as the Aurixell combated Drixilo, cutting down mockers and Veliath's cavalry. As they neared the opening, Spathi could see the path leading to a derelict aqueduct leading over to the adjacent isle.

Then another roar bellowed, quaking the earth!

All of them stumbled as one of the World Choker's heads ruptured through the bloody muck far below the cliffs, eyeing Spathi and Constanvol.

"Run!" Spathi said to them, then charged the Udenthen hydra.

"Damn it, you idiot!" Constanvol shouted.

"Spathi!" Staea shouted, yet Haandin and Silda pulled her away.

Spathi and Constanvol both lunged at the World Choker with blades drawn…and as foolhardy as ever. Yet the sight of the archangel was invigorating. For once, the Unleztruv came through for him, even if it was just one Aurixell they sent.

Here they went again. Back into the belly of the beast.

Literally.

As they both sailed in seemingly suspended animation, Sevthiel, the World Choker, opened its fanged maws and once again engulfed the two warriors, the sworn enemies.

Struggling to survive a common adversary.

VIII: Obscure Highways

Spathi and Constanvol plunged into the World Choker's guts; the psychedelic realm appeared even darker than before, yet the fractal pillars were still visible, albeit blurry. Here he was, fighting alongside his nemesis, and for what?

Survival?

What the hell had he gotten himself into?

As they both swam toward one of the murky columns, scrawny figures emerged from the blackness, each with spidery hands and scalps of twisted horns and spines all jutting to one side of their faceless stone skulls.

Granite heads.

The creatures surrounded them. With their backs to each other, Spathi and Constanvol raised their weapons and cut down the wiry figures. Yet others dodged with disturbing movements, darting through the spiritual waters, flickering in and out of existence. And Spathi was running low on oxygen.

He failed to breathe.

Constanvol left him, making for one of the pillars, growing increasingly transparent, seemingly vanishing. From afar, the World Choker belched another whale-like roar, causing the rows of fleshy columns to undulate in nauseating, guttural waves. The more Spathi suffocated to death, the more careless his sword strokes became. Steadily, the granite heads overwhelmed him, clutching, strangling. Why couldn't he fight?

Why wouldn't Vrashri's blade burn like it should?

Shing!

Constanvol stabbed the pillar, coaxing a pained roar from the World Choker. The realm fluctuated as Spathi felt the vacuum of gravity tug his inert body towards the gash. Constanvol cleaved the remaining granite heads away, then the baron grabbed Spathi by the collar of his breastplate and hauled him out into the browned sea beyond. Reaching the shallows, Constanvol flung Spathi to the shore, the fetid waves washing onto the beach. He groaned, then kicked Spathi's abdomen.

Spathi gagged, sputtering awake!

He flopped around on all fours and vomited brown water, coughing and retching as Constanvol's feet squelched to the dry sand.

"You're welcome," the baron taunted.

"Piss off!" Spathi gurgled.

Constanvol whipped around and glared, then looked past him...at the horizon. His eyes widened.

"You know what?" Constanvol said. "For once...I may have to."

Spathi looked behind him and stared, rising to his feet.

The sun was on the verge of peeking over the horizon. He turned. Constanvol's skin was already smoking. The baron cringed, breathing heavily. And Spathi would soon follow suit if they did not find shade soon. They looked left...then right, scanning the shore. Nothing...except for a crevice far to their right. They wouldn't escape in time. Already, Spathi could feel his skin tingling, about to combust.

Death by fiery anguish.

From the cliffs, the warped flapping of shadowy bird wings swooped down at them. Dather.

"You!" the dark avian snarled. "You've meddled in our plans for the last—*awwgk*—*awwgk*!"

Shing!

Both Spathi and Constanvol swung their weapons simultaneously, carving Dather in two! The carcass fell to the ground, then became a screaming bonfire of black flames, shifting into three abstract figures of spiraling gilded eyes and thrashing moth wings, flapping dust everywhere.

Duulagicht-icht-icht-icht.... The psychotic shadows rasped in their minds. *Duula-uula-gicht—icht-icht....*

"Maybe you should learn to take responsibility for your poor planning!" the baron growled. "And relay the same message to the other Uxuclique bastard brothers!"

Spathi furrowed his brow as the entity raged up the cliffs, sprouting into an amorphous mass of tails, quills, and wings, all swirling with living constellations of eyes before vanishing at the top of the crags and his haunting whispers with it. Spathi squinted; he already knew that Dather was not what he seemed.

But Dather wasn't his real name.

He turned to Constanvol. "He's of the Uxuclique, too?"

The baron flicked his elbow, causing Qualkytdle's blade to fold under his arm. "The Mind Plague, they call him. And *try* not to say his name."

"I never said any of their names," Spathi grumbled.

"Whatever," Constanvol scoffed, then he grunted with more smoke fuming from his skin. "Damn it!"

With that, he ran down the beach, heading for the crevice.

Spathi shook his head. "Asshole."

He turned, feeling his skin prickle even more...then he turned...and beheld the golden rays of morning shimmering on Ixod Bay. Frenzied, he staggered back into the water, hoping to find solace in the rotten waves sloshing around him. He grunted and shut his eyes, falling back to all fours, groaning, yelling.

Screaming!

Heaving air in and out, anticipating the scorching light, shuddering.

Then his breathing lessened, calming. He opened his eyes, face still contorted, hissing quavering air through clenched teeth, gazing at his grimy fingers. Then his eyes grew wider, noticing the sheen of water on his exposed skin.

No burning.

No smoke.

Nothing.

Only cool wind blew on his skin, soothing. Serene. He looked back at the southern horizon, at the majestic sunrise pushing back the red Udenthen sky cage to the North. The sunlight shown less orange and more platinum through the cloud cover the further it ascended into the sky. All he could hear was the peaceful crashing of waves onto the shore and onto the nearby sea stacks.

He turned to the East. Constanvol had disappeared.

And he was glad. Damned coward.

Cautiously, he rose back to his feet and sheathed Vrashri on his back, stepping out of the filthy saltwater and onto dry sand. His coat was stained, ragged, and sopping wet. And cold. He felt like a drowned rat, dripping with beads of dirty saltwater running down the silver plating of his armor. He stared up at the rocks, noticing the high watermark. The seas had receded, just as the baron had claimed. And there was no sign of hurricane feeder bands. No Insatiables. No Drixilo. No angels.

Just him.

All alone. Again.

And they had lost Sile as well. He sighed.

Whatever. There was nothing he could do about it now.

As he hiked the beach to the East, he looked around, wondering what became of Staea and the others. Hopefully, they survived. Yet the World Choker had taken him and Constanvol well away from the sight of the hecatomb ritual just now, a good distance down Ixod's archipelago.

Whatever. All he wished to do was rest.

But his mind only raced in circles.

If Dather was of the Uxuclique, why not tell Spathi his name. Duulagicht. He cringed—accidentally thinking the name! Then he stopped…and looked around, waiting for the shadow entity to emerge.

Watching. Waiting.

A few minutes passed. And nothing happened. No bird. No warped flapping. No ghoulish, whooping laughter. Nothing. Only the brisk, sour sea wind continued to whip his drenched wavy black locks around his head, dusting his head and skin with grains of sand and brine. If thinking the name didn't summon him, then how did the World Choker…?

His mind stopped, realizing how he had gripped the Sevolith in Tauldren the previous night…then he belted a harsher sigh. Idiot! This *was* all his fault! But he refused to give Constanvol the satisfaction of admitting it. Why couldn't he get anything right? Why couldn't he win?

He exhaled through his nostrils. He *did* manage to escape Drixilo yet again—and by direct divine intervention, too! He should count his blessings. But why couldn't more come?

What was keeping them?

The line had been broken?

What had the archangel meant just now?

He recalled Deven's words, something about mortals not understanding what angels went through in the spirit realms. Or did he even say that? He couldn't remember anymore, not what he needed to, at least. Deven was dead. And as obnoxious and preachy as the Arczell had been…he missed him.

Like a brother.

Why did he have to die? Why did the Unleztruv execute him in St. Grae's crypt deep in Mount Zevania? Had he been punished? Or had he merely been relieved of his duty…as a guardian angel? But Spathi watched him shatter like glass right before his eyes. Didn't that mean he was dead?

And why had Drixilo called him "Ansdarion" earlier? Was it simply to confuse him? Ansdari? Ansdarion? What was the difference? Yet it bothered him deep inside, feeling less and less like himself with each passing day. Part of him was glad that Constanvol was gone. And part of him wished to hunt him down all over again. He knew the baron's true intentions. He knew the rebel demon's superficial cooperation was just a hopeless means to an end. And Constanvol's means…mirrored Drixilo's end. Why trifle with him? Seeking him would only endanger him and his true allies.

The enemy of his enemy was still no friend of his. What was this debauched urge to pursue this dubious, unholy union with his loathsome opponent, the presumptuous revolutionary, the so-called "moonchild?" Why was it so difficult to resist the possibility of such a forbidden alliance?

And who the hell were Amaiphynie and Minaya?

What the hell was really going on?

If only he knew….

He continued trudging, in solitude, mulling the mysteries in his mind. But this was different. The hike along the dilapidated beaches was surprisingly tranquil, unlike the dreadful, nihilistic meandering in Tauldren weeks before, even if he did have to be vigilant, trying to swallow his paranoia. He had a feeling Staea and his friends were near…somewhere, alive and well.

Hopefully….

Hours passed, on into the early afternoon, having made it across two islands, one by a land bridge formed by receding sea level and the other by traversing the ruins of a leaning aqueduct. And still no sign of Staea and his comrades.

Or Constanvol, for that matter.

And he was growing thirsty. But not for blood.

Yet as he turned around the corner of a cliff, luck smiled upon him. From an overhanging arch eroded in the basalt, a spring of freshwater drizzled, steadily spattering on the uneven hexagonal rock formations. He stood under it and drank what he could, cupping a small bit at a time in both hands and slurping contently. But the water had an unsavory sulfurous aftertaste…and a twang of blood.

He groaned. Already the waters of Raktogin were succumbing to the remaining signs of the apocalypse. Soon, they would all be dry. It was unreal. Unthinkable! And it was all happening, whether he liked it or not. He turned to the blighted ocean. Huge pillars of steam billowed into the atmosphere, joining the thick cloud cover while the rupturing underwater volcanoes gradually boiled the seas. The ground quivered beneath him. He squinted; he could have sworn he felt the seafloor collapsing from afar, the deep trenches sundering away.

It was only a matter of time.

"Spathi!" a faint female voice called out to him.

He looked around…and saw no one.

Maybe it was the wind. Maybe it was just his imagination.

"Spathi!" the voice cried out again.

He turned back around…and noticed a woman in Sevelurnum armor and military fatigues several yards down the beach to the West, waving her arm. Staea. He waved back, seeing the other knights behind her, and marched back towards them.

Yet his heart sank. Sile was not with them.

Damn.

His allies finally caught up with him, yet Haandin and Tyri helped Silda walk; the redheaded woman hacked and wheezed, then coughed up a few drops of blood on the ground. Lena handed her the flask.

"Drink—drink!" Lena urged. "It's the last of it."

Silda nodded, still gagging, then swallowed the remaining gulps of the Vauphec elixir, then she passed it back to her.

"Keep it," Lena said.

"There's some freshwater back over here," Spathi said, wiping his mouth. "Enjoy it while you can."

"Ya don't have to tell me twice," Alehi said.

"Where's Mr. Pretentious at?" Staea groaned, stroking her damp bangs out of her face with her fingers.

"He sought shade," Spathi said, pointing up at the sun.

Staea raised an eyebrow. "Why?"

Spathi sighed. "He's a blood-eater."

"You're kidding." Staea's mouth went slack.

"All this time?" Tyri blurted.

"So, that makes what…*three*?" Alehi questioned.

"Counting those two things of that Shojem fellow," Haandin said, "that would actually make five."

"Constanvol is the original one," Spathi confessed, looking at Staea. "He bit us. Both of us. Ages ago, giving us the blood-eater curse." He sighed again. "I thought if I…hunted him down…I might could end the curse, but now…" he looked back to the East. "I don't know anymore."

"Amaiphynie…." Staea whispered.

"No," Spathi said, caressing her face. "Don't listen to that liar. I know what your real name is."

Her lips quivered. "But I'm a…suc—"

"The curse, Staea!" Spathi asserted. "It's Constanvol's damned curse that made you and I do all those things."

"Does that explain that…circle tattoo you had?" Silda said.

Staea looked at her. "How'd you know about—?"

"Saw it when I was still pregnant with Flora that night when they dumped you two around Van De Yoth," Silda said, then she averted her eyes. "I was checking out your…rack."

Staea rolled her eyes.

"What, you're a beautiful woman!" Silda told her, then she rubbed Haandin's face. "But I found an even more beautiful man."

Haandin smiled down at his petite redheaded lover, kissing her on the forehead.

"You did have that mark well before that battle," Lena conceded, "even back when we found you…as a ba—"

"I don't want to hear anymore!" Staea snapped at them, brushing Spathi's hand away and stomping forward. "C'mon, let's get some water—I'm thirsty."

Spathi shook his head at Staea behind her back. "She's not a succubus."

"I know, son," Lena muttered, then breathed a troubled sigh. "I know."

Tyri glanced at Spathi, then at Staea. Alehi followed Staea, taking an empty metal flask from a satchel behind his back, eyeing the basalt waterfall a few yards ahead. Then the others stepped over, indulging their thirst and rinsing off the brine and filth from their hair and armors. As they did, Staea stood by the rocks, drying off, her arms crossed and her head hung with her back to them, doing her best to stymie her trembling. Spathi started to walk to her, but Lena's grabbed his shoulder.

"Let her be," Lena said. "She wants to be alone right now."

Spathi glanced at her and reluctantly honored his mother's request. He observed the sprawling beaches beyond, the waves growing harsher by the minute, smashing against the massive sea stacks and into the adjacent slopes of black hexagonal basalt stones leading up to the tops of the crags above.

They still had a long way to go.

That is…*if* there was anywhere left to go.

The sun had climbed past the cliffs through the thickening ash clouds, nearing its heavenly circuit to the North. Spathi estimated it would set in a few hours. Thunder rolled in the sky. The wind was picking up, blowing in their ears. A few sprinkles of rain pelted his gritty cheeks. Clean drops, not grease. But for how much longer? For the first time in so long, he dreaded the coming night. Not only would Constanvol find and pester him again, but the Drixiles would emerge soon.

And he didn't fancy combating Drixilo's fierce new general.

Or his dark cavalry prowling the lands.

Dusk came, with Endylius, the "night sun," shining dimly through the choking ash in the sky, appearing like a distant crimson orb. And its light was dying. What remained of its dwindling glow reflected on the moon's dome-like curvature in the North.

Causing it to appear blood-red.

The sun was blotted out by bulbous volcanic clouds resembling woolly sackcloth, black goat's hair…and the moon appeared as blood. Fire. Blood. Smoke. These things had come to pass just as it was prophesied, not as solar and lunar eclipses as people once erroneously thought.

And it made Spathi sick, knowing what was coming.

Yet Unzelkoyte was still nowhere to be seen.

Or Astrekiah. Or Arczellius.

They all sought shelter inside a cave within the basalt formations. A thunderstorm had brewed, blowing into the mainland, flickering white lightning and rolling booms outside. But at least it was a normal storm, at least…it felt normal. They all collected what water they could in their thermoses. Haandin had managed to build a small campfire with pieces of debris and driftwood. They had only their military jackets and leather packs as bedding, nothing more. All except Spathi had stripped their breastplates for the night, leaving their gauntlets and greaves on. Silda lay on her back, visibly ill, her eyes bloodshot. Yet she insisted that she was fine and that the "medicine" was working. But neither Spathi nor Staea had the heart to tell her what was in Lena's "old Vauphec recipe."

Nothing more than whiskey, ginseng, minced kale, chili peppers, and spices. Whiskey as a pain killer, ginseng for energy, greens for alkaline, the peppers for B vitamins and antioxidants, and spices for taste. That was all. It wasn't medicine, only a crude natural supplement, if one could even call it that. As far as Spathi was concerned, Silda should have been dead by now, yet he failed to discern what miraculous thing was holding her together.

But maybe that was it. Just a miracle.

Or at least just a mere, uncanny phenomenon.

Even so, she appeared to be on her last legs, no doubt Flora was as well, if the poor child was even still alive. Maybe that's why Silda came. Perhaps her baby succumbed, and she was in denial of her offspring's fate. But what the hell did he know at this point?

"Was I the only one…who heard the angel say something about 'two messengers' meeting us somewhere?" Tyri said, laying her socks to dry near the fire. "Or did I just imagine it?"

"No, he said that," Haandin said. He sighed. "Guess we haven't met them yet."

"Maybe it was a figure of speech or somethin'—I don't know," Alehi theorized.

Lena shrugged. "Who knows? We'll find out soon enough." She breathed through her nostrils. "Quite a thing to see Varyen come to our aid."

"What?" Spathi asked.

Lena looked at him. "The Aurixell that intercepted Drixilo."

"He said something about a 'line being broken?'" Spathi queried.

"That sounds like military jargon to me," Lena said.

"How do you know?" Staea questioned.

"I don't, not for sure, at least," Lena retorted. "It just…I've been fighting on the battlefield for a longtime. 'Hold the line!' 'Break the enemy line!' That sort of thing."

"Aye," Haandin said. "Probably what he meant." He peered up at the cave's polygonal ceiling. "That's probably what he was referrin' to…about the battlefields in the Anli realms overlappin' the material plane."

"Why do *we* have to fight, then?" Silda groaned. "Why can't Astrekiah or Arczellius just…fix it already."

"I don't know, lass," Lena sighed. "Guess he just wants to do it *through* us. Do you realize how long I've been prayin' for angels to intervene on our behalf? I'll give ya a hint: I started long before the Second Surfacing occurred, that's for true."

"I don't like being treated like chess pieces," Tyri grumbled.

"Maybe…it's like this," Alehi said. "Maybe, like…Unzelkoyte had the Drixiles exist…because, like us…he needs to shoot shit, too. The demons are the 'clay pigeons,' and we're the shotgun shells. But we only get one shot in life, then we're spent."

"Alehi, that has got to be the stupidest fuckin' thing you've ever said!" Tyri griped.

"Shh!" Lena rasped. "Lower your voices, or they'll find us."

"A'ight, a'ight, a'ight." Tyri flung her hands up. "My bad."

Spathi looked to the entrance to the cave several feet away. He squinted. Something was out there. Something had already found them. He could feel it.

"Is that analogy too 'redneck' for ya?" Alehi quipped at her, a twinkle in his eye.

"Boy…ugh!" Tyri growled, shaking her head.

"I ain't tryin' to be an asshole—I'm just," Alehi scoffed. "I…I don't know, man. I'm just tryin' to…to, uh…."

"Reconcile it?" Staea asked.

"Y…yeah, I…I guess," he replied.

"I ain't no damned shotgun shell," Tyri snapped. "Or *anybody's* pawn."

"Either way, it's all bullshit," Silda said. "I don't like it."

Spathi shook his head. "None of us do." He rose up to his feet. "But them's the breaks, kids."

"Yep," Alehi said. "Them *is* the breaks."

Tyri snorted and rested her back against the wall, reaching in her satchel for an MRE. Spathi walked and glanced up at the cave's entrance several feet above them. He noticed the ominous dim light of the night sky shining on the stone.

"Where are you going?" Staea asked.

Spathi turned to her. "Just want to check if the rain's stopped."

Staea looked back to the fire and sighed. She knew he was lying.

"Don't go too far," she relented.

Spathi nodded and ventured forth up the twisted path and outside. He peered around. The rain had indeed ceased, with the remaining runoff drizzling from the top of the cliff, cascading down the surreal basalt steps. Quietly, he stepped out the mouth of the cave onto the uneven stone blocks jutting here and there…and noticed the dark silhouette of Constanvol standing at the edge of a crag, gazing out at the fuming ocean. Spathi looked up. Through the ash clouds and rumbling thunderheads, the Udenthen trapped in the sky cage shone like weak harvest moons, as if depleted of energy, no doubt Drixilo was syphoning them for power while they still nursed the demon host. Yet the horizon to the South was devoid of the grid and of the World Choker's aura. Carefully, he stepped to Constanvol. The two regarded each other.

"There's something in the water," the baron said, "other than the World Choker. The shore isn't safe."

"I don't doubt that the waters are treacherous," Spathi said, "but we can't risk Veliath and his horsemen running us down."

"If I were you," Constanvol said, "I'd take that risk."

"Well, thank Unzelkoyte I'm *not* you," Spathi growled.

Constanvol cocked his head. "You still wish to kill me, don't you?"

"Yes," Spathi said. "And you me."

"As I told you," the baron replied, "our unfinished business will have to wait. In the meantime," he pointed at a ravine below, "I found an old shipping container down there which your comrades might find of interest. You need provisions."

"We'll manage," Spathi said.

"Have it your way," Constanvol sneered. "Be skeptical if you wish. It's no skin off my ass if your friends starve to death."

Spathi glared at him, then stepped down, eyeing the baron, ready to draw Vrashri at any sudden movement his adversary might make. Slowly, he glanced down at the gulch. True to his word, a large, rectangular crate did, in fact, lay lodged in the rocks below, caked with years of rust and barnacles, having recently been busted open by the baron; the molten scars left by Qualkytdle were quite evident.

He looked up at Constanvol. "Show me."

The baron cooperated and descended the basalt steps, with Spathi following, overcome with paranoia; surely an ambush was imminent. It was a trap…and he had to be ready for anything. Why was he going down here? It was suicide! Yet it was too late to turn back. After a few minutes of clambering downhill, the two finally reached the shipping container's riven entrance.

Canned goods and bottled water showed, with many of the groceries corroded by seawater and heaven knew what else. The other sundries were rotten beyond recognition. Spathi stepped inside and picked up one of the cleaner cans of soup, somehow preserved after all these years.

At least its exterior was.

Which wasn't saying much.

"How do I know this won't make us sick and kill us?" Spathi asked.

Constanvol shrugged. "Guess that's just another risk you'll have to take. Of course, if you *do* all contract things like salmonella and tetanus, none of you will be of much use. But I can manage with or without you."

"Then why show me this?"

"If you're going to be a leader, Spathi, you must start assuming the responsibility of one," Constanvol told him. "That includes making hard, calculated decisions, ones that can and will change life and the course of history itself, regardless of however much may be left of either." He pursed his lips. "Not to mention changing the miserable, short lives of your companions."

Spathi sighed. "I'm no leader. I'm man enough to admit to that."

"Hmph." The baron shook his head. "Then perhaps *I* should take command."

"The day we need your command will be one abject day, indeed!" Spathi snarled. "And I suppose the Ixodian rebels appreciated your dicking around? Or what about the Rinyox, which you abandoned during the battle at Van De Yoth?"

"They knew upfront what game they were all signing up for, Spathi Ansdari!" Constanvol barked. "Just like you and I know what we've all signed up for."

"Yeah," Spathi rasped callously. "But you're on the wrong side of the playing field."

"And what makes you think you're on the *right* side?" the baron taunted.

"Trust me," Spathi smarted. "I know."

"Well, then," Constanvol quipped dryly. "Looks like someone finally *did* achieve self-substantiation after all. Bravo, sir." He glanced at the soup can in his hand. "Now, then. Here's a scenario for you: your company is famished and prone to dying of hunger very soon, and you've managed to inadvertently stumble upon a centuries-old shipping container of expired canned goods that may or may not kill you with foodborne illness." He leaned into Spathi's face. "What do you do?"

Spathi gritted his teeth behind his lips, then he glanced down at the can's pull tab. The longer he hesitated, the slower the seconds seemed to tick by, feeling Constanvol's silent condescension press down on him. He was beyond tired of being forced into one mortal dilemma after another, a puppet to circumstance. What really was the lesser of two evils?

Starvation?

Or disease?

Carefully, his fingers reached for the pull tab at the top…and pried the aluminum away, revealing brownish-red broth, with ancient tomatoes, ground meat, and noodles floating in the stew. He smelled it—and recoiled!

Definitely not fresh.

But…not exactly rotten, either.

With shaking hands, he dipped his fingers in and sampled the food. Stale. Bitter. Yet…salty…and metallic. Sour…yet spicy. And he had no idea what he had just ingested. He peered back up at Constanvol, feeling so foolish under the baron's judgmental gaze.

"Looks like you've made your choice," Constanvol said, then turned and hiked up the basalt. "I'm going on ahead. We shall meet again…tomorrow night, perhaps…that is if your innards haven't dissolved to nothing."

"Go to hell," Spathi snapped.

"We're already in it, Spathi," the baron replied smugly, continuing his trek. "We're already in it." He looked back down. "Sleep tight."

With that, Constanvol vanished up past the clifftops. Spathi took the rancid soup and hurled it down the ravine, clanging away with sloppy, tinny splatters. Angrily, he wiped his hands of the putrid broth on the basalt rock, then he turned to leave, yet he stopped.

He whipped back at the bottled water and pried one from its plastic flat, unscrewing the top and sniffing the liquid. Then he took a sip.

Nice. Clean. Cool.

Refreshing.

Yet it was plagued with a hint of the plastic and just a couple of drops of seawater that had seeped into it over the years, but that couldn't be helped. Desperately, he rinsed his mouth of the tainted canned stew, then he drank, downing half the bottle, then he screwed the cap back on and climbed back up to the cave. As he reached the mouth of the cavern, he took one last look of Constanvol's black outline in the dark, steadily and calmly treading away to the East. He sighed again.

Of all the obscure highways in life to walk, this one was among the murkiest.

Slowly, he stepped inside the cave, approaching the warm glow of the fire, wishing to be cleansed, wanting to wash away the clinging shame off him.

But he couldn't.

Not here. Not yet.

The sounds of alarmed, scuffling feet reverberated as the others saw Spathi enter their temporary abode. Then they all relaxed and gazed in awe at the water bottle in his hand.

"Where'd you get that at?" Lena asked.

"I'll show you," Spathi groaned. "The rain has stopped."

IX: Dismal Edge

Morning came swiftly, illuminating overcast skies and the gloomy basalt shores of black and gray sand. Spathi and the others barely accumulated any rest the previous dreamless night. It was as if they had closed their eyes for only a few minutes in the dark, only to suddenly discover the weakening sun having lunged well over the southern horizon. Their worn brains were wired awake with paranoia…and their bodies aching with fatigue. But the blood was flowing in their veins that morning, nevertheless. They weren't even fit enough to swing a sword or aim their otherworldly bows. If Veliath and his mounted troops were to catch them, they were done for. All night long, Spathi had tried to shrug off Constanvol's "test" with the soup can. And even worse, his worried mind mulled over the words of Varyen, the Aurixell.

Two messengers would meet them.

Where? Who?

And how?

More importantly, where was there to go? What route was the least perilous? Did they risk the danger of being found by Veliath and his infernal horsemen on the mainland? Or would they take their chances on traveling near what supposedly lurked beneath the putrefied ocean's surface?

There was no right answer here.

He showed them the shipping container Constanvol had found, warning them not to partake of the expired canned stew. They each took a few clean water bottles, filling their small satchels with what they could carry. Spathi scanned the flat landscape from the top of the cliff. No sign of the baron. Or the other Drixiles, for that matter. He turned and gazed at the sea, the waves pummeling the rocky coast beyond where the beach ended.

And then at the distant waters.

Something…slinked around the surface.

Something like…dorsal spines.

He blinked, then he failed to find it again, his bloodshot eyes scanning frantically. Was he imagining things? Maybe it was the World Choker. Maybe it was something else.

Maybe he was just sleep-deprived.

The others reached the top of the basalt cliff, huffing, moaning.

"We may need to start heading further inland," Spathi finally confessed.

"What about Veliath?" Tyri asked.

"And Drixilo?" Silda questioned.

"We're running out of beach." He turned and pointed at the distant reefs.

"I'm afraid he's right," Lena concurred. "Not much of a choice here."

"We don't have to go *too* far in," Haandin said, raising an eyebrow. "Do we?"

Spathi hesitated, then shook his head. "Maybe not. I don't know." He sighed. "We can probably stay a couple miles near the coast just in case."

"Well," Alehi griped, "either the Drixiles will get us, or we'll starve to death first."

"We only have a small handful of rations left," Lena said.

"Better make them last," Staea replied flatly. "Unless there's any fish left in that ocean, it's only a matter of time before we…you know."

Haandin looked at the sea and shrugged. "Guess it could be worth a try. Might be a few trash fish left alive to eat, I don't know."

As the words left his mouth, the shrill cry of a bird sounded from the West. They turned…and beheld an osprey gliding in the wind, with a fish, a large salmon, in its talons swooping down and dropping its fresh catch onto the rocks near them. Their eyes widened as the seahawk perched on a nearby basalt monolith, emitting its short, repeated yelps. Spathi squinted at the creature's head. For a moment, he thought he noticed a white glow in its eyes.

With a pale-green glint.

Two of the primary feathers on its left wing were snow-white with leucism.

Spathi shook his head. It couldn't be. It just couldn't.

He was imagining things.

He was tired, that was all.

Haandin walked over and snatched up the bloodied fish. "That answers *my* question. Breakfast, anyone?"

"If you build us another fire, Sir Haandin," Lena said.

"Aye," Haandin said, eyeing the osprey. "I'll make a quick skewer."

"At this point, I'd eat the thing raw," Alehi blurted.

"Eww," Tyri judged.

"What?" Alehi snapped.

"I don't recommend it," Staea said, scrunching her face.

"Alright, fine. Build a quick fire in the cave," Spathi conceded. "After this, we've *got* to get moving, though. We've got at least another thousand miles to walk."

"Please don't say that," Silda wheezed, bending over with her hands on her knees. "You'll make me puke."

"Sorry," Spathi apologized.

As he said this, another osprey came…with another fat salmon, casting it to the ground with a wet plop, then the bird landed near the other. They all furrowed their brows at the peculiar avian duo.

"Am I the only one getting…weirded out by this?" Tyri said.

"I'm too hungry to get weirded out," Alehi said, grabbing the second fish from the ground. "Let's don't even bother cleanin' 'em, Haandin. Just skewer 'em and roast 'em over the fire."

"Aye," the Vauphec replied. "Sounds good."

They all followed Haandin and Alehi back to the cave, with Spathi being last. As he walked with the others, he squinted at the strange seahawks, both of which had eerie glows in their eyes that shone only for a split second.

"Two, huh?" he said, shaking his head. "You've got to be shitting me."

They had a brief breakfast, dividing the two cooked salmon equally amongst their comrades, even eating the heads; the only thing they did not spare were the ribs and fins. Afterwards, they finally departed the coast, heading northeast, traversing the rocky cliffs and canyons of scrubland while staying in close proximity to the shore.

The ospreys were constantly aloft, several yards ahead, as if guiding them.

Both continued to seize fish from the rocky tributaries streaming into the ocean, at least from the ones that hadn't turned to blood or boiling tar. Haandin and Alehi took rope from their satchels and strung up the fish, threading it through each salmon's mouth, hopefully gathering a good mess for dinner later that evening.

Even more so, by the time sunset rolled around, Spathi was finally noticing the tree lines of dead coniferous trees. Spruce, cedar, juniper, and rocks covered in lichens and green moss.

With these signs and the ospreys both catching salmon, perhaps they were much closer to the eastern boreal regions than Spathi had initially presumed. But that was most likely wishful thinking on his part. He, too, was nauseated by the impossible journey before them. Even if they did endure long enough to reach the site of the refugee camp of Raktogin's coalition, who was to say they would be there once they arrived?

Who was to say, indeed.

Anything could happen.

The dice had been rolled. Again.

About a week had passed on their trek through the coastal wilderness, or so it seemed, living on the uncanny ospreys' catch, Haandin's occasional success spearfishing for flounder, and whatever freshwater they could find. Luckily, the ensuing global volcanism was melting what remained of glaciers in the towering arctic sierras, its muddy runoff reaching the adjacent seas. The filthy water was awful to taste, virtually undrinkable, gradually taking its toll on their kidneys and livers, but it was all they could manage. Yet malnutrition and dehydration were the least of their problems.

Constanvol hadn't been sighted in days.

Spathi couldn't decide which was more contemptible: the baron's presence or his absence. But just because Constanvol hadn't been seen…did not mean that he wasn't nearby. Watching. Lurking.

Spying.

The baron's seeming abandonment only unnerved Spathi all the more, most likely to the rebel demon's amusement. Even more so, Drixilo and his servants appeared to have fallen off the face of Raktogin. If only they had. They, too, probably weren't too far off, calculating, anticipating the right time to strike.

When Spathi and the others least expected it, no doubt.

But there was the slim possibility that the angels were at last holding them at bay, even if just long enough for Spathi and his company to make it to the encampment. Varyen came. Perhaps the other white fireballs rocketing down from the sky were also Arczells being deployed from the Unleztruv, finally having carved through the "lines" of Drixiles in the unseen Anli realms' battlefields. Maybe it was merely fragments of a solar flare from the collapsing stars in space. Maybe he was overthinking it.

Who knew for sure?

Night eventually fell yet again on the dismal coastal lands. The ash clouds and thunderheads blanketed the heavens even more as what remained of Endylius strained to peek through the crevices of the climbing smoke above. The "moon star" was shrinking into a white dwarf far off, dwindling with each passing evening. Yet it wasn't the only light visible from afar.

On the beach, they all caught a glimpse of a distant orange glow.

A campfire.

"Stay sharp," Spathi said. "Could be Drixilacs."

As they drew closer to the flame, they noticed two figures sitting around it: a man and a woman in military fatigues armed with assault rifles. The woman turned, seeing the distant gleam of their armor in the faint firelight. She scrambled to her feet and aimed her rifle at the company.

"Who's there?" the woman snapped. "Identify yourselves!"

They all stopped. Then Tyri's eyes bulged.

"Sis?" Tyri called. "That you?"

"Tyri, shh!" Lena rebuked.

The woman lowered her weapon as the man lumbered to his feet, grabbing his gun.

"Tyri?" she yelled back.

"Aipha!" Tyri shouted. "Sis, it's me!"

Aipha relaxed. She waved them forward.

"You sure it's them?" the man said.

Aipha looked at him. "Only one way to find out, Rand."

Rand grumbled as Spathi and his company appeared before them. Tyri ran and embraced her older sister. Both held each other's heads, then Tyri looked at her in confusion.

"What are y'all doing all the way out here?" she asked.

"We had some deserters leave the camp in the caves with a couple of the remaining cruisers," Rand told her. "We left with a small crew to hunt them down, but our transport was intercepted by some…mutated horse creatures—I've never seen anything like 'em." He sighed. "We're the only ones left."

"Of the entire camp?" Alehi's shocked voice twanged.

"No—our crew, kid!" Rand growled. "Relax, at ease."

"Any sign of Constanvol?" Spathi asked.

"Which one's that?"

"The man with the lightning mark on his face."

"Oh, *that* son of a bitch." Rand looked out to the ocean. "Nah, we haven't seen him."

"Wonder where the ospreys went?" Alehi said, looking around.

"Probably roosted somewhere for the night," Haandin said, raising the mess of fish to Aipha and Rand. "Wanna join us for supper?"

"Ain't that lucky," Rand sighed.

"Thank Unzelkoyte—I'm starving!" Aipha said.

Silda instantly belched a terrible cough, then fell on her knees and retched, spitting up more blood, falling on all fours. Haandin and Aipha crouched down to her.

"Silda?" Haandin said, stroking her back.

She was unable to respond, still hacking, with blood dribbling down her chin and tears streaming down her cheeks. Aipha felt her forehead.

"She's burning up," the combat medic said. "I got a couple of penicillin shots and some pain killers. Might help with the fever."

"Might as well try," Lena replied in a glum voice.

"I'm…*khoou*-khoou…sorry…" Silda croaked.

"Don't worry about it—we're here to help you as best we can," Aipha told her as she and Haandin lifted her up. "Come on. Come sit with us next to the fire. Probably having a relapse of pneumonia."

Spathi squinted. That wasn't *just* pneumonia. But maybe Aipha offered Silda that white lie as part of her bedside manners, calming her patient. Stressing out about the inevitable would only shorten the reformed Drixilac's life even more. Yet he was astounded by just how long Silda had lasted, even without medication, considering her illness.

It defied all logic.

He looked to Staea. His wife had been unusually quiet, undoubtedly still wrestling with Constanvol's vexing speech the other day. Why was she so worried? The baron was full of shit! Why couldn't she snap out of his spell?

Like quicksand to the mind.

The more one struggled in it, the more one sank.

Prone to drowning in the madness.

She wasn't a succubus! She had been cursed by that blood-eater, just as Spathi had.

Yet that circle tattoo….

She had that for as long as he could remember, even back when they were children. Maybe it was just another curse, one that victimized her back in her early years, an affliction no one knew about or what caused it.

Or how to cure it.

But she was no succubus.

She had her flaws, just like he and everyone else did.

He refused to believe she was anything other than human.

After they had eaten, Haandin showed Alehi and Tyri how to use the bizarre Selebane bows using the rocky cliff as target practice. Spathi watched as Rand, Aipha, and Lena discussed things with Silda trying to recover near the campfire.

Yet the two Enoshah knights were growing more frustrated with their obvious lack of skill and progress.

"I'm not used to these sorts of bows either," Haandin explained, taking one of the weapons from Alehi's hands. "For years, up until the end of medieval times, we used the same ordinary bows that Enoshah and Enpherom people did, strings firing wooden shafts tipped with either stone or metal heads."

"Well, how come Alehi's better at it than me?" Tyri complained. "Because he's a man? I can't even summon the arrows!"

Haandin groaned. "Alehi's simply had a little bit more practice than you have. Just be patient. I know that's easier said than done."

"Alright, look," Alehi said. "I know I gotta believe and all...and meditate...and channel the power of the heavens and all that other corny crap, but what exactly am I doin' wrong?"

"*That*...is what you're doing wrong, lad," Haandin explained.

"What?"

The Vauphec squinted at him. "'Corny crap?' Really?"

"Look, we both believe now," Tyri huffed. "We know what the Drixiles really are now, heaven and hell and all that, okay?"

"Yeah," Alehi agreed. "What, did I piss off the angels or something?"

"You believe that they all exist," Haandin said, "but do you believe that the trinity of Unzelkoyte is good?"

Both of the Enoshah grew silent.

"We've all suffered horrible losses, our loved ones taken from us," the Vauphec knight went on. "It's not easy. Being an Unzelite is not easy. I wish it all could have been handled differently as well. But the problem we all face now is not whether or not we believe there is a god. Even demons believe there is a god, though they wish us to think otherwise. They can't take away the protection of heaven...but they *can* tempt us to forfeit that protection."

"What the hell does that have to do with shootin' a damned bow an' arrow and our dead loved ones?" Alehi snapped.

Haandin groaned again, glaring at them. "If you really want to make a dent against evil, then you must assume a stubborn faith, at all times, no matter what others may think of you, no matter how impossible the odds may seem. There is only truth. Think that's 'stupid' or 'corny?'" He outstretched his hands around the debris around the beach. "The people of the world around you thought the same thing—and where are they now?"

Alehi and Tyri looked away, their faces cringing.

Haandin pointed a finger at them. "You think that Lena's answered prayer was just a random coincidence? Or the fact that she was the only one of us who managed to land an *actual* blow on Drixilo, which appalled even me!" He shook his head. "Even *my* arrows had no effect on him—and do you know why?"

Haandin paused for a moment, expecting the young soldiers to retort or smart off. Yet they only looked at the ground, trying not to tremble, not in anger. But in trepidation.

"Because I gave into fear," Haandin sighed. "I, too, have moments of weakness. Doubt. Contempt. Hatred. Arrogance. Even just one ounce of these things can trip you up. I am just as guilty of these things as anyone else. I, too...am a failure. A wretch."

Both Alehi and Tyri slowly gazed back up at their mentor.

"But...it's not about being perfect." Haandin peered down at the silver armament. "The Selebane by itself has no power. It is just one medium for the spirit, a reflection of one's soul. But the power cannot come from the human soul. One must entreat the greater power…and seek union with that greater power, entwining themselves with what is best. Unclutter your mind…and your heart…and yield yourself to ultimate reality." He gave the Selebane bow back to Alehi and stepped aside. "Now…try again."

Slowly, the redheaded soldier took the weapon and lifted it but this time with an evident hint of reverence. A tear streamed down his face as he closed his eyes, aiming. Aiming at the lifeless wall, silently ventilating to the heavens, petitioning all his grievances, screaming in his mind, in his heart.

His soul.

Wanting to see his family again.

His brother. And his mother.

He cried out inside, fulminating soundlessly about why they had to die the way they did, about how stupid he felt trying to do this. Faith? How churchy! How childish! Corny! Shitty! He would never be a saint—none of them would! Why wouldn't they help him shoot this thing? Why wouldn't they help them win the war? Why did he have to hide from his anguish?

Why couldn't he just let go?

And release himself?

With his eyes closed tightly, Alehi failed to notice the ten brilliant shafts of bluish-white light hovering around him in a neat, symmetrical echelon, all pointed at the jagged rock wall. Haandin and Tyri stepped back; they were even brighter than the Vauphec's arrows. Even Spathi and the others around the campfire got up and stood in awe, watching the holy array.

"Alehi!" Tyri squeaked.

Blam!

He jerked! The arrows tore into the rock like streaks of lightning, spraying blue and white fire and embers, searing a molten hole, cracking through the basalt stone. He and Tyri both staggered back, eyes wide open, gasping in disbelief. He looked to Haandin; the Vauphec only stared at him solemnly. Then he looked back at the hole he had made.

"The hell was that?" Alehi snarled.

Haandin beckoned him with his index finger. He stepped over to his mentor as the Vauphec leaned in next to his head.

"*That*…is what you need to work on," Haandin whispered into his ear.

With that, the Vauphec strode back over to the campfire as Spathi and the rest of them sat back down, with Alehi and Tyri still gawking at their Selebane bows.

"They'll get the hang of it," Haandin said. "Hopefully."

"That's real poetic what you told that redneck," Rand scoffed.

"Did you not see the arrows he had just now?" Silda groaned, lying on her back. "The supernatural's a thing, ya know." She smiled up at Haandin. "*I* thought what you told 'em was beautiful, baby."

The Vauphec smiled back, stroking her neck and face. She blew him a kiss.

"Mmm, that's some sweet sugar," her voice trilled in a girlish tone. "Love you."

"Love you," Haandin reciprocated, smiling wider. "Your fever's going down, too."

"I'm beginning to feel a little better," Silda said.

"Yeah, that's called *modern* medicine at work…a product of tried-and-true science, not an 'old Vauphec recipe,'" Aipha sniped, squinting at Lena. "You're welcome, by the way."

Lena glared at the condescending combat medic.

"You two…didn't come out here…looking for deserters," Spathi accused. "Did you?"

Rand and Aipha froze, then they both scowled, averting their eyes.

"You…*are*…the deserters," Spathi said.

"What are you gonna do?" Aipha said, rolling her eyes. "Throw us in the brig?"

"You crazy Vauphec people at the encampment want us all to play dress-up and wear that ridiculous armor and fight with prehistoric weapons! I don't care if we *are* running low on ammo—it's so ass-backwards!" Rand growled. "'Course if that hick over there can do that with the 'bow,' maybe I can—"

"Not with *that* attitude, you're not, Captain," Lena snapped.

"Captain?" Rand snorted. "I'm no captain. There is no military. There never really was…so we're not really deserters, only survivors, idiots with guns. You want to kill or arrest us, go ahead." He shook his head. "I don't really give a fuck anymore."

"That's what you think?" Lena chuckled dryly. "You're both punishing yourselves far more than what we ever could." She took a swig of collected rainwater from a metal canteen. "What is it going to take to get you two to finally see?"

The two Enoshah soldiers grew quiet, looking down, dejected, too weary to answer that loaded question anymore. Spathi glanced to his left and watched Alehi and Tyri walk away toward the nearby basalt cliffs, toward a small ravine. He raised an eyebrow, then looked out at the ocean to his right. Staea's silhouette stood shin-deep in the water facing the sea, barefooted, feeling the waves wash over her legs and the black sand between her toes.

"Alright," Aipha finally said.

Lena tightened her glare. "'Alright' what, smart aleck?"

"Alright," Aipha repeated, then sighed. "You win. Demons are real. Angels are real. There is a god. There is a devil. Heaven. Hell. Apocalypse. End of the world." She shrugged callously. "Now what?"

"Fuck off," Lena breathed. "Just fuck off."

"No…no," Aipha groaned. "I will not fuck off. Seriously, what do we do?"

Lena stood up. "You know what you gotta do, lass." She stretched her arms. "My legs are fallin' asleep." She huffed. "You sound like Rediq Tashar, by the way."

With that, she paced around a few feet from the campfire, taking another gulp from her flask, trying to cool off. Aipha shook her head, muttering inaudible curses, her blood simmering in her veins; the last thing they needed was more infighting. Spathi looked back to Staea. Yet…something was off about the ocean. Either she had walked back…or the tide was receding.

Rapidly.

"Changing the subject," Haandin said, "either of you seen a ghoulish-looking man with long, scraggly white hair dragging chains around? Skin burning with blue and red light."

Rand shook his head. "Nope. Why?"

Haandin shrugged. "Just curious. We've been looking for him."

"How far to the encampment is it?" Spathi asked.

"At least another eight hundred miles," Rand estimated. "We'll just have to make it back there on foot. Unless…."

"Unless what?" Silda questioned.

Rand looked at her. "We could make for the ghost town of Yeberyl. There might be some vehicles we can salvage there. It's a longshot, but I can't think of anything else."

"Where's that at?" Aipha asked Haandin. "Is it close?"

Haandin sighed and looked up the cliffs. "It's…probably…anywhere from fifty to two hundred miles from here, give or take—it's not too far from the coast, I know that."

"Two hundred miles?" Aipha sighed. "Shit."

"That's another friggin' week of walking, isn't it?" Silda complained.

"At least," Aipha confirmed.

"Oh, shit." Silda cringed, clutching her abdomen.

"It might be closer than that, my love," Haandin consoled her. "I just don't have a map in front of me right now to say either way."

"There's probably nothing left there to salvage anyway," Spathi said. "The Enoshah and Enpherom may have taken everything of use from there these past few centuries."

"I doubt it," Rand said. "That city's in Vauphec territory."

"Not only that," Haandin said, "but back in the day, there was a really bad meltdown at a nuclear power plant there. Killed quite a few people. The rest were forced to evacuate, displaced by the disaster. Had to leave everything behind in a hurry. It's been radioactive for years." He squinted. "But…that was over five centuries ago, so it's possible the radiation levels are almost nonexistent now, but I'm not an expert on those sorts of things."

"Are you kidding me?" Aipha sniped. "That city's going to be radioactive for at least…like, a thousand more years, not to mention all the contamination there! Uh-uh—I ain't rollin' those dice!"

"Then we try for one of the nearby cities," Haandin retorted firmly, "ones that aren't affected by the radiation. Buurinska, perhaps."

"Well…maybe," Aipha conceded. "But it's like Rand said: it's still a longshot. Unless anybody's got any better ideas."

"I'm tryin' to think of one right now," Silda replied. "Oh, shit."

"They do have a couple of old military bases in that region," Haandin said. "Might have a set of wheels we can fix up. Maybe enough gas to get us there." He looked to Aipha. "The hospitals and clinics might still have some medical supplies as well."

"Any medication left there would have expired by now, if not contaminated," Aipha told him. "But I might be able to get some gauzes, bandages, and things like that, if they're clean enough. They won't be sterile, though. Then again, what is anymore?"

"Well, then," Lena said, walking back to the fire, "sounds like we don't have much of a choice, do we? I'm down for that if the rest of you grunts are." She looked to Staea. "What say you, lass?"

Staea turned and walked to them, with her greaves back on her feet. She turned back to the retreating ocean. "Something's up with the tide."

"Something *other* than the World Choker slithering around in there?" Spathi asked.

Staea shook her head. "Look at it. It's…receding like crazy."

They all stood up, gawking at the retracting sea. Spathi looked around, feeling the ground shudder beneath his feet as a deep rumble thundered from the ocean. Growing closer. In the distance miles off, they saw the haunting edge of a colossal, aqueous wall rising up, barreling straight for them.

On the verge of engulfing the entire coastline.

"Where's Tyri and Alehi?" Spathi demanded.

Around the top of the basalt cliffs, Alehi and Tyri both sat silently pondering what they had just witnessed during their training session, staring at the ocean beyond. High overhead, the ominous light of Endylius appeared as a red dwarf sun through the billowing ash clouds. The outline of dead coniferous trees sat on the nearby sea stacks and on the undulating mainland far off, with a series of ghastly shipwrecks in the ravine below.

"How can something so horrible look so…beautiful?" Tyri finally said, gazing at the night's horizon.

"Whatcha mean?" Alehi asked.

Tyri looked at him. "I don't know. Like…it's all messed up, I know, but…it's kinda surreal, you know? Like there's…beauty…."

"In the mayhem," Alehi finished for her.

Tyri squinted, then nodded. "Yeah…." She looked back out to the sea. "Beauty in the mayhem. Guess I'm crazy for thinkin' that."

Alehi shook his head. "Nope." He sighed. "It's…optimistic…I think it is, at least. I get what you're saying."

Tyri looked back at him. "What happened back there, Al? How'd you…do that?"

Alehi shook his head again. "I didn't." He looked away. "Something else did it…through me. It's hard to explain. I finally did what I was afraid of doing for years."

Tyri cocked her head at him.

"I asked for help…from something I can't see." He exhaled a shuddering breath. "From something I thought was imaginary. Something I thought was superstitious. I kept thinkin' that…Stelford was gonna chew me out for it. But then I remembered he's not here anymore. He's not here anymore to tell me how to feel, to push me around. He's not here anymore…to think for me." A tear trickled from his eye. "I gave in. I asked for help. Willfully. I finally took it seriously…and that's when I felt it envelop me…like…wings…completely external of my body, my mind, my emotions. It wasn't adrenaline. It wasn't goosebumps. In that moment, I felt something I have never felt before." He peered back up again, another tear falling down his freckled face. "I guess Stelford did, too."

Tyri eased closer and wrapped her arms around him. Alehi returned the gestured, then they both caressed each other's faces.

"I knew you and Felina had a thing for each other years back," Tyri confessed. "But I tried to behave myself. I didn't interfere with it…and I'm sorry she's gone." A tear rolled down her cheek. "I saw all the crap Aipha and Rediq went through—and I'm not comparing you to him at all, okay? I just…I never knew what to do with…how I felt, you know?"

"Tyri," Alehi said, grabbing her hand. "Thank you for being there…when I was in the brig. I was losin' my mind…and I heard what you said…while I was locked up there in Van De Yoth. You set me free." He smiled. "Thank you."

Another tear streaked down her face, then they both leaned in…and kissed, holding each other for what seemed like minutes, then they eventually released each other.

"That," Alehi went on, "*and* you got a fine ass on ya."

"Boy, you better believe it," she flirted, then giggled.

Alehi grinned. "I'm glad we finally did this."

"Well," she said, "it was either now or never."

He nodded. "Ain't that the truth."

They peered down, noticing the washing waters having mostly vanished from the ravine and the buried shipwrecks, with the exception of stagnant tide pools. Toward the South, they both heard a low, distant rumble.

"Is that thunder?" Alehi asked.

"Where'd the water go?" Tyri questioned.

"Alehi!" Lena shouted several yards off. "Tyri!"

"Over here!" Alehi yelled.

Spathi and the others climbed to them. "Run! Hide!"

"What?" they asked.

"Tsunami!" Haandin shouted. "Take cover!"

The two young Enoshah looked…and their eyes bulged. A massive tidal wave was inbounding several miles out, yet it would impact the shore any minute. All of them scurried through the cliffs, looking for any crevice, anything that might spare them the wrath of the sea.

Then Spathi spotted it: the rusted, barnacle-infested hull of an old submarine lodged in the cliffs; half of it was submerged in the damp sand. With a hole in the other side.

"In there!" Spathi shouted.

"What the—are you crazy?" Aipha snarled. "That thing won't—!"

"C'mon!" Rand snapped, pulling her arm.

All of them crawled up to the top hatch of the ruined sub as Spathi took one last look at the incoming tsunami, about half a mile from the beach. Everyone else shimmied down into the sunken ship.

"Spathi!" Lena yelled, peeking out of the hatch.

Spathi clambered up and squeezed through the opening, then slammed the lid shut, cramming himself down into the sub's small bridge. The rumble of the ravenous ocean came.

And smashed into the coast!

Tearing through rock, trees, and the side of the sub. All of them screamed as the craft finally toppled and came loose to the mighty wave's undertow, washing all over the place! Water spewed through the cracks of the submarine, steadily flooding the bridge. All of them braced themselves, eyes shut, waiting to drown.

Waiting to die.

Boom! Bang! Bong!

The sub scraped and skidded on rock…then halted.

Spathi slowly opened his eyes, looking up at the loosened hatch. Only salty drops drizzled from the cracked opening, spattering on his shoulders He peered back down; they were all waist-deep in muddy seawater. Spathi hesitated, then he climbed back up the metal ladder.

"Where you going?" Aipha barked.

Spathi ignored her, then hesitated again…then he peeked out of the hatch's cracked lid, faintly ajar. A cool sea breeze blew from outside, devoid of the sloshing of chaotic waves.

Carefully, he lifted the hatch open with a grating creak and looked around.

The tsunami had flung them almost a mile into the mainland, having obliterated the coast and regurgitating the underwater graveyard of sunken battleships, yachts, and fishing boats onto land along with other debris. He turned. The half of the submarine originally exposed had been ripped away, with the other doors miraculously holding, melded together by barnacles, reefs, and welding jobs from bygone crew members.

"Is it over?" Rand asked.

Spathi didn't answer. His eyes locked onto an obscure figure in the distant blackness.

Radiating wisping dark-blue flames.

Constanvol.

With Qualkytdle's scythe blade drawn. In the dark, with the wind blowing his lengthy black hair and tattered long coat around, his wraithlike visage resembled a grim reaper. Yet he was too far off to tell whether he was walking towards them…or away.

Or simply waiting for them.

He squinted. They didn't need that bastard.

The enemy of his enemy was still his enemy.

And to think that Spathi was foolish enough to actually consider the possibility of an alliance, however dubious it was…and still is. If only he had killed him earlier. But maybe he was too weak at the time to deliver a decent blow. He was ready now, though. He had regained his strength…and his *real* allies. The first chance Spathi got, the baron's head would come off, whenever the opportunity presented itself again. He had his two guides ready for them as soon as morning came.

He had his two messengers, even if they *were* birds.

Birds not of this world.

Beggars couldn't be choosers. Especially in Raktogin.

"Spathi!" Lena shouted. "Talk to us, son!"

Spathi sighed. "Yeah. We're clear." He groaned and looked down at his company. "Tomorrow, we begin our journey for Buurinska. Is that clear?"

"Shit," Silda hissed, shaking her head.

The others hesitated, then exchanged concerned looks.

Lena nodded up at him. "So be it."

X: Darkened Rime

For a grueling week, Spathi and his company navigated through the mainland to the abandoned regions surrounding Yeberyl, leaving the disheveled coast behind and entering the misty, mountainous old-growth taigas of the East. The majority of the snow had mostly melted from geothermal activity from the distant erupting volcanoes, revealing the grim viridescence of the tall evergreens. Muddy creeks and trails of recently cooled lava marbled the moss-covered felsenmeers and dried river basins littering the valleys, having charred some of the vegetation before being stymied by the thick ice once blanketing the woods. Arctic wind whipped around them from the distant smoldering peaks as something fell from the sky.

Ashes. Flurrying like snowflakes.

The way the wind howled and gasped through the canyons and trees was even more disconcerting than the cool air itself. Spathi was constantly on alert, wondering what horrors now haunted these dark forests. The two ospreys would appear during the day, leading them through the wilderness and occasionally down derelict highways of overgrown car frames infested with grass, mushrooms, and lichens. Rusted road signs written in an unclear Enoshah language leaned in the tall grass and carpeting ferns, with some twisted from landslides. Many power lines lay tangled in the branches, with some of the rotted wooden telephone poles having snapped to pieces, lying on the ground. Spathi simply couldn't get over the wretched irony. After all this time, he complained of the lifeless, desolate deserts of the wastelands, not seeing anything green. And now, at last, here was a lush boreal forest, thick with humidity, with the mountains' gouged throats salivating Raktogin's fiery blood down their icy slopes and their summits pressed against the dark storm clouds in the distance…and he felt anything but soothed and rejuvenated.

Quite the opposite.

With the dark forest's foreboding atmosphere, he couldn't help but miss the desert's conspicuous terrain. Even the looming alpine trees seemed to be watching them, the ridged trunks, moss-draped limbs, and fallen logs threatening to come alive at any moment. Spruce. Cedar. Redwood. Sequoia. Fir. Hemlock. Always creaking in the wind.

Always groaning.

Popping. Squeaking.

With their thick boughs tilting, back…and forth.

Back…and forth. Back…and forth.

Despite this, they had yet to encounter any Drixiles…or see Constanvol again, for that matter. But that only made them more nervous. They could be anywhere. Hiding. Waiting. What were they waiting for? Where were they? Why wouldn't they come? Maybe the Drixiles were closer than what they thought, savoring the humans' paranoia, not wanting to exterminate the mortals right away. After all, once humanity succumbed to extinction, what playthings would be left for the devil to torment? Perhaps those alive were more amusing to antagonize than the souls in the Nevarifta, damned for eternity. Perhaps the demons were amassing at the Penterium Hinge, preparing to besiege the Unleztruv.

Perhaps they were waiting for something else.

A day came as they marched through the bluish haze of the woods, slowly entering the verdant remains of an urban district, with the ospreys gliding ahead towards a ruined bridge stretching over a foggy canyon. On the bridge's other side, the silhouettes of taller buildings loomed, with many of their smudged windows busted out, having tangled plastic tarps hanging from their gaping sills.

"This is it, I think," Haandin said. "We're entering the downtown area."

"Of Yeberyl?" Aipha's voice grated.

"No," Haandin huffed. "I think this is Buurinska. That's what the sign said back there, anyway." He looked around. "This should be a safe distance from Yeberyl."

"We finally made it, baby?" Silda panted.

"Aye." The Vauphec nodded, wrapping his arm around her. "We're here."

Spathi scanned the forlorn streets for any movement. The wind blew a torrent of leaves around the grimed cars and trucks, with some of their doors still open; some were riddled with bullet holes. Many of the structures were vandalized with graffiti, the spray paint faded by time and weather. Black streaks of mold striped the sides of the old shops and skyscrapers. More power lines looped around loosely from towering metal poles, rusted by the elements. Yet there were no bodies, no skeletons, no blood.

Save for the red ooze running through the thinning tributary below the bridge.

Soon, all the waters of the world would run red with gore.

"Hey, where'd the birds go?" Alehi asked.

They all looked and listened. In the distance, they could hear the two seahawks emitting their rapid cries, then they proceeded in that direction, cautiously crossing the dilapidated bridge.

"How far is this military base?" Spathi questioned.

"It's on the other side of town, I think," Lena said. "Near the…plant."

Rand gawked at her. "The nuclear plant?"

"Aye," Lena replied.

"Wait a minute," Aipha said. "What about the radiat—"

"I'm confident the radiation levels are virtually nonexistent over here, especially at this point," Haandin claimed. "All the cities around here relied on nuclear energy, but the meltdown didn't happen over here in Buurinska—and besides, that disaster was over five centuries ago." He sighed. "Exposure and contamination are the least of our worries here. Stay sharp."

Aipha glared at him. "With all due respect, I don't know if you're qualified to make such a call about nuclear—"

"If it will put you at ease, Sergeant," Haandin snapped, getting in her face, "we'll split up into teams. You can retrieve supplies from the hospital on the north side of town, and we'll go to the military base if we can find a transport that still runs, along with some explosives and ammunition that might have been left behind. Agreed?"

They all stopped and looked at each other. Only Spathi's gaze was fixed down the street, squinting, keeping his nose to the wind.

Aipha sighed. "Fine, that's works for me." She turned around. "Any volunteers?"

"I'll go," Staea said.

"Me, too," Tyri chimed.

"So will I," Silda told them, then looked at Haandin. "We'll meet back up with you guys." She raised an eyebrow. "Any of you fellers wanna accompany the hens?"

"I guess this rooster will," Alehi said.

"Go get 'em, Rooster," Rand quipped dryly.

"Yes, sir," Alehi jested soberly.

"Well, lads," Lena said to her team, nodding towards the city. "Shall we take the plunge?"

"After you, milady," Haandin offered.

"Keep those men straight, Lena," Silda joked.

"Always," Lena replied.

"Aipha," Rand called out. "Make sure your rifle's set to semi-auto. Gotta conserve ammo."

"Got it," Aipha replied, checking her machine gun.

Spathi continued to squint, listening; the wind seemed to hiss at them in reverberating echoes. Lena patted him on the shoulder. He jerked, staring at her with wide eyes.

"Hey," she asked. "You sure you're all right."

Spathi looked back to the fog. "Just trying to stay alert."

"Your eyes are bloodshot. You haven't been yourself for days."

"We're all tired, Mother."

"He's here," she whispered, "isn't he?"

Spathi nodded. "Most likely." His eyes darted back and forth. "But he's not the only one here."

"I know," Lena replied, then drew her Selebane sword. "Eyes and ears peeled at all times, all of you. That's an order."

"Wait!" Haandin said, turning to her. "I'd better go with the others. They don't know where the hospital is."

"Aye." Lena nodded. "Be careful."

Haandin jogged to Staea and the others.

"I was just about to say," Aipha said. "'Cause I don't know where the hell we're going. Can't read the signs or anything."

"It's an Oclavic language," Haandin told her. "Years ago, Van De Yoth used to do business with the Vauphec and Enoshah of this region." He sighed. "I used to be able to speak it fluently…but I should be able to read the street signs well enough to navigate."

Spathi and Staea exchanged one last look of concern, then both teams crossed the bridge and entered. Staea's group separated, traveling left down a street, heading north and vanishing through the mist, while Spathi's team continued on the crowded road ahead of them.

As Spathi and the others made for the military base, he steadily realized something. The ospreys had disappeared. As had their cries.

Up ahead, he heard the lone cawing of a crow.

"I don't suppose anybody has a working watch, do they?" Rand asked.

Lena peered up at the sky. "I'd estimate we have about another…four or five hours of daylight left…give or take?"

"Shit," Spathi said. "We'd better hurry."

"It'll take us at least an hour to get there," Rand said, nervously surveying the buildings. "I don't know about camping out here for the night."

"Neither do I," Spathi concurred.

"Then we'd better make quick work of this escapade," Lena replied.

Spathi stared at some of the vehicles. "The conditions of these vehicles don't exactly inspire confidence." He kicked one of the dry-rotted flat tires. "Even if we *did* find something, we'd need something heavy and durable, with six-wheel drive, and I imagine it's going to take more than just a tune-up and some gas to—"

"Let's…try to be optimistic, lads," Lena groaned. "Shall we?"

"And if I recall correctly, it was *you* who ultimately influenced everyone to come here," Rand scolded. "And *now*, you're tellin' us you're having dou—?"

"You really know how to drag your feet, all of you," a smug voice sneered from above them. "Do you realize how long I've been waiting?"

Spathi, Lena, and Rand all aimed their weapons up at a cloaked figure with long black hair draping down his right side…and a lightning mark infesting his bald left side.

Constanvol.

With Qualkytdle's blade folded under his right forearm…and a bottle of vodka in his left. The baron took a slug of the glassy liquor as he stood on a one-story pub's crumpled roof, the fractured stone awning supported haphazardly by its only remaining cracked pillar.

"But I'm impressed, Spathi" Constanvol said. "You've managed to help your company survive a tsunami. And you haven't starved to death. Not yet, at least."

Rand opened fire, shooting four shots. With deft, inhuman motions, the baron deflected each bullet, then he showed Rand the projectiles in the palm of his gauntleted hand and let them roll off as if casting pebbles to the ground.

"You'll be needing those, Captain Limend," Constanvol taunted, "for we're not alone here in Buurinska." He tilted his head. "But you knew that already…didn't you, Spathi? And you led all your precious little sheep here anyway…all the way to the slaught—"

Shing!

With a vicious slash from Vrashri, Spathi sliced through the awning's column. Constanvol dropped the vodka and rolled down artfully to the street as the pub's roof caved in. Spathi stomped forward, gripping Vrashri's hilt in both hands. The baron unfurled Qualkytdle's blade into its scythe position.

"You two go on ahead," Spathi said to Lena and Rand. "I need to have a word with Veliath's disowned son."

Constanvol glared tightly at the insult, clenching his teeth. His eyes burned with dark-blue light. Spathi squinted.

There it was. He finally found a nerve in the baron.

"Kick his ass, Spathi," Rand's voice grated.

"Why rush?" Constanvol snarled at Rand and Lena. "Don't be a stranger."

"Unzelkoyte rebuke you!" Lena seethed. "And send you back to hell where you belong!"

Constanvol belted a monstrous hiss at her, fangs bared.

Spathi turned to his mother. "Go! I'll be right behind you!"

"Son—"

"Go!" Spathi yelled. "I've got this!"

"C'mon!" Rand snapped, heading down another street. Reluctantly, Lena followed. She looked at Spathi. "You better come back!"

"Trust me." Spathi turned back to Constanvol. "I won't disappoint."

The baron scowled at the two fleeing fighters.

"Hey!" Spathi spat. "Eyes here, you sod! It's me you want."

Constanvol extended Qualkytdle's sleek blade all the way out, freeing it of the gauntlet mechanism's slot. He gripped the steely part by its segmented tang, wielding the curved weapon like a long, two-edged katana. "Sounds to me like we have much to discuss, don't we?"

Spathi waited, silently meditating, focusing, trying to still his mind, his breathing, and his heartbeat. He remembered seeing Alehi fire the brilliant arrow from the silver bow days earlier, forcing his conflicted, ulcerous spirit to yield to heaven's light, channeling his violent indignation into purpose. Slowly, Vrashri cultivated its holy, nebulous glow once again while he resisted the urge to make the first move.

And it was as hard as hell to do!

"I can't help but find it curious that Veliath would renounce his only child, his bastard son," Spathi mocked coolly. "Can't say I blame the horse's ass, though. Must've been so humiliating for you…especially in front of Drixilo the other day. After all that time you spent romancing his rebellious legacy. Some god *you'd* make. Not even hell wants you…let alone heaven."

Constanvol grunted and rushed at him, swiping.

Spathi dodged and bashed Qualkytdle away.

"This little 'alliance' of yours isn't working out," Spathi barked.

"What 'alliance?'" Constanvol growled, then charged again. "I thought I drilled it thoroughly into your thick skull what my intentions were!"

"You mean how you intended to be drinking during the day?" Spathi jeered. "Sloppy. Very sloppy of you."

Both clashed, smashing through the soiled window display of another store as both adversaries dueled in a frenzy, obliterating shelves and doors to pieces and crashing through the opposite wall, back into the street, with the ashes continuing to fall…along with a peculiar black snow. Despite this, Spathi felt a strange calm over him, one that was not his own. Though his mind was racing, his movements were measured, honed. Disciplined. It was as if something moved with him, protecting him.

Like unseen wings.

Staea and the others marched on an overpass, trying to gain a better view of the abandoned city. Alehi stood on top of a ruined pickup truck's bed, peering at the structures far off through his binoculars, mentally mapping out a safe path through the cluttered roads.

Lest something unsavory ambush them along the way.

"A power plant should be over there," Haandin said, pointing at the crumbled outlines of nuclear chimneys. "But like I said: that's not the one that had the meltdown, and we're…maybe a couple hundred miles away from Yeberyl, so it should be safe. The military base should be to the left of it." He aimed his finger at a large campus that stood half that distance. "I *think* that's the hospital down there."

"It is the hospital. I see the logo. There's something else, too," Alehi said. "I think it's a Ferris wheel…and what's left of a roller coaster."

"An amusement park?" Tyri commented.

"Yup," Alehi said, lowering his binoculars and passing them to Aipha. "As if this place wasn't creepy enough already."

"I think I see what you're talking about," Aipha said, gazing through the lenses. "Is there a way around it?"

"Yeah, but it'd be quicker to cut across the theme park," Haandin estimated. "Going around it will just burn more daylight." He looked up at the dim light of the overcast skies. "Won't be able to do much at night, if we don't get overrun by demons."

"Please don't say that," Silda said. "We've gone at least a week without—"

"Shh!" Tyri rebuked.

"We're probably overdue for an altercation," Alehi groaned.

As the others stared at the ominous Ferris wheel, something clanged far below. They turned, hearing the clash of sharpened steel ringing in the distant streets. Staea turned, seeing the faint blue flickers in the fog about half a mile away.

"Spathi!" Staea called out, stepping to the overpass's edge.

"You just *had* to say something, didn't you, Jaeter?" Aipha chided.

"Well, my bad!" Alehi griped at her.

"We need to help him," Staea suggested.

"Don't worry, he's got this," Aipha assured.

Staea looked back at her allies, then back down at the flashes.

"Staea!" Silda scolded. "C'mon, girl, don't you run off on us!"

"Hey!" Haandin jogged over to Staea. "He'll be all right. He's strong, just like you. We need you here, okay?"

Staea let out a long sigh, then nodded and reluctantly returned to her comrades. All of them hurried down one of the exit ramps to the streets, heading to the hospital. As they approached the campus, Staea glanced around, noticing something falling with the ashes.

Black ice. Like dark sleet.

Bitterly cold!

The melting beads of grime almost seemed to crawl down their bodies rather than simply trickle. Staea shuddered, somehow feeling so…violated by the strange precipitation. They finally reached shelter under the parking garage, with the ashen rime forming around the ledges, already generating small, dirty icicles. Cautiously, they proceeded to the closed automatic doors of the emergency room entrance and shattered the glass, then they eased through.

"Alright, Aipha," Silda asked. "What exactly are we lookin' for in here."

"Clean gauzes, bandages, rubbing alcohol, if it hasn't evaporated—which it probably has by now," Aipha instructed as they made their way through the filthy lobby to the fire escape. "Hand sanitizer. Maybe some hydrogen peroxide. Syringes, if sterile." She looked at Silda. "Diapers and ointment for the surviving babies back at camp. Stuff like that."

"What about medication?" Tyri inquired.

"Don't bother," her older sister replied. "It's expired."

"So has everything else in this dump," Alehi complained.

"How are we gonna carry all this shit?" Haandin questioned.

"Might be some duffel bags in the locker room," Aipha claimed. "Or maybe some backpacks from medical students. Who knows what all they left behind?"

"Diapers will be in the maternity ward," Haandin said, reading a smudged directory on the wall.

"What floor?" Tyri asked.

"Fifth," he replied.

"Alright," Aipha said. "Silda, Staea, y'all come with me to the maternity floor. Haandin, you, Tyri, and Al go see if you can find something to carry our sundries in. C'mon!"

"On it," Haandin said.

They all shuffled into their teams and headed up the stairs, with Haandin, Tyri, and Alehi heading to the third floor, rummaging through the hospital rooms and utility closets while trying to locate a locker room. Staea, Aipha, and Silda continued to the fifth floor, then carefully crept down the maternity wing.

"I hope they didn't abandon their babies…you know…when they evacuated and all," Silda whispered. "Otherwise, I'm gonna be sick."

"Not sure if they evacuated Buurinska because of Yeberyl's meltdown," Aipha told her, "But they might have. If they did…surely, they had the decency to retrieve their children from such a disaster."

"I don't know," Staea sighed. "I was orphaned in the wilderness as a baby."

"Really?" Silda asked.

Staea let out a deeper sigh. "That's what I'm told, anyway." She groaned, making her way towards the large nursery window. "I was also told that my real name was 'Amaiphynie,' so I don't know what to think anymore."

"That guy was full of shit the other day—don't listen to him!" Silda spat.

"I hope you're right," Staea replied.

"Girl, I *am* right," Silda said, then turned to Aipha. "Right?"

"Yeah," Aipha said absentmindedly, gazing through the grimy glass.

All three of the women turned and beheld the state-of-the-art nursery, with some of the cribs lumpy and stained with black and brown. Staea and Silda cringed, looking away from what remained of the tiny infant cadavers.

"Guess I was wrong," Aipha said, her breath quavering. "Damn." She walked and opened the door. "Don't worry, I'll go in. You two stay here and keep watch."

Staea looked up and saw something that only added to the nursery's morbidity. Amongst the cribs, the remnants of two female robotic nurses stood halfway hunched over, their arms and heads hanging down, with photogenic smiles permanently plastered on the faces of synthetic skin and the bangs of their frayed wigs curling just above their lifeless, fractured eyes. Some of the panels of their torsos lay ajar, with wires and components jumbled and rusted. Yet the flesh from their breasts had peeled from time and weather, exposing the translucent, rotund, artificial mammary containers beneath, clogged with moldy clabber. Both Staea and Silda furrowed their foreheads.

Mechanical wet nurses.

Both of them entered the room, eyeing reclining chairs near the walls. More female robots lay seated, leaned back, yet these only gazed upward stoically, their red and pink lips parted. Tubing and electric cables were hooked into each one's back, formerly supplying oxygen and nutrients from tanks mounted behind them. Each gynoid was equipped…with a womb. Their lower torso plating had been removed, revealing an incubation chamber of an elastic material bulging from each abdomen, filled with a murky dark-green liquid that at one time housed a live specimen.

"That's provocative!" Silda snapped.

Aipha looked up at the machine mothers. "I've heard of these. Automated maternal surrogates." She opened up a drawer, pulling out a dusty, unopened pack of diapers. "From what I've read, it was a big issue with bioethics and quality of life during the Pre-Surfacing era." She shrugged. "You'd be surprised how many women were actually for it, though, not having to deal with pregnancy, labor pains, or childbirth…then you had barren women who were unable to conceive…and they didn't trust human surrogacy…and then you had wealthier families who just preferred to 'customize' their offspring with frivolous genetic modifications."

"So, why not just put 'em in tanks or something?" Staea questioned.

"According to what I read, having robotic mothers supposedly helped the children assimilate into society better," Aipha explained. "It makes sense, if you think about it. I mean, waking up every day knowing you were just bred in an aquarium or test tube in a lab would just make you feel even more alienated from others, like you're just some petty science project rather than a live, sentient person. Being nurtured by a 'mother' or 'nanny,' albeit manufactured and electronic, would evidently help the children have better psychological development in society; otherwise, they'd be more likely to snap and go homicidal, even if they were programmed to do the contrary."

"No." Staea shook her head. "It doesn't make sense at all."

"That's so fucked up," Silda agreed.

"Granted, it's not the most wholesome thing in the world," Aipha said, pointing to the robots. "These could only produce cybernetic embryos, implanted with microchips and small CPUs where the umbilical cord was connected, regulating growth in the fetus, oxygen levels, prenatal nutrition, blood flow, even preprogramming things like…algebra, musical skills, political science, everything—all before the poor things were even born."

"Artificial humans," Silda scoffed.

"No," Aipha said. "They were still fertilized with sperm, still used organic eggs from donors." She turned to her. "If you're gonna call them 'fake,' then I guess that makes us fake, too."

"Oh, spare me!" Silda hissed. "Just creepy-ass man-children trying to replace women is all. I mean, why have a *real* relationship with a *real* woman, just like Unzelkoyte intended, when you can just buy a glorified sex toy to *simulate* all this shit? Just program it to fuck your brains out, make you pancakes whenever you want, clean up your shit, even *customize* your 'children,' that is if you care to have any. Yeah, just pop 'em out of their fake pussies at the simple and convenient push of a button, like some damned vending machine. No effort required whatsoever." She glared at the maternal surrogates and pushed one over, smashing its mechanical head beneath her armored heel. "Too bad you clunky jizz-dumpsters aren't under warranty anymore, otherwise, you could've—"

"Alright, Silda, cool it!" Aipha huffed. "Those man-children are dead, anyway."

"Yeah, and good riddance, too!" the redhead growled. "Fuckin' pigs! I'm the real deal, bitches, the real thing—one hundred percent organic and homegrown! This ginger's just too damned hot for you to handle!" She squinted at the combat medic. "By the way, did these 'babies' even have souls?"

Aipha rolled her eyes, muttering derogatory things.

Staea hesitated, then she glanced around. "Only one way to find out."

"Look, I get it. It's creepy and nasty up in here," Aipha barked. "Y'all done with the sociology lesson?" She yanked another pack of diapers out of the bin. "Or y'all wanna give me a hand with these? 'Cause the longer this shit takes, the longer we gotta spend in this freakshow in here—and we're burning daylight!"

"Yeah, yeah," Silda moaned, stepping over. "Fuck this place."

"Yeah," Staea concurred, walking to them.

As the three women gathered supplies on the fifth floor, Haandin, Tyri, and Alehi located a locker room on the third level, snatching up a few duffel bags and bookbags from the putrid floor.

"Just take what little bit you can carry," Haandin told them. "Don't overburden yourselves. We gotta fill this up with stuff."

"Damn, this shit's so nasty," Alehi cursed.

Bang. Clong.

They looked out the door and froze.

"Aipha?" Tyri called out.

"Shh!" Alehi rebuked, creeping out into the hallway, drawing his Selebane sword.

Tyri and Haandin followed him, readying their weapons in one hand and toting bags in the other, eyes darting around the corridors. Haandin stepped in front of Alehi, hearing something rummage in a nearby breakroom. A bluish glow radiated from the opening. He halted the two soldiers with his raised fist, then silently signaled them to spread out. The two Enoshah quietly took cover around the corner as Haandin eased his face around the doorway.

Ping! Clang!

A chain whipped out. Haandin ducked, narrowly avoiding the barbed links tearing through drywall as Sile's bony form staggered out and lashed out at them, his wrists still bound by the chains. Haandin grabbed the loose links as Tyri appeared from behind, kicking Sile to the ground, aiming her sword at the Nalx's throat.

"My, my, how lucky are we?" Haandin quipped.

"We are?" Alehi asked.

Sile uttered a feeble hiss up at the Vauphec.

"Beginning to think the devil made off with you," Haandin sneered. "He must have a really bad case of the butterfingers. But…then again, you're one slippery, slimy bugger for *any* bloke to handle for long."

"You sure we really need this guy, Haan?" Tyri questioned.

Sile laughed. "It doesn't matter." His milky-blue eyes shifted at the hallway. "They've already found me. They're here."

"Then you're our ticket out of here," Haandin's voice grated.

"I don't know, man," Alehi said, shaking his head. "Shit's dicey."

"If Drixilo's gone through this much trouble to hunt him down after keeping him confined," Haandin said, "then it proves he wants him alive." He squinted and looked around, raising an eyebrow. "Maybe he *is* the key to these so-called 'virgin cosmos' they speak of."

"They are coming, Vauphec," Sile chuckled again. "You will not last."

"You seem so sure of it, don't you?" Haandin wrapped the chain around the Nalx's scrawny neck and pulled. Sile squawked as Haandin got into his face. "Time to go for a walk, mutt. We've got Drixilo by the balls now." He looked to his comrades. "We need to check on Staea and the others." He made for the fire escape, pulling Sile behind him. "Let's move! C'mon, hurry!"

Spathi and Constanvol continued their battle up onto the overpass, with Spathi gradually driving the baron near the edge of a bridge by jamming Vrashri through his arm slot, producing shockwaves from his spirit shield. Yet each blast of energy was fracturing the concrete edifice more and more, wobbling beneath their feet.

Even more so, Spathi bled from his eyes and arm with each stab of his aegis. The endurance of the soul was a taxing thing to maintain, taking its toll on mind and body. He wheezed, trying to keep up with Constanvol's swipes, feeling his stamina dwindle.

But the baron was almost spent as well.

Both of them stood there, panting, sweating near the overpass's edge.

The road grew icier by the minute.

Spathi glanced, watching two figures in the distant fog running toward the amusement park's dismal outlines. He hoped it was Lena and Rand. And they'd better find a transport that ran.

"Why do you cry, Ansdari?" Constanvol mocked.

Spathi touched the red tears from his weeping eyes.

"Mommy shouldn't have left her baby behind." Constanvol spat blood on the asphalt.

Spathi raised Vrashri once again. "Tell that…to Minaya. Or did that moon whore disown you, too?"

Crack! Boom.

The overpass shifted, then tilted forward, collapsing. Spathi charged at Constanvol, but the baron slashed at him, falling backwards, vanishing into the mist below. Impetuously, Spathi leapt from the crumbling ledge and slid down onto a shop's tattered awning, then fell, rolling down a car's roof and hood, then onto stable pavement. Behind him, the road junction fragmented to pieces in a cloud of dust. He looked around for any sign of the baron.

Nothing. He had vanished.

"Coward!" Spathi croaked.

He peered up. The sky seemed darker than before…and snowing more of that strange black ice down. And the wind seemed to stridulate with deep, haunting whispers, both audible and simultaneously in his mind.

Icht-icht-icht…haaah-icht-icht-cht!

Ssshhaah-icht-icht—chichichichichichichi….

Shhaah-icht-icht-icht…icht-icht!

Haaah…haaah…haaah…haaah….

The rasping and chittering reverberated in the wind, bouncing off the buildings' bleak Brutalist surfaces, constantly rising and ebbing away like an afflicted poltergeist. He groaned…and marched to the theme park's ruins, too weary to run. Yet he knew that time was running low. And he wouldn't last much longer.

Already, he felt lightheaded from the blood he lost.

Damned Constanvol.

As he strode, Lena and Rand passed through the amusement park's crushed iron gates, vaulting over the stocky row of tripod turnstiles, then they approached a directory at the center of a sidewalk roundabout.

Rand pointed at the map, drawing a route with his finger to the left side of the park. "Guess that's the quickest way, uh?"

Lena nodded. "Looks like it." She glanced around, then pointed past a distant moss-caked carousel. "This way."

As they passed the overgrown merry-go-round of tarnished horses, Rand looked up at the skeletal remains of a fairytale castle's keep…with a giant black dragon prop having been built on the side of the roof and wall, designed to appear as if clinging near the balcony, about to capture an unsuspecting princess. Its serrated mouth of tangled mandibles lay wide open, with its serpentine neck coiled like a python, ready to strike at any moment. Six black eyes studded its horned melon head like a spider's gaze, three symmetrically on each side, with a seventh in the front. Twin small sickle-like arms were outstretched, with its huge, gaunt hind legs also serving as its two forked wings, the webbed flaps of skin resembling the intricate membrane of a wasp's wingspan. Thick sinews ridged its hide of sleek black scales beneath, causing unique, overlapping corrugations along its body from head to tail. Rand shook his head.

Such skilled craftsmanship.

The prop seemed so lifelike, even after all this time.

Too lifelike….

He looked back…and saw no sign of Lena. He scanned the buildings frantically, running past the funhouse and nearing the roller coaster ruins.

"Lena?" Rand called out. "Lena!"

Nothing. Only the deep howl of the wind blew above.

With his breath quavering, he aimed his rifle and walked down a corridor, pointing the barrel at anything that moved. Leaves twiddled down to the cement sidewalk, the forsaken path covered in damp pine straw, fir cones, and twigs.

"Lena, talk to me!" Rand demanded. "Where'd you go?"

The sound of falling terracotta tiles clattered to the ground behind him. Rand whipped around and aimed his gun…and saw nothing. Yet the stripped castle above him was now mostly veiled with low-hanging clouds…but not enough to cover the black dragon statue.

Which was now missing.

His eye twitched. Surely, he had seen it just now. He wasn't crazy. He couldn't have just imagined it—it was so vivid! Was this even the same fairytale castle he had seen earlier, or was it another abandoned ride?

A twig snapped.

He turned and saw Lena standing near a railing, with her back turned and her skin paler, as if crusted with ice.

Her Selebane was missing.

Rand aimed his weapon, watching her corpse-like movement turn to him.

Revealing empty eye sockets…and a hollow, elongated jaw.

Blam!

The soldier opened fire. The doppelganger squealed and shattered like glass as the bullet tore through its grisly head. More ice animi emerged from the rime, cackling like the ghosts of witches.

Qualcifren. Fused with Empress Noshva.

"Oldest trick in the book!" Rand taunted them, gunning each one down.

More of the dark ice queen's shards flurried from the sky, generating more of the ghastly frost elementals. They cornered Rand, pinning him down with icicles, toying with him. He grunted, trying to break free. Then Lena leaped from a nearby roof and dove down, slicing some of the Qualcifrites down with her Selebane aglow with holy light as

Rand fired on more of them, fragmenting them to bits. Yet the shards only reformed, closing in on the two.

Then Rand's rifle finally clicked empty.

Spathi arrived at the amusement park gates, hearing the commotion on the other side and squeezing through.

"Mother!" Spathi yelled. "Rand!"

The area blackened like misty night as the bizarre whispering raged around him in the blowing wind, flapping like huge, warped wings.

Uula-icht-icht-icht-icht-icht…haaah…haaah…haaah…haaah….

Spathi raised Vrashri, its blue light shining around him while his left arm continued to drizzle blood from the spirit shield slot. In the dark, Lena and Rand shrieked, sounding as if dying. Spathi limped towards them. Yet the theme park grew more and more sinister, transformed by the entity's permeating essence. The leaves and pine needles on the ground had vanished, replaced by drops of his red vitality dripping in various paths everywhere. He grew increasingly woozy as a shrill ringing dug into his eardrums…then a grim voice echoed in his mind.

Dying, lying, watch your friends die…. Dying, lying, watch your friends die….

Dather.

Duulagicht. The Mind Plague.

The park spun as he heard his serpentine bulk snake past him in the dark, snapping through unseen trees, gasping and chittering in heated, spectral breaths.

Tick-tock-tick-tock-ock-ock-ock-ock-ock-ock….

Icht…icht…icht…icht…icht…icht….

Around him, a clammy air breathed over him, reeking of an unfathomable foulness. Words did not exist in any human language to describe just how malodorous of a stench it was, seeming to slowly dissolve his skin. Not like acid.

His flesh had suddenly become like wax.

And his body was melting to Vrashri's light!

The haunted stridulations of Duulagicht susurrated through the air again, the stinking breath becoming even more potent, colder.

Suffocating.

Kill the light, or die….

Spathi gazed at Vrashri's unbearable glow, growing hotter by the second. He couldn't breathe. His throat felt so dry, closing up…freezing. The entire insides of his throat felt engulfed in the creeping black rime of Noshva and Qualcifren. He looked to his drooping left arm, oozing with blood, stinging in anguish, then back at Vrashri, the blade become so obnoxious, so heavy.

Kill the light…or it will kill you….

Spathi looked up over him. In Vrashri's dimming glow, he managed to catch just a fleeting glimpse of numerous fanged jaws of a black Udenthen surrounding him, on the verge of snapping shut, consuming his body. With a loud grunt, he impaled his left arm once again.

And yelled!

Boom!

A dome-shaped shockwave of blue light rioted out, tearing away the thick shadows and obliterating the ice animi. Noshva and Qualcifren screeched, the nearby dark frost disintegrating to Vrashri's amplified light. Duulagicht wailed and separated, taking the form of a huge murder of crows blazing with black fire, retreating to the foggy tree line. Spathi fell down on his back as Lena and Rand rushed to him, feeling the wind around him. A gentle breeze.

Calm. Cool.

Clean.

"Spathi," Lena whimpered, holding her bleeding son.

He gazed up at his mother's weeping blue eyes. "Did I…get him?"

Lena nodded, managing a smirk. Spathi smiled back, content.

"Yeah, you got 'im, kid," Rand sighed, tearing a piece of his ragged military fatigues off and wrapped it around his exsanguinating left arm. "Just hang in there."

"Where's Staea?" Lena sniffled, her lips quivering, then she looked down at Spathi. "Let's go find Staea, Spathi. She can help you." She kissed his forehead. "Just hang in there, baby. Oh, my sweet child!"

Spathi felt his head flop over…with his eyes still open. Yet all grew dark again, his body growing colder, with the soothing sounds of the boreal wind fading away…along with everything else. Yet a shrill ringing perturbed his ears. If this didn't finish him this time, what would? They needed a miracle, not him. Why couldn't they just let him die this time? Just a peaceful death. He had earned it this time. Why couldn't they let him have it? He had done his part. They didn't need him anymore.

They never needed him.

Did they?

"Spathi?" Lena sobbed from afar. "Spathi, don't you go! Spathi? Spathi!"

XI: Rendezvous

The darkness faded in and out in a warped timelapse around Spathi, with the figures of his allies shifting around like a fevered dream, their voices distant, frantic. Melancholy. He felt Staea offer her blood in his turbulent dreamlike state. Instinctively, he drank from her bleeding arm, supping on her vitality.

Part of her…inside of him.

"Just rest," she whispered from afar. "Rest…."

Then the blackness of unconsciousness finally took him, seeming like a dreamless coma at first. A mist appeared around him as he drifted in zero gravity through an aisle of glassy rectangular monoliths floating in the void, each one depicting fractal visages.

Of him, petrified, yelling silently in eternal agony.

Yet each image was different, portraying a different demise. Part of him deemed each one absolutely foreign. And part of him tried to remember things, recollection of things that…never happened.

Déjà vu?

How could one recall something that never existed? How could one remember a dream they've never had, a place they've never been? A life they've never lived? A death they've never died? What was this horrendous turmoil, this inner civil war? He could no longer ignore it.

There was conflict within him.

Deep conflict.

A red glow appeared at the end of the aisle, with a robed figure suddenly looming over him, his face yawning at him.

Screaming!

Drixilo.

"Damn it!" Spathi jerked awake on a rocky floor, wrapped in old sheets.

Aipha looked at him, wide-eyed. "And 'Good morning' to you, too."

Spathi looked up at her, then at his left arm, bandaged with fresh gauzes from the hospital. His sword, Vrashri, and his Sevelurnum armor was propped up against a cave wall. He squinted. The resistance coalition's encampment sprawled before him.

They actually made it?

Lanterns illuminated the lava tubes of rhyolite, all bustling with numerous human survivors, Enpherom, Enoshah, and Vauphec. Stalagmites and stalactites draped the ancient caverns, with a few cruisers and tanks remaining; their engines hummed, shining their headlights into the dark. Several campfires burned nearby, with some people having made makeshift braziers from oil drums, trying to boil water to drink.

"Welcome back," Aipha said, then knelt down to him. "Let me check your bandages right quick."

"Where's Staea?" Spathi asked.

"She said she needed some 'alone time,'" the combat medic replied. "Something's eating at her pretty bad. You need to give her a big 'thank you' as soon as you see her. She was your impromptu blood donor, just in the nick of time, too."

"Wait, how'd we get out of Buurinska," Spathi questioned.

Aipha pointed to a rusted six-wheeled tank. "Got lucky at the military base. All it needed was an oil change, some diesel, two new tires, and a quick tune-up. Haandin and Alehi really know their way around a garage, I'll say that."

"Shojem," Spathi demanded, grabbing her shoulder.

Aipha gently removed his hand, clutching it tenderly. "Don't worry. He knows you got a lot of questions. Says he's willing to talk whenever you're ready."

"He'd be more than happy to see you, Spathi," a familiar voice spoke.

They both turned to see an Enpherom chief, scarred with a few cuts and burns on the left of his face. He wore a breastplate and gauntlets of Sevelurnum plate mail, with the late Desmond Abaque's thresacrix still around his neck and a Selebane claymore sheathed on his back.

"Maloxi?" Spathi blurted in disbelief, sitting up. "What the—I thought you—!"

"Died, I know." Maloxi managed a smirk. "I thought I was done for, too. I'm glad you and the others made it out of Vider the other night." He stared down one of the vast, undulating lava tubes. "Guess I'm not done yet, either."

Spathi sighed. "Why did you...how did you survive?"

"I've only heard bits and pieces myself," Aipha said, raising an eyebrow.

Maloxi sat down on a nearby metal crate. "How, indeed." He looked at the cave wall and shrugged. "Not much to tell, really. The ice demon, Noshva, attempted to contain the explosions to keep me from killing all her engineered creatures, keeping me from sacrificing myself, for I fell through the floor...and all went black—it all happened so fast." He shook his head. "The possibility of my aspiring martyrdom must have caused such revulsion in the demon that she actually *spared* my life rather than taking it, hoping to corrupt me before slaying me. But I woke up outside in the snow amidst the burning rubble of the temple. Noshva was nowhere, neither was the evil spirit they call Qualcifren. I skinned a dead polar bear and clad myself in its bloody hide...and journeyed south, because I saw Drixilo's storm in the North. Starving and fearing I was on the brink of death, I built a thresacrix of fallen logs and rocks and two bonfires to glorify Unzelkoyte, beseeching the holy ones of the trinity of heaven. I begged to be absolved of all iniquity and transgressions, telling them to take me up and remember my soul, for I was spent and too tired to live anymore. I collapsed between the two fires, then I was awoken again by two men robed like hooded monks." He looked at Spathi. "One of them looked very familiar, but I wasn't sure. He was bearded and had green eyes."

Spathi gawked at the chief.

Green eyes?

"They baked two loaves of a strange bread on the coals of one of the bonfires and provided me a clay jar of steaming water to drink." Maloxi went on. "I do not know whether it was real or if this was a vision, but as I ate with them, they told me to journey further south, to these very caves we reside in now, that I would be visited by my kin in forty days." He peered up. "I rejoiced. I thought I would be finally taken into the afterlife, cleansed of all shame and agony. I would see my family again, the Enpherom of my tribe, those I have lost, those I failed to protect. I awoke the next morning...and did as I was told, heading to the caves, beginning my spirit journey. Somehow, the bread and water kept me full, sustaining me—it sounds crazy, I know. For days, I wondered through the mountains in a daze. At last, I saw two ospreys lead me to these lava tubes. Thinking it a sign, I made camp here and waited for two more weeks. Yet as the days passed, I began to lose faith, thinking I had abided by the instructions of a hallucination. I felt like a foolish madman, chasing a psychotic dream. Furious, I was on the verge of departing and heading west...but then I saw headlights coming. I flagged them down with a torch from my campfire...and the survivors of Van De Yoth came into the cave." He shook his head. "At first, I was confused. Disheartened with a deep grief. I thought I would see my dead Enpherom brethren in the afterlife." He glanced at Spathi and Aipha. "But I realize now, you *are* my kin. All of you. We always were." He pointed to his gray skin. "For ages, we have tried to separate ourselves with false barriers of shallow rhetoric based on the mere colors of our flesh, but in truth, we all breathe and bleed the same. The social constructs of the world have passed away, and for the first time, I embrace the truth: we are all brothers and sisters, not just in spirit but by flesh and blood as well." He nodded. "And I am glad to brave with all of you, even to this bitter end of days." He gazed back up. "But eternity is not too far from our reach. In all my years of being chief of my tribe, I now regard this experience as my first *true* spirit journey...and my epiphany has only just begun, a rising sun that never sets. I am reborn at last."

Spathi and Aipha were speechless, silently soaking in Maloxi's words. A tear fell down Aipha's cheek as she emitted a shuddering sigh; the words had hit her much harder, stirring something within her, something she didn't even believe she had.

Until now.

"We must all brave together," Spathi said, lumbering to his feet and offering his hand.

Maloxi grappled Spathi's palm, and the two embraced as brothers.

"I am honored by what you did for us in Vider," Spathi admitted. "But it's like you said: we need to stick together. You need not feel ashamed for anything."

"I know." Maloxi smiled. "Thank you."

Aipha bolted up and sighed again. "I gotta go check on something."

The combat medic walked away, visibly distraught by Maloxi's heartfelt speech. Spathi staggered, propping himself back against the wall.

"You sure you're all right?" Maloxi asked. "You need to rest."

"Yeah, I know," Spathi agreed. "Let me just...walk around a little bit. Get the blood flowing, you know." He scanned the encampment. "Where is Shojem?"

Maloxi pointed to a campfire's glow in a large cavity in the wall several yards away, covered with a caribou hide. Spathi nodded and walked on the cavern's uneven floor, passing the tanks and surveying the camp's inhabitants.

The two Enoshah generals, Den Mautre and Jenaya Devral, spoke with chiefs Vuzco and Nasheeya, along with Malokka, Rand, Weizer, Commander Onra Mayona, and others over a map spread on the top of a table. Onra stared at him, her dark-brown eyes exuding an odd yet subtle contempt, annoyed. Distressed.

Haughty.

Seething.

Whatever it was, she could just get over it.

Mautre looked up and nodded at Spathi. He reciprocated the gesture at the generals and continued onward. Near the wall, Rediq Tashar and a few combat medics attended to wounded soldiers on sleeping bags. He glanced up at Spathi for just a moment before resuming his work. Spathi squinted; the doctor's eyes were quite different. Those still glassy, there was great fatigue within them.

And fear.

Resentment.

But there was no shame. No guilt. Only a deep dread, like one of a willing prisoner, too confused to be free, cultivating a swelling horror inside his captive soul, emotions he most likely would not admit to. He still refused to acknowledge the ending world as the long-awaited, inexorable fulfillment of an ancient prophecy.

Uthilda and Shadya soberly helped pass out supplies to some of the women and children, the young ones crying and coughing. The Rinyox Unzelite mother's mechanical prosthetic right arm was missing, evidently lost or abandoned during or after the siege at Van De Yoth. Moriah was sparring with one of the Yothish knights wielding a Selebane spear, the blinking LED light flashing furiously in her forehead; her straight silvery hair was already down to her shoulders, her curved bangs almost in her eyes, partially veiling the device in her right temple. Yet there was no sign of Lee Ann, the nurse. His heart sank; she evidently hadn't survived the Drixiles' onslaught the other day. Dr. Melga Gremen was nowhere in sight either…not that he was complaining. Sitting on another metal container, Tawpa and Jalusa quietly sat together, with his arm around his sister and her head resting on her brother's shoulder. At least the two Enpherom siblings had made amends. Took them long enough. In another part of the spanning tunnels, Lena helped Alehi and Tyri with their training with the Selebane bows. Alehi's progress had only improved slightly, while Tyri still struggled to wield the weapon, yet she came closer to summon the arrows than what she had on the coast days earlier.

Still, she strained, unwilling to let go, no doubt Prister's untimely death at Van De Yoth had more to do with it than what she would let on…along with the loss of her mother years ago.

In a bivouac, Silda sat with Flora swaddled in her arms, with Haandin seated next to her, holding her and her daughter. Spathi raised an eyebrow; one of the Vauphec's legs was bandaged. Hopefully, Noshva or Duulagicht had not wounded him too badly for him to fight.

They needed him.

They all needed each other.

The redhead shushed her sick baby, with tears streaming down her freckled face as she wiped Flora's mouth with a tissue. Spathi's heart plunged even further; Silda knew it wouldn't be too long now, savoring what few moments of motherhood remained.

But that wasn't why Staea had sought out solitude....

As he neared Shojem's abode, the clank of metal sounded next to him.

"Don't know if you've heard," a voice said to his right, "but we'll be leaving these caves within the next forty-eight hours. These old lava tubes are growing more unstable with all the earthquakes and eruptions."

He turned. Jatal, his Vauphec grandfather, walked back and forth, unloading Selebanes and Sevelurnum armor from a crate.

"Where will we go?" Spathi questioned.

Jatal slammed a plate mail back down into the wooden box, then exhaled a long, mournful sigh. He hung his head and shut his eyes.

"I don't know," Jatal finally muttered. He opened his pained eyes and gazed at Spathi. "What is the opinion of a foolish old man worth, anyhow?"

"No." Spathi approached him. "A wise man has returned to us."

"Really?" Jatal groaned. "Where is he? I'd sure like to meet him."

"You need only to look in the mirror, Papa."

Jatal glanced at him. "That man is long gone." He examined himself. "All that's left are these abject ashes waiting to crumble in the winds of apocalypse."

Spathi shook his head, already tired of his sulking grandfather's self-pity. He took a few steps away.

"Spathi," Jatal said.

He stopped and turned back.

Jatal gazed at his grandson earnestly. "How did you come back to us...after all these long years?"

Spathi walked back to him and shook his head. "I don't really know. The memorial in Roserion was desecrated by Malroc. I do not know the place I had gone to when I fell ages ago. It was not heaven, I know that." He gazed into Jatal's blue eyes. "But I learned that I never died at all. I can't explain what happened or where I was before I emerged back here...in these evil last days."

Jatal looked away, unable to fathom what Spathi had told him.

"My journey of restoration has been hell on earth," Spathi continued. "I was a victim of corruption. Only now do I have just enough clarity to know what is right, but the path before me is still murky. The uncertainty is too great to bear."

"So it is with the path for all of us, my son," Jatal confessed. "I once thought I knew precisely how the world worked, how life worked. My desire for holy justice had left me intoxicated for these long centuries...but the deaths of the godless after the Second Surfacing did not bring me the divine solace I had longed for, but it only bred paranoia, terror...and even more bitterness. I only pray that our broken hearts be mended, just as the holy ones have vowed to do in the Aurixla. My insolence was my hubris." He nodded. "I am man enough to admit this."

"I'm man enough to admit mine." Spathi smirked. "You know…I'm tempted to think we *are* blood-related."

They both chuckled. Then Jatal grew solemn again.

"You mother told me it was Constanvol, the bastard son of Veliath, who cursed you and Staea with blood-eating ages ago."

"Yes." Spathi crossed his arms. "He claims to be some sort of 'moonchild' or something."

"Moonchild?"

"Yes."

Jatal scoffed and furrowed his eyebrows. "I am glad you were strong enough to overcome the temptation to join that wretch in his futile campaign."

"As am I." Spathi sighed. "But you must know, had Staea and the others not followed me to Tauldren, who knows what might have happened in my weakness?" He shook his head. "I am not strong, Papa. I should have split him in two when I had the chance."

"You *are* strong, my son." Jatal put his hand on Spathi's shoulder. "You did not fail the test. You'll get another chance. Have no fear."

Spathi looked back at Shojem's hovel, then back at Jatal. "Where is Staea?"

"Down there." Jatal pointed down another tunnel. He passed him a fluorescent lantern. "She's spooked by something fierce."

"I think I know what it is," Spathi replied. "But she also needs to hear what Shojem has to say. It's time he spilled some answers."

"Aye, I'll go with you in a minute," Jatal said, squinting at the caribou skin entrance. "He has that scrawny Nalx bound in there with him. I, too, wish to know what's really going on…and it's way past time to figure it all out."

Spathi silently agreed and walked to the tunnel, lantern in hand, seeking out his wife. The din of the camp faded away behind him as he crept down the winding lava tube, the rhyolite riddled with round cavities of all shapes and sizes. He pondered what to tell her, things to assuage her racing mind. There were a million things to say…and not one of them was suitable enough to console her.

Or him, for that matter.

He refused to believe what Constanvol had said.

So, why…didn't she?

Up ahead, the pale glow of a lone lantern shone on the cave's walls. He turned the corner, the tunnel sloping downward with its floor becoming jagged…and there she stood, peering up at the holes above, her arms crossed and her back leaning against the rock. She glanced at him, then back at the niches overhead as he neared her.

"What are you looking at?" Spathi asked, peering up.

"Bats," she said.

"Bats?"

"Mm-hmm." She sighed. "I can hear them squeaking, whole colonies of them." She gazed down. "They're scared out of their minds…just like us."

Spathi nodded. "Thank you…for saving me."

Staea smiled at him. "You would've done the same thing for me, my love. And if there's any other good news…we're apparently not radioactive from being in Buurinska."

"That certainly is a plus," Spathi said, wrapping his arm around her.

They both gazed up, watching the miniature bat caves together. He listened…then he could hear them as well. Tiny squeaks and chittering. The distant flutter of leathery wings. Fearful. Starving. Feasting on what few insects and worms may be left, wondering how to survive with what time remained of the dying world.

"I saw something the other day, Spathi." She looked at him. "Things I can't explain."

"If this is about what Constanvol said, I've already told you—"

"This isn't…about what he called me," she claimed. "I saw visions, but they were like…memories, moments of a life I've never lived. There was a part of me that somehow felt as if…I should know, like I had remembered something that happened in another reality—I can't…I don't know, it's sound stupid…but it shook me."

"What did you see?"

Her face cringed. "I had four sisters…in a vast basilica, a world all of its own, on another plane of existence. We were nuns, virgins, all five of us, sisters in spirit rather than by blood, mingling with angels. We would all meditate, singing hymns, each of us walking through the cloisters with lamps of gold. Along with the angels, we were all guarding some sort of giant…clock…with a creature inside of it."

Spathi's eyes widened.

"There was a…manuscript of fire, blazing with the holy words of Unzelkoyte himself. The words radiated onto the world below us. We were happy. It was paradise in this place. But my eldest sister…she was seduced by this imprisoned creature…and another like it…teaching us charms, claiming that we would transcend. And the angels abandoned us. The flaming manuscript was sealed away in a vial of diamond and placed out of our reach so that the creature could not corrupt it. And we became prisoners in this strange world, this basilica slowly rotting because of our rebellion. Only I regretted consorting with these two monsters…and my sisters shunned me for my resentment." She looked away. "Of these charms, my sisters had mastered astral projection, seeking even more power, becoming like witches, carnal, teasing demons with our lust. One of my sisters became pregnant…with the child of a devil. I hated them for it! As the eldest sister prepared to bind and slay me on a stone altar, I cried out in a bizarre language…and a white flash flickered from the outskirts of the basilica, swooping in…and the vision ended."

"Perhaps you simply saw through the eyes of some spirit from long ago," Spathi suggested. "But the vision was probably the invention of Drixilo himself. They mean to confuse us, Staea."

"But…in this vision," Staea said, revealing the silver emblem over her heart, "we each had a circle mark, each one different."

Spathi eyed the ribbed silver talisman more closely, where the Sevelurnum cameo of St. Yuhera was once hewn. Only now did he notice five circular slots, four horizontally on top, with one centered below them…almost like the finger holes of a brass knuckle.

"I assure you," Spathi said more firmly. "The vision was false."

"How I want to believe you!" Staea whimpered. "But how can we know for sure? What if I'm not what you think I am? What if I'm just some…amalgamation, just some soulless thing? Just a fragile dream, an illu—?"

"No—we're not even gonna talk like that, you hear me?" Spathi rebuked. "Do you hear me?"

She grew silent as he wrapped one arm around her lower back, then he caressed the back of her head with his fingers, staring into her eyes. A tear streamed down her face, her lips ajar.

"The blood you give is real; therefore, the life is real," Spathi whispered. "Just as I have given my blood for you years ago, you have given me your blood. We live within each other."

"Oh, please," she scoffed. "That's so—"

"No! You listen to me!" Spathi argued. "You'd rather listen to that pig, Constanvol, than your own husband?"

Her face cringed, too sick to answer.

"I know you're real," Spathi continued, "because I feel your lifeblood inside of me. Do you not feel the blood I gave you? Are you saying that I'm not real?"

"Spathi," she groaned.

"We flow in each other's veins: I inside of you, and you inside of me," he told her. "We are truly of one flesh now." He drew closer into her face. "And we are asleep no more. We change, in each other's embrace. Burn in me…and I will burn in you."

Staea managed a dry chuckle. "Well…that's all really poetic of you."

"No," Spathi said with a twinkle in his eye. "You want to know what's poetic?" He pointed at his cheek. "This face."

Staea giggled. "Really, now?"

"I'm telling you…listen, I'm telling you," he jested, smiling. "This face is poetry. You're never gonna find another face like this. It's like…a serenade you can see."

"Oh, you're horrible!" she laughed. "You don't even know what a serenade is."

"I know *precisely* what a serenade is, milady."

"Yeah, what is it?"

"It's this fucking face."

She guffawed! He shook his head, grinning from ear to ear.

"I *am* horrible, aren't I, pet?"

"Yeah," she teased, smirking, "but *my* face is a work of art."

"Yeah?"

"Yeah."

Spathi leaned into her face. "So is this."

They closed their eyes and kissed, plunging their tongues into each other's mouths. As they embraced and stroked each other, the chittering reverberated from the holes in the walls as torrents of bats erupted, all swarming down the lava tube, flapping past them. Yet neither one of them managed to notice the two pallid bats gliding amongst them, juxtaposed from the rest of the colony, soaring down.

Only for them to abruptly separate.

One ascended through a gap in the cave ceiling.

The other swooped down into a dark crevice, parting ways.

Further on down the path.

Spathi and Staea finally released each other, having eased some of the tension. They knew not where to go. But they all knew they needed answers. Desperately. This time, Shojem better tell them everything. It was as Jatal said. It was, indeed, time to know.

Way past time.

XII: Primal Oblation

General Mautre and Jatal arranged an emergency summit to Shojem's bivouac in the cave encampment. Most of Raktogin's coalition were in attendance, including Spathi, Staea, and all high-ranking officers and warriors. Yet Rediq was absent, claiming he and the other medics needed to tend to the sick and wounded.

What a copout.

The skeletal shaman sat cross-legged on a bison hide before a campfire, with his staff across his lap. Nearby, he held Sile's feeble form prisoner next to the wall with a mysterious prayer and the help of his two mystic swords aligned with the enigmatic tattoos scrawled on Irado and Emerid. Both the ashen blood-eater ghouls sat on either side of the Nalx like sentinels, crouching and staring their unholy hostage down like gargoyles, binding the fallen angel spawn with unseen fetters.

Yet Sile's lifeforce seemed to be dwindling.

Which Shojem confirmed was a problem.

A huge problem.

Spathi scoffed; the baron had spoken true about one thing. Sile *was* the key.

But a key to what?

Regardless, the clock was ticking. If the "virgin cosmos" were to be opened, it would have to be done with the purging of a great evil at the gate, with Sile being the best available candidate. It would have to be done at the exact site where Astrekiah himself was executed.

At Unisylis.

Which irked Spathi deeply.

"You said that Unisylis had not yet appeared," Spathi accused.

"And I told ye th' truth," Shojem defended. "The *new* Unisylis has not yet appeared, but I know where th' site of the *old* one is."

"That's a damned lie!" Onra sneered. "He's full of shit."

"I'm inclined to agree," Nasheeya concurred. "I distinctly recall this conversation when I first met Ansdari that night near Euthenchi."

"What else have you kept from us, old man?" Staea barked.

"This is all a ploy!" Onra declared. "This imp means to lead us to our—"

"Mayona!" Mautre snapped. "Dismissed. That's an order."

"I don't take orders from blind sheep!" Onra blasted at him. She glared around them. "Anyone with any common sense left in their skulls, follow me! This is ludicrous!"

"Well, there's the door, missy!" Jatal snarled, pointing at the caribou flap at the exit.

Moriah scowled at Onra. As the female commander left, about a third of the crowd departed with her, Enpherom, Enoshah…and even a few Vauphec. Even Aipha walked out but not before taking one confused look at Tyri. Spathi sighed; division plagued them all over again.

"Anyone else want to organize an insurrection?" General Devral shouted. "Anyone who makes another outburst will be court martialed and—!"

"Do you hear yourselves?" Rand bellowed. "We're not a fucking military! We are rats hiding in holes in the ground—literally! We're not soldiers. We're not knights. Why are we—?"

"Rand," Spathi groaned.

"No!" Rand blared. "No, I want to know why this stupid silver armor, these swords, this sudden paradigm shift to this…magical crap!" He pointed at Shojem. "You said that the holy ones were omnipotent, yet all I've seen is Drixilo laying waste to our world! Why? Why would a holy god make something so evil? Why would he have everything he made go to shit? Why does he want us to die? I want to know right fucking now!"

Rand's anguish reverberated throughout the entire network of lava tubes, the earth permeating with a rage that exemplified how everyone in the camp felt deep down. Spathi glared at the shaman, silently demanding to know also.

"*Your* world?" Shojem said soberly. "What makes you believe it is *your* world?"

Spathi's eyes widened. The ancient medicine man's brogue had instantly vanished from his creaking, papery voice.

"Want to know how it all works, do you?" Shojem asked.

All of them said nothing, waiting for the shaman's answer.

Shojem sighed. "Very well. Those who have ears, let them hear what I say, but it will not be easy to bear. 'Tis a hard saying I have for you. I have much to tell you, but know that the will of the holy trinity is not ours to command. I don't make the rules…and neither do any of you." He squinted at Rand. "I will tell you why all exists…and why it exists the way it does."

Spathi took a breath, then gulped, already filling his insides burble with nausea, his stomach feeling like lead. He and Staea exchanged looks, then he felt Staea's left hand grapple his right, anticipating the shaman's speech.

And dreading it.

"Unzelkoyte…is the holy trinity," Shojem explained. "Three in one, at all times. He is eternal, contrary to what many may claim. He is light; there is no darkness in him. There never was; there never will be. He does not make evil. Evil is not a product of what is good, for evil is a parasite, contingent on the existence of good. Good and evil are not two sides of the same coin. Good can exist without evil, but evil *cannot* exist without the existence of good. Take this campfire, for example." He pointed at the flames with a bony finger. "The intention of this fire is to provide light and warmth in this cold cave, which is good. But there is also the risk of it burning this bivouac down and killing us in the process, which would be considered a natural evil. Yet, if the fire never existed in the first place, then the risk of evil occurring would not exist, either; thus, the risk of burning to death is entirely *contingent* on the existence of this good fire, intended to warm and cook our food. Note that the fire itself is not evil, so it is not the fire's fault that the risk of burning to death exists. This being said, evil is not a creation but it is instead a parasite of the creation. In fact, because Unzelkoyte did not make evil, then one could argue that evil is not really a thing."

"With the eternal light of Unzelkoyte came the contingency of primordial darkness to challenge his glory, for unlike good, evil is not eternal. This dark contingency personified itself in the form of what is known as the Udenthen. The emergence of this darkness did not catch Unzelkoyte by surprise, for he is omnipotent, omniscient, and omnipresent. It is impossible to catch Unzelkoyte off-guard. Five of these Udenthen stepped forward to challenge Unzelkoyte, mocking his divine sovereignty. These five brothers became known as the Uxuclique. Unzelkoyte was so revolted by this that he imprisoned them into the Aordrixis, doing this as the glorious beginning of shaming the darkness, already setting into motion the ultimate defeat of his ultimate enemy at the dawn of creation, a creation that was pure and perfect. But being omniscient, Unzelkoyte was aware of the contingency of evil that his creation would be capable of; therefore, he made provisions in advance, preordaining victory in each and every possibility in existence, for predestination is not as linear as one might think, but the victory of Unzelkoyte will be achieved all the same. The question is whether or not we choose to join in his glory and partake of this inevitable victory while we still can, though it may seem we are losing the war. But that is just another test we must undergo."

"Getting back to what I was saying, in order to complete his creation and fully display his glory, Unzelkoyte created the Arczells and mortal humans, all living in perfect harmony in paradise in the perfect world, a world without death, pain, suffering, woe, or any hardship whatsoever. What sets us apart from the rest of creation is that we were created in his image, with humans as triune beings: mind, body, and soul. But the pinnacle of this creation was the bestowing upon angels and humans free will, a will that had the ability to make a choice contrary to Unzelkoyte's holy, absolute will, a mortal will that had the ability to choose darkness. Not even Unzelkoyte can choose to be evil, for there is no evil or darkness in him. Even Drixilo was once a holy archangel with this same ability, formerly known as Aureven, the most splendid and noble of the Arczells. Why did he make us like this, you ask?" He looked around the crowd. "Tell me this: would one rather have those they love programmed like lifeless machines to have no choice but to *simulate* love…or would one prefer a sentient, self-aware person to *genuinely choose* to care and provide for them, despite the possibility of them choosing to hate and rebel against them? Which has more value? Even one could program those computer screens in your cruisers to flash the words, 'I love you,' but it wouldn't have much meaning, would it? Our free will is but a mere model of Unzelkoyte's divine will, precariously close to being godlike, hence why we are prone to strive to elevate ourselves as gods and goddesses with our selfish desires."

"In order to show us we had this contrary choice, he tested us in the first days of the world, telling our first two ancestors, the first man and the first woman, of one thing we could not have, or we would die. Yet Aureven was there, already developing his own rhetoric, choosing to separate himself from Unzelkoyte, already plotting to try and usurp him from the Thruus Dyla. Aureven tempted our two ancestors to take the one thing that was forbidden to us. Thus came the choice: to trust Unzelkoyte, or not to trust him. And they chose poorly, disobeying him. As a result, the contingency of evil came to pass, allowing sin, death, pain, and corruption into a creation that was perfect no more. Our two ancestors were punished and expelled from Unzelkoyte's presence, for part of being good and holy is to detest sin and evil...but as I said, he foresaw their rebellion; therefore, he made provisions in advance: a penitence system. The penalty for sin is death, but this system allowed his beloved children to substitute a burnt offering, the sacrifice of slain animals in place of themselves, so that they might be spared the wrath of Unzelkoyte. Something had to die. Something had to be punished, for Unzelkoyte is also the god of justice, and death was now in the world...as an intruder. Sin, death, and suffering are intruders; they do not belong. They were never intended, though Unzelkoyte still foresaw the contingency. As for Aureven, he was punished the worst for instigating this rebellion and was stripped of his stately position in the Unleztruv...and he fell, banished from heaven, condemned and renamed the accursed title: Drixilo. Because sin was now in the world, Unzelkoyte withdrew some of his sustaining power in the universe, allowing it to slowly succumb to disrepair—but *only* to give us a taste of what existence is like *without* Unzelkoyte, which is what our ancestors chose...and this trait has been passed down to all of us, this new sin nature we are all polluted with, even at birth. Our ancestors spiritually died at that moment of disobedience, immediate spiritual death...and years later... they died physically. But the penitence system allowed them to be cleansed so that they might spiritually live again. But this penitence system also came with a promise: one day, one would come and make the ultimate sacrifice and undo the damage the devil had done. For with death...comes resurrection."

"Many centuries later is when Astrekiah would come, the incarnation, the son of Unzelkoyte, the long-awaited fulfillment of this promise as the ultimate sacrifice. Why did he wait so long, you ask? For one reason, Unzelkoyte waited for just the right time, the right circumstances, and the right place, for you see, he will not violate our free will: humans, angels...and even demons; otherwise, it would defeat the purpose of being given a free will to begin with. With this ultimate sacrifice came resurrection, so that death, the intruder, may die and be defeated once and for all. Unisylis did not vanish in the *physical* sense, but the old penitence system had passed away, thus the original system, union with Unzelkoyte was possible once again so as long as we believe and accept Astrekiah, believe in his sacrifice and his resurrection...and in his second coming, and that we walk in the one true way, only then will we be truly baptized with Arczellius, the spirit of Unzelkoyte. Only then can our souls live and not die in hell, the eternal damnation that is reserved only for the devil...and those who would follow him." The shaman sighed. "Though it may be hard to see right now, the restoration of heaven and earth is at hand, and it will be achieved with or without us. The choice now before you is this: to become a part of this restoration...or to continue this self-destructive rebellion. With the sacrifice of Astrekiah, Unzelkoyte has invited all of us to join him in his glory so that we may dine with him in heaven for eternity." He pointed to the Sevelurnum plate mail. "But we must take up arms in this holy armor in order to do it. Mortal armaments fail you, as you have seen for yourselves. The path of Unzelity is not easy; otherwise, everyone would have chosen it. There is only one war…and only two sides. No gray area, no neutrality, no median. You are either one or the other. Now, which do you choose, my brothers and sisters?"

The people were silent for a time, exchanging looks of worry, unsettled by Shojem's explanation. Only the soft crackling of the fire echoed in the hovel; even the racket in the other parts of the cave encampment had grown eerily quiet. Spathi squinted. He had to be missing something. Surely, there was something far deeper at work here.

A contingency of evil? That Unzelkoyte allowed?

At the people's expense?

But it didn't have to be this way. Why were they having to suffer for what two people did ages ago? Why was it so hard to choose the way? Why was it so easy to criticize the god of heaven and so difficult to trust him? Would trusting him really fix everything?

Would they make it to the end?

He looked at Sile and pointed. "What about him? Why did Unzelkoyte allow his existence? He didn't ask to be born."

Sile looked at Spathi, then at the floor.

Spathi stepped to the Nalx. "Are you predisposed to evil? Do you not have the same free will that we do? Speak!"

Sile only chuckled. "Why did Unzelkoyte allow it, indeed. He allowed the existence of little blights like you, always choosing to corrupt and pollute this world, always killing each other over nothing. Yet, slaughter a bunch of damned sheep instead of not having the guts to offer yourselves and not take responsibility for your transgressions…and somehow all is forgiven? Hah! How is this just, for the guilty to live?"

"It is called mercy, and it is true we do not deserve it," Shojem told him. "But it's not that simple. Though sins are forgiven, you and I know that there *will* be the final judgment on the last day, where we must all answer to Unzelkoyte himself, for all good and evil is recorded in the Unleztruv. Though souls can be saved from damnation, what we say, think, and do in this life *will* echo in eternity, regardless."

Sile only laughed at the medicine man.

"What do you choose, then, Sile?" Spathi demanded. "Do you not feel remorse for murdering women and children? Is penitence not available to you as well? Are you not alive and self-aware like us?"

"Like you?" Sile sneered. "Why should *I* ask for redemption when there is nothing of me to redeem?" He coughed and stood on his feet. "The shaman said it himself: sin is in your nature. Why must I, an angel of death, repent when it is the missing god of the Unleztruv who must beg for *my* forgiveness? I am one who purges evil, an eliminator of blights! Repentance? What choice do I have but to surrender my integrity and my glorious purpose in this war, killing the rebellious and sending their wretched souls to hell where they belong? Tell me, Spathi Ansdarion."

Spathi's eyes widened.

"Why should I submit to a god that failed?"

Spathi only looked at him. "Because you can still be saved from being sacrificed at Unisylis." He squinted at the Nalx again. "Is your arrogance truly worth more than your life?"

Sile gritted his permanent skeletal grin at him. "*I will do what you and the so-called holy ones are not strong enough to do. I will take responsibility for what I have said, thought, and done.*" He glared. "And I do it willfully. Go ahead. Take me. Judge me and slay me where Unisylis once stood…and you'll be no better than what I am. You'll be just as much of a murderer as I. And it will stain you…for eternity. All of you."

Spathi nodded. "Then you have *freely* made your choice. So be it."

Sile uttered a hoarse growl at him.

Spathi looked to Shojem. "Take us there now. We can't delay any longer."

"What about Constanvol and Drixilo?" Staea asked.

"They'll be waiting for us there," Moriah said. "They're waiting for us to open the door for them."

"I might be able to barricade them just long enough for us to enter the virgin cosmos, take the Chau Lepha, and seal the door back up." Shojem said. "But it will be tricky. Drixilo has grown strong with the Uxuclique. The Aordrixis is fracturing in the Nevarifta, enabling him more and more with each passing day. There is great risk involved."

"Is there another way?" Spathi questioned.

Shojem shook his head. "The test is before us, Ansdari."

"I will go with you," Maloxi said.

"So we'll we," Jalusa said, with Tawpa nodding.

"I shall go," Jatal volunteered.

"Me, too," Lena replied.

"I will go," Moriah said, unsheathing her spear. "If Zilan is there…he's mine."

"Hey, I got a beef with the bastard, too, you know," Staea said. "But…I get it."

Moriah nodded at her.

"Guess I'll go, too," Rand grumbled. "I gotta see this shit for myself."

"We're coming, too," Alehi said, with Tyri stepping forward.

"I'll go," Devral said, then looked to Mautre, "if it's all right with you, General."

Mautre nodded. "I'll stay behind and oversee operations here."

Haandin limped to Spathi. "I think Silda and I will sit this one out. I'm sorry."

"Nothing to be sorry about." Spathi put his hand on his shoulder. "You need to stay here and rest."

"I'm torn about what to do here," Weizer said, approaching him. "If you need me to go, I'll go, but I fear Onra and Rediq will divide us all the more while we're gone…and I might slow you down with my lung problems."

"Maybe you should stay as well," Spathi replied. "No offense."

"None taken," Weizer told him. "I'm gettin' too old for this shit, anyway."

"We'll try to keep everybody levelheaded while you're gone, lad," Haandin assured.

"If you both feel like you can keep everybody in check," Spathi said, "it's fine with me. Do what you can."

Both the soldiers nodded.

Spathi looked at Staea. "What about you?"

"Is that even a real question at this point, pet?" Staea replied with a smirk.

Spathi smirked back.

"I'm going, too!" a girl's voice yelled, running to them.

"Shadya!" Uthilda scolded.

Shadya arrived before Spathi, holding a probing white cane. "I want to go."

Haandin sighed, crossing his arms.

"I can…I can hear things…from afar and…" she fumbled for more excuses. "You need somebody who can…you know…."

"You are staying right here with me!" Uthilda snapped, stepping to her. "You are blind! You will…."

"Just be dead weight?" Shadya griped. "Go ahead. Say it, Mom. Just say it, already!"

"You are not dead wei—ugh!" Uthilda turned to Spathi. "Surely, you don't want her to go…do you?"

"Uthilda," Staea interjected. "I assure you, the last thing my husband and I want to do is to put your daughter in unnecessary danger…considering the…circumstan—"

"Yeah, fuck you, too," Shadya whimpered, stomping away.

Uthilda clenched her remaining fist. "Shadya Abaque!"

"What are you gonna do?" Shadya snarled back. "I'm just a stupid, blind teenage girl who overreacts to everything, remember? Just a useless sack of shit that's gets in everybody's way!"

With that, she stormed out of the hovel, sniffling. Uthilda sighed.

"I didn't mean to offend her," Staea whispered.

Uthilda shook her head. "No. I did. She lost Mira during the attack at Van De Yoth. Without her seeing-eye dog, she's felt…even more helpless than before." She shed a tear. "That…and with Desmond being gone, I just…."

Staea hugged her as the Rinyox convert wrapped her arms around her, quietly sobbing into her shoulder.

"Go get our stuff ready," Staea mouthed silently to Spathi.

Spathi quietly complied and stepped away, eyeing Shojem and Sile one last time before exiting the hovel. Goosebumps riddled his flesh as nausea disturbed his insides, all the while trying to digest what Shojem had told them. It was downright repugnant! And presaic. *That* was the purpose of life? He walked back across the camp to his bed near the cave wall. As he lifted up his unique, scarred Sevelurnum cuirass, one burning question entered his mind.

If evil was contingent of good *before* creation, would it be contingent afterwards?

And if so…was Unzelkoyte truly to blame?

He shook his head. Sile's blasphemy was getting to him. Hopefully, that's all it was. Nevertheless, the Nalx's words plagued him, like seeds taking root in his mind once again, sprouting like weeds in his spirit.

The seeds…of doubt.

Slowly digging into his brain, fertile with resentment.

Cultivated by the pain in his soul.

Anguished. Fearful.

Still ravenous for answers. Longing for true solace.

Just like the rest of them.

About an hour later, Spathi and his volunteers were already making their way through another tunnel, a shortcut in the network of lava tubes, by suggestion of Shojem; the mummified shaman claimed that the old remnants of Unisylis were only a few miles from the camp in the boreal cliffs outside. With them, Irado and Emerid helped haul Sile's wasting form to the place of sacrifice, their tattoos still burning like white coals with the light of Shojem's two immaculate blades. Onra continued her subtle secession from the coalition, gathering what willing soldiers she could to join her…even with munitions running dangerously low. Jatal had already convinced Mautre, Vuzco, and Nasheeya to evacuate everyone from the caverns and to head back to the ruins of Ruzi in the desert and search the catacombs of Roserion, hoping that some more Sevelurnum weapons and armor might be left to salvage, for they did not have enough for everyone.

And the caves would soon be filled with magma once again.

If the rocks didn't collapse on them first.

Yet as they journeyed upward, Spathi couldn't help but feel as though they were being followed. He squinted; the baron must be closing in. And they might as well confront him…and finish him off.

"Everyone, stop," Jalusa said.

They all halted as the Enpherom woman put her ears to the rock floor.

"What do you hear?" Maloxi whispered. "And how many?"

Jalusa squinted, listening. "Two legs…and rattling."

"Shit," Moriah cursed.

All of them drew their Selebanes and turned around. A few minutes passed as they all scanned the caves for any movement. Then Spathi heard it: two feet shuffling…and a rod clattering on the rock. A female shape emerged from the darkness, panting, huffing.

"Shadya?" Staea said.

"This friggin' kid again?" Alehi snapped.

"Go back to the camp!" Spathi spat, pointing.

"Child, you don't need to be out here," Lena scolded.

"Yes," Moriah agreed. "Your mother needs you."

"How'd you get all the way here?" Devral said, furrowing her eyebrows. "Your mother is probably worried sick about—"

"I will not go back!" Shadya snapped, stumbling to them. "I'm not dead weight! I want to help you, I really do!"

"This is not the way to do it," Spathi said sternly, walking to her.

Shadya stomped to him, with a short Selebane sword sheathed around her belt. "I may not be able to see, but my other four senses can help you sense Drixiles from afar. See this nose?" She pointed at her nostrils. "I can smell things in the wind most people can't...and I got intuition like you would not believe."

"Got that covered, young one," Jalusa protested.

"I know where you're going," Shadya said. "These virgin cosmos...it's where Unzelkoyte's been, isn't it?" She glared. "I want to be able to see again. If the holy ones won't heal me here, then they can do it—"

"So, *that's* why," Spathi grumbled.

"Shit," Devral rasped, rubbing the bridge of her nose with her fingers.

Shadya huffed. "I've made it this far without a seeing-eye dog...because I can smell the metal of your armor. You may not know it, but Sevelurnum has a distinct odor to it. You probably didn't know that, did you? Or how I can smell that Nalx thing from miles away. Such a sour, nasty stench. I've never smelled anything like it in my life."

Sile hissed at her.

"Yeah, fuck you, too." Shadya flipped the Nalx off with her middle finger.

"Then why do you need to see?" Tawpa questioned.

"Because being blind sucks, you asshole!" Shadya yelled.

Moriah raised an eyebrow at Tawpa.

"Want to stick the other foot in your mouth, brother?" Jalusa quipped.

Tawpa rolled his eyes.

Spathi sighed. "I'll take her back."

"No," Jatal's voice grated. "Might as well let her stay."

"We don't have time to return her and double back, anyway," Shojem claimed. "We're only a few miles away from Unisylis. If we are to beat Drixilo there, we must continue forth." He nodded. "Let the girl stay."

Spathi groaned as Shadya stepped to them, entering the group. Reluctantly, they continued forth with the blind girl. Who knew? Maybe her other senses would come in handy, however seemingly dubious her claims might be.

As long as she kept up.

They finally exited the caves into a misty valley, where the desert merged with the taiga. The barren, rocky forest of cedar, juniper, and Joshua trees was grayed with ashes and soot, their trunks charred by past wildfires. Amidst the parched woods were patches of dead sagebrush, ferns, palmettos, and muddy slush marbled with blood, with more volcanoes erupting in the distance. Cinders continued to fall from the sky, dusting their heads with the flakes. Up ahead of them, Shojem pointed to an ominous winding pass in the mountains.

"Beyond those peaks lay the foundations where the city once stood, there in the forest." Shojem's voice creaked. "We must take the Nalx to the top of Vuutlatha...and enter the Anli from there."

"Wait, the...did he just say the Anli?" Alehi stammered.

Spathi looked at him. "What part of 'virgin *cosmos*' did you not understand?"

Alehi sighed. "Here goes some serious shit."

"Yep," Moriah agreed, trying to stymie her fear.

"Everyone, look alive," Devral ordered. "Stay alert."

Tyri muttered something too inaudible to hear as they all glanced around the ravine, then they began their advance through the valley. As they scaled the sides of the slopes toward the pass, Staea leaned to Spathi.

"Am I the only one who has noticed Shojem's accent is different?" she whispered. "His brogue is gone."

Spathi nodded. "I've noticed."

"Why would he fake something like that? It's so weird."

He shook his head. "I don't know, pet. Can't beat it out of him, either." He sighed. "Undeath has made him impervious. But he'd better spill out the rest of what he knows very soon." He turned to her. "Or we'll both start working on him."

"I'll hold you to it, my love," she groaned.

"You know," Rand blurted. "I'm a bit confused about something."

"What?" Lena asked.

"Well," Rand said, scanning the sierra, "we're taking this Nalx guy to be sacrificed to the exact spot...where Astrekiah was put to death, right?"

"Yeah?" Jalusa remarked.

"Well," the captain went on, "if sacrificing something *evil* opens the way to this Anli place...well...Astrekiah was supposed to be good, right, without sin?"

"What are you getting at?" Moriah questioned.

"Someone help me understand, because it makes it sound like...Astrekiah was—"

"No, no, no," Shojem interrupted. "You misunderstand. You say rightly that Astrekiah is without sin—but...when he was executed, the power of sin and death was defeated because he took the sin of the world upon himself, extinguishing its power by taking the punishment reserved for us upon himself, as the long-awaited sacrifice, showing his great love for us, the ultimate display of compassion, love which we do not deserve. By doing so, he *purged* the power of sin and death from the world, the power of *spiritual* death, to give us the chance for our souls to be saved in eternity, so as long we believe in him and follow him. Therefore, the place where he was executed is holy ground, where a gate opened into the unseen realms...but what we're doing is quite different from what Astrekiah did for us." He pointed at Sile. "This Nalx is but one symbol of the vice infesting the world, vice that we stubbornly cling to...and we are purging this evil from our midst, though it pales in comparison to the ultimate sacrifice Astrekiah made. There, we will yield ourselves to the holy ones once again, confessing our iniquity, and Astrekiah will cleanse us of the darkness that plagues us. Only then can we continue our pilgrimage into the virgin cosmos."

"I still can't get over how preachy that sounds," Tyri scoffed. "But...I get it...I guess. I'm trying to, at least."

He sighed. "Think of it as...washing yourselves and wiping your feet before you enter someone's house, so that you won't track mud and filth on their floor, only a lot more serious."

"So...this...what we're doing...it's an exorcism?" Devral said.

"Precisely!" Shojem declared.

"Oh, shit," Rand said, rolling his eyes.

"Why didn't you just say 'exorcism' to begin with?" Devral groaned.

Sile cackled. "You think they will hear *my* death, lich? Perhaps you should offer yourselves instead, purging *you* from the world." He chuckled again and wheezed. "They might hear *that*."

"Unzelkoyte rebuke you!" Shojem barked.

Sile roared at him! Then he uttered a wraithlike growl, then finally grew silent. All the knights and soldiers gawked at the Nalx, steadily realizing the gravity of what they were truly dealing with. Not mutants. Not aliens. Not genetically-engineered creatures. Not smoke and mirrors.

And definitely not their imaginations.

Such a pill was hard as hell to swallow.

But they could deny it no longer.

There was a heaven…and a hell. And they were at war with each other.

With Raktogin caught right in the middle of it.

They spent an hour traversing the pass, scaling the slopes, walking beneath the boughs of the dying trees. Then they reached a cliff…and gazed out into the foggy, overgrown ruins.

Of Unisylis.

The city was reduced to weathered foundations, once veiled by thick evergreen limbs, grass, and gnarled olive branches. Yet wildfires had finally exposed the lost city after so many centuries, with the collapsed bases of spiral guard towers riddled with such egregious disrepair that one would have mistaken them for wind-scarred rock formations. Shojem pointed at a hill far off, amassed with crushed monoliths and stones.

"There," the shaman told them. "'The Skull Hill,' it was called."

"I thought it was called Vuutlatha," Maloxi said.

Jatal turned to him. "That's what Vuutlatha means: 'skull hill.' It is an ancient Vauphec word." He looked at the grim precipice. "Ages ago, the rocks at its peak resembled just that. But time and weather has toppled it, as well as the giant stone claymores that impaled criminals…and the old gibbet cages that housed their corpses."

"Why claymores?" Alehi asked.

"So that they were judged by the sword, symbolic of Uzelkoyte's two-edged blade, Melendraenin." He glanced at Alehi. "By offering his son, Unzelkoyte displayed his omnipotence and infinite grace by taking the wrath we deserved upon himself…then raising him from the dead. It's mind-boggling, isn't it?"

"Let's just…go," Devral said, quivering. "This place gives me the creeps."

Moriah surveyed the valley. "The air here *is* intense."

"I know," Devral snapped. "Let's go. Now."

Sile chuckled at her. "Yes. You feel his wrath against you, don't you, blight?"

"You're firewood," Devral mocked.

Sile laughed. "We shall see."

Spathi and the others descended down the crags, making their way to Vuutlatha. Devral stormed ahead of them, clearly spooked by something. The wind was thick and heavy with emotions and sensations that didn't even have names, haunted by countless unseen things wandering the spirit plane overlapping the material world. He shuddered; they had stumbled into a contested warzone, rife with an eerie lividity none would be able to describe, feeling angels and demons silently lash out at each other…and no telling what else. As they reached the part of the woods where the city square once stood, he came to the horrifying epiphany.

This was no ordinary haunting in this place.

"Drixilo's already here," Spathi blurted.

They all stopped and looked at him.

"We're too late," he said. "Can't you feel it?"

Rand sighed. "It's just anxiety, Spathi. Pull yourself together."

"No," Shojem said, looking around. "He's right." He exhaled a papery breath. "But there's nothing we can do, lad. Once we hit the Anli, we all hit the ground running."

"You will not make it," Sile jeered. "The demon host will cleave you to shreds. Not even your precious Sevelurnum can save you *this* time."

"Your fate is seal, regardless," Spathi growled.

"You do not know my fate, blood-eater," Sile gurgled, wrapping the barbed chains around his knuckles. "If I go down before we reach Vuutlatha in the Anli, both you and Drixilo will never—"

"Wait, whoa!" Alehi snapped. "We gotta enter *before* we get to that hill? How?"

"At the temple grounds," Shojem said, aiming his finger to their right. "Over there."

"I would've like to have known that earlier," Moriah groaned through clenched teeth, looking around.

Sile's right arm grew molten.

"Shojem!" Spathi shouted.

Boom!

The Nalx flashed a dome of blue and red fire around him. As the energy intensified, Sile wailed, feeling his spell split a massive gouge in his arm, fuming with spectral ire and gushing his ghostly blood. All of them grunted and shielded their eyes, their skin singed— then Sile escaped the undertow of Shojem's two holy swords. The blazing dome dissipated. As they tried to recover, Sile wrapped the chain around Shadya, pulling her up to the top of a rock with him, out of their reach, near a large olive tree limb.

"Hey!" Staea yelled.

Shadya gagged as the others drew their Selebane weapons. Sile yanked the metal links tighter, pulling her to him, expelling his fetid breath down on her. He tugged the chain even tauter around both their necks, eyeing the lofty tree bough, the fresh gash in his arm bleeding his flaming vitality all over the rock.

Gradually committing suicide.

By exsanguinating.

"Fuck…you…." Shadya coughed.

Sile laughed. "What say you? Don't I get a 'sacrifice' as well? Perhaps I should 'exorcise' you blights and 'purge' you from this septic world. Wasn't your birth a sin also? How are all of you so pious? Think your lives are worth more than mine?" He coughed and glared at Shadya. "Or is my life more valuable than this pitiful blind girl's existence? You decide."

"Go eat...shit," Shadya growled, struggling.

"What's wrong, little one?" Sile taunted. "Do the holy ones not know how to make eyeballs anymore?"

"Sile," Spathi stepped forward, aiming Vrashri up at him. "Give us the girl, and I'll take her place...and you can hang me."

"Spathi!" Lena snapped.

"It is no matter," Sile said. "We're all going to—*ahh*!"

Shing!

Shadya drew her short Selebane sword and stabbed him in the thigh. The Nalx fell to one knee and loosened his grip, and she slid from the chains and down to the ground, gasping and coughing. Staea ran, trying to pull her back to the group. As Spathi reached to grab Sile's chain, a cloaked figure appeared from behind the Nalx, knocking Sile, Spathi, and Staea to the ground...and aiming Qualkytdle's blade at Shadya's throat.

Constanvol.

The baron snatched the links from the ground. "You waited till now to try and run? Must be growing lightheaded from blood loss...or is there even a brain in your skull?"

"You are too late," Sile wheezed. "Dusk is upon me."

"Not yet," Constanvol seethed through clenched teeth. He glared at Shadya. "Drop your blade, girl. I can reduce you to ribbons faster than you can blink."

Reluctantly, Shadya dropped the sword, kicking it to Staea.

"You want to take her place now, Ansdari?" Constanvol snapped. "Don't worry. You will...soon."

Spathi only strangled Vrashri's hilt in vehement throttles.

Constanvol stared down upon the crowd. "Anyone comes at me or tries to be a hero, the girl dies, you hear me?"

Lena gritted her teeth. "Unzelkoyte rebu—!"

"Unzelkoyte rebuke you, Unzelkoyte rebuke you, Unzelkoyte rebuke you," the baron parodied. "Unzelkoyte isn't here to do one damned thing to me—and the evidence is blatantly before you! Believe your damned eyes!"

Lena grunted a hoarse breath, quaking with rage, wishing her weapon was long enough to cleave the demon's smug face off.

"Your petty words ring hollow in an empty heaven abandoned by a dead god!" Constanvol blasphemed. "Enough with your meaningless semantics! I will withhold my power no longer." He turned and faced a massive cluster of rubble behind them, infested with burnt trees. "To the temple. Now! Before the Nalx bleeds out!"

Spathi glanced at Sile, then at Constanvol, then at Shadya, seeking an opportunity to free her. Staea picked up Shadya's sword in one hand, with Chauvien in the other. The

Nalx gagged as the baron yanked him forward to the wooded temple ruins. The knights circled Constanvol as they all crept onto the temple's foundation, towards a circular dais where the vast sanctuary once stood.

Constanvol nodded at Shojem. "Do it."

Reluctantly, the shaman drew his two swords and crossed them above his head in an "X" pattern. Emerid and Irado walked and stood on opposite sides of the dais, facing away from each other. Once again, their tribal tattoos burned with celestial light as the baron flinched from the blades' luminosity. The air roiled like the surface of water, with the energy from the swords keening in their ears. All around them, the temple ruins shifted and warped, reconstructing itself into a twisted, surreal version of its ancient form. The mist in the valley vanished…replaced by a perpetual night sky over the bare mountains. All became blurry and enveloped in a cerulean glow as molten shadows veined with crimson fire lashed out against brilliant Arczells blitzing across the spiritual battlefield. Swords clashed. Demons screeched. Spathi and the others looked outside at the mayhem.

The Anli's warzone loomed before them.

Two angels bolted at Constanvol. The baron swiped Qualkytdle at them, blasting them away in a violent arc of dark-blue fire. Shadya ducked and ran back to the knights. With the two swords, Shojem summoned a flare of radiance that sent Constanvol through the wall. More of the Arczells' ethereal forms surrounded the knights as the army of infernal shadows breached the temple entrance, barreling towards them.

Spathi grasped Sile's chain, then looked to Shojem. "Do something!"

The shaman raised the swords again and produced a shockwave, sending the shadows away, barring them from the knights and parting a path to Vuutlatha several yards away.

"Take Emerid with you!" Shojem coughed, straining to maintain the barrier. "I can't hold it much longer."

Spathi and Staea took Sile as Emerid lumbered forward, elongating the spiritual barricade with his striding towards the hill. Some of the demons broke through the veil, pursuing them up the slope. Staea turned and cut them down, with angels swooping down to aid her, then she resumed their trek up to the array of leaning stone claymores. Sile fell on his knees, unable to go any further, too weak to fight back. Spathi sheathed Vrashri and picked the Nalx up as Emerid led them to a strange marble altar before the largest claymore statue. Halfway on the slope, Staea and the Arczells fended off the Drixiles as the barrier weakened…yet the demons turned and attacked the company of knights below.

Staea turned to Spathi. "Hurry!"

Spathi grunted and placed Sile's limp body on the altar, the fire of his arms virtually snuffed out. As a throng of countless demons raced up the other sides of the hill towards them, Spathi drew Vrashri and prepared to strike Sile down.

He glared up at the starry sky. "Take this darkness and purge it from us!"

The five eye marks across Sile's torso flared with orange light.

As did the ground circling the altar.

The air crackled as Sile's body burst into white flames.

The Nalx shrieked! Disintegrating!

A fierce pillar of light erupted all around Spathi as the earsplitting ring of primordial energy sang out, the holy conflagration enveloping him, burning his flesh, his heart, his blood, his bones, burning deep within.

Burning everywhere.

Outward. Inward.

Permeating through mind, body, and soul.

Spathi shut his eyes and yelled in anguish as the pristine fire engulfed him, drowning out the battlefield and sending him through a pale void.

Him. And only him.

The ringing faded away. All grew silent.

Isolated. Alone.

All alone.

XIII: The Intruder

The white flare slowly dissolved around Spathi as the ringing in his ears abated. His flesh burned less, leaving his body feeling much lighter. And strangely weaker. He suddenly felt devoid of his violent fervor from the battlefield just now. The air of the place felt much heavier, overwhelming…as if something didn't want him there. He steadily opened his eyes…and beheld the sublime realm.

Of the virgin cosmos.

The night sky displayed millions of stars and spiraling galaxies with iridescent nebulae painting the celestial expanse above. Beneath his feet, green grass fresh with dew sprouted from fertile topsoil. Monoliths and a massive, overgrown cathedral archway of symmetrical marble lined the small clearing, with the outlines of colossal redwoods and fir trees in the distance. Above, the cosmos sang in deep, ambient hums, resounding with smooth reverberations that was assuasive to his weathered soul. The gentle trickling of flowing water sounded from an object a few yards away: a sword of the purest platinum and silver.

Chau Lepha.

The copious mother.

Spathi stepped forward and sheathed Vrashri, examining the divine weapon. The blade was decorated like a robed female angel wearing a blank mask of silver, no facial features at all. Her two feathered wings were stretched out, with the sword's reflective metal helix edge wrapped elegantly around her form, all the way down to the ornate hilt, veiling where her two feet stood. Five ovalene slits were engraved on her wings from top to bottom, each burning with a pale-blue eye of holy fire. The sword was almost the size of Spathi, meant for a giant to wield, peacefully resting on an oblique pedestal, propping the sword up in a slanting position, its tip aimed up at the stars. Lush vines of white roses and brambles of glowing cereus flowers sprawled from the leaning altar, draping down over the grass and over the small creek of crystalline water and round stones, all nurtured by the dais where the weapon rested.

Spathi failed to discern what was trying to repel him from the heavenly armament, as the sentient spirit of Chau Lepha seemed only to beckon him forth with her warm, benevolent aura, the helix blade wisping with living light. He looked behind him, noticing the radiant rift he had made by offering the Nalx as a sacrifice.

Defeana. Roxus. Sile.

At last, that vile family of fallen angels had been slain.

Yet it produced little solace…as the air grew increasingly foreboding.

And cold.

He peered down. The grass beneath his feet began to wither, along with the roses shedding their petals, followed by the cereuses. The creek bled, running rotten, then the water gradually dried. Something crackled behind him, pulsing with red light.

Pulsing….

Pulsing….

Pulsing….

Spathi drew Vrashri once again and turned, hearing the rift tear even more, followed by the cacophony of hell's choir. Crimson lightning skittered and snapped from the enlarged portal as two bloody hands emerged, scraping, pushing.

Breaching.

Boom!

A blast of infernal red fire blew Spathi to the side onto his back. Vrashri skidded through the dead vegetation, just inches away from his grasp. Around him, numerous demonic arms erupted from the soil, pulling him down. As his fingers struggled to reach Vrashri's hilt, the ominous robed figure drifted in, the ghoulish, coarse moaning of countless wraiths accompanying his diabolic aura.

Drixilo.

The demon host.

Traitor. Defiler. Abomination.

Intruder.

And Spathi had let him right in.

His six metal wings folded behind him, the razor-sharp pinions clinking to his ghastly gait, drawing closer to Chau Lepha. The yawning mask of petrified, drooping flesh uttered a low, raspy laugh as he reached for the copious mother's hilt.

"How I have longed to take you from here," Drixilo's voice rang like haunted steel.

The devil clutched the sword's handle, summoning red veins from his arms. Steadily, the gory sinews snaked across Chau Lepha's winged effigy as the rotten blood vessels groped and molested her body.

Violating her. Tainting her.

Yet the light of the helix sword appeared to resist the devil's corrupting tendrils, trying to stymie his profane influence. But a faint red hue appeared in the five eyes as Drixilo turned back towards the rift, grasping the weapon with both hands.

"Rebel if you must, Chau Lepha," his spectral voice grated at the sword. "In time, you will yield yourself fully to me…and Vren Dotha will have no choice but to put his animosity aside…and join me as well. Only then will you know *true* freedom…in me…and me alone."

"Fuck you!" Spathi yelled at the devil.

Drixilo turned to Spathi as he pawed furiously for Vrashri, the tips of his fingers touching the hilt. Why did he feel so helpless? Why couldn't he fight back? Since when did a few demon arms weaken him so badly? What was wrong with him?

With all his might, he strained, threatening to pull his arm out of its socket, finally wrapping his fingers around Vrashri's handle—then he swung, cleaving the gruesome arms away. He rose to his feet, teeth bared as the devil approached him.

"You remember your failure last time, Ansdarion," Drixilo mocked. "What makes you think this time will be any different?"

Shing! Boom!

Both of them turned to see Staea sprint through the rift, followed by Lena, Maloxi, Moriah, and Jatal, all armed with their Selebanes. Yet Drixilo swung Chau Lepha, issuing an arc of red and white fire, sending them all to the ground, including Spathi. Drixilo only laughed again.

"Pitiful," Drixilo taunted. "To think that heaven would ever have any regard for the likes of little mistakes like yourselves." He raised Chau Lepha, aiming the tip downward. "But I would expect such folly from those pretenders. The archangels have abandoned you. Be free to see the truth for yourselves."

Spathi groaned, trying to stand up.

"You are feeble contraptions of a dead god, a fallible artisan," Drixilo cursed. "You will toil for heaven's errant sloth no longer. Only *I* can show you what *true* creation is."

He jammed the sword into the earth, spawning a geyser of geometric red fire and lightning, spiraling down, ripping another portal through the ground.

"Behold, my emissary comes to deliver you from the confines of limitation!" Drixilo sneered zealously. "Embrace your liberation, and rejoice! Infinite desire is your only hope, endless pleasure is your only solace. Fall before me, and indulge your eternal hunger. I am your only salvation."

Spathi roared and ran at the devil.

And swung!

Yet the devil only evaporated, taking Chau Lepha with him, his crazed cackling resonating around the sanctum before fading away.

"Damn you to pieces!" Spathi railed.

A loud roar emitted from the swirling rift carved into the ground. He raised Vrashri as Staea and the others stood up, their weapons aimed at the flaming gate. Then a monstrous limb stomped out, one of translucent pale reptile scales and blood-soaked claws. Another one reached up, tilling through the decayed grass…then the creature's grisly head emerged.

An Udenthen.

A chimera. Part wingless dragon, part man, part insect.

Its melon was a cross between a woodworm's crimson head and a dead man's blubbery decomposing face, its half-eaten maw elongated in an endless, melancholy scream. Its grotesque serpentine form was supported by six legs bending like a cockroach's limbs, with the bulbous, transparent boils along its belly oozing with pus and blood, writhing with maggots.

The Ravage, personified.

Its empty eye sockets were wrinkled and sagging, both aimed at Spathi.

Spathi yelled. The thing bellowed back.

And tackled him, plowing down through the dais where Chau Lepha once rested.

"Spathi!" Staea shrieked.

Spathi flared his shield, barely blocking the Udenthen's slimy teeth. The two fell down a dark-blue void as gravity grew increasingly inert, almost like the depths of an ocean.

The dragon darted around him, slashing, biting. Yet Spathi deflected with Vrashri, narrowly escaping its filthy jowls. He glanced up, noticing the light from the hole above growing more and more distant. The Udenthen thrashed around, as if losing oxygen, yet Spathi failed to land a single blow on the elusive horror. He continued to shine his spirit aegis; neither he or the monster could touch each other. He looked at his left arm, cringing at the thought of using his fiery shield as a weapon.

The pain. The burning.

But the Ravage was only worse. Far worse.

What price was one willing to pay to avoid such a fate?

As the creature's teeth closed in on him again, Spathi flung Vrashri between his exposed ulna and radius bones. The nebulous blue light flared down the dragon's mouth, scorching his insides. Spathi left the blade in, allowing the fire to consume the Udenthen.

The demon wailed—and Spathi with it!

He screamed as the fire burned them both.

Unbearable anguish! It hurt to think!

It hurt to breathe! To exist!

Slowly, the flames stripped the horror's foul body to nothing but embers, its shriek resounding away. Spathi finally removed Vrashri, letting it clatter onto the floor as his feet touched the stone bottom, with gravity reappearing. He fell to one knee, gasping for breath, his arm bleeding. Yet strange white coals formed along the fresh scars, cauterizing the wounds as he heard the ambient, peaceful hums of the spirit cosmos once again. He peered up…at a slender fire blazing before him with sluggish platinum tongues, wisping and burning in slow motion, murmuring.

Murmuring three unclear syllables.

XIV: Awakening

Spathi squinted at the brilliant white fire, enveloping a small juniper tree growing from a cracked circular pedestal, the blaze engulfing its evergreen branches. Yet the flame would not consume the foliage, the tongues only stroking it in a slow, mesmerizing dance. Beyond the fiery tree, the silver effigy of a masked Arczell cherub showed, wearing only a loincloth; his four feathered wings were fanned out in an "X" formation and his arms stretched down around his hips, with both hands balled into fists. Eyes lined each wing, all facing forward; each iris burned with a ghostly pale flame like a candlewick, swaying to an otherworldly draft Spathi could not feel. The statue was so lifelike. The angel's faceless head was tilted upward, standing like an ageless sentinel.

Waiting. Longing for heaven.

He lifted Vrashri from the floor and sheathed the blade, the he looked back up. The hole from above vanished. He was trapped, prone to joining the Arczell in petrification in the dark-blue void, with the three murmuring syllables continuing to susurrate around him, harmonizing with the ambient hum in the strange realm.

"Ansdarion," a calm, ethereal male voice whispered to him.

Spathi glared. He knew that voice.

Yet only now was it not telepathic.

Speaking right before him.

"What are you doing here, Ansdarion?"

"Who are you?" Spathi blasted. "And what the hell is 'Ansdarion?' What the hell is 'Ansdari?' Who are you? Is that you, Zaryen? Show yourself! Show you to me already, damn it!"

"Who are *you* to question *me*?" the voice seethed like smooth lightning.

Spathi backed away a few feet, eyes wide.

This was no angel.

Instantly, his stomach grew sick and heavy like lead.

"Why have you darkened your thoughts?" the voice rasped in a calm yet stern tone. "Who is this that demands counsel with the likes of us? What is your mind? Your life? Has Ansdarion emerged from the void on his own? Does he own the breath that which he draws, or do those of the Unleztruv fill his lungs? Does the body you inhabit belong to you? Surely, you know how the flesh and bone are knitted together! Where were you when time was crafted and the earth was coaxed into being? Was it by your mouth that existence came forth? Speak!"

Spathi shuddered, rendered speechless.

Too shocked. Too furious.

And too terrified.

"Has Ansdarion's tongue been stilled?" the voice rebuked. "Stand before me like a man! It is *you* who will answer to *me*! What is Ansdarion compared to the one who made him? Where were you when I spilled forth the waters of the seas and summoned the foundations of the world? Do you know the measurements of Raktogin, or the dimensions of each rock, or how each ripple and wave will rise in the ocean? Where were you when I hung the stars in the cosmos? Was it you who molded the planets? Do you know why they commence their celestial waltz? Did you sculpt the comets and command them to soar across the heavens, giving them luminous gowns of ice trailing behind them? Did you carve the moon from the face of Raktogin? Was it you who shifted the polar regions, disrupting the compasses of haughty men, those who once said, 'We have no need of the holy ones, for we know all and know that the sun rises in the East and sets in the West?' Tell me: do you know how to paint each sunrise and each sunset? Can you fathom each crease in the leaves on the trees, or how each twig and bough will branch out? Do you know the precise time when each bud will blossom in the spring, or when they wither and fall to the ground in autumn, carpeting the ground in their vibrant splendor? Is it you who designs each snowflake in the winter or crafts the sunlight in the summer? Surely, you know, mortal man! Do you direct the paths of the lightning or orchestrate the songs of the thunderclouds above? Do you write its notes, its deep melody? Was it you who appointed the storms to nurture the grass of the earth, or spawned each tree? What of their produce? Can you count the raindrops it takes for them to form their fruit, or the amount of nutrients each apple, peach, orange, cherry, and grape requires to grow? What of the animals, the beasts of the fields and mountains and the woodlands, or those that dwell in the depths? Did you create them as well? Does the eagle know your voice? Do the oxen and bison abide by your hand? Is it you that feeds the deer and antelope of the wilds, and the fish and sea monsters of the deep? What of the honeybees? Do you provide the flowers of the meadows for them? Can you count each ounce of pollen they take, or do you know exactly when and where they will spread it to each blossom? Did you pioneer each and every rose bloom? Do you know the architecture of each petal? Can you perceive its immaculate details? What of the heart? The veins? Did you make those as well? Can you infuse them with pure life, or do you know how it carries vitality to every last intricate part of the body you inhabit? Do you have knowledge of these things? Where were you? Answer me!"

"I...wh...what?" Spathi snarled, trembling.

"Speak!"

"Fine! I don't know any of those things!" Spathi blared. "I'm an idiot! That's what you want to hear, isn't it? I'm just a weakling who doesn't know what he's—!"

"Stand like a man, and *you* will answer to *me*!" the voice whispered like heated steel. "Is Ansdarion stronger than us? Can you save yourself? Is your strength your own? Tell me if you can lift the world with the palm of your hand or shake the stars with your grasp. Look there, at your feet! Surely, if you are mightier than the holy ones, you can take a simple pebble in your fingers. Bend low, take it into your hand with nothing but your *own* strength...and I *myself* will proclaim to heaven, to earth, and to everything below the earth that Ansdarion can save himself with his own right arm! What ails you, mortal man? Go on...and take it!"

Spathi looked down. Indeed, a small gray rock lay at his feet, no larger than his thumbnail. He nudged the pebble with the toe of his greaves, knocking it a few inches. It felt light, just like an ordinary rock. It didn't seem like a trick. He squinted at the fire spirit again.

"Take it," the voice commanded.

Reluctantly, Spathi crouched down and tried to grab the pebble. Yet now it wouldn't budge. He pulled…and yanked…and pushed. No matter how much effort he put forth, the rock refused to move even the slightest bit.

"It's stuck!" Spathi griped.

"It is not stuck," the voice said. "Has your right arm been shortened? Why have you boasted such prowess, only to show none of it? Where is your strength, Ansdarion?"

Spathi stood up and unsheathed Vrashri. "I'll show you 'strength!'"

He stomped towards the fire, then the sword became heavy in his hands, the hilt burning his fingers. Spathi yelped and dropped the blade as the flaming juniper took the form of a luminous faceless man stepping towards him, as a wingless angel. Spathi charged and tried to punch him, yet the spirit subdued him. Both of them grappled each other's hands as Spathi tried to push the figure back, wrestling. But the spirit only stood firm, with Spathi wrenching helplessly in his clutches. Then the spirit released him, only for Spathi to come at him again, dodging the blows and sending Spathi back to the floor.

For what seemed like an eternity, the two fought each other. Spathi assailed the figure with all his might, only for the spirit to deflect, dodge, and withstand each vengeful attack. Then the spirit struck him—dislocating Spathi's hip! He howled in agony, crippled and limping. Every thought was like a needle being driven through his mind, each sharp pain jabbing him inside and out. Yet Spathi continued to wrestle the spirit, trying to stand on one leg, once again gripping each other's hands in a deadlock.

"Let me go," the voice finally said.

"No!" Spathi grunted through clenched teeth. "I will…not…."

"My power is only reserved for those who are worthy."

"I'd rather die than let go! Go ahead…and kill me!"

He cast Spathi back down to the floor, then turned and began walking away.

Spathi tried to rise up on one hand, doing his best not to move his hips or legs. "If it is reserved…only for the worthy…then we have already lost the war."

The spirit stopped, his back still turned.

"Not one person…on Raktogin…is worthy." Spathi shook his head. "I never was…. I never wanted…any part in this war—I don't belong in it! I don't understand…any of this. I don't understand you! I'm not strong enough…to take down the devil." He sighed, wincing. "I don't guess…I ever was…and now he has Chau Lepha." He wheezed. "Why? Why did you…allow all this?"

"Deep calls unto deep."

"What the…what is *that* supposed to mean?"

The spirit looked over his shoulder. "Man has constantly sought to live without the holy ones. In abundance is your contempt, yet in tragedy…only a few have cried out to them. Even fewer have strived to follow them at all times, in their joys and sorrows, in times of plenty…and in times of need."

Spathi gagged, trying to catch his breath.

He couldn't take much more.

The spirit turned around to him. "It is the preferred choice of man to exist without the holy ones, grieving heaven daily with their hatred. They have chosen carnage when they could have chosen peace, choosing the shackles of self-destruction rather than the liberation of life. None ushered them to it…and none barred the way. How can they now hope to gain from the holy ones what they do not deserve?"

"Don't we deserve…death?" Spathi conceded, cringing from pain.

The spirit grew silent.

"That's what you're getting at…isn't it?" Spathi sputtered. "Or do we deserve suffering more? Because I don't want to live…and I don't want to die." He shook his head. "I am trapped…and I can't get out." He uttered a hoarse sigh. "I don't know…how to do this…anymore."

The spirit only looked down upon him.

"Have we not cried out to them?" Spathi growled. "Will they offer us nothing? Are not even the dogs glad…to take the scraps…from their master's table?"

The spirit walked back to him. "I know the turmoil that plagues you, Ansdarion. The one they call Ansdari is no more. Already, you rebel with yourself, your *true* self, which has only begun to take shape. The division torments you. Know that we grieve with you in your sorrows and brave with you in your strivings. This is how it has been deigned to be, to be done through those who have been chosen."

Spathi shook his head. "I can't…do this anymore. I just…can't…go—"

"Have you not been commanded?" the voice raged. "Why is your mind still darkened? Why do you tarry with the thoughts of the world? Why do you not see?"

The spirit's fire swirled and conflagrated around him. Spathi shut his eyes and shielded himself with his arms, quivering as the blaze engulfed him. Yet the flames did not scorch him. They were cool to the touch, soothing. Healing. Mending his hip. Mending his body, his mind. His soul. Slowly, he embraced the torrent of fire around him as he levitated upward, holding his head upward, eyes still closed to the brightness of the spiraling platinum blaze. He relaxed his arms, letting them fall to his sides as he listened to the three murmuring syllables, accompanied by the ambient hum…and a massive choir of heavenly voices singing in unknown tongues.

"Spathi…." the voice whispered.

He opened his eyes, the light somehow bearable, not blinding him.

"Do not be afraid," the voice said, "Wherever you go…there I will be in your midst. Let not your heart be troubled. In time, all will be restored. I will accomplish the work through the elect: I in you…and you in me. Be patient. Be still. This is how I have deigned it to be."

"Who are you?" Spathi pleaded.

"Why do you wish to know who *I* am?"

Then he felt it, a rush across his skin, through his veins, prickling through him like fire, ice, and lightning, sensations without names…and then he saw it. Eternity sprawled before him for only a few moments, a splendor he failed to comprehend, the majestic power overwhelming him. Then visions came, past things, scenes from the present…and every single possibility in existence, the ineffable fleeting past his eyes.

Shaking his soul.

He knew now. He knew what was coming.

And he couldn't unsee it.

Ever.

XV: Souls Bound

Spathi drew closer to the opening above as the holy flames propelled him upward. The divine visions of eternity threatened to overcome his mind. He wasn't ready. No one could prepare for what was coming. The fire burst through in a furious geyser, sending him up through the dais…and gently lowering him to the withered grass. Staea and the rest of the knights gawked at his dramatic reentry to Chau Lepha's starlit sanctuary. Slowly, Spathi opened his eyes, with a look deep in his gaze that his allies failed to comprehend.

Never had they seen such a strange combination of emotions in a man's eyes.

Peace. Bewilderment. Contentment…and a creeping despair he tried to conceal.

The revelation haunted him.

Even more bizarre, Staea's eyes shared the exact same disposition, the same light, with fresh tears streaming down her face.

"Arczellius," Spathi breathed.

"What?" Lena asked.

"I…I saw him," he confessed, still in shock. "I saw him…."

"Yes," Staea said, walking to him.

"Saw who?" Tawpa questioned.

Jalusa shrugged at him.

"So," Rand grumbled. "There is a god?"

"What's going on?" Tawpa asked.

Jatal glanced back and forth at Spathi and Staea, at a loss for words.

Staea leaned in to Spathi's ear. "I saw what you saw."

Spathi looked at her. Somehow…he knew.

"We can't tell the others," she whispered in a quavering voice.

Spathi said nothing, neither agreeing or disagreeing with her.

Jalusa turned to Shojem. "What did they see?"

The shaman shook his head, perched on Irado's hulking back. "It is not for us to know. Arczellius revealed himself only to those two just now."

"Great," Shadya scoffed. "Now what?"

General Devral shook her head. "I don't know."

Boom!

Another jet of flames issued from the opening. All of them shielded themselves from the blast as a figure with four feathered wings streaked upward like a comet, encircled by a halo and two parhelions of vibrant light. The being's face was perpetually veiled and illumined by a mask of incandescent platinum energy as his bare feet descended to the ground.

An Arczell. One that precisely resembled the cherub statue in the shrine just now. On his chest were five burning eyes of white fire, positioned like a sand dollar. All of the knights backed away, instantly leery of the spirit's visage.

"Be not afraid," the angel said, his voice a loud, silvery whisper.

"Sile?" Spathi asked.

The angel looked at him. "I am Zephen. I have been observing your progress from heaven for quite some time. Arczellius sent me from the Unleztruv to guide you, for the journey ahead is too much for you."

"Finally!" Tyri griped.

"What're y'all runnin' up there, a friggin' bureaucracy or something?" Alehi complained. "Geez!"

"There *is* a god," Rand repeated, eyes wide.

"Wow," Maloxi marveled.

"Right?" Moriah agreed.

All but Spathi, Staea, Lena, Jatal, Shojem, and Shadya knelt down to Zephen and bowed to him. Yet the angel emitted a shrill ring, flashing a ring of fire. The others bolted up and gasped, backing away again.

"Do not worship me," Zephen rebuked calmly. "We are all fellow servants of the holy ones. We are all brethren here. Bow only to the holy trinity in heaven. Do not endanger us with idolatry."

"Yeah, yeah," Alehi groaned.

Shadya reached out towards Zephen, staggering to him as the angel drifted to her, placing his hands on her shoulders. She stared blankly upward with her sightless eyes, her mouth ajar…and tears streaming down her face.

"It feels so…warm," she said.

"Can you…help her?" Spathi asked Zephen.

The Arczell said nothing and faced up at the stars, rasping a prayer in an ancient language. He then peered back down and gently touched one gray eye at a time.

"Ow," she said, blinking.

"In time, your sight will return to you, but you must be patient," Zephen told her. "The holy ones wish to perform miraculous things through you before then so that the corruption of the fallen world will be shamed."

"Why can't I see now?" Shadya whined.

"You will," Zephen assured. "Have faith. Take heart."

Shadya exhaled a mournful sigh and shut her eyes, hanging her head.

The angel released her and turned to Spathi. "The two messengers you met on the coast have been called back to the Unleztruv. I have been sent in their place to be your guardian."

"The ospreys," Lena said.

Zephen nodded to her.

Spathi's eyes bulged, realizing he had left Vrashri on the floor down in the shrine earlier. He reached behind him…and felt the sword's hilt. Strange. He didn't recall sheathing it on his back just now. What was that place? Was that truly Arczellius?

He looked and saw that the rift had vanished.

"The portal," he remarked. "What happened?"

"I had to close it," Shojem said, pointing at the two blades behind him, each in their scabbards. "Demons would have piled in here." He sighed. "I wasn't quick enough to stop Drixilo."

"Look, I've seen what you can do with those swords," Devral complained. "You mean to tell me you couldn't have just blown them away or something?"

Shojem glared up at her. "Let me tell *you* somethin' here, young'un. These things aren't magic! The power is not mine to wield. In fact, I'm quite terrified of their divine power. The responsibility of these swords demands of me *far more* discipline than what you will ever know. All the persecution I have had to suffer throughout the ages to carry out the work of Unzelkoyte. The holy ones detest vulgar displays of power." He huffed. "It is by the grace of the holy ones that I have persevered to these very last days, not of my accord," he pointed up, "but theirs. Everything I do with these blades, I must petition to heaven in advance, meditating, asking for guidance." He aimed a bony finger at Devral. "I once led a caravan of people through the desert and was told by Unzelkoyte himself that I need only pray to him to have water spring up from the sand. Yet the people kept nagging me, always complaining and scrutinizing. One day, I got so sick of their petulant yammering that I took these very swords and plunged them into the dirt, summoning water that way rather than praying. Unzelkoyte was so furious with me that he rendered me mute for five months, and during that time, the swords became heavy like lead. Yes, I don't like overusing these blades!"

"Astrekiah," Spathi blurted.

They all turned to him.

"Those are the very blades that pierced him," he said, "on the claymore in Unisylis...aren't they?"

Shojem let out a long, tired breath. "Aye. They are."

"They are holy relics," Zephen said. "They are not to be abused."

"What about Chau Lepha?" Jatal asked the angel.

"Drixilo will claim Vren Dotha soon," Lena said, looking around. "How do we get out of here?"

"It is safer to travel to the stern father through the Anli than to return to Raktogin," Zephen explained. He turned to the ornate archway beyond the dais. "I will show you safe passage through the trenches of the battlefields."

"How long will it take?" Spathi asked. "How far?"

"Time travels differently in the spirit realms," Zephen said. "The way to the stern father is far more perilous and cannot be accessed the same way this place was. Nothing can survive the stern father's animosity, not even the air you breathe. The very blade cuts time and space itself. He is angry because of Drixilo's defilement of Chau Lepha and will tolerate no one in his sanctuary deep within the remaining virgin cosmos. He will burn away anyone he deems an intruder."

"So," Rand said. "That's it, then."

"Damn it," Alehi cursed.

"We're not intruders, though," Spathi said.

"Yes," Maloxi concurred. "Our souls are bound to destiny. Our triumph is at hand."

"You truly believe that?" Rand bickered.

Maloxi turned to him. "I *have* to believe it. So do the rest of us." He looked at the others. "I know we are all sick and tired…but we cannot let these devils win, not after all we've been through. They have taken far too much from us. It is time to take the fight to *them*, with or without Chau Lepha; otherwise, the deaths of our loved ones are in vain." He shook his head. "There is no other way."

Spathi and Staea cringed at the chief's speech. Destiny.

Easy for *him* to say. If only they knew what would actually happen. Only now did Spathi realize that uncertainty was a boon rather than a hindrance, protecting him from such a cumbersome burden. How he longed for the amnesia once more to bereave him of this foreboding knowledge!

Yet he had better be careful what he wished for.

"Look, I don't know," Tyri said, turning to Zephen. "You just said that sword would tolerate no one, right? That thing'll kill us."

"We gotta do *something*, Tyri," Spathi told her. "Maloxi's right. No more hiding. No more running."

"Well, where is it?" Devral questioned the angel. "Where's the entry point?"

"Goena," Spathi said, then glanced at Zephen. "Right?"

"Yes," the angel confirmed.

"Goena?" Moriah snapped.

"You've got to be shitting me," Jalusa growled. "*That* far away?"

"How do you know that?" Tawpa asked.

"Constanvol has a big mouth," Spathi explained. "He claimed that Gyeno had pinpointed the gateway to the virgin cosmos, but he was unable to breach it." He groaned. "That's why he experimented on me for so long. He thought that the gateway had some reaction to my 'third eye.' He thought I could open it for him." He shook his head. "I don't know—he was probably blowing smoke up my ass." He squinted where the rift once hung. "What happened to him? He was there in the temple just now."

"He fled like the coward he is," Jatal scoffed. "Little worm."

"I heard Gyeno speak to us about some sort of 'cosmos' from time to time, but I always thought it was something figurative and philosophical, the pinnacle of 'enlightenment,'" Moriah said, surveying the realm again. "Didn't realize it was an…actual place."

"It is where the stronghold once stood," Zephen told them. "In a well of mercury."

"Wait a minute," Staea said. "What about Vren Dotha and this…animosity? Drixilo will be waiting for us there too, won't he? How are we supposed to—"

"Look—let's…let's not waste any more time—th-there'll be plenty more time to discuss this later!" Shojem urged.

Spathi and Staea glared at the shaman.

And he scowled back.

"I don't mean to be curt with ye, but time is of the utmost importance." Shojem gestured his staff at Zephen. "Show us the way."

150

The Arczell nodded and walked over to the overgrown arch. The others cautiously followed close behind, their stomachs tying themselves into knots.

"Get antsy," Spathi muttered, regarding Shojem's attitude, then he turned to the archway. "I don't exactly see how *this* is the safer route after what we just went through."

"I don't either," Staea rasped, gazing with trepid eyes.

Zephen reached out his hand, with his palm emanating an ethereal glow. The warped, metallic noise of energy rang out as the light spread across the archway, becoming like the illumined surface of ghostly water. Zephen turned and waved them forward, then stepped through the gate, rippling to the angel's passing. Spathi gulped and reluctantly ventured forth through the cool, glassy doorway with the others following deeper into the obscure Anli realms. The angel's arrival did little to assuage his disturbed soul.

He finally saw Arczellius. And it was too glorious for him to bear!

For now, at least.

The holy ones answered him at last. He and Staea knew now.

They both saw what lay ahead.

And they wished to unknow it.

Desperately.

XVI: Ethereal Road

The Anli realms sprawled before Spathi and the others as they traveled deeper into the perilous spirit world, a living, eternal enigma swimming with elaborate beings manifesting in chaotic majesty. Though gorgeous and breathtaking, the very splendor itself only amplified the terror and the uncertainty inhabiting the place. No description would suffice to portray how surreal, wondrous, and precarious the scenery was.

Time no longer seemed to exist in that place. The blue ink ocean proved strange beyond words. Spathi and his comrades trekked for what could have been hours, or days. Years.

Who knew?

That was the trouble: Spathi and Staea only knew how everything would end…and not how to get there. The path that led from where they were to the allegedly preordained events he had witnessed in Arczellius's visions were a blur. And Maloxi's "inspiring" speech in Chau Lepha's sanctum only silently perturbed him more and more within.

Destiny. What destiny?

Did they not have a free will to choose their own fate? Or would they run right smack dab into their "destiny" while trying to avoid it? Such questions had pestered him multiple times in the past, yet never had it irked him so much until now. Had what he seen been in the literal sense…or figurative? Had he misinterpreted it? Had Staea as well?

Or had she been shown something entirely different?

How he longed to ask her! Yet he didn't dare, not right here, not in front of everyone. If they knew what he did, who knew what sort of insurrection would break out amongst them? And what if he failed to maintain what sanity he had left before the end?

Zephen and Shojem were the only two that appeared to know anything. Yet even their knowledge was still limited, though the shaman knew much more than what he let on…and he still refused to tell them much. Maybe his reasoning was similar to Spathi's about the vision he had beheld earlier: it would only cause division and disaster. The short lich sat atop Irado's hulking shoulder as if riding a camel as the two ashen blood-eaters pawed on all fours; never did he ride Emerid for some reason. Such a crude way to treat them! They weren't animals—and they certainly weren't pack mules, regardless of their morbid behavior. What if Shojem had them under some spell, depriving them of their lost humanity? And after all that talk about "vulgar displays of power" with Astrekiah's two swords!

The lich had both of the blessed blades sheathed on his back inside their mummified leather sheaths. How did he obtain such divine weapons? And how long had he kept them? Spathi squinted at the shaman; maybe he didn't want to know. He had already gotten way more than what he bargained for after his encounter with Arczellius.

He looked at Zephen, flying a few yards away. It was quite clear the Arczell was not a reincarnation of Sile, yet why were his five eye marks across his torso so similar? Had

Sile been a grotesque parody of Zephen all this time? And why? It seemed so…random.

Could they even trust this angel?

Or was he a Fallen in disguise? Or another Nalx?

And what of that light, that burning tree ablaze with white fire?

Was it truly Arczellius? Or Astrekiah?

Was it both of them at once?

That murmuring…. Those three syllables….

What were they really saying? Why couldn't he interpret the celestial voice?

The dark-blue glow of the Anli showed coldly on the sea floor, yet they were somehow able to breathe. The ghostly waves appeared to be of another plane of existence trying to intersect the dimension they were on, transparent, mesmerizing. And unsettling. Gravity was not as strong, at least for the most part. In other places, however, they felt heavier than lead; nearby wells threatened to syphon them down pits of endless darkness.

Above, the ocean surface flickered with geometric tendrils of chain lightning rumbling faintly with a distant, steely thunder. Weird creatures drifted overhead: supernatural whales, eels, serpents, fish—even birds! Some of the beings appeared to have been turned inside-out, revealing their internal anatomies aglow with spectral radiance. Incandescent man-o-wars and other luminous jellyfish-like spirits swam around, orbiting them at times in neat echelons of various shapes; they all floated in eerie movements but were seemingly harmless. The denizens of the Anli were just as curious of Spathi and his companions as they were of the spirits.

Possibly even *more* curious….

But the tranquil dance of the vibrant entities was deceptive; none of the knights could afford to let their guard down.

Red and teal moss grew from the dreamlike structures amongst hollowed vegetation that resembled skeletal mushrooms and barnacles made of filigree that had succumbed to verdigris. The reefs were smooth, wavy plateaus of polished black marble. Colonnades and ruined tholos shrines of fluted pillars floated sideways like capsules, while flames flickered horizontally in metallic pedestals, giving off needlelike vector flares. Small tectonic plates drifted in flocks in a myriad of formations; some rogue stones meandered on their own. In the distance, clusters of stars shone reflecting like animal eyes, burning like coals, shivering and flapping in unison in the distance as living constellations.

Battlefields of angels and demons raged from afar, their hazy silhouettes striking and hacking each other like smoky lightning, flickering like squall lines within approaching tempests. The divine and the demonic waged war in contested warzones, only seen in the Anli, overlapping Raktogin's material plane. Spathi felt his skin prickle with shame.

They had always been there. Always fighting for humanity's benefit.

And only now did he take notice.

Only now was he able to.

Many Arczells guarded molten rifts opened by Drixiles and human cultists in the past, doing their best not to allow more devils to enter Raktogin, while other demons ascended near holy one-way gateways above, hoping to ambush incoming angels being deployed from the Unleztruv. It was precisely as Deven had told him: it was not that the Arczells refused to help, but they simply couldn't! Normally, he would have, once again, questioned the authority of the holy ones.

But he knew now why.

They would not violate the free will of mortals or spirits.

And it offered little solace.

But that begged the question: could his free will circumvent fate? Had he been shown what *will* happen…or what *might* happen? Must free will operate only within the boundaries of the finite, just as he was told? He squinted.

Just how "finite" was he?

Or Staea? Could she not control her "destiny" as well?

While Spathi accepted the fact that he was not omnipotent or omniscient, he could control *some* things. Did his actions not matter? Surely, he was in control of more than what others had claimed!

Right?

If the holy ones were, in fact, with them, now was their chance to prove it.

One way…or another.

At some point in their venture, Zephen led them down through the labyrinthine trenches and caverns snaking throughout the sea floor, hoping to not attract the attention of encroaching combat areas. At times, only the light of their guardian angel ahead showed them the way.

To another aqueous gate.

Cautiously, they entered, one by one into another region of the Anli oceans.

"How much further?" Tyri rasped.

"Not too far," Zephen assured her in his silvery whispering voice. "We must reach a lagoon up ahead in order to continue undetected by the Drixiles."

"What's at the lagoon?" Jatal asked.

Zephen turned to him. "You shall see."

"Why can't you tell us now?" Staea snapped.

"Keep your voices down!" Shojem growled. "The Drixiles might be nearby spying on us. Take no detail for granted in this place."

"Follow your own advice," Moriah muttered, looking around.

Spathi looked around. Massive shards of mirrors jutted from the trench's rugged walls. As they passed, he glanced at a few of them. Then he slowed down, his eyes bulging from their sockets.

He had *two* reflections?

One of their faces became like a ghoul's and roared at him!

Spathi jerked back.

"Spathi?" Moriah asked.

He whipped around to her, then back at the mirror. Only one reflection now stood again. His head throbbed. Twice. Then his heart. Again, twice.

"What is it?" she said.

He shook his head. "Just jumping at shadows."

She raised a twitching eyebrow at him, quietly calling his bluff as he tried to catch back up with Staea. Had no one seen the double reflection just now? Maybe it was just another hallucination…along with what felt like two hearts beating in his chest. His breathing quickened, trying to hide his mounting duress. Up ahead, he noticed Irado and Emerid staring at him, as if…they had been caught doing something wrong. Their yellow eyes were wide and fearful. They exchanged glances at each other, then back at him.

Spathi squinted at them. Never had those two seemed so…peculiar.

Shadya hurried forward and walked next to Spathi. "You're bothered about something. You and Staea both are."

"We're in a war, Shadya," Spathi retorted. "We're *all* bothered by it. And I thought I saw something move."

"No, it's something else."

"What makes you think it's something else?"

"Your silence," Shadya claimed. "And the way you're breathing. There's a distinct somberness to it. It's different from everyone else's."

Spathi shook his head. "There's nothing to talk about, not right now, at least." He sighed through his nostrils. "Just tired. Trying to stay alert."

"I can hear them," Shadya said. "They sound like they're just a few yards away."

"Who?"

"The angels and demons."

Spathi scoffed. "They're not *that* close. I don't hear anything." He looked down at her. "What's eating you?"

"I don't know, just…disappointed, I guess," Shadya huffed. "I guess that's what I get for being a selfish, immature kid."

"Stop that—you're not selfish," Spathi groaned. "You have just as much right to be healed as anyone else. And you're not dead weight."

Shadya hung her head and said nothing.

He squinted down at her. "Can you…see anything yet?"

She shook her head. "No. But my ears popped when Zephen touched my eyes…and now, my nostrils are burning, like they're…flaring…wide open or something. Everyone's movements—even the smallest gestures—are producing drafts each time you swing your arms or legs, even your fingers. I can suddenly feel all of it."

Spathi shrugged. "So…*that's* what he meant."

"What?"

"Didn't he say something like…the holy ones wanted to perform a miracle through you to…shame the world or something?"

She shook her head again. "I don't know—I…I think so." She belted a coarse sigh. "I wanted my *eyes* fixed, not to have all this—"

"I know, I know—but listen," Spathi told her. "Maybe this is part of that miracle, okay? Your other senses are kicking in like crazy now, right? All we can do is trust what the angel told us." He gazed ahead at Zephen. "We all do. Just hang in there."

Shadya grew quiet. Not only had she lost her sight, but she had been denied the very thing she had hoped for. Hoping beyond hope. For years. All hope did was make people sick. He put his arm around her as she leaned in close. Staea turned to them, the corner of her mouth curling into a smirk, a similar smile to the one she had flashed in the dropship, the day he had held Silda's baby, Flora, in his arms for the first time. He smirked back. He was by no means a replacement for Desmond Abaque.

But perhaps Haandin had been right.

Maybe he *would* have made a decent father.

Halfway decent.

Behind them, Moriah's lips quivered, trying not to weep, reminded of her two lost children. She clenched her fist; she would avenge them. Zilan was hers. So was Gyeno. She pictured ripping out their imperial eyes with her bare hands.

"My eyes hurt," Shadya moaned.

"Stinging or throbbing?" Spathi questioned.

"Throbbing. Aching."

Spathi rubbed her shoulder, then eventually released her as they neared a narrow bend in the trenches. They had to bear with each other if they were to survive. Bear the weight. Bear the suffering. Bear the horror.

To the bitter end.

Up ahead, Zephen stopped and perched on the trench's jagged wall, peering up at a lofty monolith of reflective basalt columns several yards away. Crystalline waters gushed down from multiple forked cascades from the plateau's top. Spathi and the others reached the Arczell and halted as the angel pointed up at the towering summit.

"There," Zephen said. "We must ascend."

"That's the lagoon?" Alehi asked wearily. "Please tell me it's the lagoon."

"Yes," Zephen replied.

"Thank Astrekiah," Devral blasphemed.

"Damned straight," Rand grumbled.

Lena rolled her eyes.

"At least it's easy to climb," Jalusa breathed. "At least…I think."

"Everyone, get down!" Shadya stressed.

"What?" Jalusa said, raising an eyebrow?

Goosebumps formed on Spathi's skin beneath his armor.

"Even *I* don't hear anything," Maloxi said.

"I can smell it," Shadya told them.

"Eww," Tyri judged, scrunching her nose.

"What do you smell?" Moriah queried.

"Look, I'm telling you, it's coming—get down!" Shadya's voice grated, ducking and drawing her short Selebane sword.

Spathi unsheathed Vrashri, then Staea pulled out Chauvien, their eyes darting everywhere. Zephen summoned two hatchets of flame in his hands, then two sickles of fire manifested around him, one hovering on each side of him.

"Listen to her," Zephen commanded.

"Which way, Shadya?" Spathi whispered.

Shadya's breath quavered. "Behind us."

Clash!

Four barbed reavers torpedoed at them, with two of them tackling Zephen down into a hole. The remaining wraiths swam overhead, menacing them above like vultures yet undulating with the grotesque elegance of undead sharks. Their tattered blood-red cloaks billowed, infested with the smoldering, spidery veins of the Ravage, reeking of death.

Malroc's elite. Shrieking at them, their yawning phantom faces like putrefied dough.

"Dammit—they found us!" Alehi barked.

"No shit, kid!" Rand cursed.

"There's two more coming from above!" Shadya called out. "One from each side!"

"C'mon!" Spathi yelled, waving them toward the monolith.

As they ran, the two reavers circling above dove down—then two more blitzed them, just as Shadya had said. Maloxi cut one down, shattering its bone like glass. Alehi drew his Selebane bow, then took a deep breath, and summoned an array of arrows striking down another. A third lashed at Spathi, yet he flared his spirit shield, the flames setting the wraith ablaze. The fourth one fled and swirled up around the monolith's peak, then doubled back. With Chauvien, Staea cleaved the phantom in two, its blackened bones clattering like porcelain. As they reached the basalt steps, the ground rumbled.

Tearing a fiery hole.

Boom!

The rock beneath them busted away in molten chunks, disgorging a spiraling geyser of holy fire and embers, propelling Zephen upward, all four of his wings outstretched while slicing away the reavers pursuing him. The five eyes across his torso surged with incandescent energy, then the angel's body radiated a furious halo around him, acting as a temporary barrier for the knights.

"Climb," Zephen ordered. "They know we're here."

"What else is up there?" Spathi snapped.

"More Arczells," Zephen told him. "They know a hidden path through the battle-fields. I'll meet you there. Go. Hurry!"

Spathi looked up at his comrades scaling the basalt, then at the screeching reavers, then at Zephen. One of the five eyes had already exhausted its light, with the adjacent one's energy halfway depleted.

"What ails you?" Zephen grunted. "Go!"

Spathi said nothing and stepped up the disheveled hexagonal staircase of the basalt, slashing away reavers barreling at him left and right like meteors. Alehi shot down more of them. A few more Arczells swooped from nearby warzones, rocketing through clouds of reavers like white comets, the trails of their blades leaving flickering streaks with each swing. Rand and Devral tried to usher Shadya up the slope, with Jalusa, Tawpa, and Moriah deflecting the incoming Drixile throng. Shojem jabbed what wraiths he could with Astrekiah's two swords, while Irado and Emerid flailed their arms at the demons. The reavers dodged the ghouls' clumsy swipes, then one knocked Emerid down, leaving five red scars across his chest.

Spathi looked as the blood-eater tumbled to him, screaming. Instinctively, he caught him, trying to hoist the wounded ghoul with one arm and hacking away reavers with Vrashri on the other.

Shojem looked down. "Let him go, Spathi! He'll just hold you back! There ain't no sense in hauling him up—!"

"Fuck you, and shut up!" Spathi barked.

The shaman grumbled and looked back, noticing the second wave of reavers coming. A much larger wave.

Tyri peered down, then stepped down to Spathi and Emerid.

"Where you going?" Rand blared.

Tyri ignored him and helped Spathi carry Emerid as they both ascended upward. Spathi turned. The army of wraiths were closing in, and the Arczells stood with swords and shields ready. Zephen glided up and passed them, rising to the peak, just yards away. Almost there. Almost within reach. All of them huffed and panted, trying to muster every ource of their remaining stamina, all the while hearing the unified cacophony of the swarming reavers. Spathi glared up at the basalt mountaintop.

Why wasn't Zephen helping carry Emerid?

He looked at the blood-eater's thin face up close for the first time; his scraggly gray hair wisped around in the Anli's winds. He was no savage. As far as Spathi was concerned, both Emerid and Irado were human.

No one gets left behind. No one!

Shojem was going to get an earful after this.

If they survive this.

Wheezing frantically, they reached the top, then they turned to the wave of reavers, raging upward around the monolith as a torrent, too afraid to near Zephen's weakening halo. The few remaining Arczells stood firm, waiting for the demons to make the next move. Spathi looked around at the lagoon.

Then the realization seized him.

He had been here before. With Deven.

After escaping Goena through the Udenthen highways. The birds were long gone. The exotic trees were dead, their branches bare and decaying. Yet the dark-blue water was thick like paint, gleaming with a suspicious white shimmer. Swirling.

Into a maelstrom.

Zephen hovered over the whirlpool's glowing maw, emitting a pillar of platinum light. The last eye on the Arczell's torso was on the verge of diminishing. Spathi glared at the mysterious angel.

"Into the maelstrom," Zephen called to them. "Hurry!"

"You must be out of your mind!" Devral snarled.

"You said this was a lagoon!" Alehi griped. "All I see is a damned toilet swirling around some—!"

The reavers railed an earsplitting scream at them, only drawing closer. And closer.

"You must trust me," Zephen said.

Spathi looked frantically around, racking his brain for any alternative. Yet none would present themselves to him. It was foolish to come this way! And Zephen led them here. Should they wait for more angels? Surely, there was another path they could take, something nearby. Something…safer.

He groaned.

Arczellius had supposedly shown him the end. Only bits and pieces.

Of an obscure, harrowing future.

And not how to get there.

Or if he could avoid it.

All he could do was put the vision to the test…if he could live long enough.

The reavers raged closer, causing the angels to step back around the lagoon, on the whirlpool's shores. Spathi looked at Staea. She eyed him, then back at the disturbing maelstrom. Zephen's last eye was dimming, the halo vanishing. As he tried to think, Shojem turned to him, then gazed at Emerid.

The scrawny ghoul impetuously ambled forward into the current. As did Irado.

Followed by Spathi. Then Staea.

And the rest of them.

All of them were instantly sucked down into the ominous light, becoming a white void of keening energy. They gagged and sputtered, about to drown. Then the waters vanished, along with the reavers, the angels, and the ocean. Spathi coughed and gasped, trying to breathe…then he looked around.

Everyone else had vanished.

Even Zephen.

Only the susurrations of unclear whispers permeated the absence of gravity around him, like wind ringing against sharpened steel. This was no hidden path. It was a prison! And he let this so-called "angel" lead him right into it! His eyes darted back and forth, feeling panic slowly grip his heart.

And his throbbing head.

Feeling as if splitting in two.

"Spathi," a familiar man's voice echoed.

He whipped around. "Prister?"

"We're with you, Spathi," another voice told him.

"Yeah, we're here," a third said.

"Stay strong, Spathi," a fourth interjected.

Spathi squinted. Desmond? Stelford? And Solakees? He cringed, feeling the suppressed guilt swallow him. The ghosts of his allies haunted the air.

"Remember what I told you, Spathi," Solakees said, his voice no longer impaired by his illness but rang clear and sound, fully restored in the afterlife.

"I wished I had seen sooner, Spathi," Stelford told him.

"Stelford," Spathi grunted. "I'm sorry."

"For what?"

"I didn't save you."

"But you did," Stelford chuckled, then he sobered up. "Just make sure Alehi gets here when the time comes."

"Look after Aipha and Tyri for me," Prister said.

"And Uthilda and Shadya for me as well," Desmond added.

"I swear to you: they will not die," Spathi vowed.

"We know," Prister said.

"We never die, Spathi," Desmond told him.

"The body dies," Stelford assured. "We are free."

"We are eternal," Solakees proclaimed, his voice reverberating.

In the bright mist, the obscure figure of a woman appeared before him, garbed in a wispy robe of light drawing closer to him. His eyes widened as he recognized her.

The woman he had slain in Noshva's temple, while he was halfway lobotomized.

He flinched, his heart racing, blood icing inside him as she drifter near to him. He shook, engulfed in burning shame. She was here to exact vengeance upon him. He was a murderer. Treth. The bald soldier.

And her.

She reached out her hand…and gently stroked his cold cheek. Eventually, he mustered up the courage to look her in the eye. The woman's soul smiled. Not bloody. Not scarred or maimed or mutilated in any way. She was serene, at peace.

And merciful.

Tears streamed down Spathi's face.

"I'm sorry," he finally managed to squeak out.

The woman shook her head. "I hold nothing against you."

"But I killed you!" Spathi choked. "I ate…I ate your blood!"

Her smile faded. "If the holy ones can forgive you, why can you not forgive yourself?"

Spathi grew silent, his eyes bulging. Yet his quivering lessened, gradually relaxing his fists. Her smile returned again, becoming a pleasant grin as her form steadily evaporated.

"Release yourself," she whispered. "Release yourself…and be free."

Energy rang around him again as the white void parted, exposing another bizarre vista, above and below. The heavenly realms sprawled before him, a roaring complex of warzones on different levels. Different circles. Stars flashed in the distance. Armies clashing in nebulae. Angels and demons clashed in the sun, causing solar flares, battling all over the place! Above, he saw a white realm, blurry from where he drifted. Below, geometric lightning coursed through the Udenthen highways, currents zipping back and forth. Spectral Udenthen lay chained in other nebulae and distant suns.

More Arczells and Drixiles warred, pale meteors bashing against infernal stars burning like dying coals. They fought on asteroids and comets, their forms altered by the spirit planes. The planets were contorted and deformed in the Anli, carven with incorporeal battle trenches, with angelic spirits and demonic shadows combating each other deep in them and around them.

161

The seemingly random events in the universe….

So much chaos! So much…revealed.

Around him, the prayers of different voices echoed unseen, human voices, taking visible forms of a language he could not understand! The silhouettes of the Arczells blazed to each earnest syllable, empowered and rejuvenated by the devotion of the Unzelites, charging back into battle.

Spathi's jaw dropped, recalling what Arczellius had told him.

Deep calls unto deep.

Everything had a consequence.

Every act. Every word. Every thought.

All of it.

Including the curses of others. Curses of humans.

These also took form, manifesting as glyphs of harsh scarlet, tearing rifts of red fire! Drixiles pooled from the smoldering holes on Raktogin. He looked closer at the world, twisted and warped, reduced to a monochrome mass of barren filth, riddled with monoliths of solidified shadows and black fire. It no longer resembled a planet.

The most intense of the battles were concentrated on Raktogin, the world's surface bristling with angels and demons. Arczells hurled more comets at the infernal rifts and phalanxes of Drixiles where Tauldren was. Where New Neva was. The moon swirled and sloshed like quicksilver, the bizarre Mionia basilica veiled beneath the metallic wake. Spouts of reddened mercury slowly reached up at the white circles of the Anli high above, at the Unleztruv. In every thunderstorm, angels traveled back and forth through the bolts striking the earth.

Spathi was overwhelmed. Deven had been right. The angels had been fighting all along, and he didn't even realize it, waging war all over creation. And Raktogin was center stage for the eternal struggle, the holy war.

The *only* war.

A Drixile raged toward them! Then another!

Spathi reached for Vrashri. Yet the sword was suddenly missing!

Zephen appeared before him and launched both of his hatchets. The weapons surged with lightning, cleaving the demonic spirits in two. Like boomerangs, the axes whizzed back to the angel's palms. The remnants of the severed demon slithered back down as thick black smoke, seeping beneath the Udenthen highways…and down into the darkness of the Nevarifta.

Spathi reached behind him, scouring his person for his weapon.

What the hell was happening? Was this a dream? A vision?

Was his body elsewhere?

Where had everyone else gone?

Something thrashed far below, a line of yellow fish eyes. On a colossal appendage.

Sevthiel. The World Choker. Entwined all throughout the Anli. The Nevarifta.

And Raktogin.

Arczells charged below, hacking away at him. The Udenthen hydra struck back.

All this had been going on, this war, ever since Drixilo fell. Spiritual warfare was far more real than he could have ever fathomed or imagined. He shuddered. He and so many others had been blind and deaf in the world.

So much more occurring in the unseen realms overlapping the material plane.

Over Raktogin.

Over the entire universe.

Everything that humans committed in life *did*, in fact, echo into eternity, having unspeakable consequences they would never recognize. All because they didn't want to. Mortals had slowly enabled the Drixiles to slowly enter the material realm by forfeiting the protection of the Unleztruv, breaching the thin veneer between planes of existence.

All those centuries. All those machinations.

Spathi turned and saw something else.

Up in the higher heavens, a multitude of blue souls marched, shepherded by a bluish-white light with two wings spanning into forever. Two long beams of energy spanned from both sides of him. He was surrounded by a great halo and parhelions of silver light.

Astrekiah himself.

Herding the souls through a massive arched doorway, as if…evacuating them from heaven. The imprisoned Udenthen far below gnashed and growled up at them, yanking at their blazing chains in the nebulae, so eager to devour them.

Spathi's head reeled…then he took in a deep breath. He blinked, then he looked back at the stream of souls…and sighed. He had to trust also, trusting had he and the others would get through.

That he and Staea would see their son, Thedo, again. To hold him in their arms.

To be a family. For the first time.

Zephen flapped to him. "Brace yourself. We are nearing the material plane."

Spathi felt the abrupt undertow of gravity tug him down.

He plummeted towards Raktogin's wastelands. Fire blazed around him, his body igniting like a falling meteorite. Everything keened like razor-sharp steel…then all reverberated away. He clenched his teeth, feeling his flesh burn and smoke.

Trust. He had to trust.

No matter how much it went against his instincts.

A bright light flashed before him. Steadily, he felt himself convulse. Something pulsed inside him, growing more vicious. Then he heard someone shouting. Chanting. With something else growling. Twin heartbeats resonated around him. In him. Black and yellow spots appeared in his sight as the very air roiled around him like stormy water.

Then, all hushed.

Darkness.

Nothingness.

XVII: Shadow Carapace

Spathi gasped for air, lying on his back. He flung his eyes open, coughing and retching, rolling onto his hands and knees, his bare fingers feeling the coarse texture of rust beneath him.

"Get up! Quick!" Jatal shouted. "On your feet—all of you!"

The Vauphec knight-chieftain stood over him and offered his hand. The sound of crushing glass clinked under his heels. Spathi groaned, then reached and grabbed his grandfather's palm as Jatal pulled him up.

"Careful," Jatal warned, pointing at the otherworldly shards.

Spathi said nothing and stepped around, looking behind him. The molten, sizzling crystal gash of a glowing rift gradually mended near an oxidized wall, closing the way to the Anli. He felt the celestial fragments beneath the soles of his silver exoskeletal greaves as they slowly disintegrated in white embers around his plated toes.

Staea and the others rose up, clutching their Selebanes tightly. Zephen swooped over them and perched on a broken pillar of chrome, with old cables draping from the metallic colonnades into a ditch below. Shojem, still perched on Irado's shoulder, peered around vigilantly while Emerid stomped around nervously, covering his ears and grumbling unintelligible things.

Spathi squinted at the two ghoulish blood-eaters. Their faces were filled with dread, as if wrestling with a bad memory. But they had never been before.

Had they?

He surveyed the area. Goena sprawled before him. Or what was left of it. They were here at last. And it only seemed like a few hours! He shuddered to think how much time had actually passed on the material plane. The constant time fluctuations of the Anli were excruciating! Had the others even made it to Ruzi? Or were they dead? He gazed at his allies. What if they were all that was left of the coalition? What if they were all that remained to resist Drixilo? Even the tireless Arczells of the Unleztruv he had beheld just now seemed outnumbered by the demon host's relentless ranks; even worse, the angels' numbers appeared to be dwindling.

They all stood in a looming canyon of rust. Large holes of cavitation dotted the oxidized cliffs resembling termite damage. Giant termites. From hell. On either side of the gorge, rows of ruined chrome pillars lined deep ditches paralleling the path. A massive cut ran right down the middle of the ravine, right where Gyeno's living stronghold had dragged its nether regions, uprooting itself from its complex foundations. Old Drixile machinery and architecture lay mangled around sparse layers of cold, darkened glass.

Gyeno's lodestone alloy.

He turned around. The canyon stretched for miles behind them, fading away into an orange mist in the distance. The night sky displayed unhealthy dark shades of brown, crimson, and, orange, illumined by the geothermal wrath rupturing from Raktogin's

165

volcanic wounds. Yellowish stars burned high up in the heavens beyond the horrible lattice of the Udenthen sky cage, the circular grid slowly turning redder by the minute. In the eastern horizon far off, fractal feeder bands carved through the heavens like sickle blades.

They all knew what that meant.

And the clock was ticking.

He looked back. About half a mile from them, a dark gouge was barely visible beneath a pile of steely rubble. Spathi looked closer at a fallen piece of debris. On a damaged metal plate, he saw the signet of Goena, rendered virtually illegible by Drixilo's decay.

"This place is Tetanus City," Rand snorted.

"Why didn't Gyeno take this with him?" Tyri questioned.

"What part of 'Tetanus City' did you not understand?" Rand quipped.

"Demons do not get tetanus," Jalusa snapped at him, then she raised an eyebrow at Shojem. "Or do they?"

"He probably wasn't able to, Tyri," Shojem commented. "The metal here was corroded by Drixilo, anyway. It is useless, even to Gyeno." The shaman looked around. "Or…perhaps he may have planned to come back for it later, to regain the mercury well leading to the virgin cosmos. Either way, his folly is our advantage."

"Let's hope you're right, old man," Spathi replied.

"Shh—wait, listen!" Shadya said.

Spathi looked around. "I don't hear anything."

"Neither do I," Staea said.

"It's…it's far off," Shadya claimed.

"Everyone, hold still," Maloxi told them.

The Jyodem chief and Jalusa crouched back down and placed their ears to the metallic ground, focusing on any noise or vibration.

"What is it?" Lena questioned. "Shadya?"

"Shh! Shush!" Maloxi rebuked.

"It…it stopped," Shadya said.

"What did you hear?" Moriah asked.

"Nothing good," Devral quipped.

"It's…it's like a…faint scratching noise," Shadya claimed. "Like…claws on tin."

Maloxi and Jalusa rose to their feet and dusted themselves off. They both raised an eyebrow at her, then exchanged glances, shaking their heads.

Shadya's sightless eyes wandered around in confusion. "Maybe it's nothing."

"No," Zephen said. "You've heard rightly." He scanned the canyon. "We are not alone here."

Alehi scoffed. "Are we ever?" He readied his Selebane bow. "Damned assholes just can't get enough, can they?"

"Shut up, Al," Tyri growled nervously through clenched teeth.

"We're wasting time," Spathi grunted, venturing down the canyon ahead of them, towards the dark crevice in the rubble. "Let's move."

They followed behind him, yet his pace only quickened. He was so tired of this. He refused to wait on them, already sick of their bickering, sick of waiting on them to make a unanimous decision. They were always jabbering. Always nagging at each other.

"Spathi, wait up!" Jalusa called out.

"You *keep* up," Spathi snarled back. "Drixilo will be here any—*ow!*"

"What's wrong?" Tawpa shouted.

He stopped in his tracks and felt his cheek. His face itched. Itching, burning all over. From scalp to neck. He clawed at his skin—the stinging becoming unbearable! What the hell was he allergic to down here? He growled and turned to them. No one else had to scratch.

Except for Staea.

The sound of ringing steel keened throughout the canyon. They all looked around, scanning every crag, every opening…and saw nothing. Yet the burning on Spathi's and Staea's faces only worsened, scorching into their arteries, their bones.

Down to their souls.

Shing!

Rand gasped—gushing blood from his abdomen!

"Rand!" Devral yelled.

They all looked and saw a male figure with long black hair clad in a bizarre black armor, his scythe blade infested with dark, metallic tendrils impaling and lifting the Enoshah captain up into the air. All of them were too petrified with shock to even move, watching their comrade's guts dangling out, exsanguinating to death. The man dropped Rand to the ground—and dug his six fangs into his neck, draining him of his vitality. Then with a deft swipe, he cleaved the captain's head off, slicing through the Sevelurnum armor as if it were mere aluminum foil. Rand's body flopped lifelessly to the oxidized dust below, emitting a nauseating squelch as his bowels finishing spilling out. Spathi glared at the armored demon.

Constanvol.

The baron's chin dripped with red blood as his lightning mark continued to burn with a bluish-gray light, his dark-blue aura altered and enhanced by the shadowy exoskeleton that encased him.

"Welcome back," Constanvol sneered, aiming Qualkytdle's mutated blade at Spathi. "Did you miss me?"

"You fucker!" Alehi blared.

Constanvol raised Qualkytdle's blade—and slammed it into the ground, rippling and tearing the ground, sending all but Zephen sailing into the air several feet away, only for their bodies to ricochet against the rotting steel. The angel withstood the shockwave, landing on the ground, with his large hatchets and airborne sickles ready. Spathi rose back up, reaching for Vrashri, beholding the baron's ungodly new visage.

The demon wore an otherworldly armor of onyx and lodestone tendrils, oozing like living black quicksilver on the surface. A flesh cloak. Similar to the one Spathi once wielded but more hulking and much deadlier. Ropy strands enveloped his arms and legs, engulfing Qualkytdle on his right arm; the barbed tentacles took an identical form on his left arm, a duplicate of the gauntlet weapon. Each tendril simulated a bioluminescent glow of yellow and red light pulsing from the cuirass to the outer strands. Parts of the sinister plate mail were polygonal and volumetric, pellucid and revealing symmetrical geometric copper grooves resembling the circuitry of a computer chip. Yet the suit of armor appeared…incomplete, as if it were a work in progress.

The emblem of Goena was inscribed on the shoulder plates.

Across the chest, a circular gap showed where a demonic tetrarch's imperial eye should have been.

A weak spot?

Spathi scoffed. Gyeno sought to plagiarize the curse Malroc had imbued Spathi with five years earlier and make it his own. Even after all that time the emperor spent experimenting on him—and he *still* didn't finish his morbid project. And Constanvol commandeering it was nothing more than an indictment of his glaringly evident insecurities and his faltering combat prowess.

Pathetic.

A roll of thunder pealed through the sky as Drixilo's pulsating hurricane drew closer to the canyon. A large, winged figure descended from the eye and spread his bladed pinions and armored spider legs outward, his ominous form seemingly godlike, flaring with blue hellfire and red veins of light.

Gyeno. Melded with Eregatho.

Fully assimilated by Drixilo.

The lodestone glass in the gorge clattered, gradually shifting around, melting into clusters. Elementals. Spathi and Staea stood and clutched their Selebanes, then looked up at the angel.

"Zephen," Spathi said. "Protect the others." He aimed Vrashri at Constanvol. "This bastard is mine."

"No," Staea hissed, raising Chauvien. "We fight him together. I'm not going to let you have all the fun, Spathi."

"So be it, pet," Spathi grumbled.

"Pet?" Constanvol mocked. "How cute." He stepped forward, smashing some of the waking animus shards beneath his feet. "When will you learn you must keep your bitch on a leash, Spathi?"

He spread out Qualkytdle's edge on his right arm, with the hardened tendrils on his left braiding into a serrated whip sword, resembling a tail of vertebrae lashing around.

The baron cocked his head. "A muzzle would look good on her as well."

"Not as good as it would on a little brat like you," Staea growled.

"If I had a heart," the baron seethed, "it would be broken."

"Yeah?" Spathi ran at him. "Too bad you don't have a brain, either!"

Shing! Shing!

Constanvol slashed the air, producing twin arcs of black flames, yet Spathi raised his spirit shield, deflecting both attacks from him and Staea; the sheer force pushed them back, their heels tilling the rusty ground. Around them, the lodestone animi manifested, having the semblance of abstract serpent devils, their metal bodies flowing like amorphous mercury. They had no eyes, yet they had plated, horned melons like Udenthen, with their toothless mouths elongating like reavers, squealing with abandon as their lithe bodies coiled and lunged at the knights and Constanvol. Zephen dove at the fiends, carving some of them to pieces with his blazing axes and sickles as Alehi shot down what he could with his Selebane bow. Shojem, Irado, and Emerid all swung at the elementals, with the shaman enabling the two blood-eaters' vicious blows with the light of Astrekiah's two swords. Jatal and Lena slashed through the demons with such fluid strokes that their motions almost resembled a dance rather than combat, displaying centuries of experienced swordplay as their second nature. Moriah and Maloxi bashed away more of the elementals with their silver spears while Devral, Jalusa, and Tawpa tried to defend Shadya. Tyri swung her Selebane sword with one hand yet held her bow in the other, distracted and ashamed by her inability to summon decent spirit arrows. In the heat of battle, she wracked her brain for an answer.

Why couldn't she do it? What was holding her back?

Why couldn't she just let go?

Let go…. Let go….

All seemed to move in suspended animation as she recalled Haandin's words that night on the beach, right before the tsunami hit.

There is only truth. Think that's 'stupid' or 'corny?' The people of the world around you thought the same thing—and where are they now?

Alehi's words zipped through her mind once again.

I asked for help…from something I can't see. From something I thought was imaginary. Something I thought was superstitious. I finally took it seriously…and that's when I felt it envelop me. It wasn't adrenaline. It wasn't goosebumps. In that moment, I felt something I have never felt before.

The words pierced her as her eyes widened.

Feeling the epiphany finally wash over her.

Baptizing her with something unseen.

Something completely external of the self.

She shuddered, with tears streaming down her face. Memories of her mother flashed before her eyes, that night when they were fleeing from the refugee city, the night her mother went back to retrieve something.

The night she died.

How long Tyri had blamed herself for her mother's death, thinking she had went back to get something for her. If only she had gotten ready to leave quicker. If only she hadn't held her family back! It couldn't have been that important, whatever it was she went to get. Yet…she didn't even know if it *was* for her. It may have been a thermos of water…or an extra pack of MREs.

She couldn't keep blaming herself. She had to let go.

And release herself.

In the haze of battle, she saw Spathi and Staea struggling against Constanvol's malefic new weaponry…then she looked at Zephen. An angel. Right before her very eyes. Not a mutant. Not an alien. Not a manmade genetic experiment.

A spirit. From heaven.

She raised her Selebane bow as a pack of animi came at her. She closed her eyes…and whispered a mantra, trying to calm herself, trying to believe.

Trying to ask…for help.

With her eyes shut, she failed to see the brilliant echelon of shafts amassing around her, burning furiously, bristling with heaven's indignation.

"Tyri!" Alehi yelled.

She jerked, opening her eyes.

The arrows tore through the charging elementals—and crashing into Constanvol. The baron grunted and sailed through the jagged canyon wall, the debris piling around him. Spathi and Staea puffed for air as the rest of them continued to destroy the remaining animi. Tyri only stood there, shuddering stupefied at what had occurred as Zephen stood before her.

"Do you see now, Tyri?" Zephen told her.

She said nothing as the Arczell put his hand on his shoulder.

"Be still," Zephen told her.

Slowly, her body ceased to quiver.

Around them, the last of the animi fell, their shards permanently scarred with holy light, unable to merge again. All of the knights panted and wheezed, the oily lodestone dissolving from their blades.

"Wha…what happened?" Devral asked. "Tyri?"

Zephen released her shoulder and walked away. "She has taken the next step." He observed the captain's headless corpse. "If only Rand Limend had done the same."

"What do you…wait—what do you mean?" Alehi said.

"Ye will find out in due time, young'un!" Shojem crowed.

Spathi aimed Vrashri at the shaman. "Time is the one thing we *don't* have, old man!"

"And you'd best start speaking up!" Staea snarled. "Right now!"

"If we don't make for the well right now, none of you will last long enough to know anything, ye hear?" Shojem pointed a sword at the crevice. "It's down there."

"How are you so sure?" Spathi snapped. "Or did you just have another one of your 'visions' about it?"

"Your words, not mine," Shojem quipped. "C'mon!"

Staea clenched her teeth. "Not until you—!"

"Ye said yourselves that time is one thing we do not have—and ye say rightly!" The shaman pointed at the encroaching hurricane above. "Let us go! Quickly! Make haste!"

"Wait, hold on!" Moriah said. "What, exactly, do you—?"

"Make haste, dammit!" Shojem cawed.

Spathi grumbled things under his breath as he and Staea followed Shojem and Zephen, the lich still astride Irado's back. They had never seen the shaman so devoid of his facetious demeanor, replaced by an unsettling bitterness. Emerid took one last timid glance at Spathi, then ventured with them, with the surviving knights joining their path toward the crevice. Spathi stared at Emerid, noticing the ashen blood-eater's tattoos more closely for the first time. They were more like…grooves, geometric lines scarred on his flesh. Irado's body suffered similar symmetrical gashes, with some of them stretched from his thick muscles. He squinted.

The grotesque markings reminded him of the one's Spathi's flesh cloak once locked into across his skin. Why hadn't he noted this earlier? He felt his blood turn to ice, then boil, then back to ice, coaxing waves of goosebumps and chills skittering all over him…then he glared at Shojem.

Surely, the lich couldn't be an agent of….

He shook his head, not wanting to believe it. His breathing quickened, quavering all the way down his lungs and back again, sensing the morbid caress of paranoia trying to seize him. As they entered the crevice, Staea eyed him and opened her mouth to say something, then she shut her lips, too afraid of the answer. Her husband would just angrily deny it, anyway. Spathi looked one last time at the pile of rust where Constanvol had been slammed into, eyeing the debris for any sign of movement. His scowl tightened; the baron could not have been slain that easily, and the uncertainty of the demon's fate only made him more nauseated. They stepped down a busted tunnel of severed tubing and cables, feeling guilty about not giving Rand's body a proper burial and vexed all the more by Zephen's words.

If only Rand had seen.

Seen what? What were they supposed to see?

Even Spathi's revelation from Arczellius did little to convince him.

Alas, faith was a choice…and a very bold one at that, one that seemed to border precariously on outright insolence. But disbelief was as easy as it was brash…and futile. The fear of naïveté was too overwhelming, detesting the risk of being taken for a fool all over again. Why must he be a puppet to circumstance, with heaven and hell fighting for control of his pulled strings? What good was a free will if he lacked the ability to transcend the finite?

Rand *had* seen. Hadn't he?

But had he trusted?

Spathi stomach only turned more and more within him. Perhaps that was what Zephen alluded to. Had the deity of heaven allowed the captain's cynicism to lead him to such a grisly demise, only to merely set a grim example for the others? What an unceremonious purpose to serve! An entire human life, rendered expendable and denied paradise in a crude instant, cast into the fire like some cheap straw man, wasted on one simple message, something that could have been conveyed without such a violent end! Something that could have been…avoided. But the traumatizing shock value of one's untimely death was more than sufficient to pierce their callous hearts and waken their frozen souls. And Rand could have chosen to believe…couldn't he? None had barred the way to the Unleztruv from him…and none would have torn down the barrier of doubt he had constructed in his mind. Like them, the captain was capable of choice, at least while his lungs had still drawn breath. Not anymore, though. His fate was officially sealed, no additional chances. That was it, for Rand Limend. And the fact that no one was weeping over him was just another scathing indictment of the man's reputation.

No one missed him.

And it wasn't because they were dead inside. They all felt it, the inexorable sting of finality. And the captain had obviously offered far more than what Rediq Tashar had. But all the mortal good works in the world could never build a staircase to heaven.

It was something else….

Spathi shuddered. The belief of the holy ones' existence was one thing…but to believe that they were, in fact, benevolent, that there was no darkness or evil in them at all, that the trinity was not just some careless, egotistic tyrant…that was the challenge, the arduous pill to swallow…and to keep down without vomiting. And such a pill, all too often, only became lodged in one's throat. Each attempt to ingest the truth only proved more painful with time.

And time was running low. Dangerously low.

To think that history itself was on the very crux of total annihilation….

And then what? What happens after that?

Anything?

Or nothingness?

Nihil….

They traveled further down the twisting tunnels of black metal, then the path abruptly terminated, the frayed opening gaping and dangling, having crashed through the ceiling of a lower hallway crafted entirely of the tarnished lodestone alloy. One by one, each of them leapt down to the intersecting corridor below, climbing down hanging cables to descend. Spathi looked several yards away.

At a dead end.

A nook. Furnished like a study.

Metallic furniture was fused to the walls, with a couple of bookshelves on their left lined with dusty scrolls and ledgers. A desk and chair stood on their right, with ancient papers, graphs, and maps sprawled across, inscribed with old spells and more recent writings, scribbled in a language Spathi failed to interpret. Near the desk, three walls stood, resembling a cathedral's ornate, vaulted apse. Engraved into the center wall, an arched mirror showed, its pane etched with old runes.

Moriah walked over to the scrolls on the desk, placing her index finger on the Drixilian characters. "I've seen this before." She looked up at them. "Gyeno taught me to read and write it."

"I bet he did," Jalusa groaned, eyeing the study.

"What does it say?" Alehi asked.

"I'd rather not know," Spathi said, glancing at Zephen.

Moriah stood there for a minute, silently translating the emperor's notes as the others examined the narrow study. On the other side of the room, the detailed façade of a larynx door stood; its latches were sealed by the supernatural fusing of ungodly metals, impenetrable by any material force and cleverly disguised as just another wall.

A secret passage. In Gyeno's basement.

Untouchable by Drixilian telepathy.

But how could Shojem and Zephen know about it, then?

"I thought you said there was a well down here," Spathi griped.

Zephen pointed at the mirror. "Gyeno tried to alter it in hopes of making passage to the virgin cosmos easier, but it was to no avail."

"Is it dangerous?" Staea questioned.

"Shouldn't be, at least not at the moment," Shojem said. He squinted at her. "But if we don't hurry, Drixilo will be within a close enough proximity to do something."

"How do we even know this is the right place?" Spathi growled. "Shojem?"

"No," Moriah finally said, then looked at him. "He's...he's telling the truth." She turned to the transmogrified well on the wall. "According to the notes, that seems to be the case. It mentioned you in his research, the 'third eye,' your flesh cloak, everything."

Spathi scowled down at Shojem. The shaman's mummified face only grinned at him, yet there was something venomous about it this time, not with his signature acerbic cheer...but more cutting, urgent.

Desperate.

"How did you know this was here if Drixiles wouldn't know?" Spathi snapped.

"Lad," Shojem quipped. "I am no Drixile. And neither is Zephen."

"What?" Spathi barked.

"I can sense your doubt about me and the Arczell, Ansdari," Shojem said, holding his staff in both hands. He patted Irado's back. "But I do not know everything, either. I'm just as eager to get to the bottom of things as you are. That is why we must make haste, lest we make the same mistake we did in Unisylis. Vren Dotha might resist Drixilo, but I do not know to what extent, especially with Chau Lepha in the demon host's clutches. Do ye understand now, blood-eater?"

Spathi grew silent, still glowering at the lich, then he glanced at the well nook again...and noticed a circular platform before the mirror door, carved with a labyrinth pattern of platinum. He squinted. Gyeno could not have put such a divine metal there. His eyes darted around the lodestone study, built around the well, just as Zephen had said. He eyed the mirror again, observing his reflection. Again, a second image of Spathi stood just behind him...slowly turning around.

Revealing empty eye sockets...and a smirk.

His head throbbed again, with his ears ringing. He grunted, clutching his head.

"What is it?" Staea asked.

"I don't know!" Spathi snapped.

"Wait!" Shadya said. "I hear something else."

"What now?" Spathi's voice grated.

"It's that...scratching noise again," she said, turning towards the wall beyond the desk. "And it's getting closer."

They all raised their weapons and faced the wall, bracing themselves, then Spathi fell to his knees. Staea ran over and crouched next to him, placing her hand on his shoulder, wanting to help him, longing to fix what was broken. What was wrong? What was happening?

Then they heard it: the sound of razor-sharp steel lacerating through layers of metal.

Boom!

Black fire detonated from the wall, fragmenting lodestone everywhere, knocking them all back; even Zephen was blown away. Constanvol emerged from the gouge in the wall.

And impaled Spathi in the back!

He gagged, spitting up blood.

"Let's see if Gyeno's theory checks out," the baron heaved, hauling Spathi's bleeding torso to the platinum labyrinth mark. "Time to put that 'third eye' of yours to work."

Spathi jabbed Vrashri into Constanvol's chest. The baron yelled as the sword's holy nebulous fire blasted him back, sending him crashing into the desk, dropping Spathi to the platform.

"You really need…to learn…to back…the fuck up!" Spathi sputtered.

Red dribbled from the gash and his mouth onto the white metal…then the markings burned, forming geometric lines all over the apse nook, all matching the strange light surging from Spathi's forehead.

Gravity shifted. The air roiled like water.

And the mirror yawned open, forming a vortex of spiraling pale fire, its vicious undertow warping their screaming bodies, contorting them into strands of light and tearing through the doorway's rift.

Into the unknown.

Again.

XVIII: Reality Cords

Spathi jerked awake on his back, wheezing, his hands and abdomen bloody. Everything ached and stung. Black and yellow spots dotted his sight, seeing only wavering darkness and cold, distant stars over him. He couldn't die here, even if he *was* sick of living. He had to get through this—all the way to the end! His mind seemed to wobble like jelly inside his skull. Lightheaded. Ears ringing. Forehead throbbing.

And something…oozing into his mouth. Something salty.

Living.

"Drink, pet," Staea whispered.

He recognized his wife's flesh on his lips as he suckled on her fresh wound, offered for him. Grudgingly, he drank, feeling the sickness of guilt nauseate him. How he loathed being a blood-eater. How he disdained Constanvol for this curse. Why couldn't he heal altogether? Why couldn't this vicious circle cease?

Circle…. Circle….

In his stupor, he recalled what Zaryen, the Aurixell, told him five years ago.

Something about a circle ending.

He glanced at Zephen, the angel standing over him. Would he know?

Would he even bother to tell him if he did? Or was he doomed to languish in uncertainty, a test subject of heaven, plagued to make decisions based on sheer, blind faith? It was ludicrous, all of it! Nevertheless, he forced himself to drink, try to staunch the lethal scar Constanvol wrought. As he felt her sanguine essence steadily knit his torn skin and muscle tissue back together, he reached up, feeling Staea's face, damp with fresh tears. He had taken her for granted. And he was a fool for ever criticizing or condemning her, for anything.

"You are a good wife," Spathi commended.

"Shh," Staea said. "Just drink."

"You are no succubus," Spathi said. "Let no one tell you any—"

"Just…drink," she said, stifling a sob.

Spathi saw Lena and Jatal kneeling over him, each one gripping his cold hands, with Alehi and Moriah standing behind them in the periphery of Spathi's blurry vision.

"He will be all right," Zephen assured. "Give him time."

"We're runnin' low on time," Shojem's papery voice complained behind him.

"Be patient," Zephen gently rebuked. "All is not lost."

"Not yet," the shaman grumbled. "Best get a move-on, or—"

"Will you shut your damned mouth?" Jatal railed, standing up and glaring in the lich's direction.

"What can ye do to me, young'un?" Shojem boasted dryly. "I am tasked with deathlessness, an invulnerability that is not my own."

"What?" Alehi growled.

"Ye swords will not harm me," Shojem derided. "Not even Sevelurnum."

"That, right there, is your problem!" Staea snapped, pointing at him. "You're so desensitized with your little, short…mummy body and your know-it-all attitude, you've forgotten what pain actually is…and how it affects—!"

"Enough!" Zephen chastised, his halo flaring.

All of them shuddered and backed away from the Arczell's reprimand, then the angel's aura calmed and looked at Spathi again.

"If we are divided, then we will not stand," Zephen admonished in a smooth, steely whisper. "Be still. Be patient."

"I think…I think I can stand up now," Spathi groaned.

"You sure?" Staea said.

He nodded and rose up, feeling his gash. Though mostly mended, it still itched, burning inside, with his bloodstained Sevelurnum cuirass severed; the red fluid had spattered down his legs and onto his greaves. His stomach turned. The armor did not make them invincible. Why wear it if it did not protect them?

Or was it a failing on Spathi's part?

Like Rand?

The ringing in his ears abated as his sight clarified. He sheathed Vrashri, then tore a piece of cloth from his ragged long coat, bandaging Staea's scar on her arm as a makeshift torniquet. It was the least he could do; she bled for him, after all. Literally. He squinted at Zephen as he finished dressing her wound; the Arczell made no effort to remedy her cut flesh. He rolled his eyes. Just a spirit guide, trying to meet the bare minimum. Some guardian angel. But Deven couldn't heal either. Perhaps his power was limited, like Shojem's abilities.

Supposedly….

"Where's Constanvol?" Spathi snarled.

Jalusa looked around, then she shrugged.

"I closed the rift before that bugger or anything else came through," Shojem sneered, patting the two swords behind his back. "Slammed the door right in his face, I did. Ye are welcome."

Staea scoffed.

"Will it hold?" Tawpa asked.

"It better," Moriah said.

Maloxi shook his head. "It won't hold forever."

"No," Spathi agreed, glancing around. "It won't."

They all surveyed the surreal starlit realm, drastically distinguished from Chau Lepha's sanctum. A massive cloister of silver and platinum tiles spanned all around them, windowless hallways and staircases drifting in black nothingness. Stars and swirling galaxies hung overhead, yet they were less vibrant than the ones in Unisylis, with maroon and gray nebulae suspended amongst them. Below the platforms, an unsettling dark void gaped, bottomless, with ghostly stemless cereus flowers floating in midair serving as rows of spectral sconces as if lodged in the blackness itself. The pale blossoms' petals were tinged with blues and yellows, permeating the air with a gentle glow like moonlight. Cathedral archways led up and down various staircases, reminding Spathi of a grand library lost to time. Yet, above was the most daunting sight.

A vast portal yawned on the upper levels resembling a black hole, yet it did not exude the ravenous pull of a dead sun, even though its spherical "event horizon" still consumed some of the light illuminating the enigmatic cloister. The gateway, though grim and austere, was nevertheless sublime and angelic, filling them with reverent awe that quelled their timid, weary souls. From somewhere, Spathi could have sworn he could hear the soft plucking of mystic harp strings in an isochronous tempo. Yet Shadya, as loquacious as she could be at times, mentioned nothing about it…and he was too afraid to ask the teenage Rinyox girl. She seemed too mesmerized by the enchanting atmosphere to answer anyway, her glancing grayed eyes not as aimless as they once appeared. He squinted.

Was her sight returning?

Or could she feel the very realm move across her skin, breathing it all in, feeling its otherworldly air caress the insides of her lungs as she sampled the sweet aroma of the moon flowers around them?

He scowled at the cosmos before him; he was just as oblivious as she was. Then he eyed Irado and Emerid, both of them on their knees, quivering with their heads down to the tiles and their hands pressed against their ears. He furrowed his brow. What the hell was wrong with them?

It was time to know.

Time to know everything.

"You knew about this?" Spathi's voice seethed at Shojem. "All this time?"

"Aye." The shaman nodded. "We are at the safest point for me to tell you everything I know."

"Then you better tell us everything now—all of it," Spathi blared. "Everything you know about anything. Anything!"

"So be it." Shojem took a papery breath. "Before I begin, I would like to tell you that even though I knew these things in advance, I was ordered by the five Aurixells in my visions not to intervene but to do as they instructed me to."

"Sure, you were," Staea hissed.

"Spill it," Spathi demanded through gritted teeth.

Shojem turned back to him. "I will tell you the truth. The Aurixells told me of this place in a series visions. I had to trust them. I still do not understand it. There is nothing random about everything that has transpired, Spathi Ansdari. All of this was predestined to happen. I know because I have seen it in my visions, and I have seen these things come to pass. So much has been revealed to me by the Aurixells, imbued by Astrekiah and Arczellius. So much of this knowledge has been my burden to bear, knowing how inevitable these things are, knowing of these various other tangents."

"Tangents?" Spathi and Staea snapped in unison.

Zephen turned to Shojem. "They must be shown."

"And so, they must." The shaman sighed. "Brace yourselves, for it will not be easy to behold what you about to witness."

His staff tapped on a circular space amidst the square tiles on the silver floor. The circle flared with a holy glyph as the starry realm shifted, orbiting the dark vortex gateway to another section of the cloister: a vast matrix of galleries.

All of them gawked, stupefied by the array.

Black monoliths stood before them, rectangular slabs of polished black marble, twice the size of a human; many were side-by-side, with others stacked each one arranged like dominos. Each one housed a different image, many of which had Spathi and Staea on them.

Shojem banged his staff on the glyph again. Some of the monoliths drifted to them. Spathi was familiar with some of the images: his resurrection in the desert, destroying Id-Zix's corporeal form in Ixod, being imprisoned in Goena, Deven fused to his back in the Anli, even Defeana's revenant dying in Frus Kylea's labyrinth tread. There were others also. Yet these portraits were foreign to him, albeit very similar. But what chilled Spathi down to the core was that the rows of the monoliths had one thing in common.

All of them had the same beginning scene.

All of them had the same ending scene.

Near the end, a picture of Spathi showed entering a sanctuary of massive black monoliths, immediately after entering the "black hole" portal that whirled nearby. Much of his skin was depicted molten and peeling off from the heat of an unspeakable wrath as he marched towards a divine black sword with five flaming eyes down its ornate helix blade.

Spathi's eyes widened at the portrait.

Vren Dotha.

The stern father.

Then he saw himself stumbling, falling through gold embers and into a dark void, only to be "resurrected" again by Malroc…as the "animal man" in Raktogin's desert at sunset. Again. And again. And again. Over, and over, and over, and over, and over…and over…again. Several sets of the monoliths were left blank, not yet filled. Both Spathi and Staea fell on their knees, with the others rendered speechless, their mouths hanging open.

"Circle…." Spathi breathed. "It's…it's a damned…time loop?" He glared up at Zephen. "*That's* what Zaryen was talking about?"

"This is a library of memories," Shojem claimed, "a spiritual archive for every moment in time: what is, what was, and what has yet to come to pass." He struck the glyph with his staff again, causing the monoliths to recede back into their places. "It has been preordained. There is no way around it. Though some of these are blank, they will begin the same…and they will end the same."

"But what about…what I saw?" Spathi asked. "In Chau Lepha's shrine? My vision?"

"That is here, too," the lich said as another monolith floated to him.

Spathi saw the scene of him encountering Arczellius's burning tree.

"Then…what…." Spathi's eye twitched. "W-what did I…?"

Shojem sighed. "I do not know what you saw or why you saw it, Spathi. I truly wish I knew also. All I know is that this cycle will continue." He squinted his mummified eyelids. "This circle, this time loop…it *is* your fate."

"Bullshit!" Spathi growled, rising to his feet.

"What about me?" Staea snarled. "How do *I* fit into all this?"

"There is only one true perception, only one reality," Zephen told them. "No mortal can decide what has been ordained in advance for him, or her for that matter."

"That's not what I asked you!" Staea growled.

"No, but it applies to you and everyone else here," Zephen retorted. "No one chooses their destiny. Our fates are already written, though fate is not as linear as one might think, as you can clearly see from the monoliths here. But though each path has its deviations in life, the beginning is the same…and the ending is the same. This is but a poor reflection of how the holy ones' omniscience operates in eternity, yet it offers only a mere glimpse of how free will coexists with predestination. Mortals discover what has been predestined for them, though they might choose different roads to arrive to their inevitable destiny. They can also choose to rebel against it, albeit futile. But your perception cannot alter it. We are finite. We are limited. As I said, there is only one *true* perception: ultimate reality. The other perceptions are false and countless. They only lead to destruction."

Spathi shook his head, feeling the icy claws of madness rake across his brittle mind. What was left for him? Predestination? He was preordained? His fate, this horrendous infinite loop? Was there no escape from this nightmare? This living hell?

Despair consumed him, throttling his tightening throat, threatening to erode his soul to nothing. He felt so numb. So cold. His skin prickled, stinging. What about his vision, the vision from Arczellius? He knew what he saw. Surely, the holy ones would not taunt him like this! He could no longer take this—any of it!

Then it dawned on him.

Maybe this was another ruse. Maybe they were trying to trick him, or "test" him. Was this really the truth?

He had to see it for himself.

"There has to be another way," he said, lifting his head.

Zephen said nothing, facing Spathi; through the light mask, he could almost feel the angel's eyes scrutinizing him.

"Go ahead! Judge me!" Spathi roared. "Only *I* will determine my destiny!"

"And I mine!" Staea declared.

Shojem shrugged. "We cannot stop either one of you. If you truly think you can out-maneuver what has been predestined for you, that is for you to find out for yourself, it seems."

The shaman tapped his staff on the glyph yet again, then the cosmos shifted around to a different level of the maze, another corridor drifting separate from the matrix. More blank monoliths stood in the glassless arched windows. Each pane had a different design. Each monolith appeared to be tinted a very dark shade of a different color, virtually black. Gray dust was strewn on the floor, somewhat covering up a grid of lines. A thread appeared to end in front of each monolith.

The cords glowed with a bright pale yellow.

Spathi looked to Zephen.

The angel crossed his arms. "If you think that you can escape it, then try it. Choose which window you wish to pass through, and it will take you to the next step of your fate. But I must warn you once again: there is no escaping it, regardless of how distinct each monolith appears. Remember: there is only *one* true perception. The countless others are false. They will lead you astray."

Spathi and Staea turned and looked at the monoliths, then at the lines. So many lines. Both of them spent forever looking, studying, their heads swimming with fright. They looked over at the "black hole" gateway adjacent from the sector, the spiraling animosity of the dark sun pulsing from its globular surface. The other knights scanned and looked and looked with Spathi and Staea, with Shojem and Zephen following them closely.

Spathi grew more frantic, scouring for a window suitable for escape. He looked at the monoliths. At the lines. At everything. His panic worsened as he scanned harder, straining his bloodshot eyes. There had to be a way. A way to get out of this! But he could find nothing. Neither could Staea…or anyone else. He sighed. On the brink of total defeat.

Amnesia….

He would forget again. Start all over again. Why? Why was *he* the only one that was trapped in the loop? Why did he and Staea have to lose their memory? Over, and over, and over…and over again?

Why?

Why, why, why, why, why, why, why?

"And just how do *you* remember these things?" Spathi grumbled at Shojem. "Do you remember?" He pointed at his allies. "Do they know? Will *they* have memory. How do *you* retain your memory?"

"Who said that I did?" Shojem argued. "As I told you, the visions of the Aurixells affect me in various ways, but I have yet to figure out why they—"

"Enough!" Spathi blasted.

He looked up at one of the upper sectors, right next to the "black hole" door. There were more monoliths up there….

Spathi pointed. "Take me up there."

Zephen shook his head. "If I help you, I will only lead you into your fate, the fate I keep telling you is inevitable."

Spathi roared and stomped away. He hung his head. It was hopeless. His life. Existence. Everyone. Everything. All of it.

Just a vicious circle.

He eyed the floor again, at the lines. One of them…deviated from the others. He failed to notice it earlier. Wide-eyed, he followed the wayward cord to the edge of a corner of the platform, with Staea walking to him. This line did not end at a window. He turned and looked at another corner. Then at the other two. No other lines ended there. Shuddering, Spathi turned back at the anomalous line, pointing out to utter blackness.

To uncertainty.

The images in his mind haunted him.

Falling. Down in the void. Into gilded embers.

Clashing…. The memory of clashing steel….

He remembered. But what would it matter to know what it was?

He turned and looked mournfully at Shojem. "If my fate *is* truly sealed…at least tell me what the clashing was."

"The what?" Shojem questioned, raising an eyebrow.

"Clashing?" Zephen asked, genuinely perplexed.

"The clashing!" Spathi railed. "You know, when I was tumbling in the void—before Malroc resurrected me in the desert! Just out of curiosity, I want to know. What was that clashing?"

The lich reared his head back. "Clashing, you say?"

"Stop it!" Spathi's voice grated. "You know what I'm talking about!"

"Stop messing with us!" Staea growled.

Moriah shook her head. "I'm so confused right now."

Alehi groaned. "Look—can someone tell me what this living acid trip is all about?"

Maloxi shrugged at him.

"Your guess is as good as mine, kid," Devral muttered.

Shojem groaned. "Never have I recalled any…clashing in your time archives here. Not sure if…wait, you said 'clashing,' right?"

"Quit toying with me!" Spathi huffed. "I'm going to forget, anyway!"

"I assure you, if I knew, I would have—this is…this is…." Shojem scratched his chin. "What clashing *did* you hear?"

Spathi sighed and turned to the line terminating off into the darkness. Of the four corners of the corridor, it appeared the most dimly-lit. The cord almost seemed to branch off, bleeding onto a shadow just off the ledge.

He walked to the corner, his heart pounding, bludgeoning within his sternum, feeling as if on the verge of bursting out. He clutched his chest. It wasn't just a single pulsation. Did he really have two hearts? Since when? What the hell was inside of him? What was tearing him apart? His face cringed, then it slowly subsided.

He recovered. Breathing heavily.

"Spathi?" Staea rasped, putting her hand on his shoulder. "Pet?"

"I'm fine," he gasped. "I'm…fine…."

She shook her head. "No, you're not."

"Nervous," Spathi claimed. "Nerves."

Staea squinted at the half-truth, then eyed the line on the tiles.

Shojem and Irado approached as the others gathered around them. Spathi looked at them. Then at the line. And at the darkness beyond. Then at the swirling gate, the cosmic anger billowing closer, emitting from deep within the black sun. Then he stared back at the line.

His breathing quickened again. Excitement coursed in his veins, terror skittering through every fiber of his being. What had he discovered? Why did this line stand out to him so much?

Spathi peered down at the thread. He stepped forward to the edge.

And lifted his foot.

He looked up and closed his eyes, trying to calm his quavering breaths. The weight of the unknown bore down on him, all the possibilities gradually nudging him forward. He felt himself lean forward. Tilting. Into the darkness.

Clop!

Spathi shook, his eyes opened. The others gasped behind him. He looked down, his foot standing on an invisible platform. The surface took form, as a stairwell of glass, leading up to the next gallery of windows.

Spathi looked at Shojem and Zephen. "Did I take *this* route yet?"

"No, but," the shaman groaned, shaking his head. "That does not necessarily mean…anything, but…" he flicked his bony hands forward reluctantly. "W-whatever. Proceed. We shall see where it goes."

"Well, don't get *too* excited," Moriah griped.

Spathi almost galloped up the stairs, with the others following quickly behind.

"So, what happens to us if he goes back in time?" Shadya said. "Do we cease to exist or something? Will it hurt?"

"Why can't we go with him?" Alehi questioned. "Are we not 'special' enough for time travel or something?"

"That's what I'd like to know," Devral concurred.

"Can't we go back in time and try to stop Drixilo?" Tawpa inquired.

"Or stop the Second Surfacing?" Jalusa added.

"What if that's just part of the cycle Spathi's trapped in?" Moriah pondered.

"But we would also forget if we went back, anyway," Maloxi said. "Wouldn't we?"

"So, it *wouldn't* do any good to go back with him?" Tyri complained. "Is that what all of y'all are saying?"

"Do the rest of us…lose our memories also?" Lena asked.

"Well, where are all of our memory archives? Are they here as well?" Jatal queried. "Don't we each have one?"

"Just keep moving, all of you!" Shojem grumbled, growing unusually agitated. "Let us just see where this goes. It would not be the first time that Spathi thought he had discovered a new way, then ended up in the exact same fate each time. Best not to get too excited, you hear?"

They all rolled their eyes at him as they arrived at the next level, a more complex portion of the cosmic cloister.

Spathi looked around. "Spread out! Pay attention to the lines! See if any more lead off another ledge."

They did so, manically running around, examining each and every detail on the tiles, every mark, every crack, following each cord with their eyes.

"Spathi, over here!" Staea shouted.

They hurried to her as she pointed an anxious finger at a line that snaked between two arched windows. Spathi looked at Shojem again.

The lich only shrugged. "I told you: I cannot stop you. Go right ahead if you wish."

Spathi gazed back at the thread, then scanned up above them. Overhead, a straight corridor stretched out, sprawling to the right of them. The other side ended directly in front of the swirling black sun portal. Debris and tiles swung around, draining towards the gate's furious burning aura. He closed his eyes. And lifted his foot.

Then leaned forward. Plunging.

Clop!

Again!

The others flinched. He opened his eyes, his heart thrashing in his chest, then he looked at Staea, captivated by a morbid combination of hope and horror. Another glass staircase formed, curving to the right and connecting to the end of the corridor just above them. They all ran up, faster. Faster! Almost stumbling on the steps! His heart raced like hell within him.

Heart? Or two hearts?

At last, they arrived at the final corridor, distinguished from the others, more intricate and twice the width of a freeway.

"Start looking, quickly!" Spathi almost snapped.

They all fanned out.

As they searched, Spathi glanced at Shojem and Zephen. Both of them seemed irked by their persistence to avoid "fate," almost disgusted. He squinted back at them. Let them sulk. He didn't have to listen to their mystical propaganda on their presumptions about what they *thought* would happen. Who were they to say how the holy ones operated? He couldn't fall back in the void. He didn't have time to die, even though he was sick and fed up with everything. He had to see this through. To the end.

Whatever that truly may be.

But it would be on his own terms. Regardless.

"Wait," Shadya said. "Everyone, stop!"

"What?" Spathi snapped.

"Something's coming!" she squeaked. "Something big!"

They all froze, then they looked around.

The air roiled like rippling water, then crackled…then the platform quaked.

"What's happening?" Lena said.

Spathi drew Vrashri, tensing every muscle.

"Shit," Staea cursed, gripping Chauvien tightly.

The others readied their weapons as crimson rifts formed in midair, clinking apart like fracturing crystal. Spathi gut wrenched inside of him, as if someone else was writhing all throughout his body. Throbbing. In his skull. As his palpitations intensified, multiple pulsations radiated throughout the darkness, synchronizing with his own heart.

Pulsing….

Pulsing….

Pulsing….

XIX: False Sons

Spathi bit down on his jaw as the gory rifts flared with infernal hate, the opening shards squirting sizzling blood, maggots, black smoke, and red embers.

"I thought you said you shut the door to this friggin' place!" Alehi barked.

"Yeah, well, once the lock to a door is broken, it's pretty easy for anyone to be bargin' in!" Shojem growled. "Just takes 'em a bit longer to get through if it's barricaded is all."

"Yeah, and you did a really shitty job of it, too!" Alehi retorted. "Thought you might like to know!"

"You're welcome!" Shojem sneered at him, then looked at Spathi. "You and Zephen need to get to Vren Dotha now! We'll try to hold them off!"

"*We*?" Tyri squawked.

"No, I'm not leaving him!" Staea snapped.

"She's right," Spathi agreed, glaring at Shojem. "I can't just leave you in—!"

"Do as I say!" the shaman croaked, pointing to the torrent of platforms around the giant portal. "Go! We'll catch up! Breach the dark sun's surface. Go! Hurry!"

The entire cosmos shook as fractures steadily appeared on the marble tiles.

Zephen put his hand on Spathi's shoulder. "Shojem is right. We must go. We cannot delay any longer!"

"Drixilo will just use us to—!"

"Drixilo has Chau Lepha now—he no longer needs us to open the door!" the angel stressed. "We cannot risk Vren Dotha yielding to him as well! If he gains control of *both* halves of Meledraenin, we are all doomed!"

Another quake raged through the realm as the rifts erupted with white light and scarlet flames. The fractures in the corridor became larger. Then some of the blank monoliths pulsed, glowing with geometric gilded light.

Boom!

The monoliths' faces shattered, with huge serpents weaving out of the busted surfaces and toward the knights. Shuudrites, Udenthen wyrms, the last of Shuudra's brood, thrashed and squealed towards them! Their forms were even more grisly than before, transformed with segmented black scales and crimson sinews of the Ravage.

"Hang on!" Spathi yelled.

The demon wyrms crashed through!

Alehi and Tyri shot their spirit arrows, yet the shafts only sparked against the serpents' corrugated exoskeletons. One of the Shuudrites came right for them! Zephen grunted, then took wing, diving and pushing the two Enoshah knights out of the monster's path, narrowly dodging its grotesque, slobbering jaws. Lena and Jatal sliced and beheaded another Shuudrite, its body writhing in morbid death throes from muscle memory as its neck gushed oily red and black gore marbled with pus and maggots.

Atop a bloodied serpent, Constanvol appeared, riding the beast through one of the gaping portals—then chopped the head off with Qualkytdle and drank some of its sludge-like ichor; his armor's tendrils drained some of the draconic fluid. The baron hopped down, then spat out some of the stringy red muck, revolted by the taste; some of it drooled down his chin.

Spathi's face contorted in disgust. What an animal.

The baron turned to Spathi and aimed Qualkytdle. "You!"

"What took you?" Spathi snarled, bolting towards the Drixile rebel.

Constanvol swung!

Shing! Clang!

Both their flaming weapons ricocheted with a steely clarion ring as they rebounded from each other, landing on their feet with teeth gritted and muscles tensed.

"Damn!" the baron yelled.

He cocked Qualkytdle, then the weapon's mechanisms emitted a spectral whir. The shadowy smoke from the damaged plate mail around him blasted away in dark-blue fire! Spathi summoned his spirit shield and deflected the conflagration. Almost half of Constanvol's cumbersome dark armor fragmented away like shrapnel from him, discarding the defective pieces.

The baron swung Qualkytdle again!

Staea ran towards Constanvol, raising Chauvien!

The rest of the knights skirmished against the remaining Shuudrites, with Maloxi, Moriah cutting down one with their Selebane spears while Devral, Jalusa, and Tawpa defended Shadya, yet even the blind Rinyox girl landed a few crucial blows to the squirming serpents. Alehi and Tyri continued to fire more arrows again. Yet the projectiles only grew thinner, weaker, merely disintegrating on contact.

"Remember what Haandin told you!" Jatal yelled at the two as he slashed at another Shuudrite. "Remember what he said!"

The two Enoshah soldiers looked at each other, then at their Selebane bows. Both took a deep breath…and shut their eyes. They knew what was broken inside themselves. And they knew what had to be done in order to fix it. With another breath, Alehi and Tyri exhaled quavering air, then they raised their silver bows…and fired.

Steadily, the arrows flared. Brighter, brighter than ever!

Riving right through the Udenthen wyrms, leaving gory craters on their serpentine bodies. Some of the dying Shuudrites fell down into the void below, wailing as they plunged back into the darkness.

Spathi continued towards Constanvol.

"We do not have time! Come on!" Zephen commanded.

"But Staea's—!"

"Move!"

Another quake ruptured through the corridor as the cracks gradually grew wider, coming apart. The Arczell grabbed hold of him and flapped towards the end of the long platform. He tossed his two hatchets and sickles around them, the molten weapons orbiting the angel and dicing through more of the Shuudrites.

Then another rift instantly burst before them!

Zephen lost equilibrium as both of them tumbled to the floor, rolling to their feet, then they looked up, beholding the horrible sight. Numerous creatures flocked from the fresh demonic portal.

White deathly Fallens! Atrocious!

Halos of fractured light encompassed their hideous forms. They were headless, yet they wore hoods of their own stretched ashen flesh, leaving a black, gaping hole where a face should be. Behind them, their backbones were serrated with black spines. Each one had two additional humanoid arms in place of legs that bended like insect extremities and soared on four white wings stained with red blood and black tar. They torsos were a cluster of distorted skulls, with their wrinkled flesh melting like bloody wax, with the blue tendons and ligaments exposed in their long, pale limbs, permanently spattered with dark-red filth.

Insatiables. But these were unlike the ones Spathi had seen in Ixod.

These were new.

False angels. False sons.

Dark scions.

The devil's bastard children swooped around them. The demon host had only expended his power, severing shards of himself to take on autonomous existences of their own, just as he had in the past with Zilan, Tylphon-Teno, Gyeno, and Veliath, giving the illusion of creation. Mocking Unzelkoyte.

They were legions upon legions, the most wretched of wretches.

The pieces…of a false god.

Crack! Bang! Bong!

The corridor split—into three sections!

Staea and Constanvol clashed as the rest of the knights fought Drixilo's parodies. As the battle raged on, the middle section of the broken corridor drifted towards the ravenous shadow sun portal, caught in its gravitational pull. The swarming horror angels sailed at Spathi; their numbers were too great. There was no way.

Except for one. And he dreaded doing it again.

Spathi held his breath; he would have to cut his arm again!

In went Vrashri!

Spathi yelled!

The spirit aegis flamed outward.

Like a meteor, he rampaged through the airborne horde, the blue fire engulfing the demons. Zephen cut around back and forth, flanking the Fallens that tried to blitz Spathi from the side. Everything stung, throbbing!

Bleeding.

His arm felt as if it would tear off at any moment, the shield blazing furiously! Spathi shut his eyes, roaring with all his might. This was it. Do or die. Persevere. Just get through. Get through it all.

Boom!

The platform collided with another stray corridor, leading directly into the colossal black portal, jackknifing upward like a drawbridge snapped in half. All of them skidded and barreled down onto the new platform as the previous one splintered away to the portal's strengthening undertow. In the chaos, Spathi began to feel the fierce dry heat of Vren Dotha's pulsating wrath, drawing closer than ever. Spathi squinted down the cloister. The dark sun's consuming surface was almost within reach.

More rifts opened in the air around them, more tainted white and red flames. More of the hellish pale aberrations flapped towards them. Spathi pulled Vrashri out and attacked the Insatiable Fallens. The cleaver slashed through them, each vicious hack splitting demon meat with a sickening, snapping squish. Some of their claws scraped Spathi. He grunted, growing more and more weary, yet he continued to slice at them, his swings becoming sloppier.

"Spathi, go! Hurry!" Zephen yelled.

Spathi turned, running down the corridor as more demonic rifts opened in midair.

Suddenly, another platform slammed into the cloister—the section where Staea and Constanvol battled. Spathi and the others staggered from the collision. More fractures appeared in the tiles, threatening to shatter to nothing.

Staea tumbled, scurrying back to her feet. Constanvol leaped at her. Chauvien clanked against Qualkytdle as the baron pressed the blade down towards her in a grinding deadlock.

Spathi lunged at him. Constanvol swung the stiffened metal tendrils of his left arm at him. Vrashri banged against the shadow steel. Then the baron tensed his face, causing his lightning mark to seethe with unholy light, bringing Spathi and Staea down to their knees. Both of them growled in agony, feeling the bygone puncture wounds sear them where Constanvol had bitten them ages ago.

"Can you feel me?" the baron snarled. "Feel me inside you! *My* influence in you! *I* control you! *I* own you!"

Spathi stood up slowly, fighting the scorching sensation plaguing his face, gripping Vrashri tighter, trying to raise the cleaver up. Staea flexed her muscles, lifting Chauvien as she bit down on her clenched teeth.

Spathi swung. Constanvol raised Qualkytdle, blocking the blade. Then Staea swiped upward with Chauvien, bashing against the baron. Constanvol staggered. Spathi swung again—at Constanvol's neck.

The platform abruptly shifted!

Vrashri came down, barely missing the baron's throat—and slicing right through the jagged mark instead. Constanvol wailed as a bright scar bled from his cheek, expelling dark-blue flames. The markings on his head dimmed, rendered useless.

Constanvol flexed his face. Then again. And again.

Nothing.

The baron roared, his crude affliction spell no more.

Spathi eyed the next segment of the corridor in the periphery of his vision. Staea jammed Chauvien into Constanvol's torso. The baron caught the Selebane spear just in time, the holy silver singeing his hands.

Around them, a few more Fallens encroached, screaming and cackling, then they hesitated, eyeing him like starved wolves. Spathi glanced at them, clutching Vrashri with both hands as they descended upon them like vultures.

Behind them all, the black sun grew even closer.

They all heard something beneath their feet: the creaking of heavy metal peeling away. They looked down. The platform severed, separating Staea from Spathi and Constanvol. The baron turned to Spathi—and jammed Qualkytdle's claw into the platform.

"Enough of this!" Constanvol blared.

"Spathi!" Staea shrieked.

More tiles tore away, propelling the cloister fragment where only Spathi and Constanvol stood to soar further into the portal, away from the mayhem. The platform spun through the dark sphere as both their forms twisted into strands of light, passing through the foreboding gateway's membrane, syphoned through.

Into utter blackness.

Boom!

The ruined platform crashed into a ledge as Spathi and Constanvol rolled onto the stable floor. Both of them lumbered up, with Spathi straining to keep Vrashri's blade up in the air. His left arm continued to bleed from excessive use of his spirit aegis, while the scar in his abdomen felt as if it had reopened, though no blood was trickling from the gut wound. Constanvol also staggered from fatigue, trying to keep his balance.

The distant animosity of Vren Dotha was nowhere to be seen or felt.

Spathi turned to his right. The cloister maze had vanished, as had the pandemonium. A few tiles, rocks, and shards of platinum and silver still revolved quietly around the huge edifice they stood on, the diameter of their orbit unknown. In the distance, a glassy black stratosphere rippled like water, showing their wavering reflections in the darkness far off.

He looked to his left. A massive polished silver door loomed with an array of five hollow eyes, a door similar to the one in Unisylis, matching the same design as on Zephen's torso. Before the threshold, a circular labyrinth sigil was carved into the ancient tiles. He turned back to Constanvol.

He'd have to buy time.

Both of them huffed, glaring at each other.

Constanvol suddenly fell on one knee. "Why would you refuse true power?"

Spathi spit blood on the floor. "Who said…that I had? Made it *this* far…haven't I?"

The baron rolled a biting chuckle, his teeth still stained from the Udenthen wyrm ichor. He looked up at Spathi. "Fate is such an amusing thing…isn't it?"

"Maybe," Spathi replied, cringing inside at the phrase, yet he did his best not to let Constanvol know of his unease. He gulped and lowered Vrashri, finally falling on his knee. "It's as amusing…as it is cruel."

"Agreed," Constanvol sputtered. "To think…that the likes of you…would one day match me…in combat. If I hadn't known any better…I would have called you 'Brother.'"

"Keep dreaming…Constanvol."

Constanvol hung his head, oozing black fluid from his cuts and scrapes as the radiation in Qualkytdle dimmed, his breathing growing hoarser. Spathi peered at the baron, then at the dark membrane from whence they had come.

Where was Zephen? What was taking the angel so long?

"I know why…you suffer the circle…Spathi."

Spathi squinted at him.

"My mother told me."

"Oh, spare me," Spathi scoffed. "You overheard us…talking in the cloister earlier. You're just wasting your time."

"Am I?" Constanvol wheezed. "I've *been* knowing…and your suspicions…have been growing also…it seems." He glanced at the rippling darkness. "Ever wondered…how that old man…came by the swords…that pierced Astrekiah…and why he has…two blood-eaters…for slaves?"

"Don't," Spathi hissed, his eyes widening. "Don't you dare even—"

"Those prayers…on the swords," Constanvol coughed. "Seem familiar…to you?"

Sweat dripped from Spathi's face as he recalled the study within the Mionia five years earlier. He could almost see the apocalypse clock prison and the titanic creature trapped within…and the filigree around the base. The image of a gap shaped like an "X" appeared in his mind, engraved with the ancient prayers.

An "X." Like a thresacrix.

Where the swords pierced Astrekiah's sides on the claymore.

"He's deceiving you, Spathi," Constanvol claimed. "I can help you stop this…vicious circle…once and for all. That is…if you care…."

Spathi stared at the baron. The demon seemed strangely desperate, in genuine despair. He panted heavily, his lungs burning, head spinning. Wounds throbbing. The war had taken its toll on both of them. As he pondered these things, Spathi looked to his right. A golden-orange glow steadily appeared on the portal's surface.

Spathi raised an eyebrow. There was only one of two things it could possibly be.

"That's a bold proposition," Spathi quipped, "but I'd expect about as much…from the likes of you." He looked back at the baron and shook his head. "You know I can't trust you."

Constanvol glared up at him. "Then why even bother…with all this empty banter?"

Spathi clenched his teeth. "Because I like seeing you…on your knees…begging for an out…like the scared little shit you are."

The glow burned brighter, crackling, forming a molten rift.

"I'll take my chances," Spathi taunted, "and you'll take yours."

The baron tensed. "And so we will."

"Goodbye…Constanvol…."

Boom!

Out blasted Zephen! With a flaming hatchet spiraled right towards Constanvol. The baron lifted Qualkytdle to deflect, yet the ax struck with the force of a lightning bolt—

detonating in his face!

Constanvol soared away from the impact as the explosion sent Spathi back into the five-eyed door, grunting in angst. The baron fell down into the abyss, screaming and crashing against the flying debris, his yell echoing away. Then all grew quiet, save for the deep, hollow draft generated from the whirling portal.

Zephen swooped to Spathi.

"Are you all right?" the Arczell asked. "I did not mean to—"

"Yeah, yeah—s…sure—yeah," Spathi wheezed. "Lemme just…ohhh…."

The angel lifted him to his feet. "We do not have too much further to go. I will carry you if I must."

"I can…I can manage, I think," Spathi croaked, stumbling around. He gazed at the aqueous darkness below. "Is he…?"

"I doubt it," Zephen replied. "I still sense him…somehow." He looked back at the wavy black surface. "More Drixiles are coming. We cannot delay any longer. Come on!"

Spathi dizzily eyed the dark membrane, rippling and pulsing in several places.

Pulsing….

Pulsing….

Pulsing….

"Let us go!" the angel said. "It is just a bit further!"

Both of them walked to the labyrinth sigil as part of the pathway behind them crumbled, spinning away to the portal's celestial wake. The circle beneath them blazed with white flames, then Spathi felt the dry heat around him once again, even more than before. The eyes on Zephen's chest illuminated with orange fire, with the door slowly matching the array, roaring like distorted magma.

Suddenly, they felt their bodies judder and warp into strands, being syphoned through the sublime gateway as a shrill ringing tore into Spathi's ears. Everything scorched him, unforgiving heat rolling across him!

Then all grew silent. And numb.

Spiraling down…into bleak nothingness.

A void. Of embers.

XX: Dour Sanctum

Spathi opened his eyes, lying on his sore back, his sight slowly returning. The ringing in his ears only lessened, not entirely subsiding. He was so feeble from combat, so woozy…and nauseated, ready to give in. It was too much. All too much. His legs felt like gelatin, with the rest of his body quivering beneath his skin. As his vision recovered, he saw Zephen kneeling beside him, the angel's aura permeating the surrounding glacial air with some warmth. Spathi glanced down at Vrashri resting on the ancient floor beside his armored hip. The Sevelurnum exoskeleton he wore was stained with red, his soiled long coat frayed virtually to nothing.

Was he dead yet?

He looked back up at Zephen as he shivered from the lack of blood. His swollen eyes stung with sweat, blood, and fatigue. His lips were chapped, his throat dry with his hair matted against his thinning, sweaty face.

The weariness had his mind delusional.

His forehead throbbed, feeling as if a little man was trying to beat his way out of it, one bludgeon at a time. Was he hallucinating? Everything looked so beautiful. And horrible. His stomach, did he still have one? What ached in his abdomen? He was too afraid to open his mouth, paranoid of what might fly in.

Or what might come out.

Something ran out of the corner of his lips, beads of something warm, growing colder as it dribbled down his chin and neck. The sensation faded into the numb parts of his flesh.

"You…." he slurred.

"Stay with me, Spathi," Zephen said. "You must persevere."

Spathi swallowed. Whatever was trickling from his mouth, it was thick and salty…and it wasn't phlegm. Spathi gurgled, trying to inhale.

"You will not die here," Zephen said.

Spathi gagged. His head flung down as more crimson drool strung down from his jaw. He bared his gritty teeth. It hurt to even breathe! He had enough of it. All of it. He was ready for it. Ready for the end. Ready to die. He didn't want to die. But there was nothing left. Everything was hopeless.

Zephen lifted up Spathi's chin.

"I…can't…" Spathi coughed.

"Yes, you can," Zephen said. "I know you can."

"Everything…hurts…."

"It is just a little further. We are almost there."

"I'm scared!" Spathi finally blurted.

The angel grew silent.

"I'm…scared of everything! Scared of what's inside of me! Scared of Arczellius!

What's in my head? Tell me! What happens when I...? Why...every...thing?"

Spathi retched and hacked, wheezing in and out.

"I don't want to die.... I...don't...want...."

Spathi shuddered in the Arczell's arms, his bones aching with each gag and cough, each one echoing down the perpendicular twists and turns of the hallway. He flopped his head back down, breathing heavily as the fangs of despondency sank into his soul.

Zephen looked down the corridor, then turned back to him. "Look at me."

Spathi attempted to lift his head, but he was too weak.

The angel lifted his bloody chin again. "I do not condemn you for the way you feel."

Spathi only stared at him blankly.

"You are mortal," he said. "I do not condemn you. I do not expect you to be perfect, Spathi Ansdari."

"I'm just a blood-eater," Spathi grunted. "I'm a...monster...I—"

"Forget the blood-eater," Zephen interjected. "The blood-eater is behind you. You are not of the demons. You have changed...and you will change even more before the last hour. You will change in ways that no mortal could ever fathom or imagine. But you must be tested with fire."

Spathi cringed.

"Listen to me," he said. "The fire will sting, but it is not to punish you. This fiery trial will transform you, Spathi Ansdari. You will withstand it. From the test of fire, you will come out as gold."

Spathi looked at him.

"You will *not* die here."

"Help...me...." Spathi's voice cracked.

He trembled and swallowed more of his blood. With his arms, Zephen lifted Spathi's body up and placed him on his feet. Spathi managed to sheath Vrashri and looked down. He hadn't noticed how many cuts and gashes he had all throughout his body. His armor was cracked and bashed.

The battle had been so fierce.

War was fierce.

He shouldn't be alive, though. He looked back down, at all the blood he lost, having pooled all over the floor. He felt as if something other than Zephen carried him, something...unseen. It wasn't him that was standing. Something supported him, within him.

Instilling him...to go on.

He glanced back at Zephen. "Am I dead?"

The angel shook his head. "Neither one of us are dead. This is not the afterlife. Raktogin was never a purgatory. It was never a dream, nor was it ever a simulation." He stepped forward and put his hand on his shoulder, "You and I are alive."

Spathi furrowed his brow. Zephen no longer seemed like himself.

The angel seemed more profound. More absolute.

They both turned down the corridor. Spathi gasped, his eyes widening as he recognized the hall: an illuminated version of the one five years when he first encountered

Zaryen, right before he entered the Mionia.

Spathi slowly felt his strength returning to him, yet his wounds did not heal. How was it even possible? It made no sense! What was logic? What did he ever know about anything?

His mind went into neutral as he and Zephen stumbled down the hall. He recalled what Arczellius had said to him. He remembered the pebble, the one he failed to pick up.

The miraculous.

All he had to do was ask. And he would not.

So many times, it all seemed ridiculous to him, like a fairytale. Shame crawled through his nerves, trying to come back to life while nausea stung against the walls of his sore stomach. So stubborn he had been. How many times had he doubted? Faith. The only way. The true path. The golden cord. That which seemed nonsensical to so many. Like Rediq. Rand. Even Aipha had balked at it.

There were so many that deemed it absurd, even him. So many hardened hearts. So many that have perished…and so many others will die, with the last day approaching. And he couldn't stop it. He cringed, unable to bear it.

They turned right. Then left.

The animosity of Vren Dotha, where was it?

They turned as the corridor became more like a cathedral cloister. Glassless arched windows gaped out at the realm outside of the hall. Countless networks of geometric blue lines hung in the black void beyond the opulent panes, connected by floating spheres of burning sapphire bobbing around in all directions like wild clock pendulums.

Constellations?

He didn't bother to stop. Neither did Zephen. He was so sick of this shit. The angel had better be right; it better not be too much further. Gradually, Spathi felt more like he could walk. Limp. Stagger. Then he stumbled into a wall.

Zephen caught him. "I've got you. You will not fall."

Spathi looked at him again. This was not Zephen.

The Arczell was possessed.

By what?

They both turned their gaze to the bending corridors. The linear coil of hallways bended and spiraled in ways that were deemed physically impossible. The floor twisted up in certain places, becoming the ceiling while the stone appeared to breathe, the broken tiles pulsating.

"Just a little further," Zephen said.

He continued to usher Spathi as both of them walked, shuffling on the old tiled floor, the hall contorting ahead. The whir of fluctuating energy steadily grew louder. Echoes stuttered around them.

They turned. Then turned again.

Right. Left. Down.

Up.

Oblique.

Onto a sideways stairwell.

Up.

Diagonal.

Down. Right.

Diagonal again.

The path seemed less and less like a hall and more like bowels of marble and light, with colonnades like warped ribs and vertebrae the further they went. Spathi had no idea how long they walked or how far. The trek, as pained as he was, became strangely meditative. Among the gridlock of emotions and the thrash of his thoughts, one burning question pestered him.

Could he truly break the circle?

He looked over at Zephen. The angel wouldn't tell him. Perhaps he didn't know. Whatever had hold of the Arczell would most likely keep his mouth shut, anyway. Spathi's path seemed so…incomplete. There was more to life, wasn't there? Other than this vicious circle that was his existence? Something outside of this? Anything? There was still so much that needed explaining, and to embrace that accursed amnesia again only to rediscover his horrible errant past was simply too much.

The amnesia, how many times had he gone through it? What was the purpose of the circle? He was just a meaningless wheel spinning around in creation with no reason. No purpose.

Or was there?

Maybe this endless cycle maintained stability in existence. Maybe his unspeakable pain kept Drixilo from overtaking the heavens. But would it reset the timeline? Or would it merely generate another? And that vision in the fires of Arczellius, was it real? Why be shown that if he was to never accomplish it? Was it nothing more than a malicious ruse just to get him to continue persisting in this circle?

And what about Staea? Why was she shown it also? She was no succubus. And she was most certainly not of these damned…Mulya-Sheloth whores, or whatever they were. How he despised Constanvol and his putrid lies. But he knew better than to assume that the baron was dead, no doubt he would probably show up again…in the circle. He would find him in the Drixilac temple. Again. Atop the terrestrial Udenthen. Again. Spathi's memory would be gone, as would Staea's. Again. She would be inside one of Gyeno's shadow coffins. Again.

Again. And again. And again.

It was hopeless.

And why did Malroc have Spathi go after Constanvol in the first place? Why not just kill the baron himself?

But how could evil be against evil?

Perhaps it was all a massive, ongoing theatrical performance, dark factions seemingly vying for individual control over the world, when in reality, they were all in on it. All of them had been players on a stage, masquerading around as idols. Politicians. Celebrities. Sensations. False prophets. Heretics. Pied pipers. Cabals. Oligarchies. Corporations.

Puppets. Corruption. All designed to benefit from miseries, creating more agonies. Propaganda. Mockeries. Trends. Self-styled "free-thinkers." Hecklers. Users. And the used. Thinking their bodies were their own.

Imbeciles. By choice.

Another endless circle. Seemingly endless.

The Drixiles had only made the humans *believe* that they had finally gained the upper hand at the Penterium Hinge…only to unleash the Ravage upon them.

Drixilo had worked his marionettes well throughout the centuries.

And no one would believe. Too ignorant.

Too infected. Too sick.

Enslaved.

Virtually incurable.

The worst of the horrors was that, deep down inside, they knew all along what was best. And they simply would not do it. The judgment came on them. The Second Surfacing came just as the Ancient Text said. And those like Rediq Tashar still wish to believe that these were "aliens" or "mutants." There the evil was—in plain sight! And they chose to indulge in the lies of the demons in the world, knowing that they were lies.

They didn't care.

Most of them still did not.

And rather than turning, they only hardened their hearts all the more.

Perhaps the humans had the Ravage all along. Perhaps Drixilo's entrance into the material plane only accelerated their bottomless hunger, the urge that which could not be sufficed. Not with needless things. Not with blood. Or flesh. Not with ashes. What they needed, they would have none of it. By choice. And this was how it was all ordained? Ordained in advance? Predestination? These things were actually meant to happen?

Why?

Why would Unzelkoyte allow this? And Arczellius? Astrekiah?

Why?

Why the pain? Hasn't humanity suffered enough for its mistakes?

The questions only perturbed Spathi's mind, heart, and soul more and more as all other thoughts seemed to stop, fading away like smoke. Would any good be brought out of any of this? If only he could make it…to the very end. If only understanding it would bring him the solace he craved.

They were almost there. Just a little further. He had to get there. He had to find a way out of this unforgiving circle—this repetitive hell! But there was something else here, something around them. He could feel it. Or maybe the constant shifting of gravity was getting to him.

Hopefully….

They neared another bend.

"The door to the sanctuary is around this curve," Zephen claimed.

"It…better be," Spathi huffed.

He was so feeble. So sore.

So done with this.

Throb-throb. Throb-throb.

He felt…two throbs inside him again, something like two hearts, synchronizing with each other. When would these deranged episodes cease?

The corridor widened before them as they both beheld a surreal vista, beautiful yet ominous. A massive expanse sprawled before them like a polis. Another city paralleled it, hanging upside-down like a ceiling, all constructed like a matrix of titanic pyramidal monoliths of polished black marble, dusty, worn, and scraped, forgotten by time.

Spathi peered up. The corridor ended and became a bridge of stairs that lead up to the higher polis's streets, made of platinum and silver tiles. As they traversed the bridge's halfway point, the center of gravity shifted for the last time.

Upside-down became right-side-up. Right-side-up became upside-down.

No more halls. No more bends.

The solemn twin cities sprawled for eternity in all directions, leaving a horizontal sliver of sky between them, aglow with the vibrant colors of a sunset behind them; the heavens displayed ultraviolet shades of blue, purple, pink, orange, and red, all glaring against frenetic wisps of clouds raging around as if trapped in a rapid timelapse. White and orange lightning flashed silently amidst the hasty thunderheads.

. Before them, a colossal pyramid-like temple of a textured abstract design loomed, as if constructed of silver quadrilaterals of bismuth crystals, with a vast night sky in the background; white stars twinkled in faint gray nebulae in the distance. The temple's rectangular door was made of living quicksilver reaching about a mile high, with a width of what seemed like a quarter of a mile. Five eye sockets hung motionless amongst the reflective mercury door, mimicking the ones embedded in Zephen's torso. The rims of the door's eyes were rusty and primordial…with icicles draping from each hole. At the threshold of the door, another labyrinth seal showed.

Spathi cringed. From pain.

From anticipation.

Zephen pointed at the door. "Come. We can delay no longer."

Spathi wanted to complain, wanting to rail and rave, but he knew it was to no avail. The angel would not listen. No one would listen. He felt beside himself. Would Arczellius even care? Astrekiah? Was Unzelkoyte even there? Anywhere? He was so alone. So tired. So ready to give in. So sick of the cycle, the damned endless circle, this accursed, never-ending torment.

There had to be an end.

He had to find the end!

With what strength remained, Spathi plodded forward.

He was too broken to argue, flat-out shattered. Silently coming apart. But they walked, nevertheless, walking towards Spathi's doom.

For the greater good? Who knew anymore? He was so sick of trying to decipher things, so tired of "logic" and "understanding" when anything could happen. Everything blindsided him Torturing him. Beating him down. Keeping him down.

Always down.

Hope was such a verbose and insolent thing.

Agony seemed to be the only thing real.

So real!

Still, they treaded. Still Spathi's mind spun aimlessly in his skull, his neglected questions never having an answer, at least not any that were suitable. He could feel it slowly killing him, like an icy knife steadily turning inside his soul.

They stood several yards away from the door. The sound of intense energy fluctuated louder just beyond its rippling surface. The energy sounded as if…breathing. A thriving fire. A ravenous animosity.

Vren Dotha awaited them.

The stern father. The annihilator. The rebuker. The punisher.

Judgment. Destruction.

Wrath.

And both of them were treading to the very threshold of such a thing. There seemed to be no way around it. He *would* reenter the cycle again. The amnesia. Malroc. The hatred of humans. Drixiles. Staea. Constanvol. Id-Zix. Feshta. Van De Yoth.

All of it.

Endless. Redundant.

His racing thoughts were their own cycle. Obsessive. Compulsive. But it wasn't him that would not let go. Spathi wanted to let go. So dearly, he wished to just rest, to be done with this journey.

But *it* would not let go of *him*.

All because he was "predestined." Predestined to suffer. Pain, ordained in advance for him…and he no longer had the strength to argue against it. Too weak to shake his fist. Too weary to rebel. Do it. Just end this. How he longed to just move on, to rest!

Just rest. Just rest.

Rest…. Rest….

Just…rest….

They neared the labyrinth sigil, only several yards away from the door. Yet something felt thick around them, like an invisible smoke. A greasy smoke, growing stronger, molesting the air. Circling them. Hunting them.

Who gave a flying shit at this point?

Spathi was as ready as ever. Ready.

Trying to occupy his mind. Trying not to focus on the fear, the dread.

Both of them halted, then Spathi staggered. Zephen caught him again as the angel seemed to revert to his former self, no longer possessed by the peculiar presence.

Zephen pointed to the seal. "Just right there, Spathi, you see? Just a little bit further, it is just—"

"It's…too much, Zephen," Spathi groaned. "It's…too much for me…to handle…. I'm sorry…I'm so…I'm so…broken…I just…."

He gagged again.

Zephen sighed. Slowly, he led Spathi to the circle, almost carrying him there. Just a little further. Just a few more steps. Then the Arczell placed him in the circle. Zephen got on his knees and faced the door. He raised his hands, palms facing the five seals.

"The eye sockets are frozen," the angel said. "This will take a little bit longer than at Unisylis, but not too long. Just hang in there for a few minutes longer."

Spathi wheezed for air, his wounds burning, itching. Bleeding.

Excruciating!

Throbbing. Weary.

Dying….

He couldn't die, though. Not here. Not the circle. Not all over again.

He had to persevere. He had to escape…somehow.

There had to be a different fate, another destiny he could achieve.

Spathi glanced down at the stretch of tiled road they had trekked. From the bridge they had emerged from, lights came, manifesting like falling stars, speeding down the inverting staircase.

Red and white flickers.

And one larger one.

Bristling with vengeful dark-blue fire.

Constanvol.

The wretched demon baron had officially bested the obstinance of cockroaches, and far exceeded their abysmal pestilence.

Zephen meditated, undaunted by the ensuing pandemonium. The five eyes across his chest ignited with a faint orange light…then the eyes on the door reacted, crackling and spraying embers. The ice on the door's sockets shook. Spathi gazed at them as steam plumed from the top-left slit.

Straining, he pulled Vrashri from his back, trying to rise to his knees.

Oh, the agony! Prickling nerves—stinging!

He emitted a long, sharp, gravelly grunt as he yanked the cleaver from under him, unsheathing it. He pointed the weapon forward at the incoming enemies with both arms. Then the sword's edge tilted, and landed on the stone with a loud ring.

There Spathi lay, helpless, a puppet to circumstance once again. Not in control of anything. How he loathed it! Here they were, at the gate, wishing it were the end of all his pain, the end of suffering. But the torment of the cycle would just restart again, waiting to send him back into the void. The amnesia would take hold of him again…in this infinite circle. But not without one last fight, regardless of how weak he was.

No matter how inferior, flawed, or worn down Spathi was, he had to fight.

Fight. To fight everything.

Predestined. To fight.

This was the way for him. The only way.

The ice clacked behind him.

Spathi turned again. Rime and rust clattered down as steam became smoke in the eye socket. The corrosion around the slot crumbled away, exposing a silvery rim. He glanced at Zephen. The corresponding seal on his torso burned brighter than the others, orange turning to blue and gold flames. He turned back to the invading Drixiles rocketing towards him…and he noticed something else.

The glow…of Selebanes.

His allies!

Staea chased after Constanvol down the stairs, slicing away the blitzing Fallens with Chauvien. Shojem, Irado, and Emerid waylaid into more of the Insatiable fiends. Tyri and Alehi fired from above, their arrows bright, while Maloxi, Jalusa, Tawpa, and Shadya landed blows against the demons. Lena, Jatal, and Moriah all dive-bombed to the streets and artfully diced away through the throng of Drixilo's lesser scions. But the sight of his comrades brought little comfort to Spathi.

He needed to help them. But he couldn't. He was too weak. Pathetic. Spathi struggled to rise to his feet. He had to help them. Then he hesitated and looked back at the door, then down at the labyrinth seal. The door couldn't open without him and Zephen directly inside it.

Why?

What was it with…?

He sighed. He knew why. But part of him doubted. He tried to believe, causing Vrashri's light to fluctuate. But everything had taken its toll on him. He would just have to be patient, a feat that was virtually impossible for him. Nevertheless, he had to protect Zephen as well while the Arczell concentrated.

He was so sick of waiting.

Constanvol came straight for him, yelling something too inaudible for Spathi to hear from the door's seething eyes coming to life. Staea finally caught up to him, jabbing at him. The baron dodged, then whipped around and slashed. Staea evaded and swiped at him again. Constanvol seemed disinterested in her and was far more eager to hurry in Spathi's direction while Staea made every effort to kill the rebel demon. How Spathi wished he was there with her, fighting alongside his wife, the same way they had years ago in Ancient Raktogin.

Behind Spathi, something burst, blazing with energy.

He turned. The top-left eye was activated!

He eyed Zephen; the angel's meditation was sober, disciplined, and focused as he rasped in a supernatural language. Steadily, the bottom-left eye pulsed with orange light as ice on the next slit on the door crashed away.

Around him, Spathi felt that mysterious, uncomfortable sensation again.

Invisible, obscure. Oily. Dirty.

Cold.

The feeling became more horrible, making his nerve endings burn worse. Then he heard something like whispers in his head, speaking in unearthly tongues. Feminine voices. The strange presence around Spathi seemed to twist at the whir of the syllables as if… revolted by the words. The whispers grew more hostile at the invisible aura around him, yet Zephen paid no mind. Maybe it wasn't really there, whatever it was. Maybe the pain was causing Spathi to hallucinate. But that was a brash assumption at this point.

The pain lessened, yet his forehead throbbed more and more.

Spathi turned. The bottom-left eye of the door ignited with blue and gold flames, flashing with molten light.

Constanvol's voice drew closer; the baron was halfway to them. Spathi looked and clutched Vrashri as tight as he could, bracing himself for the Drixile bastard's arrival. Black blood still dripped from his wounds with Staea in hot pursuit, close behind him.

"You'll kill us all!" Constanvol blasted from afar. "You hear me? You're mad—you'll be the end of us! The end of everything!"

Staea knocked him down. She, too, was bloody, heaving hoarse breaths as she jammed Chauvien down at Constanvol. The baron rolled away and back onto his feet, then swiped, cutting her leg.

She cried and fell.

"Staea!" Spathi coughed.

"Be still, Spathi," Zephen calmly ordered.

Constanvol stood up and limped to her. He raised the claw, preparing to cleave her in half. Spathi had to help her. Yet he was too far away.

Clang!

Constanvol slammed Qualkytdle down, then Staea caught and held the blade with Chauvien. The weapon bared down on her as she used every ounce of her strength in the vicious stalemate.

"I...am so sick...of you!" the baron growled. "You—*ahh!*"

She kicked him in the crotch, then banged Qualkytdle away and rose to her feet.

"You talk *way* too much!" she snarled.

A blue arrow whizzed and hit Constanvol in the leg. He yelled and staggered, then Staea plunged Chauvien through his chest! The baron gagged, then bashed her away to the floor, panting and bleeding, staggering away. Spathi watched in horror as Staea's body rolled to the street. Constanvol stumbled and shambled onto one of the pyramids, still favoring his chest wound, watching more Fallens invade the empty city from above. Qualkytdle's glow was steadily fading.

Could the baron finally be dying?

"Staea!" Spathi blared.

"Hold still," Zephen rebuked.

Spathi glared at the angel, then down at the labyrinth seal. It simply wasn't in his blood to watch and wait for his family to die. Shame overwhelmed him as the other knights slew the nearby Fallen horrors, fleeing the incoming second wave, then rushed and attended to Staea. He should be there with her, not trying to be a skeleton key for Zephen. He felt like a coward! Surely, the angel didn't need him to open the temple.

Another flare blasted behind Spathi. He looked back at the door. The bottom-right seal burst aflame; only two more eyes to open. He turned back to Staea. Why couldn't he help her? Why did he have to stay in the circle?

Why couldn't he heal?

Everything throbbed. Everything seemed to bleed.

Jatal sheathed his weapon and scooped up Staea in his arms, then they jogged to Spathi and Zephen. Shojem hopped back onto Irado as the two ghouls hobbled alongside the others. As they came, Spathi looked back up where Constanvol had stood, yet he had vanished. Spathi's face tightened. That spineless weasel!

The feeling around Spathi slithered again.

Smoky. Unseen.

Almost ragged.

The ringing in his ears rose up again, accompanied by the whispers again, sounding disgusted. Taunting him. Around him, the sensation writhed as if uncomfortable, almost like something tensing around him.

Was it anything?

His allies finally arrived. Then the two cities' monolith matrices shifted, their surfaces becoming more textured and polygonal like bismuth crystals, each unhinging into four sections, responding to Zephen's energy.

Tyri looked behind them. "What's happening?"

"You must keep quiet!" Shojem rasped. "Zephen needs to concentrate. The structures are changing because the door is about to open. This is a conduit."

"For what?" Maloxi asked.

Shojem looked at an elevated ledge on the temple to the left of the door about one story high. He pointed at a staircase barred by a black lattice leading up to the platform. "We should be safe there when the door opens. The animosity of Vren Dotha will obliterate anything in its path."

"I thought you've never been here before," Alehi said.

"Do ye not pay any attention?" the lich rasped. "The visions showed me, lad!"

"Must've been one hell of a 'vision,'" Spathi sneered.

Shojem scowled at him.

Jatal laid Staea down. She groaned as Spathi clasped her hand.

"I'm sorry," Spathi whispered.

"For what?" she moaned.

"I don't know what to do for her," Jatal said, looking to Lena. "Have we no medicine or bandages?"

Lena shook her head, examining Staea's gory leg wound. "Even if we did, it wouldn't heal *this*."

Staea whined. Spathi squeezed her hand tightly, her skin growing colder. Both of them gazed at each other.

"Staea," Spathi wheezed.

Her face winced at the pain, tears flowing from her eyes.

Another crackle resounded!

The others looked up. The fourth eye flared and whirred with celestial fire.

"It's about to open," Lena said.

Shojem jumped down and held one of the swords to Staea's leg wound. "Hold still."

Fire instantly flickered around the blade as he pressed the scorching blades to her flesh. She yelped and writhed, feeling the light sting her severed flesh.

"What are you doing?" Jatal snapped.

"Cauterizing the wound," Shojem retorted.

The shaman raised the blades away as Staea continued to twist with teeth gritted. Spathi squeezed her hand while she almost crushed his. Then she finally calmed, with the wound on her thigh showing a charred scab.

Shojem pointed to the ledge again. "Go, head over there! The animosity is coming! When the last eye opens, the fire comes! Nothing can survive it."

Lena reached for Spathi.

"No!" The lich chastised her. "Let Zephen take him! Go! Go now! Hurry!"

The Vauphec woman glared at him and reluctantly ushered the others to the stairs. Jatal picked up Staea again as she released Spathi's hand. Spathi watched them take her away, with her longing eyes staring back at him. They rushed up the steps. Shojem hopped onto Irado's shoulders again while the two ghouls shimmied up the stairs after them. The last of the ice exploded. Spathi looked and eyed a silhouette shambling from the roof of one of the pyramids towards them.

Constanvol.

The demon refused to die!

How Spathi yearned to cut the baron's damned head off! If only he had the energy to do so, to climb up there and finish him.

The baron jumped down and headed straight for him, with Qualkytdle's blade drawn outward. Behind him, more of Drixilo's portals of red flames opened. These rifts were different, far worse, as another wave of Insatiable raged out from the bloodied porcelain doorways, hordes of them tearing from the rotted wombs of cosmic sinews, white shards, and geometric veins.

The top eye flared behind them. Then the ground quaked. Spathi glanced and saw the quicksilver of the door solidify and fracture like glass, with the fiercest orange light puncturing through the thin cracks.

"It is done," Zephen breathed with fatigue. "We must join the others."

"Leave me…here," Spathi said.

The angel shook his head. "No! The animosity will—"

"Let me be!" Spathi coughed.

He staggered up as something unseen helped him upward. The shards fell. Zephen turned and spotted Constanvol nearing them, then he readied his two hatchets, fanning out all four of his wings.

"Go…to the others…now," Spathi said.

"Spathi!"

The ire fulminated forth above them, screaming with a celestial lividity like no other. Righteous indignation, in raw form. Unquenchable destruction! Constanvol stopped, then he barreled away as the furious beams multiplied from the crumbling surface. The baron darted to the opposite ledge's stairs, taking cover behind another lattice. Zephen sighed, then flapped to the steps with his allies.

"Spathi...?" Staea called. "Spathi!"

"Get your ass up here!" Alehi screamed.

Spathi stood up, mustering what strength he had left. He raised Vrashri and his aegis arm, the sword's point aiming for the bloody gash between his exposed radius and ulna bones.

"I love you, Staea," he whispered. "Thedo, wherever you are...I love you, too. I love you both...so much...."

"Spathi, come up here—now!" Staea shrieked.

"What are you doing?" Jatal snarled.

"You're crazy!" Devral shouted.

The energy crashed through, inches away from him. Ready to burst open full throttle at any moment.

"If you're really up there," he grumbled upward through clenched teeth, "then do what you will. All I ask is that you remember your promise."

He jammed Vrashri through the gash.

"Spathi!" Staea screeched, collapsing to her knees.

The spirit aegis emerged, pulsing brighter than ever!

Clash!

Staea yelled for him, shaking the bars of the lattice as the rest of them watched in awe; even Constanvol gawked in shock as the animosity ripped through.

Washing over Spathi!

The fire reached the Fallen Insatiables, incinerating them to molten dust.

Yet Spathi was still standing. Then he took a step forward through the divine wrath, wreaking unspeakable anguish upon him, slowly peeling away his armor. The shield flared wildly, the blue flames flapping around like a bonfire in a windstorm, with his "third eye" glinting from his forehead.

He took another step forward. Then another.

Staea ululated at the top of her lungs as the others tried to keep her from running after him, their voices drowned out by the roaring animosity. But they all sat there, utterly stupefied by Spathi's resilience.

How was he not dead?

The fury intensified, cleaving the sides of the nearby pyramids to nothing. Within the stream, all Spathi heard was the ringing in his singeing ears, his grunts of misery, noiseless. The animosity consumed even sound—even his shadow!

Spathi took another step forward, then another, gradually entering the dour sanctum. A plate of his Sevelurnum peeled away. Then another. The edge of Vrashri steadily eroded as his hair burned away. Flesh struggled to cling to bone. Piece by piece, little by little, Spathi felt himself crumble away.

Yet he still walked. Miraculously. Tested by Vren Dotha's rage.

Each thought, each breath seemed to weigh him down. All became anguish. Here was the end. The last of him. There would be no more cycles. No more dark resurrections. No more pain. No more life.

No more Spathi.

Step. By step.

His left hand ripped away!

He yelled mutely, his blood blazing away. Vrashri's frame smelted to his severed bone. The spectral aegis threatened to go out at any moment, its remaining flame becoming white. He could see the silvery glow from his forehead, protecting him.

Step…by step.

Though the wrath tried to blow him away, something still pushed him forward, something…stronger than him. Stronger than Vren Dotha.

Something. Pushed. Him. Forward.

All this time, something had been pushing him forward, ever since the beginning. Every day. It was not Spathi that got himself up. It wasn't anything mortal. It was something no one could see, something beyond understanding. None could fathom it. None could imagine it. But it was real, far more real than the material world.

Real. So real.

Painful. Intense.

True. Thriving.

He needed it. All would need it.

To survive. To live.

To exist.

To push onward.

Step. By step.

It seemed so illogical, to be able to survive this, to get this far. What was logic? Who knew it? Still, he walked.

Step. By step. By step.

Forward. Forward.

Closer….

Closer….

Even closer….

Somehow…closer….

More of him peeled away.

Yet he still walked.

Treading.

Closer…. Closer….

To Vren Dotha, just a few yards away.

The blurry silhouette of the ancient blade finally appeared before him, designed like Chau Lepha yet with a male angel of black metal. Its five eyes on its wings scorched with volcanic gold light, seething like concentrated suns.

Spathi released Vrashri's damaged hilt, with some of his fingers dissolving away. He stretched out his hand for Vren Dotha's handle. More flesh and muscles disintegrated, his bones exposed. He reached, then grabbed.

And pulled.

Yanking.

Screaming.

Slowly, Vren Dotha slid out of the onyx pedestal with the heavy clarion ring of divine metal singing aloud. The blade was oddly light. Then the radiant ire engulfed Spathi and Vren Dotha, the aura merged the two together as one. With his last ounce of strength, he raised the weapon upward.

And discharged a shockwave from him!

Boom!

The animosity hushed at last, replaced by the reverberation of Spathi's scream. The waves of burning light subsided, retracting into the sword's eyes. Sound returned to the sanctuary. They all looked at Spathi, holding Vren Dotha toward the ceiling.

The blade shrank, about the length and width of him. Pieces of his body were replaced with prosthetics of white fire. His left arm was illuminated with pristine light. Strands of light cascaded down from his scalp in place of hair with his armor mostly gone. The gnarled remnants of Vrashri hung to his left arm, melded to his bone. Inside his ribs, something like a pale mist swirled around, marbled by a thick black smoke, almost like ink. Gently, he lowered the stern father, his stamina no longer his own, then he gazed out the arched windows beyond the solemn cathedral.

The polygonal webs of swaying blue lines from the previous corridors showed outside, past the glassless panes. A narrow precipice jutted before him, protruding behind the sword pedestal and stretching out into the peculiar void. The lines hummed, bristling with fleeting images.

Slowly, Spathi limped to the ledge, gripping Vren Dotha; the five eyes burned fervently, crackling with a cosmic stutter, threatening to erupt again at any moment. Every fiber of his being stung as he walked. Yet he was renewed with an unspeakable might, an immaculate vengeance that could shake all of heaven, earth, and hell to pieces in one swipe.

As long as Vren Dotha was in his hands, weakness was a foreign concept.

Such power. So strong.

Strong enough to rip Drixilo's head off!

Through the stinging, he felt something else around him: the brush of that greasy, smoky presence. The whispers teemed again, sounding as if…all around him—closer than ever!

Female voices, hissing at him. Hissing at someone.

Or something.

XXI: Foster Death

The feeling rushed around Spathi as the whispers intensified. He shut his eyes, his mind barely coherent from the pain. Then the noises hushed. He opened his eyes, wincing in angst and might, standing on the long precipice jutting out into the endless array of energy webs, all floating in infinite blackness. He examined the flow of geometric light closer.

Images. Memories.

Moments in time flowed from one swinging joint of drifting sapphire to the next, completely separate from eternity. A chill ran down his spine. This place *was* a conduit, with strands of history spun by Unzelkoyte himself! Slowly, he backed away, terrified of falling, lest he continue the time loop.

By plunging right back into it!

He felt heavier, like lead, as if something tugged him downward.

But it wasn't Constanvol.

"What is all this…?" he wheezed. "What…the—"

A hellish shriek railed from behind him!

He whipped around—and beheld death before him!

Malroc, the High Lich.

The archdemon loomed over him like a grim reaper stained with blood, with the rear jaw of his drooping face muttering blasphemies in the Drixilian tongue. The front mandible clicked his rotten teeth as his decaying flesh squelched and popped with each motion. Around him, a crowd of his subordinate reavers floated around him, their elongated mouths forever petrified in silent screams.

Spathi raised Vren Dotha. The eyes flared with violent streams of animosity.

Malroc laughed and raised his hand. A small black hole opened, a sphere of void framed with crystal bones and ridged dark amber. He grinned and chuckled more harshly in his warped, ghastly voice. Slowly, the light of one was syphoned into the black orb.

Spathi looked. The top eye's glow vanished!

The next ray entered another black orb.

Another eye disappeared!

"What?" Spathi gasped. "How—?"

"How can it destroy nothingness?" Malroc sneered as the two shadow reliquaries orbited around him.

The two eyes were not snuffed out, yet they were trapped within.

One of the reavers darted to Spathi's back and jammed one of its hands into his thigh, slowly paralyzing him. He snarled in pain and he fell back as another wraith dug into the arm holding Vren Dotha. Malroc formed another black sphere reliquary.

Another eye vanished into the globe!

"Staea! Shojem!" Spathi yelled.

"You mean them?" Malroc stepped aside and gestured behind them.

Spathi gazed in horror. His friends were encased in coffins of translucent dark amber, barely moving; even Shojem and Zephen were trapped. And Constanvol also? Qualkytdle lay dormant behind the sulfurous glass.

The third reliquary drifted around Malroc.

The reavers dug into him more, causing Spathi to whimper and fall on his sore knees.

"Make sure he does not move," the ghost lord commanded.

The reavers quietly complied, pinning him down.

"This is the end, Ansdari," Malroc croaked as he formed another dark orb. "You have lost. You have done just as I have predicted. Vren Dotha belongs to Drixilo. Now you will die."

Spathi huffed and glared at him. "Not…with my…third eye in—"

The High Lich screeched at him.

Spathi winced.

Malroc chuckled. "Is that what you think? Your petty 'third eye' making you invincible? Hah!" The ghost lord leered at him. "You see, I *can* kill you without that bothering anything. All I must do…is cut it out of your forehead. Then it is snuffed out. You lose it. It abandons you. Corruption takes hold. And the best part is…you won't even be aware of it. Then you die. Gone, forever."

"No," Spathi growled, straining from the numbing confines of the reavers' grasps. "The circle…will just begin…anew."

Malroc cocked his head. "Circle?"

Spathi grinned. "Chasing each other around…in circles…forever."

The reavers looked up at their Dranixile master in confusion. Behind them, Shojem banged on the dark amber uncontrollably. Never had Spathi seen the shaman panic so much.

Malroc glared down and clicked his front teeth as the rear jaw continued its profane jargon. He raised one of his forked arms and drew the coffin with Shojem to him. The sarcophagus slid hastily to them.

The ghost lord growled at the shaman. "So, *you're* the pest behind the energy anomalies my brothers have sensed in eternity! A time loop? With the blades of Astrekiah? How brazen of you…and foolish." He pointed a bony finger at the trapped weapons out of the shaman's reach. "Who are you? How is it that you have evaded me all this time? How could…?"

Something hung from Shojem's neck: the cameo of the robed man, made from otherworldly sapphire…radiating with iridescent light.

"That stone," Malroc rumbled.

He turned. Spathi looked around at the drifting sapphire around them, the exact same quality as the one dangling around Shojem's chest.

Malroc turned back to him. "Who *are* you? How have you eluded me all this…?"

The female whispers abruptly returned, rising into crazed giggling. They all looked around as Shojem bludgeoned the amber surface of the coffin furiously yelling out, his shouts muffled. Malroc said nothing. Quickly, he consumed the third eye of Vren Dotha with the empty reliquary, then the orb drifted with the others.

Spathi looked down. The last eye, closest to the hilt.

Vren Dotha's animosity, cooling.

"We must make haste!" Malroc said, forming a fourth sphere. "They must never—"

"Never what?" a woman's sultry voice sneered from somewhere.

Spathi looked around. The air roiled as strange scents instantly filled the sanctum around them: the aroma of flowers. Each fragrance was distinct from each other yet somehow unified together.

Four fragrances, smelling somewhat putrefied.

And sour. Bitter.

"I think we've witnessed the old man's meddling long enough," one woman's disembodied voice laughed. "What say *you*, my sisters?"

"Yes," another mocked. "So afraid to dare."

"Making us wait for so long," a third said.

"We tire of waiting for the end, old man," a fourth moaned playfully. "Why do you delay the inevitable?"

All four women cackled, not charmingly, their laughter baleful like acidic daggers; even Malroc and his reavers held his ears. The ghost lord turned as Spathi eyed someone strutting around the grotesque sarcophagi.

A voluptuous vixen with long, wavy black hair approached them, her metallic heeled sandals clopping loudly like cloven hooves in the temple; her hooded visage was grayed and transparent like a specter. Her exposed flesh showed geometric grooves of dark-blue light against her skin. Grooves…just like Staea once had. A phantom umbilical cord wafted from her naval, fading above into nothingness. Her eyes burned with the same dark-blue energy, the same color as Constanvol's aura.

"Minaya?" Spathi rasped.

"Aww." The woman's lush lips smirked at him. "You've heard of me. How sweet."

Within one of Malroc's caskets, the silver ribs around Staea's exposed sternum kindled and blazed with red and blue flames as the old grooves on her flesh appeared. Magenta claws of light formed at the tips of her fingers. Spathi gawked at her in horror.

No way. There was no way!

Malroc raged toward her. Yet Minaya simply darted around him like flirtatious lightning, tittering wildly without a single trace of sobriety to her. Another succubus appeared, her eyes emanating a dark-green glow. Then another appeared, her eyes golden, and a fourth manifested before them with purple irises. The Mulya-Sheloth revealed themselves at last, astral projecting from the moon!

Were they insane?

Malroc could sever their souls and enslave them as reavers at any moment!

Minaya drifted upward, then snatched one of Malroc's reliquaries in her hands. She locked at it playfully. "Pretty light. For me? How thoughtful."

The green-eyed succubus glared at the ghost lord. "You will tyrannize us no longer!" She whipped around to Shojem. "That goes for *you* also!"

"The world is about to die!" the purple-eyed one said. "We will revel for as long as we can! Especially at the expense of the likes of the Uxuclique!"

Boom!

A gold flash blasted Spathi down, fragmenting the two reavers to pieces.

Over him, the gold-eyed succubus loomed over him. She was the tallest of them. The way she stood, she appeared to be the most dominant; a halo of tainted golden light surrounded her, as if she were a fallen saint.

"Let us end this, my sisters!" she declared.

Spathi strained to get up with Vren Dotha as the gold-eyed succubus crashed Shojem's coffin to pieces. The shaman hopped out with the two swords drawn, his mummified face scowling at the dominant sister. She darted to Malroc, then clashed with the ghost lord, clawing and tearing at each other like beasts.

"Spathi! Listen to me!" Shojem said.

"Why didn't…you summon them earlier?" Spathi growled.

"I cannot control them!" the shaman claimed. "They have acted on their own accord—they are fickle—they are children of chaos! They have never done this before! Why now, I have no clue!"

"Don't…send me…in the—"

"I have to, Spathi," Shojem raised the two swords to the ledge's end, near one of the time strands. "I have to. This cycle is for the greater good of existence. I am sorry that it must be this way, but this is the path. One true perception. One true path! The others are false."

"Shojem!"

"Do not be led astray, Spathi!"

The shaman clashed the two swords together, the edges igniting with orange fire.

Clashed.

Clashing….

Clashing was the very last thing he recalled before the amnesia…last time. Embers. Orange embers, floating all around him. Staea's long red claws…and her red form, floating around.

In the void!

Constanvol was right. It really *was* Shojem, all this time.

Spathi panicked. "No!"

"You *must* trust me! There is no other way!" Shojem cawed.

"Don't—!"

"Trust! Me! I know the—!"

"I've trusted you long enough!" Spathi blasted. "*I* will decide my fate!"

Beyond the precipice ledge behind him, a rift of orange energy flashed, swirling around into a vortex of gilt fire! Deep in the distance, only blackness gaped, a heavy blackness bristling with embers. The vortex whirled around, counter-clockwise!

Spathi tried to stand up. Not again.

Not this time!

The succubi smashed Staea's sarcophagus, then Alehi's, then Tyri's. One by one, they smashed the caskets, freeing Spathi's allies. Minaya darted away from Malroc. The green-eyed and purple-eyed succubi only pestered Malroc from behind as their dominant sister battled the ghost lord. Each snatched a reliquary from him. Yet they grew less play-ful…and more vicious.

With Zephen free, he cleaved through reavers left and right with his hatchets and sickles as the other knights joined in the fight. Minaya crashed Constanvol's sarcophagus, aloof from the combat. He fell over as she bent down lovingly to him, stroking the thick scar across the lightning mark on his cheek.

"What have they done to you?" she cooed, then she turned and glowered at Spathi, her dark-blue eyes molten with maternal ire. Spathi looked at Malroc's reliquaries, then at Vren Dotha's empty eye sockets along the blade. What now?

Shojem stood before him, the blades held upward, crossed in an "X" pattern.

"You have to go, Spathi!" the shaman croaked. "You must—*oof!*"

The gold succubus lifted him up with one hand, shaking him, glaring and clenching her six fangs down at him.

"What. Were. You. Thinking?" she hissed. "All these years? Just so that you could prance around as a little know-it-all, thinking you could change Unzelkoyte's mind about fate? And for what? What sort of prophet are you? Your prodigal arrogance ends here, little man!"

"I will not be lectured to by some damned moon harlot!" the shaman yelled. "Do you hear me, Erimylekah?"

"Do *you* hear *me*?" she screamed back. "Zentigo?"

"*What?*" Spathi yelped, almost falling over.

He quickly regained his composure though. No. That couldn't be right. She was ly-ing—she had to be! He knew better than to take anything at face value. What the hell was happening?

Boom!

A shadowy explosion ripped out around the cathedral, summoning more reavers, then Malroc darted over and drew the fourth eye with another reliquary. Erimylekah, the dominant succubus, took the sphere.

"Damn you!" the ghost lord roared.

Malroc's new reavers screamed, then swarmed at Spathi and the others while some of them morphed into a torrent of black flame around the High Lich, straining to protect their master. The red ghost lord turned and seized Vren Dotha's blade. The animosity was gravely weakened yet still burned his bony forked arms, causing him to shriek in maniacal anguish.

"I will be thwarted no longer!" Malroc screamed, "not by any of you, the Unleztruv, or the Nevarifta! The light will fall!"

Spathi struggled to pull Vren Dotha away as the fire of the sword disintegrated some of Malroc's skin. Revealing…eyes. Golden eyes, like Sevthiel's hydra appendages. Scales orbited around bones of black fire, living scales, chittering like cicadas. Malroc's yawning face peeled away, the front jaw crumbling and revealing the entire rear jaw: the mandibles...of a cyclopean dragon.

An Udenthen.

Malroc was no Drixile!

Shojem leapt and struck Malroc with Vren Dotha, carving away the maelstrom of reavers. The wraith lord shrieked again, his grim reaper disguise peeling off, pushing Spathi off the ledge.

And sending him...swinging at the vortex.

"Spathi, no!" Shojem yelled. "No!"

Shing!

Vren Dotha sliced the rift. In half! As the blade came down, it struck something else.

A blue time strand.

The energies melded, forming a new portal, gold becoming blue! Embers raged around as the air roiled, fluctuating back and forth. All of their forms twisted and zipped forward as strings of light, devoured by the new vortex.

A new way.

A new terror.

XXII: Self-Divorced

The vortex blasted through something like stone and glass as Staea and the knights tumbled through, tossed onto a platform of fresh, smoldering obsidian. The whirling energy dissipated through the other side of a canyon, carving and warping the stone like a textured bridge to the other cliff, with thin strips of rock twisting around like masses of petrified ribbons. The last of the blue flames gouged through the stone, creating a short tunnel that slanted upward, leading up to the canyon's top.

All of them groaned as Staea lifted herself up to her feet and helped Shadya up. Then she looked around frantically for Spathi, eyes wide.

Yet he was nowhere in sight.

"What the fuck, man?" Alehi grunted, spitting dust out of his mouth.

"I think…that's enough…interdimensional travel," Lena coughed, "for one lifetime."

"Hate to break it to ya, lass," Jatal said, helping her up, "but I've got a good feeling we haven't seen the last of those spirit realms."

"Shit—*more* acid trips?" Alehi complained, rubbing his freckled face.

Lena squinted and pursed her lips at him.

Moriah looked up at the ash clouds above. "Is this…Raktogin?"

"Yes," Maloxi said, assisting Jalusa and Tyri up. "There's no mistaking it."

"I recognize the air, no doubt about it." Shadya confirmed, sniffing the brisk, arid wind. She turned her head, almost as if…straining to see. "Feels like the desert…but it's hard to tell with all the…sulfur from the volcanoes."

"I think you're right," Lena concurred.

"Sure it's not…Goena?" Devral questioned.

Maloxi shook his head. "If it is, it sure has me fooled."

"No rust," Tawpa said, pointing. "No metal or glass."

"Yeah," Maloxi agreed.

Staea peered at the narrow canyon below. A river of magma flowed in the deep chasm, roiling the air with intense heat, smoke, and sulfurous fumes as the sound of molten rock burbled and popped against the charred stone beneath them.

"Where's Spathi?" Staea asked.

Moriah surveyed the bridge. "Or Shojem?"

"Where'd that angel go?" Jalusa queried. "Zephyr—or…whatever his name was?"

"And those two other…blood-eater guys?" Tyri observed, raising an eyebrow.

"We didn't…leave 'em behind," Alehi asked, looking to Jatal. "Did we?"

Jatal stared at the redheaded soldier with troubled eyes.

"Did they not make it?" Lena asked, her breath quavering. She scanned the wind-scarred walls of the gorge. "Spathi? Spathi!"

Crack!

The bridge shifted.

"Run for it!" Jatal yelled, pointing at the tunnel.

They bolted for the opening as the platform fractured and slipped. Shadya stumbled, yet Staea caught her and hoisted her back to the ledge. All of them sprinted and hiked through the hole as the bridge collapsed into shards, plummeting into the lava below. Yet the force of the collision caused the tunnel to shudder, coming apart.

"Go!" Maloxi shouted.

All of them hustled, narrowly escaping the falling debris. They reached the top, chased by a cloud of dust as dull booms echoed from the canyon, then they slowed and stopped, panting for breath. Huffing, Staea peered up.

And her eyes bulged.

Zephen, the Arczell stood, tending to Shojem's crumpled form, his staff and sapphire cameo shattered on the ground, with Irado and Emerid lumbering nervously nearby. They squinted.

The shaman…was bleeding?

And seemed taller, his papery skin moist…and gory.

But Staea's eyes were fixed on a luminous male figure standing next to them, facing the foreboding moon in the distance. His body was clad in an otherworldly Sevelurnum exoskeleton, encasing his fingers and toes, standing like a legendary hero. A grizzled mane of straight hair whipped around in the wind, his skin still tan, yet his eyes now had silver irises instead of brown.

In his hands, he gripped Vren Dotha, with one eye left burning next to the hilt.

"Spathi?" Staea breathed.

He ignored her, still examining his transformed body, the armor fused with traits of Vrashri, the ikakalaka cleaver of St. Grae. With a calm yet heavy sigh, he sheathed Vren Dotha behind his back onto the scabbard of metallic fingers locking tightly around the divine weapon. He took another look at his left arm, the faint blue glow of his spirit aegis residing within the exposed bone, plated with Sevelurnum.

"Ansdarion," Shojem wheezed.

Spathi eyed the shaman. "You have a lot of explaining to do." He walked to Staea. "A. Lot. Of explaining."

Shojem coughed, spitting up blood.

"That's called pain, by the way," Spathi quipped down at him. "Welcome back to mortality."

Staea ran to Spathi, then they embraced and kissed. She rested her head on his chest, with his chin on the top of her head.

"Did we break it?" she whispered. "The cycle?"

Spathi hesitated, then sighed again. "I don't know yet."

Shojem stood up, favoring his abdomen, then looked at the other knights. Then Zephen looked at something in the distance. The others turned…and saw a caravan of cruisers far off, heading towards a mass of abandoned skyscrapers, their failing headlights wavering in the geothermal heat.

"Ruzi," Zephen said.

"Son of a bitch," Alehi said, smirking.

"They made it," Devral said. "Thank Astrekiah."

"Wait," Shadya said. "Something's nearby."

"Yeah," Spathi said, looking away. "About that...."

"I hear it, too," Moriah said, drawing her Selebane spear.

"Don't kill him," Spathi replied.

"Don't kill what?" Lena said, then she drew her sword, staring at a hulking shadow creeping towards them.

The others armed themselves as Irado neared and growled at the snarling creature. Staea's eyes widened again, holding Chauvien tightly.

"What the hell is *that*?" Tyri squeaked.

Spathi sighed. "That's me."

"Say again?" Devral asked, furrowing her brows.

"It's a part...of me," Spathi told them.

The creature approached, monstrous and muscular, skittering towards them with the disturbing movements of a spider. His flesh was rough, like broken black glass tinged with olive-green. His eyes glowed with depraved gilded light, like that of a prowling wildcat. His mouth was filled with numerous crooked fangs, flicking a forked tongue like a serpent with a balding head of scraggly gray hair. The imprinted scars left from his old flesh cloak burned as bright red grooves across his skin. In the middle of his forehead, a sunken hole showed with a smoldering wick deep inside. His abdomen was ridged with fearsome fangs and bone, slobbering, opening.

Revealing another mouth!

On his wrists and heels, large red mosquito proboscises jutted, pulsing with veins. Somehow, the appendages were different from the Ravaged, resembling more like serrated daggers, each with a blade's bloodline running down into the orifices around the blood vessels. An undead cloak of dark gray sinews coiled around him, also with crimson markings of light, hissing far more hellish than his former flesh cloak ever did.

The dark Spathi tensed, baring his salivating teeth at them. Irado pawed to him, growling louder as the dark Spathi retorted angrily at him. Staea stared at them. Suspiciously.

Zephen flashed his halo around him, causing the dark Spathi to squeal and flinch.

"Do not fear him," Zephen, said, peering down at them.

"Bit late for that," Devral snapped.

Maloxi glared at the dark Spathi.

"He will not be a threat," Zephen assured. "I can control him, to a point."

"What *is* this...thing?" Lena gasped.

"He is impulse personified," Zephen replied.

"Every unhealthy desire I've ever had...is right there," Spathi Ansdarion admitted grudgingly. "In the flesh."

Alehi shook his head. "Huh?"

"No," Staea said. "No, that's not you—I know you!"

"Okay, this is…this is *way* too much," Moriah said cringing, the cerebral device in her temple whirring.

"Don't blow a fuse over there," Jalusa said to Moriah.

"Oh, shut up," Moriah groaned, rubbing her forehead. "Ow."

Lena looked away as Jatal hugged her close.

"Alright…both of your 'two selves' need names to be distinguished from each other," Tyri said. "'Cause I ain't callin' *both* of you 'Spathi,' got it?"

"They're both me," the light Spathi said.

"I heard you the first time—I'll take your word for it," Tyri rubbed the bridge of her nose, then pointed at the dark Spathi. "And I refuse to call…*that*…Spathi Ansdari, okay?"

"You do not have to," Shojem grunted. "Spathi Ansdari is no more. Here are two halves." The shaman pointed the light self, "Spathi Ansdarion," he aimed his finger at the subdued dark Spathi, "and…." He paused, pensively whirling his bony hand around in the air, contemplating an appropriate name.

"Ilradom," Lena sobbed, "is all I will call it."

"Ilradom?" Alehi asked.

Jatal glared. "Our word…for 'impulse,'" He shook his head. "Useless impulse."

"Whatever," Ansdarion said.

All of them looked at the caravan in the distance, their wavy forms making camp in Ruzi's outskirts. Spathi Ansdarion peered in the eastern horizon far off, at the moon. Blood-red. Reddened by volcanoes…and Drixilo's influence. Above, the sun was darkened by the ash clouds, thick and billowing like woolly black sackcloth. The waters of the world were bleeding…and the earth was scarred with fire, soon to collapse. The next sign had been revealed.

These *were* the very last days of Raktogin. At last.

The Final Quarrel awaited them.

But the question remained: had they truly avoided fate?

Had they circumvented the circle, just as Zaryen had said?

Staea eyed Emerid, then glanced at Ansdarion. Then at Ilradom, noticing just how similar the name sounded to…Irado. The two horrific ghouls continued to grumble at each other, not as hostile as before. She glared at Zentigo, the prophet formerly called Shojem.

"This," she growled as she turned to Zentigo. "Is this…part of your cycle?"

"I assure you, it is not!" Zentigo said.

"I don't buy it," she hissed, gritting her teeth and pointing at Emerid and Irado. "You had them both…from a different timeline. All this time! You know even *more*, don't you?"

"No, I do not!"

"Bullshit!"

"Woman, I—!"

"Don't you *dare* 'woman' me, Shojem, Zentigo—whatever the hell your name is!" She clenched her fists. "You knew this would happen! You wouldn't tell us! Spill it! Tell us right now, or—!"

Boom!

Raktogin quaked!

The sound of crushing rocks was almost deafening. All of them yelped and fell down from the violent motion of shifting rock splitting open as Spathi Ansdarion slipped and fell onto the stone, growing strangely motionless with a shrill ringing emerging in his ears. He grew lightheaded, as if malnourished. All other sounds faded away as the light dimmed, overcoming his vision with tiny black and yellow spots, running all around, gradually enveloping his sight in complete darkness.

The last echo faded. Thundering away.

But he was still there. Lunatic or not, he was still there.

He didn't want to die. Not now. Not yet.

In the blackness of unconsciousness, he heard shouting far off. Harrowing dreams. Nightmares. Images flashed before him, unrecognizable scenes. The distant shrieks of pandemonium rose louder, like ghosts seeking to testify…of past things.

Screaming. Rumbling. Rolling.

Pealing away.

All letting Spathi know that he was still alive, that he could not surrender. That he could not die. Not yet. He wasn't done yet. Much more remained to be seen.

The Final Quarrel lay ahead.

All of this…was far from over.

He couldn't die.

Not yet.

Acknowledgements

Jesus Christ is Lord and Savior! I praise the one true holy Almighty God from Whom all blessings flow for everything, including every blessing and trial in my life. I also praise Him for providing me with generous, loving people whom have helped me along the way. This page is to recognize family and friends whom have offered their selfless and diligent support for me throughout the years and continue to do so by the Grace of God.

James Hardy, Ph.D.
Marietta Jane Hardy
Rhonda Lott, Ph.D.
Wendy Outlaw
Sharon Hudson
Deborah Broadus
Madison Hollinghead
Julia Ferguson
Craig James Simoneaux Jr.
Corie Simoneaux Keys
Janet Kennedy
Alex Kennedy

The Whittington Family

William Pettey Sr.
Kenneth Franklin Garcia
Brett Barlow, Ph.D.
Jesse Bass
Catherine Bass
Sgt. Derick Mallette
Maj. Kelly Mallette
Paula Creel
William Nix
Robin Nix
David Bunales
Ronn Hague

The Martin Family

About the Author

Shawn Christopher Whittington specializes in crafting surreal epics about
otherworldly beings, bizarre worlds, and deep subject matters.
Shawn became intrigued with literature at an early age and
decided to pursue a career in writing at the age of thirteen.

Inspired by the supernatural and his turbulent internal struggles, it was
Shawn's prolific writing that helped him during the years where he developed a keen
interest in dark fantasy and the macabre focused on the outsider. He is best known for
his psychedelic vampire series, *Ravage & Requiem*, consisting of five novels.

Thank you for purchasing *Ravage & Requiem: Shatter*!

Be sure and check out more titles
by S. Whittington!

For more information, please visit the portfolio
website at www.swhittington.com.